EVEN WHEN
I'M GONE

Even When I'm Gone

Copyright © 2019 by Nicole Fiorina

Publication Date: October 29th, 2019
ISBN: 9781695914407

All right reserved. Without limiting the rights under copyright reserved above, no part of this publication may be reproduced, stored in or introduced into retrieval system, or transmitted, in any form, or by any means (electronic, mechanical, photocopying, recording, or otherwise) without the prior written permission of both the copyright owner and the above publisher of this book.

This is a work of fiction. Names, characters, places, brands, media, and incidents are either the products of the author's imagination or used fictitiously. The author acknowledges the trademarked status and trademark owners of various products referenced in this work of fiction, which have been used without permission. The publication/use of these trademarks is not authorized, associated with, or sponsored by the trademark owners.

Published by Nicole Fiorina Books | Poetry by Oliver Masters
Proofreading by Annie Bugeja | Cover by Nicole Fiorina Books
Formatting and Editing by BohoBooks Publishing Ink

nicole fiorina

NOTE FROM AUTHOR

Even When I'm Gone is the second book in the *Stay with Me* series. If you have not read *Stay with Me*, you will be lost and confused.

A lot of research went into this entire series, beginning with Stay with Me and continuing throughout the trilogy. Please keep in mind that the discussion regarding medication is based on my personal experience with it over the years, and how it affected *me*. Medication reacts to everyone differently. I am not a doctor or licensed psychiatrist, and I do not recommend altering medication without first speaking with your doctor. Between my personal experiences, as well as speaking with those who have lived with the subjects discussed, and countless hours of research, I've learned that every person's experience is unique in their own way. No two journeys are the same. This story isn't meant to change your mind, but to open your mind. For you to embrace those who are different, and see that there are two sides to every story—both sides being correct depending on how you look at it.

Difficult topics are discussed in this story. *Their opinions may or may not reflect my own.* Mature content, adult language, graphic sexual content, and disturbing matters may trigger an emotional response. Read at your own risk.

I hope you enjoy my creative spin and this world I've built.

Even When I'm Gone Playlist Available on Spotify:
https://spoti.fi/2mlHWFF

Streaming available at
https://www.nicolefiorina.com

Dad,

If you were here, you would have told me to let it go, but we both know I was always the wild card with my mother's fierce spirit and your honest heart. So, I did it, anyway. Perhaps not in the way you would have expected, but I finally found a way to give you a morsel of justice compared to what you truly deserved. I wish I could do more, and I'm sorry I couldn't have done something sooner.

    This is for you, Dad.

    This story is your justice …

            … and my revenge.

    Love,
    The daughter who can't let it go

PROLOGUE

*"I'm not so sure what's more terrifying,
the violent storm inside my head
or the silence."*

OLIVER MASTERS

Ollie

had been an arsehole.
   And I'd known it at the time.
   You would think knowing would have made things easier.
But it hadn't.
It had made leaving her worse.

"Ollie's back," a familiar voice called out. I turned my head to see them both standing there—Jake and Mia. My eyes connected with hers, and though I wasn't ready for it, everything I feared had become my verifiable truth. I'd once loved her, and it hadn't been long ago when she was my everything. I remembered the way she'd made me feel, but now those feelings were replaced with something else.

Betrayal? No. Anger? No.

Something worse.

Nothing.

She looked at me, my little explosion of hope, eyes filled with belief. Only I didn't have it in me. Instead, I turned and walked away.

It was easier, Mia.

I walked back to my dorm, and it was her footfalls echoing through the corridor. I should have known she wouldn't have given up so easily, but I wasn't ready to face her. Not yet. Not until I could give her the answers I knew she needed.

I'd warned her this would happen, and now that it had happened, I saw everything so clearly. How could I ever love a girl that had been corrupted by my brother?

Her hand grabbed my arm and spun me around. Before our eyes met, I knew it was her. I would always know her touch. Every inch of her had seared into my soul like a permanent tattoo—because we once belonged. Though I was gone, the pills could never erase the imprints her hands had left behind on my skin; the places she had touched.

I hoped for a connection like I felt in the mess hall from day one—instead, nothing. I flashed her a smile. It was probably worse than anything else I could have done, but again, I didn't have it in me.

Dammit, Mia.

"I don't know what to say," I deadpanned, unwilling to look her directly in the eyes, but only because I was scared. *Fuck, was I scared.* I didn't want to feel anything. Because what if I did? Feelings made things more complicated. It was easier not to care, and that was what my body wanted me to do. So, I looked past her as if she were a fading shade of my past.

"Say anything," she pleaded, taking my hand in hers. It was all I ever wanted before—her touch. All I wanted at this moment, though, was the silence.

Pulling away, I looked into her golden-brown eyes. I remembered it was all I'd used to search for in every room I'd entered. It was all I'd hoped to see when I would wake in the morning, praying for the golden-brown days over the dark-brown days.

I had to push her away because I would only disappoint. It was for her own good.

"You fucked my brother. I should have never allowed it to go on as long as it did," I reminded her, which was all true. She screwed my brother, and even though our love couldn't be tainted before, now it was. Tainted, because now my immune heart and soul lived in a world of the impervious.

"Allowed what to go on?" she asked. Despite her chin pointed up, challenging me, tears shook in the corner of her eyes, and her lovely lips trembled.

I breathed in.

I breathed out.

"You and I."

My eyes moved past her, and the all-familiar struggle in her breathing broke like the times I'd laid her over my mattress and pleased her with the same lips and tongue that just spoke those three simple words.

She was acting strong. Hell, she was strong, and I showed her how. But I could strip her of her strength with a snap of a finger.

"Ollie, it's the medication. You don't mean that. You promised me," she showed me my ring on her pointer finger, "You fucking promised me, remember?" Her hand shook between us.

"Don't curse, darling. It's a turnoff." I took one step, but so did she—right out in front of me.

"Tell me what to do, Ollie. How am I supposed to remind you?" she asked, desperation twined in her tone and beaten eyes—my little desperate explosion of hope.

There was nothing to remind me of. I remembered everything.

"You can't. It's over. You have to let me go," I said, forcing out each word.

She touched my face, and my entire body went rigid under her fingers. Standing at least a foot over her, I could easily pick her up and throw her

11

to the opposite end of the hallway with little effort, yet she disarmed me with the tips of five soft fingers.

My incompetent body and helpless mouth surrendered under her touch. Even my heart went on standby, obeying like a damn fool, awaiting orders.

"Please, look at me," she pleaded.

Only a fraction of a centimeter to my left was needed to see her, and that small effort demanded every ounce of strength I had, and I had a lot.

But it still managed to wipe me out.

Our eyes met, and despite my lack of giving a damn, my hand covered hers over my face. My intention at first was to pull them both away, but something snapped inside me.

And again, I couldn't move.

Mia inched her way closer, lifting off her heels, and my eyes closed before her lips barely brushed across mine. She pulled away slightly, and I opened my eyes to see her.

Twelve freckles spread across her nose and under her eyes. Golden-brown eyes blazed from the fire in her soul. The sweet taste and heavenly aroma of … "Mia …" *Poetry.*

An abrupt crusade fought within me.

A villain and a hero. An angel and a demon. Heaven and hell.

A rush of emotions crossed over me in an instant, and I dipped down, immersing myself in them. I couldn't help it. She was to blame. She always had the power.

My reckless mouth grabbed onto hers, holding on for dear life. But not even her anchor was strong enough against the waves of the paralysis.

Because then it was gone.

I pulled away.

"I'm such an idiot," I whispered, and the dark side inside laughed like it was no big deal. I looked her over, thinking how my brother's hands were on her. Thinking of how he had touched her. How she was his before she was ever mine. "Stay away from me, Mia."

Five bloody words.

Despite the alarming, gaping hole it left, I walked away.

She cried out for me in the place I left her. My feet stayed in front of me, one right after the other, but the small fraction of my heart that hadn't been corrupted by the pills screamed along with her, clawing at me from the inside out.

I shoved my hands into my pocket to clench my fists.

And I closed my eyes.

ONE

"The two slowest deaths
are absence and time."

OLIVER MASTERS

Mia

Seven Months Later

He stared at me, his eyes fixed, steady, and without a smile. If one didn't know better they would think he was bored. But I'd known Zeke for almost a year now, and this was the face of contentment.

The room where we typically held group therapy was vacant on the weekends, and at first, I'd come here to ease my thoughts of Ollie and my itching fingers, but now I've continued to play the piano every Saturday to relieve Zeke's troubled mind.

Dr. Conway said she had seen an improvement in Zeke since I started playing for him. I was just glad it was because of my own doing. For once, I'd improved life for someone instead of destroying it, and it felt good.

Despite Ollie being gone, the time spent with him still changed me. Ollie changed me.

"Okay, Zeke. Hour's up." I rested my palms over my thighs. Zeke didn't speak, as always, but communicated "thank you" with a simple motion of his hand—*as always*.

I'd picked up gestures here and there but mostly learned from a book I'd grabbed from the library. I wasn't fluent in sign language, but Zeke's patience never hindered.

As soon as I stood, Zeke held up an "O," and I already knew the direction of where the question headed. Zeke survived on routine, and just like every Saturday before, after I stood from the piano, Ollie's name was brought up.

I hadn't seen Ollie since the day he slipped away. No one gave me any indication as to why Dean Lynch removed him from the program, but rumors spread as wide as Maddie's legs here at Dolor. Some blamed it on Lynch's carelessness and favoritism as if they understood the entire story. Supposedly, the Dean had decided to cast Ollie out to prove his dedication to Dolor's core values. Others assumed he was removed temporarily while he and his brother were investigated. Both seemed plausible, and Lynch wouldn't tell me otherwise.

One thing I was sure of: I missed him.

The first three months without him were unbearable, and these last three benumbing. The unknown only made it worse—not knowing if I would ever see him again, not knowing if he was okay, not knowing if he had gotten better.

"*Stay away from me, Mia,*" were his last words to me, but I refused to. He hadn't been in his right mind, and that much he had warned me. And whether he was here or not, I would stay with him. Those last words were replaced by others he had said to me the night he snuck into the Looney Bin and confessed he was in love with me. "Stay with me, even when I'm gone."

Right now, he was gone.

And over the last seven months in his absence, I stayed.

Like every other Saturday, I provided Zeke with the same answer, "Close your eyes." I forced a convincing smile. Ollie's slow and haunting voice flowed through my head without admission. *"If reality becomes unbearable, close your eyes. We were made with an imagination."*

Clenching my eyes closed, I fought the tears threatening to fall.

Not in front of Zeke.

"Stop right there," I ordered, peering down the corridor after closing the door to my dorm behind me. The blond hair boy froze and I narrowed my eyes. "Jake? Is that you?"

Jake slowly turned around, and his thin lips managed to disappear under the force of his broad smile. "Crap-bag!"

The next thing I knew, I was swept off the floor and engulfed in Jake's arms.

After the school year ended, Jake's father signed him out of the program to attend a mission trip for his church. With Jake and Ollie gone, Bria and I had grown close.

"I honestly wasn't expecting to see you again," I admitted once he set me back on solid ground.

Jake's blue eyes beamed down at me. "Yeah, well, I'm still gay," he giggled, and I never thought I would have missed his giggle until I heard it.

"Thank god for that," I said through a laugh. "Heading to dinner?"

Jake nodded, and we continued to walk down the hall side by side. "Catch me up on things. What's happened over the last two months?"

"Ollie's still not back, and Alicia's gone."

"What? No!"

"Yeah, last year was her final year. I thought you knew that," I said, tilting my head up to face him.

Jake kept his eyes in front of him. "I knew it was her last year, but I was still hoping to catch her one last time," his hand smacked his forehead, "Bollocks, I don't even know her last name."

"Bria's here, though," I added in a hurry, hoping it would lighten his spirits and nudged his arm with mine, "and Liam, and a really cute new guy."

Jake's brow spiked in the air. "New guy for me or you?"

"Ha! New guy, period. For no one," I shook my head, "Just some eye-candy to keep your thoughts entertained."

"Name?"

I took a tray from the buffet line. "You know, I don't know his name. He's quiet, doesn't really talk to anyone."

Jake's baby blues scanned the mess hall on a mission. "Is he here now?"

I glanced over my shoulder. "No."

"We should go to his dorm and introduce ourselves, offer an invitation to our 'pity-party,'" he said with a slight mock in his tone, and flashes of the time Jake and Alicia had shown up at my door to introduce themselves came forth. I smiled to myself. It seemed like ages ago when I'd first arrived here but it had only been a year.

"You're relentless."

"Girl, and don't you forget it." He lifted his tray and followed my lead over to my table. Jake and I both greeted Zeke before Jake took a seat at the end. "Any news on Isaac or Oscar?"

Every time someone mentioned those names, my skin crawled. Oscar's dark eyes, hands on my body, and taunting tone haunted me every chance they had. New Year's Eve night still haunted me. Oscar, Ollie's brother, was the very reason Ollie wasn't here any longer.

"Lynch confirmed Oscar's behind bars for good," I fell back in my chair, "he got thirty years after linking him to other sex crimes."

"And Isaac?" Jake asked with a mouthful.

"Five. Isaac wasn't a repeat sex offender. Was only here because of drug addiction, or at least that was the little amount of information Lynch would give me."

Jake nodded. "How's Bria holding up?"

"Good. She should be here soon," I said, looking over at the entrance for her. "We've grown pretty close over the last few months. Dr. Conway and Lynch approved for us to hold an open support group once a week for those who suffered from sexual abuse."

Jake's eyes danced like a proud brother. "Look at you!"

"Yeah, I put it together and convinced Bria to do it with me. Use our experiences for good, you know? Plus, I needed *something* to keep my mind occupied …" I trailed off as Ollie, once again, invaded me.

Jake dropped his fork and wiped the corners of his mouth with a napkin before crumbling the paper up in his fist. The words sat on the tip of his tongue. He wanted to spit it out, but his eyes studied me for a moment before he finally stated, "You miss him."

I exhaled. "You have no idea."

Brief silence wrapped a noose around my neck, and I wondered if this was how the rest of my life would be—silently suffocating in the memory of him. I knew I would never find what Ollie and I shared again. *"Embrace it, Mia. Every moment, no matter how long it lasts, it's all worth it, yeah?"* Ollie had once said.

Yeah, Ollie. It was all worth it.

"Sweet mother of Jesus," Jake whispered, reeling me back to reality. "I forgot how fine Prince Harry over there was. His sweet ass is turning my bigger bollock blue,"—Jake leaned into me— "What's his name again?"

Shaking my head, I pulled the fork from my mouth. "Ethan Scott."

"That's right." Jake picked up his fork, but his eyes stayed on the security guard, opened mouthed and watering. "Never been into redheads, but I'll gladly start a forest fire with that one."

I laughed. An honest laugh. *God, I missed Jake.* "Good luck with that."

"Oh, c'mon. You can't tell me he isn't fit as hell," Jake dropped his head closer to me, "Can you imagine what he's hiding behind the uniform?"

I lifted my attention from my food and found Ethan's electric blue eyes from across the mess hall. Ethan sent me a wink with a slight head nod.

Jake dropped his fork. "Yup, my john just jerked."

"Jake!"

"How the hell do you know him like that?" he asked me, but his eyes we're still on Ethan.

"We're friends," I casually said, remembering the day so vividly. Originally, Ethan and I met when he had questioned me in the nurse's station after Oscar's attack. He had been the officer to take my statement. Now he was a security guard at Dolor, and the day Ollie slipped away, Ethan had scooped me from the hallway, carried me outside, and held me until I thawed from the mental state I'd been stuck in. His only explanation at the time was he didn't want anyone seeing me like that—didn't want them to send me back to the psych ward. Ethan had sat quietly at my side until day turned to night and I had no tears left to cry.

"Friends?"

"Yes, friends. He was the one who convinced me to start a support group." I glanced from Ethan back to Jake, and Jake's disbelieving grin didn't falter. I pointed my fork to his tray. "Whatever, eat your dinner."

"I'd much rather be eating something else."

"If it isn't Jake-the-bollock," Bria chimed, taking a seat beside me.

"I prefer Jake-the-bull," Jake smirked, "the *raging* bull."

"Oh, you wish," I laughed.

Bria and Jake exchanged summer adventures as we finished our dinner. Hearing Bria gloating about our program made me smile. Her eyes lit up every time she talked about the plans she made for the upcoming year. If Ollie were here to see this change in her, he would be elated. Of course, I took a little credit myself.

"So, we're heading to new guy's dorm to see what he's all about," Jake explained, lifting his tray. "You coming, Bria?"

Bria nodded as she finished her juice before tossing it into the nearest trashcan.

As we made our way out of the mess hall, Ethan ushered me over with a small nudge of the head. "I'll be right there," I called out to the two of them.

"Jake Tomson, he's from last year, yeah?" Ethan asked, looking straight ahead with his hands fastened securely to his belt.

I'd known Ethan for seven months now. Over the summer, we'd established an unusual bond no one could know about. He'd become overprotective of me, and at times I believed Ethan used me to replace the relationship he used to have with his sister before she died. Other times, I wasn't so sure. Ethan was very back and forth, treating me like a child, but also looked at me with pining blue eyes. He was hard to read, and I'd always been fascinated by him and his ways.

Ethan was a challenge—a tough case to crack.

But I was determined to figure him out.

"Jake Tomson is harmless, Ethan."

Ethan tilted his head down, and for a brief moment, his icy blue eyes met my gaze before turning back to the mess hall before him. "No one is harmless, Jett," he drew in a deep breath and adjusted his stance, "Don't be stupid. There's a bunch of dodgy blokes at this school. I can't be looking after you at all times."

"I never asked you to look after me."

"Fine. You're on your own tonight then." His arms crossed over his chest, and my nerves twisted into knots.

"Fine."

"Fine."

Rolling my eyes, I walked away before picking up into a light jog to catch up with Jake and Bria.

"No running in the halls," Ethan called out, sarcasm dripping from his tone. A slow smile stretched across my face knowing Ethan turned back to watch me, and I didn't slow down either because I was still the rebellious badass.

This was our relationship: hitting me with such comments, but his eyes held a different story. Though Ethan never smiled, he was the first one to help me find mine after Ollie left. The rest of last semester I'd spent in a fog, but Ethan pulled me out. If I'd never met Ollie, I could have easily fallen for Ethan, despite the way he treated me like a little sister. But I did meet Ollie, and there would never be anyone else.

"Is this the right door?" Jake asked as I approached them down the second wing.

"Yeah … this … it's the one," I panted with my hands over my knees.

Jake looked me over with wide eyes. "Damn, girl. You seriously need to exercise more. You were in great shape when Ollie was here."

Bria laughed.

I didn't.

Jake swung an arm over my shoulder. "Come on, lighten up a little bit."

The door before us swung open, and the three of us immediately straightened our posture. A man over six-feet-tall stood over us, long dark hair just above the shoulders, and drooped earlobes from those big hole earrings, I'd assumed. The guy's pale skin glowed against his black clothing, and his lips were perfection. Frosty blue eyes sliced through the three of us between his long black lashes. "Can I help you?"

"I… um… ye…" Jake shoved my shoulder for assistance as he fell into a hypnotized state.

"I'm Mia. This is Jake and Bria. We just wanted to welcome you to Dolor." Being new at this whole introducing thing, I tried to remember how Jake and Alicia did this when they appeared at my door on the first day. "Want to be a part of our pity-party?"

The dark-haired guy raised his brow. "Pity party?"

"Well, no. That was a joke. You see, when I first arriv—"

Bria dug her heel into my foot to silence me. "What she means to say is, if you're ever looking for a good time, let us know."

"Ah, a good time? What makes you think I'm down?"

Bria rocked on her heels and ran her finger across her lip. She had this in the bag. "I guess there's only way to find out. Friday. Meet us after breakfast."

He leaned over and planted his palm over the dorm frame. "In the morning?"

"I-it-it's kind of an all-day event," Bria stammered.

Great, she was buckling. I had Jake to my right who was still in shock and drooling, and Bria who forgot how to use her voice box.

"What's your name?" I asked.

The dark-haired guy's pale blue eyes slid to me in the middle. "Jude."

"See you on Friday, Jude," I grabbed both helpless humans from beside me and dragged them away from his door. "You two need to get a grip," I whispered when we got at least ten feet away. I turned back around to find Jude's head hanging out of the door frame, and his lip turned up in the corner.

"Easy for you to say, you only have eyes for the one bloke who isn't here," Bria finally spoke after coming back from her Jude-induced coma. "Ollie's not coming back, Mia. It's been seven months. Time to have some fun."

"You mean to tell me Mia hasn't ... in seven months?" Jake's expression was utterly shocked.

"Bria either," I countered with my eyes shooting daggers at her.

"I have a good reason. I'm still adjusting," Bria said defensively. Instantly, guilt washed over me for mentioning it. Bria was still recovering from what happened New Years, but I became proud of all she had accomplished since then. "Although, Jude is just what I needed to push me into full recovery."

Turning the corner, I'm face to face with another wall of books rising to the ceiling. Colors of their bindings blur together along with my vision as I spin in circles, looking for a way out. There is no way out. Running through the maze, my heart pounds inside my ears and it hurts to breathe. The moment I stop running is the moment I give up. I know this, and I keep running.

"Ollie, I can't find you!" I cry out, my head turning in all directions. All I see are books, dozens of them closing in on me. "Call out to me!"

The books laugh back at me, taunting whispers flow through their pages. Their words wrap around my windpipe. Each aisle I run through inch smaller and smaller, shelves cave in, and before I know it, I have to squeeze through the aisles.

My legs give out and my body collapses to the ground. I drop my head into my hands as my senses overpower with defeat.

"Wake up!"

My eyes flew open to see someone leaning over my bed with a hand over my shoulder. "Ollie?"

His jaw clenched. "Ethan."

"Ethan…" I echoed through a sigh, blinking rapidly. Sweat built up between me and the sheet and my hair stuck to my face. I kicked the top sheet off me. The room was dark, but I managed to make out Ethan's silhouette as he took a seat beside me on the edge of the mattress. He wiped a cold towel over my face like he did every other time in the middle of the night. "You said you wouldn't come anymore."

Ethan stayed silent, gathering my hair in his hand and pulling it off my neck. The cold towel at my nape soothed the fever of my night terror.

"Ignoring your screams is torture," he mumbled.

The night terrors had come every night since Ollie left, and I could rarely recall what my nightmares were about, but for seven months, Ethan had been the one to pull me from them.

My breathing steadied, and I rolled over and looked up at Ethan as he moved the towel across my neck and over my collarbone. He never touched me with his bare hands, only the cool hand towel he always had prepared.

And every night I needed it.

But tonight, I needed more.

Slowly, my fingers inched to his over the wet towel. My mind raced, and I didn't know what I was doing, but my body starved for any source of physical comfort. Ollie was gone, and I was desperate. My irrational thoughts spun, thinking Ethan's hands could heal me from the loss. Or perhaps I just needed someone to hold me because when my eyes closed, the ache surfaced. Ollie wasn't here to take it away, but Ethan was.

Ethan didn't move. He froze, seeing what would come of it. His eyes stayed on mine as I pulled his hand to my face. I closed my eyes against his warm skin. It was nothing like Ollie's hand, but comforting in its own way. Releasing an exhale, I held his hand there, waiting.

Ethan rubbed his thumb against my cheek and let out a small breath of his own. When I opened my eyes, I found him again. "Please, don't leave me," I choked out. "Stay with me for just a little bit. Until I fall back asleep?"

Ethan's mouth set in a hard line as he pushed more strands away from my face, but his eyes never wavered from mine. "Don't put me in that position."

He removed his hand and turned his eyes away.

Then he stood and adjusted his belt. I used to fear the jingle of those keys, but Ethan's presence had replaced that fear. I no longer flinched at the sound. Now, I begged to hear it.

Ethan turned back around to face me, and his eyes wandered up and down my sweaty body until they landed on my face. "I'll see you in the morning, Jett."

He'd never call me by my first name, and I never understood it. Rolling back over in the bed, each of his footfalls gripped my already broken heart before the door clicked closed behind him.

TWO

"You're desperate, I know, but
his touch is never going to fix it.
You're empty, I know, but
he can never fill the place I once did.
I warned you, my love, but
you're stubborn and never listen."

OLIVER MASTERS

Mia

// "I have to say, Mia, I'm very impressed with how far you've come over the summer compared to where you were last semester," Dr. Conway said as we sat in her office. "Do you have any goals for this year?"

One more week until school started, and between the support group I conducted once a week and my night terrors, there was still plenty of time for my mind to stray to Ollie. No matter how busy I tried to keep myself, he was everywhere.

"Goals," I laughed lightly from the leather couch, "There's a word I would never have attached to my name before."

Dr. Conway's face sank under her bangs. "Stop with all this self-deprecating…" she mumbled before turning in her chair and raised to her feet. My eyes followed her as she walked toward a small side table on the opposite side of the room and pulled out a drawer. "Ah-hah." She held a green velvet notebook in the air, waving it around as if it were the winning lotto ticket.

"What's that?"

"This, my dear, is your first assignment for the new school year," she handed me the notebook, "I want you to start writing in a journal. It will be therapeutic."

I groaned and fell back into the couch. "Why do all your assignments include reading and writing?"

"Because it stimulates the brain."

"My brain isn't the muscle that needs stimulating."

Dr. Conway shot her palms over her ears. "No, you didn't say that. I didn't hear it."

I laughed, and she re-took her seat in her swivel chair, recovering from my comment. "Have you thought about what you want to do once you leave here? Will you continue school?"

"Haven't given it much thought."

Ollie and I had made plans. We'd talked about his dreams of publishing his poetry, traveling across the world, and giving back to those who went without. We'd talked about my dreams of watching him fulfill his because truth be told, Ollie had been my dream all along. That was until he took it all away from me. Though he was gone now, my plans of running away with Ollie were still in motion. One more year left at Dolor, and I would find him and remind him of what we had.

"I want you to start thinking about it. You have your whole life in front of you, Mia. By the second semester, I can help you apply for colleges in the states."

"Thanks." I ran my hand over the front of the fuzzy journal. The shade changed as my fingers swiped down, then lightened as they swiped back up. I did appreciate Conway's offer, but I didn't want to go back to Pennsylvania. There was nothing left for me there.

The UK became my home.

Ollie was my home.

On my way back to my dorm, footsteps sounded behind me. Each time I paused and turned around, the noise stopped. After waiting a moment, I continued again. The footfalls started shortly after, growing louder and closer together with each step I took. My feet picked up the pace and I snapped my head behind me right before I turned the corner when I slammed into what felt like a brick wall.

My notebook fell to the floor, and strong hands grabbed my elbows to keep me steady. "Whoa, darling," a low voice said.

Glancing up, Jude peered down at me with pale blue eyes and my arms in his secured hold. My muscles tensed. "Sorry, I thought I...." My head whipped around to see nothing behind me, and I shook my head. "I don't know. I thought I heard someone behind me."

Jude released me and took a step back.

"What are you doing on my wing anyway?" I asked, crouching down to pick up the notebook. "Your dorm is in second wing,"

Jude shook his black hair from his face and lifted a shoulder. "I got lost."

An awkward silence loomed over us as Jude's eyes kept me pinned in place.

"Everything alright over here?" Ethan's level voice came from behind. He laid a hand over my shoulder. "Jett? Is he bothering you?"

I swallowed. "No, I—

"Just looking for the loo, mate," Jude interjected.

Ethan withdrew his hand and pointed behind me. "Your loo is that way. Different wing. And I'm not your mate."

Jude dropped his chin and scurried off around the corner.

I turned to face Ethan. "You didn't have to be so rude, you know. It was *me* who ran into *him*."

Ethan's gaze followed Jude, watching intently. "He had no business being down here."

"He was lost, Ethan."

Ethan's eyes shifted from Jude's back to me. "Don't call me Ethan."

"Okay, *Officer Scott*," I blew out air, "I'm starting to think you should be a patient here instead of an employee."

Ethan pinched his brows together and his eyes bounced between mine. Without giving him a chance to reply, I turned and walked away.

Over the summer, Ethan and I spent many nights together, talking until the sun came up. Our conversations typically consisted of differences between the states and the UK, television shows, and music. I'd learned Ethan was only a few years older than me, but he hardly talked about himself. He mentioned he had to complete a year here to advance in his career. Out of all the institutions, he was stuck with Dolor.

He made it very clear he did not want to be here.

But it was the similarities between his sister and me that made Ethan so interested. When we first met last year after Oscar had attacked me, I'd learned his sister had also been raped, then passed away shortly after. Ethan didn't go into the details about his sister, but wanted to know every aspect of my traumatic past. I didn't mind, either. If it helped him come to an understanding about what happened to his sister, I'd do whatever I could to help.

A strong scent of death drifted up to my nose upon entering my dorm room, and I quickly covered my nose with my hand as my door closed behind me. I tossed my new notebook over my desk before following the source.

The unbearable smell curdled my senses, and bile burned the back of my throat in warning. Crouching down, I pulled out the rolling cart under my bed. The sight before me sent me back on my hands, crawling away until my back slammed against the desk. A scream belted from my throat, and my eyes bulged at what I was seeing.

A dead, mutilated animal laid in the cart.

The color of red and fur mixed with my clothes.

Crawling to my trashcan, I leaned over right as the contents in my stomach came up.

"Mia?! What in God's name…" I heard before hands gripped my shoulders.

I recoiled at the sudden touch and twisted around, pressing myself closer to the wall. Once I noticed the hands belonged to Ethan, my arms flung around his neck, and I cried into his shirt collar. Ethan's body went stiff for a moment before he relaxed and pulled me in closer. His hands grasped the back of my head.

"Who would do this?" I cried out.

Ethan's hold around my waist tightened as his hand moved over the back of my head, "Some sick fuck," he muttered through an exhale. "Come on. I have to get you out of here and call this in."

Ethan shielded my eyes from what waited for me on my pull-out cart and walked me just outside the door in the corridor. He led me against the wall as I tried shaking the image out of my head. His blue eyes stayed on mine while he unclipped the radio from his belt and talked into it.

"Yes, wing four…" he repeated into the radio. Ethan clipped the radio back over his belt and hunched over with two hands on my shoulders. "Has anything like this happened before?"

Shaking my head, I tried to control my trembling hands.

"Has anyone threatened you?"

Shaking my head again, I said, "No one. It's been quiet all summer."

Another tear fell down my cheek, and Ethan reached out to capture it but paused before contact could be made. He sighed and dropped his hand and head at once.

"Ethan …" My voice broke and I let his name hang in the air as both a plea and a question. I wanted to tell him to make this go away—to find a way to erase the last ten minutes, but I could no longer speak. I bit the inside of my cheek to avoid showing emotion and fight back any more tears from escaping.

Ethan lifted his head and held my face with one hand. "Stay here while I look around?"

I nodded, and he took off.

My back fell against the wall and I slid down until my bottom met the ground.

"So, where are you going to be staying now?" Jake asked over the running water of the showerhead.

No matter how long I stayed under the water, the visions of the dead cat wouldn't disappear. Scrubbing my body until it turned pink, I replayed the last couple of weeks over and over, trying to find a flicker of a hint as to why someone would do something like that—nothing. "Take a wild guess," I said through a sigh.

"Please don't tell me a different wing."

"No, Officer Scott wouldn't allow it," I said low, hoping he didn't latch onto the comment or make something of it. No one knew the friendship Ethan and I shared, not even Bria. My friendship with Ethan stayed hidden in the middle of the night and far away from everyone else. It was all mine, and something I cherished. Up until the dead animal was found in my room, he had the ability to separate work and me. It was only a matter of time before his two worlds collided, and I wondered how this would change things between us.

"Then, where?"

I turned under the water and tilted my head back, massaging my fingers into my scalp. "Ollie's old room." The room where we had first kissed. The room I'd slowly fallen in love with him. The room we'd made love on countless occasions.

"No way," I heard Jake laugh from the opposite side of the wall separating us, "Oh, you poor thing. That's pure torture right there."

"Tell me about it."

"Do they know who did it?"

"No, but they opened an investigation."

I turned off the showerhead and rung out my hair. "Shit, I forgot a towel. Can you grab me one?"

"Yeah, one second," Jake said, and I waited naked as the cold slowly crept over my wet body. Moments later, Jake pushed a towel through the opening of the curtain. "Thanks." I wrapped the towel around me and opened my curtain. Jake was already in his boxers and standing in front of the mirror, squeezing toothpaste over his toothbrush.

I cocked my head over to the entrance of the bathroom to see Ethan standing against the wall. As soon as our eyes met, he turned his head away and adjusted his stance.

Since last year, security presence doubled around campus. A security guard was assigned to each wing, Ethan was ours, and the guards rotated between the mess hall and the community bathroom. I tightened the towel around me and grabbed my toothbrush from the sink. "And I have to wear the looney bin clothes until I can get new everything," I added, eyeing the tasteless clothes waiting for me on the counter. My old ones, including my "Cute but Psycho" shirt, had been ruined.

Jake spat a mouthful of toothpaste. "Oh, this just keeps getting better and better."

"Yeah, you should see the underwear they gave me, too."

He rinsed off his toothbrush before tapping it over the edge of the sink. "I don't know why you care. It's not like you'll let anyone see your knickers, anyway."

Though I couldn't see, I felt Ethan's eyes on me again. I turned my head, and my eyes met his piercing-blue, narrowed eyes. The way he treated me like a child annoyed me, but then he looked at me like this, and I figured screwing with his head a little would help with the day I had.

The few stragglers emptied as the steam gradually lifted. We had half the students here during the summer, and it wouldn't be long before the community bathroom crowded again, and I would have to start taking my showers in the morning.

"Alright, I'll see you in the AM." Jake tousled his blond hair and high-tailed out as I finished brushing my teeth.

It was just Ethan and me. Turning to face him again, he tensed against the wall; eyes fixed on me, hands clutched to his belt. He wanted to turn away, struggle carved in his features, but a more powerful force kept his eyes trained on me.

I released my towel and it dropped to my feet.

Ethan's jaw clenched behind his light red stubble, and his eyes scanned up and down my naked body. The rest of him stayed glued against the wall. The thick air swirled around us as we both breathed deep, staring at one another and chests rising in sync.

Finally, a look from him I'd been waiting for—admiration and appreciation.

"Get dressed, Jett," he finally said from the throat, clearing it afterward. "Please."

"I never said thank you," I picked the towel off the floor and towel-dried my hair, "but I'm tired of you treating me like a kid."

He turned his head away. "Then stop acting like one."

"Do I look like a child to you?"

"Don't do this," he warned.

"No, look at me," I forced out with a finger pointed at my chest. Ethan dropped his head momentarily. My heart plummeted as I waited, begging to be looked at again—waiting to be appreciated again. The same way Ollie did. "Do I look like a child to you?"

Ethan lifted his head, and his eyes soaked me in as the rest of his face fell. "No, Mia, you're definitely not a child."

He slapped the wall behind him with his palm before walking out.

Ollie's dorm looked like every other room now. It no longer screamed "Ollie" and now had a desk, a lifted bed, and a rolling cart—prepared for the next prisoner, which was me. My notebook sat on the desk, and I took a seat before opening it. Blank pages waited to be filled. It didn't take long before ink colored an entire page before I moved on to the next. The day became my muse, writing about everything between the sick surprise in my room to Ethan's gaze in the bathroom to Ollie.

My thoughts always ended with Ollie.

That night, my own screams woke me. Ethan never showed. I kicked off my covers and peeled off my sweat-drenched looney bin sweater clinging to my body and tried to catch my breath.

The days that followed were the same, Ethan avoiding me during the day, and by nightfall, the fear of a terror kept me awake. Some nights I cried myself back to sleep, and some nights, I didn't go back to sleep at all.

"You still having nightmares?" Bria asked as we sat around the circle during WASA—*Women Against Sexual Abuse*. We held our support group in the group therapy room before dinner on Thursdays. During the summer, we only had one other girl attend, but I was sure once the semester officially started in just a week, more would trickle in.

"Unfortunately," I sighed, crossing my legs in front of me. We never sat in the chairs, always took it to the floors. It seemed less official that way. "And it's like I'm back pedaling because I don't even know what they're about. My slate wipes clean every time I wake up."

"You might have a sleeping disorder. Like sleep apnea, which can prevent you from remembering." Tyler shrugged.

Tyler had started Dolor this summer. Her, Bria, and I became friends during our meetings. Come to find out Tyler was as much as a know-it-all as I was. Our stories were similar. Tyler was raped about a year ago and couldn't overcome the anxiety that came along with it. She'd hurt herself multiple times. After being thrown into a mental hospital twice in one month to protect her from hurting herself, she ended up here—cast and thrown from society like the rest of us. Tyler had long, blonde hair, but we shared the same brown eyes. She was shorter than me, but only by an inch. Her figure was fuller, but after a few more months, her weight would drop. It was inevitable, and she couldn't wait.

"When did all this start?" Tyler asked.

33

"I had them when I was little... after the incident. But they didn't come back until after Ollie left..." Missing him only strengthened with each passing day, and putting on a face for everyone to see became a daily battle. Torn between two worlds—life with Ollie, and life after him. Only, I never wanted or expected an after. My body and my heart both refused it, keeping me up each night, inducing the night terrors. He lingered inside my head, words always haunting me, his voice always reminding me of what we had. He'd left this beautiful trauma inside me, and the flame of what we shared burned.

This time, though, I wanted the flame to blow out.

The burn was too much to bear alone, incinerating me to nothing, only to wake up and relive a new day without him all over again.

"Oh, right... Ollie," she sang his name. "It's a shame I never got to meet this Ollie that I hear so much about."

"Maybe Ollie's absence is your trigger," Bria chimed in. "Ever thought about that?"

"He did help me out of the long-term funk. Maybe I relied on him too much... I don't know ... anyway, let's focus on you," I pointed to Tyler, "You still on that medication the psychiatrist prescribed?"

"Yeah, Dr. Butala is a godsend that stuff is the holy grail. No anxiety. No depression. I've never been happier."

Bria rolled her eyes. "I'm wondering at what point it will wear off. You have to get immune at some point, no?"

"Way to be positive," I muttered.

"I'm just trying to be realistic. Medicine will only get you so far, and eventually their effects will wear off and you either have to switch to different pills or find the root of the problem," Bria countered.

She had a point, but I didn't want Tyler feeling defeated. We all needed to take it one day at a time.

"I don't know, but this prescription I'm on has increased my libido or something. I haven't thought about sex since the incident, and now I'm looking at every bloke that walks by having thoughts I shouldn't," Tyler confessed. "Not to mention ... fantasies about Jake."

With that, we all fell into a burst of laughter.

"This is good!" I laughed, trying to catch my breath, "We all sound like a bunch of horny teens."

Tyler raised her hand. "Technically, I'm still a teen."

And she was right, Tyler was still nineteen. I had just turned twenty while Bria turned twenty over the summer.

"Hey, New Kid looks like he could use a little fun." Bria smiled.

"Jude gives me a bad vibe," I admitted. After bumping into him in the hall before the cat incident, I haven't been able to shake his grip or stare.

"Everyone gives you a bad vibe," Bria countered.

That was true.

After crying myself to sleep, I woke to a dark room with a cold towel pressed against my forehead. "Ollie?" I blinked my eyes open.

"No, Jett. It's Ethan," Ethan answered, leaning over me with worry struck in his eyes. "It's always Ethan."

Without an afterthought, I wrapped my arms around his neck and pulled him closer, only wanting his security and comfort to clothe me as I gasped for a steadfast breath. Unexpectedly, Ethan abandoned all principle and rolled over beside me, pulling me close. His strong arms pinned me against the heat of his body as his fingers moved the hair from my face.

"I'm mad at you," I whispered.

Ethan sighed. "I'm mad at you, too."

I pulled my head from his chest and searched his face. "What did I ever do to you?"

"You're a constant distraction," he explained. "Now roll over, Jett."

Listening, I flipped over on my other side away from him and closed my eyes as the tears for Ollie fell like clockwork. Ethan gathered my hair and flipped it up off my neck before placing the cool towel at the nape like every night before.

Though, tonight was different.

Tonight, was the first night he had ever climbed in beside me. I wanted it to be Ollie next to me, but having Ethan did lessen the blow—*a little*. The tears still came as the memories preyed on me, weakened me. I clenched my eyes, and the visions emerged as my cries drifted into the night.

I was held captive by the love Ollie gave, and the future he built for us. But the day Ollie slipped away, I shattered. For seven months, I was left behind picking up the pieces.

And Ethan was on his knees, helping me.

I'd never asked him to, either. Though here he was, holding me as I broke away all the pieces he just picked up the night before—a recurring nightmare.

There was little Ethan knew about Ollie, only the fact he was Oscar's brother who had been arrested for drugging Bria and myself and almost raped me. The first night I'd cried out for Ollie in my sleep, Ethan asked me why it was his name I screamed out for. Ethan couldn't understand, and he never would.

Talking about Ollie only hurt more, so I avoided all unnecessary self-infliction.

Ethan's fingers ran down my arms, giving my body silent permission to fill my lungs completely. "He's gone, Mia," he said in my hair with confidence. His arm reached under my arm, crossing over my chest, pinning me to his as if I couldn't be close enough. "I'll stay until you fall back asleep."

After day bled into night, it became impossible to hide. Ollie wasn't here to get me through it, and I was angry. Ollie had taught me how to save myself, but this time, I was drowning, and I didn't have the strength to swim against the current of the pain.

But, Ethan kept my head above water.

At least when I closed my eyes, I could pretend it was Ollie.

And I was desperate.

THREE

"What's keeping me up at night is the haunting memory of that last breath you took right in front of me."

OLIVER MASTERS

Ollie

"Can we at least stop for tea? I'm in need of a caffeine fix," I asked, all-knowing the answer, but this drive dragged. Plus, my restless legs needed stretching from the three-hour transport from the jail.

The security guard didn't bother entertaining my request, keeping his focus out the window of the small van. I didn't remember him. He was dark-skinned with a shiny bald head and slim physique. The restraints pinged against the metal as I attempted to lean my elbows over my knees to steady my bouncing knee. The cuffs pierced my skin, and I groaned, throwing my head back against the torn leather. "You must be new at Dolor, yeah?" I asked the guard, slicing the awkward silence. "Haven't seen you before. What building are you stationed?"

"We have another hour until we get there. Let's make the next hour relaxing for both of us, alright?"

Turning my head out the window, I wondered what could be waiting for me at Dolor. Maybe jail wasn't so bad. Aside from being thrown into interrogation on numerous occasions for hours on end, I'd been treated fairly. It took five months for the detectives to piece together a strong case against my brother, Oscar. At first, I hadn't been cooperative, but only because I'd been angry.

After the second week without my medication, I had completely lost control as my emotions raided me from all directions.

The only thing I could think about was her.

All I asked for was her.

All I wanted and needed was her.

Regardless of whether my eyes were opened or closed, she invaded every piece of me like a raging storm. To get me under control, they had reached out to Dolor and retrieved my medical paperwork before putting me right back on the agony-reducing pills, and finally, they had me right where they wanted me.

Oscar had gotten what he deserved. And me? I had been cleared from all sex crimes. I'd never voluntarily been associated with the prostitution ring, only a product of a prostitute.

Unfortunately, they couldn't clear me from the crime I'd been placed at Dolor for originally. Even after explaining to the detectives I was innocent for the crime against Brad, the punter that had been on life support by the hands of my brother when I was seventeen, they still didn't have enough evidence confirming it was Oscar.

Oscar had a false alibi. I hadn't.

Brad had passed away two months ago.

Now, I was charged with homicide due to mental illness instead of unlawful injury.

Dolor was my only chance at freedom.

Back to square fucking one.

With one more year left, they sentenced me back to Dolor to finish what I'd started since I'd helped take down Oscar.

I'd made a friend from my seven months in jail. His name was Travis.

We'd exchanged our life stories like they were lived by other people. Travis was a good mate, only got caught up in the wrong crowd. Travis's story was much like every other desperate bloke needing quick cash. He was the look-out guy during a robbery, and had a clean record before. The bloke grew up much like myself with an absentee father and shitty mum. There was hope for Travis, who mentioned he had a girl waiting for him. He had asked me if I had a girl. I'd told him I didn't. I couldn't bring myself to talk about her, let alone say her name out loud. Though, she always lingered in the back of my mind.

I remembered the way I felt for her, and glad through these last seven months the medication had dulled the ache I knew I would have without it. Detoxing from the pills had caused my Emotional Intensity Disorder to heighten those emotions and had driven me into utter insanity.

During transport back to Dolor, I was three days free from medication, teetering back and forth on whether or not it was worth feeling again—back and forth on whether or not I'd ask Dr. Butala or Conway to keep me off of them.

Was it worth fighting through the pain?

It didn't feel like I had much of a choice.

My feelings for her slowly raised from the ashes over the last six hours. Every hour more painful than the last.

"We're here," the security guard announced as we pulled off the main road and onto a single path leading up to the gates of Dolor. The pavement beneath the tires turned to rock, and I glanced out the window to see Dolor under a grey sky.

My body reacted to the closing distance of hers and nerves set in. I drew in a long and uneven breath. Three days without the pills, and I needed to take them every twelve hours. Already, I felt myself losing control and was thankful for these restraints. My hands shook, and I closed them into fists to ease the tremors.

The van pulled up to the front of the campus before it came to a stop. The security guard zip-tied my wrists together before unlocking the cuffs from my wrists and ankles, and escorted me out of the van and through the double doors.

"Oliver Masters," Lynch greeted at the security checkpoint, "I'd like to say welcome back, but that all depends on you." It had been seven months since I'd seen Lynch, and it looked as if the chap aged twenty years. His tailored suit didn't mask the tiredness in his brown eyes or the apparent stress causing his hairline to recede at a much faster pace.

"I'm not here to cause trouble. I want to make it through the year smoothly just as much as you," I said, meaning every word. I refused to join my brother in prison.

Lynch nodded and guided me through the scanner without beeps. As I walked through the halls to the office, I kept my head down and feet in front of me, unable to bring myself to see the library doors—the place her and I ran off to each Saturday morning to escape.

Still, her laugh echoed through my head, reminding me.

Her brown hair whipped in my memory as I chased her.

Her heart-stopping smile projected in my thoughts against my will.

"This way," Lynch said, rescuing me from the moments of my past.

The dean's office hadn't changed.

Lynch held up a finger, picked up the phone, and I took a seat in the chair across from him on the opposite side of his desk. I wiped the sweat from my forehead across the sleeve of my shirt, shivering in a cold sweat.

"Dr. Butala, yes… I have Oliver Masters in now… mmhmm…" Lynch nodded and hung up without a goodbye. "Your psychiatrist is on his way down now, so we'll wait." Lynch's brown eyes met mine briefly before turning away. The color of his eyes matched a bottle of Jack, the same as hers, and my heart twisted from another reminder of her.

Dr. Butala and I never agreed on much, but his intentions were good and honest.

He believed in a chemical imbalance in the brain, and she—still not thinking or saying her name—thought it wasn't a disorder, but a blessing to feel wholeheartedly. She loved me the way I was, but she had only ever seen one side of me. I never allowed her to see the other side of my disorder—the evil side.

Butala knocked before Lynch welcomed him in.

"Masters, glad to have you back," he said with a hand on my shoulder. He was a small gentleman from India with a slight accent.

I dropped my head in a single nod. "Glad to be back."

Butala took a seat beside me and rested my file over his lap.

"First and foremost, I want to apologize again for putting you in an improper position with Oscar," Lynch said, his tone soft and sincere. "If I'd known, I would have never allowed it. Can we put that in the past and start over?"

"Yes, sir."

Relief flashed in his eyes, but only for a moment. "Very good. Now that is out of the way, today marks the new school year, and we have already had a few mishaps over the last week. Though you didn't advise me about your brother, can I count on you now to come to me if anything seems out of the ordinary?" Lynch asked, brow raised. "All I ask from this point forward is open communication."

Though I understood each word he said, his voice came in and out as if my head was submerged underwater. Hoping it would clear the fog in my eardrums, I shook my head. "What happened?"

Lynch's eyes darted from Butala then back to me. He drew in a breath, rolled his chair forward, and propped his elbows over the desk. "You'll hear about it anyway so you may as well hear it from me," he folded his arms, "It didn't start until early last week, so it's hard to say who is doing this, but there have been vulgar pranks. Now, I know it may be too much to ask, but you're the only person I know that isn't behind it, so I'm asking if you can keep your eyes and ears open."

"Vulgar pranks? What happened exactly?"

"Cat mutilation found in a student's dorm early last week. Then just yesterday there was a target sign written in blood outside a door," Lynch said with distaste in his mouth. "Now I'm not asking for you to get involved, Oliver. I only need you to let me know if you hear or see anything."

My stomach jumped.

I tried to swallow it back down.

"Absolutely." I had a hard time focusing, my body slowly defied me, and I ran my zip-tied hand up my forehead and through my hair.

"Good, now let's talk about your treatment plan," he said, nodding approval to Butala.

Butala opened my file as I processed the pranks and why it was so hot in here.

"When was the last time you took medication?" Butala asked.

"Over three days now."

"How do you feel right now, Oliver?"

"Sick…"

"Turn around, let me see you."

Pivoting my chair, Butala took the stethoscope from around his neck. He brought one end to his ears and the other under my shirt against my chest. It was cold to the touch, and the room fell silent as he stared at his watch.

"Heart rate is abnormally high," he glanced up, and our eyes met, "Pupils are dilated," he turned to Lynch, "He's already experiencing the beginning stages of withdrawal."

Ha. Withdrawal. Such a simple word for the turmoil thrashing around within, eating away at the dead parts of me, only exposing the remanence of regret and guilt. Perspiration rolled down my hairline like ice against my hot flesh.

"Get it under control, I don't want a repeat like the last time," Lynch stated.

Butala turned back to face me. "Oliver, other than sickness, what else do you feel? Angry, sad, happy?"

My knee bounced again, and I stretched out my leg. "Nothing. I don't feel anything, just this sickness."

"We can restart his treatment today, but with already three days of skipped dosages, it could take a few days for it to take effect. You could keep him in solitary until the medication kicks back in, but I don't recommend it. Keeping him confined may extend the recovery time."

"What do you recommend?" Lynch asked Butala.

Butala sat back in his chair, studying me like a science project. "Get him set up in his new dorm and have him start his new schedule in a week or so."

"Very well," Lynch sighed and leaned back in his chair. "Oliver, please don't make me regret this. It wouldn't be a good start to the year."

While the security guard escorted me to the nurse's station, I kept my head down. A few times up the stairs, I lost my balance and quickly fought to regain it. Having both my wrists bound didn't help.

It was mid-morning, and since classes started today, everyone should be on the third floor. Nurse Rhonda didn't hold back and flung her arms around me. "Get these zip-ties off him, Jerry, this boy doesn't belong in these!" She yelled at the security guard as she held me at arm's length.

"Rhonda, you always had a soft spot for them," Jerry chuckled and took a blade against my ties.

My wrist freed, and I rubbed the insides.

"Oh, Ollie. You need a proper haircut," Nurse Rhonda shook her head, "I'll do that, then you can go over there and take a shower. I'll have Jerry get your belongings you left from storage while you shower, yeah?"

"Yeah, sounds good." I strained a smile despite my dizziness.

She pulled up a chair and grabbed the scissors and comb from the cart and gestured me to sit. "You don't look so good. You're pale." The back of her hand pressed against my forehead before she disappeared behind me.

"Going through withdrawals," I explained and kept my head steady. "Not too short."

Rhonda smacked the back of my head. "I've been cutting your hair for over a year, boy. I know what I'm doing."

Despite my small laugh, it was enough to remember laughing was all I had done before.

Six months didn't seem like a long time, but it was enough time. I'd known I loved the girl who owned my soul the second I felt her, and I'd spent six months convincing her we were meant to be together and loving her completely.

The last seven months I'd spent numb and without her.

Three days were spent off the pills, suffering a heat stroke in a winter storm.

And the last sixty seconds were spent counting the days since I'd met her to avoid the ripping my heart was doing during this wintery hurricane under the sweltering sun.

Yeah, my body was fucking confused … to put it lightly.

I rubbed my palms up and down the rough material of the blue pants I wore from the jail, allowing them to absorb the proof of my weakness. Even through my struggles, she dominated every breaking fragment. The thought of her alone kept my blood pumping while the rest of me wasted away.

I had to know. "Ms. Rhonda?"

"Yeah?"

"How is she?"

"How's who?"

I drew in a deep breath.

"Mia," I exhaled. "How's Mia?"

It was the first time I'd said her name out loud, and as soon as it left from my lips, the ache intensified, the need for her taste conquered the need of a numbing fix. Her name was both a stifling curse and a vital prayer. Her name invited more rips inside my chest and more memories of us together.

Memories of the way she made me feel.

Memories of the way I'd made her feel.

Perfection.

She'd always fit perfectly in my arms. She'd fit perfectly on top of me. I'd fit perfectly inside her. She'd fit perfectly beside me, against me, under me, bodies entangled and aligned.

Every way, we'd fit without flaw.

Her body was my kingdom come.

Her divine kiss was my salvation.

Her soul was mine's paradise.

Mia was my evermore.

And I'd known since the moment my soul felt hers.

My lungs shrunk as my heart shook in her name.

"Mia's holding up, that one. You'd be proud of those girls, you know. Her and Bria spent the summer organizing a support group for girls suffering from sexual abuse. She's been keeping busy, that's for sure."

Freeing a steady breath, I smiled. Mia was okay—a temporary fix until I could see her.

"It's a shame what happened," she added.

And just like that, my smile dissolved. "What do you mean?"

"The bullying against her, Dean Lynch didn't tell you?"

"Bria?" *Don't say my girl's name, Rhonda.*

"Mia. Found the dead cat herself right under her bed last week," she snipped another layer of hair as it fell at the corner of my eye, "Poor girl has been through enough."

My fingers gripped the arms of the chair, and the ache twisted into anger. She had to be mistaken. Mia had never gone out of her way to upset anyone, at least not since I'd found her. "Has she had any meltdowns? Made visits in here or solitary since I left?"

Was she still the same light-brown eyed girl?

Was she still my Mia?

"No, as I said, she's been doing real good," she sighed and tousled my hair, "alright, you're good for a fortnight. Time to hit the shower."

Jerry, the bald guard, came back with my belongings in a trash bag, and I spent my shower thinking of Mia, trying to control my emotions at all costs.

I needed to see her.

But not like this.

My hands ran up and down my face over and over under the water, in an attempt to drown out the slow-building rage inside me.

Someone had targeted Mia.

My clothes had been washed, and I slipped into my gray pants and black tee, feeling more like my old self, though the spells of sickness still loitered inside me and my emotions grew after each passing second. Rhonda checked me over before Jerry walked me back to my dorm.

"This isn't my dorm," I stated, standing in front of Mia's door beside Jerry.

Jerry didn't bother with an explanation as he unlocked the door and turned the knob. The door swung open, and a gust of new memories engulfed me. Swirling memories. The ones I'd buried deep in my subconscious.

The padded walls had been removed.

A desk sat against the wall on the right.

A bed complete with headboard and footboard welcomed me.

"Where is the girl that was here before?" I asked, my gaze touching every place I'd made love to her. *There. There. And there.*

"Hell if I know. This isn't my wing. I'm on third," Jerry said and gave me a nod. "Don't forget, dinner at five-thirty."

Then the door closed behind him, leaving me to fend for myself against the pictures inside my head. After dropping my bag on the floor, I sat at the edge of the bed and closed my eyes. It was all too much. Nausea whipped around in my stomach, anguish seeped through my pores and stabbed every part of me, and above all, I was bloody exhausted. The clock above the door read lunch had passed, and she would be with Dr. Conway for another forty minutes.

Collapsing over the mattress, I closed my eyes.

Unavoidable images of her lying under me, light brown hair sprawled across the pillow while her hips swayed in eagerness to be filled flashed like a movie. I remembered her supple pink lips turn raw from the damage mine had done while the rest of her shook under the pleasure I gifted her. Watching her come undone while still inside her, being a part of it, the purpose of it, the pulsating…

Mia…

Over three hours had passed before my eyes sprang to life. Rolling into a sitting position over the side, I ran my palms through my shorter hair and down my face. Every cell, muscle, and vein pounded against my skull as the rest of my body shivered in the bitter abandonment of Mia and the pills.

I could only choose one.

The pills were a necessary evil right now.

But Mia was my endgame.

I tilted my head, and the room swayed around me as I tried to find the clock. Dinner was almost over. Bringing myself to my feet, I jumped up and down on my toes to bring myself to life and wake the fuck up.

The last thing I wanted was for her to see me like this, but we didn't have much time. It wouldn't be long before I'd be back to the heartless asshole, and right now, all I wanted was to see her eyes. I needed to make sure she was still with me. I wanted to feel her touch, kiss her lips, and have her eyes on me. My feelings for her flowed from my pumping heart to the rest of my body, screaming out for her.

On the verge of an utter breakdown, I left the dorm and shuffled down the hall, looking like hell, I was sure. The closer I made it to the mess hall, the more my nerves twisted with bashing thoughts. *Did she hate me? Did she forget about me? Did she ever want to see me again after I all-knowingly pushed her away?*

It wasn't me that day. She had to have known that.

With every step closer to the mess hall, my soul felt like it was one step ahead of me, leaving my body only wanting to be closer to hers. Adrenaline pumped, keeping my body up with my eager soul.

I paused just before the entryway and leaned my shoulder against the separating wall, keeping my eyes on the swirling marble below and drawing in a deep breath.

I turned the corner, counted to three, and looked up.

My eyes immediately went to her.

A full smile appeared on her face, and her beautiful brown eyes squinted as she waved whatever Jake said away with her hand. A million emotions filtered through me, and my hand fell over the wall to hold me steady from the chaotic rush. It all happened at once, everything I'd told her about—the air left my lungs, an ache pierced my heart, the pounding in my head, the lightning in my eyes. I screwed my eyes shut, thinking it would keep me from falling apart, but it was no use. When I opened them again, she found me from across the room and tears sprang in my eyes.

Her entire expression changed, no longer smiling and laughing like she was moments before, and it was because of me. Mia stumbled to her feet, and I pushed off the cement, wanting to run to her, but needed her alone.

She would follow me.

Turning, I walked in the opposite direction to the community bathroom where we first exchanged words almost a year ago. My hands shook as my body drained with each step until I was behind the door. My back fell against the tile near the door.

She would come.

Then the door opened, and my body reacted instantly. My arms wrapped around Mia's waist, pulling her into me. Her smell whipped around my senses, the scent of coconut blended with jasmine in the spring rain.

Her face pressed against my chest as she held me tight, her small shoulders shook as she cried silently in my shirt. The last thread holding me together snapped and I broke down. My breath released in a staggered rush and tears outpoured as my cheek pressed against her head.

My nervous hand ran through her hair and held the back of her head, pinning her against me. *Perfection.* I kissed the top of her head, her forehead, her wet cheek. Her grip around me tightened, and my hands moved to the sides of her face, and I tilted her chin to see her eyes.

Golden-brown and beautiful.

"Mia... I'm..." I tried to get the words out, but my emotions strangled me. Her eyes shined like glass, and her chin trembled as tears freely spilled from the corners. She held on so tight, but we weren't close enough.

We could never be close enough.

Our lips crashed, and my body instantly let off the wall, wanting to merge with her. With the familiarity of her scent and taste, my soul fed on her, satisfying its only deprivation. But just as quickly as she pulled me together, she pulled away from me, and her hand came across, striking my face.

My face didn't feel it, but my heart sure did.

She stood before me, her eyes mixed with emotion and her bottom lip shaking.

"Seven months!" she cried out, "Do you have any idea what you've done to me?" My head shook, and I took a step forward, but she backed away from me, and that small distance she created cut deeper. "I let my guard down for you, I loved you with everything, and in the end, you…" her palms hit my chest, and I did nothing but take the beating, "I was on my knees, Ollie, then you pulled everything out from under me and for seven months I crawled through every fucking memory and every empty promise!"

Each word penetrated me, tore me open worse than her hands on me. Over the last seven months, I had been able to get by without her because I was already dead inside. Yet, I helped her destroy her walls for me only to leave her unarmed.

And the way I left stripped her of the belief I created for us.

I took another step forward, and she shoved me against my chest again.

"How dare you," she choked, her voice defeated. Her brown eyes filled with hatred—hatred toward me. Strands of her hair glued to her wet cheek as tears continued to fall from her eyes. "I'm scared to close my eyes because every damn time, all I see is you, and when I open them, you're not there! You were gone!"

I'd seen this side of her before, but it was during a time she fought against herself. She'd held the same terror in her eyes before when I'd taken her down in the shower room and I clutched onto her under the water.

In her eyes, I was the new enemy, but I refused to accept it.

She came at me again, but I snatched her wrist and pinned her against me, holding her close to my chest. "I'm here now," my mouth hovered over hers as she trembled in my hold, "I'm right here."

She fisted my shirt at my chest and yanked me down until our mouths collided. The rest of me turned to liquid as her soft wet lips stroked mine, speaking her pain and unwavering love she still had for me. I inhaled a more stable breath through my nose upon her exhale, breathing her in.

Mia.

Poetry.

As if no time passed between us, our lips moved in sync while the rest of my body forgot about the sickness and caved to our needs. I spun Mia so her back was against the wall and mine fused to her where it belonged. Her lips parted for me, allowing me in and I took what I unknowingly craved for the last seven deadly months.

"I love you, Mia," I grabbed her face and waited for her eyes to open to see this is real, "I'll always love you."

Lights sparked in her eyes like it did the first time we kissed, and though I never needed confirmation, it was all I needed to dive into her again.

Slowly, my tongue caressed hers, the taste of apple juice still embedded in her buds. Ignoring the tremors in my hands, I held her soaked face as she sucked my lip. Warm hands glorified my bare skin under my shirt, fighting to ease the bitter withdrawal.

For her, I fought to be strong, but I only grew dizzier from the sickening affliction. My head dropped to her shoulder, and the door to the room swung open.

"Jett?"

My head snapped up, and a red-headed security guard stared at the two of us from the doorway. Instantly, I lifted myself off her, and my gaze darted between Mia and the red-headed wanker.

Mia's face was blotchy and wet—golden-brown eyes, battered.

Her breathing faltered from what just occurred between us.

The security guard's eyes jerked between Mia's condition and me, and suddenly, he launched at me. The cracking sound of my nose came from inside my ears as my head bounced back. My hands shot over my nose and eyes when another force sent my back into the sink. A weltering pain stabbed my lower back.

"Stop it!" Mia's screams echoed in the bathroom. "Ethan, stop!"

FOUR

"The truth is, I'm not normal.
Is that too much for you to handle?"

OLIVER MASTERS

Mia

"Ollie ... oh, my God ..." I cried, pulling Ollie to his feet and leaning him against the sink. His elbow rested over the edge, unable to hold himself up fully.

"Ollie?" Ethan asked surprised from behind me, but I ignored him as I frantically pulled paper towels from the dispenser and ran it under cold water. The tears hadn't stopped flowing as I turned off the faucet and returned to Ollie's side.

Moving Ollie's hand away from his nose, I replaced it with the paper towels and tilted his head back, holding them in place to stop the bleeding as he grumbled incoherently.

He came back, and my mind couldn't keep up with what my heart was doing to me. Ollie closed his eyes with the cold towel pressed against him, still partially leaned over the sink.

"I can't believe this shit," Ethan growled and smacked the tiled wall with his palm.

The seven months of living in hell reached a boiling point and spilled out of me as I turned against the one person who had been on my side since Ollie left. Taking three harsh steps toward Ethan, I pushed him once in the shoulder. "Why did you do that?"

With the last ten minutes, I'd physically hurt the two people who ever cared about me. I knew what I was doing, but I couldn't stop myself at the same time. There was an abundant amount of emotions hitting me at once, and the moment Ethan walked in and hit Ollie, he became an easier target to release seven months of the pure hell I'd been living in.

My hand swung at him, but he rapidly lifted his arm as a shield and took a step back. "Coward!" I yelled, taking another step toward him.

Ollie's arm snaked around my stomach and dragged me away. "Stop, Mia. We don't have time. I don't have time." He pinned me to his torso with one hand and walked me backward until my back hit the sink. Ollie's other hand pressed the blood-soaked towels to his nose as his hips leaned into me, caging me in. "Listen to me. I don't know how much time I have. We can't risk either one of us going to solitary."

"He punched you for no reason!" I looked around Ollie to face Ethan. "You punched him!"

Ollie pulled me back in front of him. His hand cupped my face to redirect my attention. "I deserved that, love."

"How are you back?" Ethan asked with nervous hands moving from his belt, over his stubble, then behind the back of his head. His face paled. I'd never seen him so bothered.

"Please, I need a moment with her," Ollie stressed, leaning over until his palm caught the edge of the sink. I studied his stance. Sweat pricked his temples, his eyes strung out, and he couldn't sit up straight. Something was wrong.

"You're on your own, Jett," Ethan shook his head, "Just know, I'm not picking you up this time." He pulled the handle to the bathroom open hard enough to send the door flying against the wall.

Ollie looked down at me, his green eyes blazing, and his muscles tensed to control whatever thoughts strained his mind. "I would ask what that was all about, but I'm not sure if I want to know," Ollie muttered, and dropped his free arm over my back to pull me close.

My arms wrapped around his torso. There was a slight tremor in his hand as he rubbed up and down my back. "You need to see the nurse, Ollie," I tilted my head up to see his face, "You don't look so good."

Ollie shook his head as a student entered the bathroom, then his head rolled back as another girl followed in behind. Both student's eyes swept over us briefly as they passed by.

"Come on, let's go to my room before the auto-lock sweep." He grabbed my hand and led me out of the bathroom and down the corridor through a crowd walking to their nightly shower routine. He approached my old room, and before opening, he looked down at me with the paper towel held over his nose. "Out of all the rooms here, they put me in this one."

"You got my room?"

He nodded, then pushed the door open.

Stumbling, Ollie fell back against the mattress and tilted his head up over the pillow with a low moan. He waved me over to lay next to him. "Please, I'm going to pass out any second."

This whole disposition wasn't like him. "Are you sick? What's going on with you?"

"I'm just not in a good place right now,"—he turned to face me— "Please, come here. The last thing you owe me is your forgiveness, but your distance is killing me worse than how I'm feeling right now."

No matter how angry I was with him, my body wasn't. Like a reflex, my feet move forward, my knees hit the mattress, and in no time, I melded to his side. He pulled the paper towel away and threw it to the end of the bed before swiping his fingers under his nose to see if the bleeding had stopped. When he realized it had, he turned over and nuzzled his face into my neck.

Though my brain hadn't quite caught up fully on everything that just happened within the last twenty minutes, I finally let go of a breath. I was finally home. Though this home was different, yet all the same like a fresh coat of paint. My heart didn't know the difference, but my hands ran through his sweaty hair and over his trembling skin. His shirt was damp while his breathing was shaky. "Are you on your medication?" I hesitantly asked, afraid of the next words he would say.

"I wasn't then I went back on them today. It's the withdrawals until they hit my system. I think all this back and forth made me sick. I can't think straight. I'm sorry," his fingers dug into my waist as his body quivered through the dark spell, "I'm so sorry, Mia. I'm a bloody mess right now…" each word muffled by his refusal to leave my neck, "I don't know what to do anymore."

For months, I thought about the moment of us re-uniting, but being the one comforting him never crossed my mind. His hot body shivered in my hold, while his breath, lips, and sweat all soaked my neck. I rocked him as a soft and hardly inaudible mantra of "I'm sorry's" flowed from his lips until he fell asleep. It didn't take long, and after he was out, my own mixed and confused tears freed from their private prison.

I cried because he was back, and those happy tears mixed with the sad ones—sad ones because he was riding an emotional rollercoaster, and I knew from experience what it was like, but this was one I couldn't fix.

If what he said was correct, it meant it was only a matter of time before he'd turn right back into the unreachable asshole who left me in the hallway seven months ago.

Zeke stared at me from across the table during breakfast the following morning. He seemed to be in a good mood, and I wondered if he somehow picked up on Ollie's energy and knew of his return. I didn't dare tell him—not yet, anyway. If Ollie was back to only leave at the hands of oblivion, I preferred preserving Zeke's hopes.

In a year, our table had grown from only the two of us, to now Zeke, myself, Bria, Jake, and Tyler. Ollie used to sit beside me, and I wondered if he'd find his way back to my table or his old one which was now occupied by Maddie, Jude, and Gwen.

"You're quiet this morning," Bria said, sitting one chair over from Zeke. "Up all night again?"

I shook my head. "Surprisingly, I slept all night. First time in months." And it was odd. For seven months, without fault, I'd woken from terrors without remembering what they were ever about. But the night of Ollie's return, I slept peacefully. There was no such thing as coincidences.

"Then what's got your knickers in a twist?"

Ethan's gaze caught my attention behind Bria by the doorway, and he glanced away. "Nothing, just one of those mornings." They would all find out eventually, hopefully after I'd come to terms with it. Returning my attention back to my uneaten tray, I wondered what this all meant when Tyler slammed her fist over the table.

"Dibs!" she shouted.

Zeke flinched, and I snapped my head in her direction beside me. "Watch it, Ty. You're going to freak him out."

"I call dibs," she said again, pointing in the direction toward Ethan.

Looking back over, Ollie stood before Ethan, shaking Ethan's hand. My smile stretched across my face. Ollie fixed his black tee down over his joggers and turned to head in our direction. When our eyes met, the recognizable bright green beamed, and his hair was back in its usual tidal wave.

"Oh … my … god," she sighed in awe. "Who is that guy?"

"Ollie!" Bria squealed as she jumped out of her chair.

It didn't take long before Ollie's arms were around Bria, then Jake, and even Gwen as she rushed over. Ollie's eyes never left mine as he swiftly got through everyone, and I couldn't help but beam as he greeted his friends.

"Zeke," Ollie nodded his head over to him as he came up behind me. Familiar arms wrapped around my waist, and his head dropped into my neck. "My love."

"Hold up," Bria said, pointing at me. "You knew he was back?"

Ollie took the empty chair between me and the window. "Only got in yesterday."

"So, you're not available…" Tyler mumbled to no one.

"Good question, I'm not sure," Ollie squeezed my thigh, "Mia, am I available?" Turning to face him, he flashed me a smug smile. "Is it you and I, or are we shagging other people?"

I narrowed my eyes, trying to process what he'd said. The three words that stuck were, *"I'm not sure."* Even the suggestion of fucking other people should have stuck, but it didn't. Since the day I'd met Ollie, he had always been certain. He'd never questioned what we had, and those three words were a reminder there was a morsel of the guy who left me crying on my knees in the hallway seven months ago still inside him.

"I'm not sure," I said, matching his uncertainty with a shrug but pain cut through each word. The truth was, I was sure. I just wasn't sure which man was sitting in front of me. Was it the man I fell in love with, or the one who left me stranded? That day haunted me ever since, and it didn't help the fact I had to walk down the same hall every damn day and relive the moment over and over again.

Ollie's face twisted into a look I'd never seen before and raised his brows. "You're going to embarrass me like that, yeah? In front of your friends?"

His facial expression and tone weren't him, and I was sure my Ollie hadn't returned. My Ollie never cared about what other people thought. His eyes, touch, and tone conflicted with one another, all contradicting. He didn't hold the same low and carefully controlled tone. *No.* His voice had a hint of hostility, dripping with the reminder of him slowly slipping away before my very eyes once again. "And you didn't?"

His mouth set in a hard line, and I shook my head, backing my chair from the table and gathered my belongings all at once. His hand caught my wrist, but I snatched it away. "The Ollie I know is certain," I said through gritted teeth.

"I'm sorry, I didn't mean for it to come out that way," his leg bounced under the table, and he pressed down on his knee before standing. "Mia, let's go talk."

"I have class." With my books clutched to my chest, it was my turn to walk away from him. The green eyes staring at the back of my head burned a hole, but I kept my feet in front of me. It hurt to be around him, only bringing back the day he slipped away. All I wanted was for my Ollie to be back, and I wondered how long I would have to wait.

"You alright, Jett?" Ethan asked as I passed him while leaving the mess hall. Without stopping, I nodded and picked up my pace. "Wait up!" Ethan followed after me, and I didn't stop until his hand rested on my shoulder and spun me around. "Listen, it's none of my business—"

"You're right. It's not," I snapped.

"Just listen to me for a second." His electric blue eyes burned as he peered down at me, and he scratched the back of his head. "You've been doing so good. I don't want to see you fall back into that same place."

"Why?" I asked, my voice on the verge of breaking. "Why do you care?"

"Don't play coy. It's no secret we're close, or at least I thought we were close," Ethan rolled his head back before returning his eyes to me, "We're friends, and I'm not going to sit back and watch him bring you down again." His blue eyes went cold, and there was something he wanted to say, but he bit his tongue, refusing to cross a line.

"What's this?" Ollie's voice came from behind. His arm draped around my shoulder like he was marking his territory. The tingles shooting up my spine blended between what my heart wanted and what my brain couldn't understand. It was Ollie, but it wasn't. Twisted confusion. Total mind-fuck. My head snapped up to see Ollie's eyes darting back between Ethan and me. "Ah, it makes sense. You got a thing for security guards, don't you? You're screwing *him* now?" Ollie turned his chilling tone to Ethan. "You banging my girlfriend?"

Ethan shook his head and took a step back. "You have the wrong idea."

"No, I don't think I do." Ollie pulled his arm away and shoved me forward with enough force, my books fell to the floor and my face crashed into Ethan's chest. "Have her, mate. I have no use any longer."

I went into shock, and I pressed my face further into Ethan's chest, gripping his shirt into my fist. Ethan took a step forward, taking me with him and a calculated chuckle came from Ollie while his footsteps faded behind me, adding more distance between us.

Ethan's hand pressed against the back of my head. "He's gone," he mumbled and tried pulling me away, but I refused. "What a fucking prick."

"It's not him. That's not Ollie," I cried, "He's never done that before…I don't…"

Ethan's grip tightened around me before his chest rose against my cheek, then fell as he released a long, exaggerated breath. "Don't make excuses for him."

FIVE

> "I'LL WAKE UP
> WHEN THIS NIGHTMARE
> IS OVER."
>
> OLIVER MASTERS

Mia

It had only been a week since Ollie's return, and already he'd proven I could hate him. He warned me this would happen, as if his forwardness would have prepared my paper heart. It would have been easier if he just stayed away. Luckily, classes kept me occupied, and Ollie kept to himself.

Knowing he was within touching distance, talking distance—within distance, period—didn't help. Three times a day, I'd seen him throughout the week. Breakfast, lunch, and dinner. I felt his eyes on me as if he were watching me from across the room from his old table with Maddie, Gwen, and Jude. But each time my eyes drifted, all I'd ever catch was the side of his face.

"So, I'm thinking we should get together in the woods. It will be like old times," Bria announced as soon as she sat down across from me on Friday morning in the mess hall. "Think of it as a *welcome-home-Ollie-get-together*."

"No, I don't think that's such a great idea," I stated.

Jude's mysterious behavior turned Bria utterly smitten with him, and the get-together had nothing to do with Ollie. The smile on her face when she looked at Jude told me so. All Bria wanted was to get Jude in the woods, and though I'm not a cock-block, I didn't know which side of Ollie would show up, or if he would show up at all.

"We need something to cheer us up," she whined, turning to see Jude at the same table Ollie sat at.

My gaze followed hers until my eyes landed upon Ollie once again. He looked the same in his black jeans, faded tattoos, and dirty-brown chaotic hair, though his smile was different and his eyes never found me like they used to. Some moments, I swore I'd caught a glimpse of the old him, as if a light bulb went off inside his head. But mainly he paid no attention as if our time together never existed.

Since he pushed me into Ethan, he hadn't made an effort to talk to me. Ollie was back to his medicated self, and I'd rather him be gone than see him like this. At least with him gone, I could imagine the old him and the memories we shared.

"Mia?" My attention moved away from Ollie and back to Bria. She stared at me from across the table with her black brow in the air. Her expression transformed when she noticed mine, and a sigh escaped from her lips. "You don't have to go."

Bria needed this.

"I'm going," Tyler piped up from beside me. "I've never gone to one of your get-togethers before. Should be interesting."

Tyler had never witnessed the nightly parties I suffered through. She had never met Isaac, never met Stanley, had never known the old Ollie, or the old me for that matter. At this point, I missed the former me. Not caring and no heart. "I'll go," I uttered through a sigh, wrapping my rebellious lock of hair around my index finger, pretending all was right in the world I lived in. "Just no games."

"No games? Do you know who you're talking to?" Bria laughed and pushed out her chair as she stood. Her black pixie hair grew into a short bob, and it swayed as she walked over to Ollie's new table and leaned over, surely informing the four of them of today's get-together.

"And she's back," I moaned.

A recent storm brought a tree down at our old spot in the woods. Bria sat beside Jude on the broken tree while the rest of us grouped over the ground. Jake's hands thread through Tyler's blonde hair, finishing off a French braid, whilst Ollie sprawled out along the leaves with his hands behind his head, looking up into the sky beside Maddie.

The late morning August sun filtered through the branches, raising the cold temperature a few notches. Brisk winds blew scarcely, reminding me summer was over and it was only going to get colder from this point forward. Between the constant rain and the location of Guildford, it rarely reached temperatures over seventy degrees, even through the summer. A commotion from Ethan and Jerry breaking up a fight during a ritual poker game took place a couple of yards away, filling our background noise.

"Ya finally gonna tell us your story?" Maddie asked Jude, breaking the silence. I wondered if the other's felt the disconnection in the air, or if it was just me.

Jude brought one leg up on the tree, his knee poking through the hole in his black jeans. "Nope."

"Probably an addict," Ollie muttered with his eyes glued to the sky, speaking the first words since we'd come out here. His statement only confirmed my Ollie was gone. "Pill poppin' addict," he followed slowly, popping the P's and tugging my heartstrings.

"No, I know an addict when I see one," Bria said beside Jude. "You don't have to say anything." She flashed him a small smile, and Jude gave her a sideways glance before looking back out in front of him. Jude was a walking contradiction. The fact I couldn't quite figure him out yet annoyed me. *Was he into Bria? Was he not into Bria?*

Ollie lifted himself on his elbows. "Alright, this is boring. I have better things to do than sit around and watch the fruit loop braid hair."

"Hey," Jake whined. "What's your deal?"

Ollie shook his head. "How about a game, yeah? Power? Strip or Dare?"

"You don't like games," I reminded him, ripping a leaf in half.

Ollie's gaze fell over me, his green eyes dim and narrow. His head tilted to the side. "You don't get to talk to me," he said with a finger lifted in my direction.

Pretending his words didn't hit me like a tornado, I trained my eyes and fingers back on the leaf, ripping into smaller pieces. No matter how many seconds passed, I was still wrapped up in the cyclone of his sentence. Spinning and spinning and …

"Bloody hell," Jake blurted, finishing off the braid. He jumped up to his feet and stood in the middle of us all. "You guys have fun, I'm leaving."

Jake took off, and I wished I had the nerve to follow him, but Ollie's wayward presence and tone kept me glued to the ground with my fingers tearing the leaf until there were no more pieces remaining. The small bits glittered my combat boots.

"What do you want to do?" Maddie asked Ollie in her sweet sing-song Irish accent, and my eyes rolled to the back of my head.

Maddie and I managed to steer clear of one another all summer, but since Ollie's return, she hadn't left his side, clinging to him like a damn groupie.

"How about a welcome home present, Mia." Ollie's lips curved into a smile as he swayed his hips back and forth.

I raised a brow, and he wiggled his in return. "Fuck off," I mumbled and dusted the remaining pieces of the leaf away from my boots. His intentions were unclear, and my heart and ego couldn't handle any more blows.

Ollie's smug smile grew. "Love to." I flipped him the bird, and in seconds, Ollie jumped to his feet and walked toward me. My insides buckled, not listening to my brain. My hand dropped, and so did Ollie—right in front of me. "I'll take that as a yeah."

"What are you doing?" My eyes darted around, and everyone else's attention trained on us, waiting to see what would come next.

"I miss you," he whispered with a jaded voice, but his words sliced into me, cutting me open and tearing at an already present wound he put there. His hand wrapped around my thigh as he crawled between my legs, and my limbs failed me. I couldn't find the will to push him away. The bulge in his pants pressed between my thighs as he lowered me onto my back. Leaves crunched beneath us. "You see what you're doing to me?"

"Get off me," I warned, but my desperate hands had a mind of their own as they gripped his sides, resisting my words.

"You don't mean that Mia, do you?" His eyes flickered a darkness I'd never seen in him before, and his fingers reached for the skin under my shirt. Flashes of his brother entered my mind, triggering bad memories of last year, and I crawled backward out of his hold. Ollie's fingers gripped me tighter and pulled me back under him. "Where are you going?"

My hand instinctively slapped across his cheek, and his face whipped to the side. His, once smug, smile disappeared and he dropped his head as he stayed idled on all fours. I stumbled to my feet and looked down at him, trying to catch my breath. "What the hell is wrong with you?"

Ollie rolled over to sit on his ass and dropped his arms over his bent knees with his back facing me. "Alright, I get it. You're only into men in uniform." A low, incredulous laugh came from him, and I forced down the tears building up behind my eyes. Shaking my head, I took a seat with Bria and Jude on the tree branch.

Bria shot me a confused look. "You're going to let him treat you like that?"

"He's not himself right now." The more those words came from me, the more it sounded like utter bullshit. Ethan had been right. I continued making excuses for him, seeming more like a broken record.

Ollie whistled Maddie over, and she crawled into his lap, side-eyeing me. "She's stupid for denying you," she sang as she ran her fingers through his hair.

"What in the actual fuck is happening?" Jude whispered. I ignored him as my body recovered from being close to Ollie's all while Maddie continued to brush her fingers over the mark I left on his face.

Ollie wrapped Maddie's legs around his waist. Bria and Tyler's eyes darted to me, waiting for a reaction, but all I could do was stare. How could he have been so indulged in the two of us when he first got here, and be a completely different person now?

"Ollie, what are you doing?" I asked, worry laced in my tone while the rest of my body tensed under prying eyes and un-prying bodies.

The woods turned quiet. The only movement was Ollie's hand appearing behind Maddie's head before her tongue darted inside his mouth. My jaw clenched as Ollie lowered himself until his back hit the ground with her on top of him. My knees wobbled as I stood back to my feet. I opened my mouth, but nothing came out. Bria's eyes grew wide, waiting for a reaction out of me, but I couldn't give one. All I could do was turn and walk away.

"Oh, come on, Mia," Ollie's voice boomed from behind me, "What did you expect?"

My walk turned into a run back to the main building and straight into my room.

Unable to keep still, I pulled out the desk chair and withdrew the journal Dr. Conway gifted me and wrote, driving the pencil into the paper as if it were Ollie's heart. The truth was, Ollie was my hell, but it wasn't until now that I truly understood the meaning behind my own words. He was both the hero and villain in our love story, saving me only to ruin me. But I'd been there before. I understood low points. I understood mixed emotions and the inability to feel. I'd understood it all, but it wasn't until now, on the receiving end, to understand the shit I'd put him through. It was my turn to help him, but would helping him lead to my own undoing?

A knock at the door grabbed my attention. "Mia, it's Tyler."

The breath I let out mixed with both relief and disappointment. A part of me still expected Ollie to follow. After opening the door, I let it hang there and returned to my desk chair. Tyler closed the door behind her and glanced over at me, feeling out my mood before taking a seat at the edge of my bed. "I don't know what that was all about, but it didn't last long."

"I don't care to know, Ty," I rushed out, wiping my palms down my face. "It's not him. He's not the same." Broken. Record. The automatic words became more natural to say, like "hello."

Tyler's doe-brown eyes scanned over me before she brought her hands into her lap and fidgeted with her fingers. "Listen," she hesitated, "even he knows it wasn't him. As soon as you left, something clicked. I may not know him like the rest of you, but it's so obvious the bloke is a mess right now."

"Good, he deserves it."

The night terrors came back full force, but it wasn't my cries that woke me. "Ollie …" I heard myself say, but the moment Ollie's name slipped from my mouth, the day before dawned on me and the ache returned.

"Ethan," a muffled voice said before my mattress dipped from Ethan sitting beside me. "I thought with Ollie back this would be over." The cold towel pressed to my forehead and instantly eased almost every worry.

"Ethan," I whispered, and opened my eyes. His mouth parted slightly, then closed. The lump in his throat bobbed. Blue eyes glowed against the moon's light, and the red in his hair flared. "Why don't you smile?"

Pulling away from me, Ethan removed the towel and rested his elbows over his knees. "I don't have a reason to smile, Jett," he scratched his stubble, looking back at me, "Not yet, anyway."

"Why do you refuse to call me by my first name?"

Ethan wrapped the towel tight around his hand, thinking about his next words or avoiding them altogether. "What's with all the questions?" He finally asked. "Go back to sleep."

"Answer me."

"No."

"Lay with me."

"No."

"Just until I fall asleep?" My voice cracked in a plea, but I knew if I continued to push, he would cave. Somewhere inside, deep down inside, Ethan needed me this last year as much as I needed him. For different reasons, I was sure, but I never had to push too far for him to give up on his morals.

Ethan groaned, but the sound of his keys coming off his belt had my hopes take off like a rocket. Next went the taser, then the radio, laying each item over my desk carefully. He lifted the sheet draped over me. His eyes flitted up my bare legs, panties, and tank top. I inched back to give him more room, and he shook his disapproving head before climbing in.

"Turn around," he ordered, his faint breath falling from his lips as he held up his head in the palm of his hand. Ethan bent his knee, planting his left foot over the mattress and twirled his finger.

"No." I grabbed his hand and placed it at my side. Ethan froze for a moment and chewed his bottom lip. "I want to remember what it feels like to be close to someone," I finally added. "Someone who makes me feel safe."

Ethan dropped the arm holding up his head and sank beside me. His fingers moved over the exposed skin at my side while his other arm snaked beneath me, pulling me closer against him. "What are you going to do about Masters?"

My chin tilted to meet his gaze. "You know?"

I didn't care if Bria, Tyler, Jake, or anyone else knew about what happened earlier in the day, but Ethan was different. I cared what Ethan thought about it. Every decision I made, for almost a year, depended on his approval. *What would Ethan do? Would Ethan be proud of me? How would Ethan see me?* It was strange, the way I starved for his approval like a father figure, looked up to him as a brother, wanted to be looked at by him as a lover, and wanted to feel close to him like a security blanket. I didn't know exactly what I wanted from him, only the mere fact I was attached to Ethan.

"I know everything."

My head shook. "It hurts, but I just have to keep reminding myself it's not him."

Ethan's callused fingers traced circles over my back as his chest rose and fell heavily against mine. "Stay away from him. He's going to kill you slowly, and I'm tired of cleaning up his mess."

"I'll stay away from him, but I'll never stop loving him."

"How do you know this?"

"Because love is constant. When you love someone, you can be angry with them, you can hate them, you can be upset or disappointed in them, but you never stop loving them because love endures all other emotions."

"Yeah? And where did you learn this from?"

"Ollie."

Ethan drew in a deep breath, and that was the last sound between us the remainder of the night. With his stubble pressed against my forehead, he rubbed my back until I fell back asleep.

SIX

"I'm stuck between I'll never be enough, and no one else will ever love you more."

OLIVER MASTERS

Ollie

"Oliver Masters, you're back," Arty declared as soon as I took a seat on my usual chair during group therapy. My attention automatically sailed to Mia across from me. A constant reminder I was absolute rubbish. I'd tried talking to her all weekend, but she was smart and stayed away.

Maddie took a seat beside me. I rolled my head back and crossed my ankle over my knee. "Yeah, glad you're back, Ollie." Her filthy hand landed on my thigh, and I dusted it off with a bad taste in my mouth. Another reminder of the piece of shit I was.

Turning my head toward Jake beside me, I nudged him with my elbow. "I'm sorry, mate. I shouldn't have said those things on Friday."

Jake pursed his lips and crossed his arms.

The silent treatment? *Real mature, Jake.*

Arty cleared his throat. "Let's get caught up on everyone's summer. I went back home to Egypt to spend the holiday with family, which can be demanding," he chuckled, "I couldn't wait to come back. How about you, Maddie? How was your summer here on campus?"

"B-O-R-I-N-G," Maddie spelled out.

Mia laughed. "And here I thought she couldn't spell."

I stifled my laugh with the tips of my fingers and adjusted in my seat, stealing a look at my girl across the room. Mia smiled, but her eyes remained locked on Maddie. Even her fake smile was no longer intended for me.

"Oliver," Arty re-directed. "Your summer?"

With eyes fixed on Mia, I responded, "Locked in a cell. Nothing to it."

"Well glad to see you made it out in one piece."

Arty continued to ask around the smaller group as my eyes feasted on Mia, waiting for her to see me. For a little trace or indication she still held on to us. Her finger twirled around a strand of hair as she bit her lip, and I could hardly sit still. My knee picked up the bloody bouncing, and all I needed was to feel myself inside her again. It was selfish, what I'd done and what I knew I'd continue to do.

As soon as I'd allowed Maddie to kiss me in the woods, I'd wanted to drive my head through a tree. My heart had demanded me to run after her as soon as she took off. But my brain had laughed at the incident like I'd told a ridiculous joke. If I'd run after her, I would have made things worse for myself, digging an even deeper grave.

Each time my mouth opened, it said things I didn't mean.

Each time I moved, it contradicted everything my heart screamed.

I had no control.

"How's your support group, Mia?" Arty asked, and even her name coming from someone else's mouth sounded like poetry.

Her pretty lips moved as her voice flooded my ears. "Good, and I'd like to take this time to invite anyone to come talk to me afterward if they are interested in attending. The group is closed and anonymous."

"Oh, for girls who are sexually abused?" Maddie huffed, "You mean for little bitches who can't take it—"

Arty quickly silenced her. Mia paid her no attention.

She was clothed in strength, but it no longer was because of me.

I wondered if this redheaded bloke had something to do with it.

Once I approached our wing, my sights landed on Maddie's tall and skinny figure as she walked out of Mia's room. "Whoa, what do you think you're doing?"

"Looking for you," she said with a wicked smile and met me halfway in the empty hallway. Everyone must be in their rooms or gathered in the mess hall awaiting dinner.

"That's not my room anymore, and why are you looking for me?"

Maddie's lashes fluttered over her eyes under her bangs. She had similar features to Mia, and it wasn't until I met Mia when I understood how my heart could have been confused. The eyes were almost the same, though Mia's were a golden-brown when we were together. Maddie stood a few inches taller, with hair a tad lighter. My body reacted to the familiarity of what it thought it wanted, but it knew for certain when Mia came around.

"We're always around people, we haven't had a chance to talk," she said through a small smile. Her hand reached out, and I took a step back.

"There's nothing to talk about."

"I knew you would come back around, no? I just needed to get ya back on the meds."

"You've gone mad." I took a step away from her, but she blocked me.

"You and me, it's going to happen. It's only a matter of time. You'll fall right back into becoming the man-whore again. I know everything. You think she'll stay with you after seeing that side?" My hand found her throat, and before I knew it, she was against the cement wall. Maddie's eyes mocked me, not one ounce of fear clouding her face. Her hand slipped over my dick, and she sucked in her lips. "There he is. There's the Ollie I remember."

"Stop," I warned through a clenched jaw.

Maddie laughed, and I tightened my grip while she tightened hers. Both of us daring the other to pull away first. Her fingers rubbed over my swelling cock before I snatched her wrist and slammed it against the cement.

"Funny thing is…" her voice cracked against my hold, "Ya into it, Ollie. You're just like your brother."

My hand released from her throat, and I backed away, shaking my head. "I'm nothing like my brother."

The taunts followed me back to my room before I slammed the door in her face. Maddie grew too close to Oscar and knew too much. The scary thing was, she was right. The summer on the pills over a year ago drove my dick into almost every girl as if it were looking for something.

It was Mia all along.

And perhaps I should keep Mia away, but nothing would let me.

She was my life source, and though I was confused by a lot, I was certain of one thing: I needed her. Like breathing, I fucking needed her.

Strolling into dinner late, I hung back and stood beside Ethan under the archway.

"Masters," he said casually, keeping his eyes in front of him—keeping his eyes on Mia. "I told you last week. I'm not getting in the middle of whatever tosh you're involved with."

"You're already in the middle of it." I already knew. *Hell*, I knew. I saw the way Mia looked at him, and it was the same way she used to look at me. "I'm not all together, I know, and I appreciate you being everything that I can't right now." Ethan shifted in place and crossed his arms over his chest as I continued, "But I'm not an idiot either. No matter how bad you wish it could be you, it will never be. It will always be me."

Ethan tore his eyes away from Mia to me. We stood there, same height, same agenda, different hearts when he finally spoke up. "You think you can fuck up and expect her to be unchanged by it?" Ethan averted his gaze back to Mia. Both of us watching her smile and sign words to Zeke. "Look at her, Masters. She's not the same person you left seven months ago. She's already learned how to live without you."

Ethan dug his hand into his pocket and smacked the contents against my chest. "Don't ask me for any more favors."

I took the pack of gum from him without looking, counting on it being my flavor. A tenner for a pack of gum seemed ridiculous, but I needed it. Others gave into other addictions like caffeine, nicotine, or pills. My only addiction to calm my nerves was to occupy my grinding jaw with gum, which cost me more now that Oscar was gone.

The new bloke, Jude, walked in late, eyeing our exchange before I stuffed the gum into my pocket. I looked back, noticing he came from my wing. "Fucker came from the wrong direction."

"He has a habit of getting lost," Ethan mumbled with his hands back on his belt like it was no big deal.

Running my twitching fingers through my hair, I caught up to Jude at the buffet line. "Where are you coming from, mate?"

If there was one thing Oscar had taught me, it was not to trust anyone. The problem was, I trusted everyone my whole life, but not on these pills. While medicated, I walked on eggshells and paranoia. And the eggshells and paranoia enabled a spidey-sense telling me Jude was up to no good. There should have been zero reasons for him to be walking through the third and fourth wing. He should have entered through the opposite walkway, not mine. Not Mia's.

Jude turned around, his greasy black hair slicked behind his ears and faint-blue eyes wide. "What's it to you?"

Jude instantly went on the defense and throwing accusations wouldn't get me anywhere. He grabbed a tray, and I followed his lead. "If you need another tour of campus, let me know."

Initially, I planned on eating alone, but I needed to keep an eye on him. Be-friend him. Get to know him, and find out why he was here.

I pulled out the chair beside Maddie and stretched my legs as Jude sat across from me. Maddie's fingers found my thigh, but my eyes found Mia.

Her golden-brown chestnuts glowed against the dying sun beside the window. For four seconds, she gave me the look I so desperately needed. The same one reminding me all was going to be okay between us, at least until her eyes fell underneath the table at Maddie's hand on my dick.

Shit. "Fuck, Maddie," I spat out, pushing her hand away, "Keep your hands to yourself." My gaze returned to Mia's, but she'd already turned away.

Maddie giggled and pressed her breasts against my arm as she leaned into my ear. "It's only a matter of time," she whispered.

I threw my fork against the tray as her brazen hand returned to my disobedient cock. Despite my agitation and sole purpose of sitting with them in the first place, my growing knob wasn't agreeing.

It was the medication, and Dr. Butala had me on some magic pill, giving my dick permission for instant arousal by a single touch, not helping win Mia back. Like an annoying fly, I pushed Maddie away for a second time. "A tad late for dinner, mate. You almost missed the buffet," I said to Jude.

Jude's eyes darted over to Mia's table before meeting my gaze. I picked up my fork, ready to get the bangers and mash in my mouth before I ground my jaw down to the bone.

"I could say the same for you," he smirked and ripped off the end of the sausage between his teeth.

Dammit, he was right. "Touché."

A silence played out between us as Mia's contagious laugh traveled throughout the room. It had been a while since I heard that laugh. My eyes slid to that laugh. My entire being grew envious of whoever caused it.

"So, fucking annoying," Maddie deadpanned.

I pointed my fork at her. "Watch it."

"I don't understand you, Ollie," Gwen piped up. "All last year, you denied the relationship. But every time someone comments on the bird, you get all narky, protecting her as if she means something to you. So, which is it?"

"It's none of your goddamn business." Falling back in the chair, I stole another glance at my girl. Mia had that smile that caused her eyes to disappear along with her top lip, taking up her whole face. She never hid her smile, only leaned forward into it as another giggle escaped. Though I was over here, screwed up in disarray, her smile proved everything Ethan said was correct.

She learned to live without me.

And she was doing just fine.

Mia was on top, out of the hole in which I dug her out of. I lifted her arse up there, and she promised me she wouldn't forget about me, said she'd always take me with her. Her independence should have angered me. Instead, seeing Mia happy brought me peace.

Her smile washed over me like the bloody plague, and I brought my fingertips to my mouth to hide my pleasure. I didn't deserve it, not yet, but her warmness still engulfed me like a blissful disease—a disease I could die happily from.

All week I'd kept my distance from Mia and the damage I'd done.

Like every other Saturday over the year, I'd escaped to the library in hopes of seeing her. I wanted to get her alone, to talk to her. To apologize. To explain myself. But she wasn't there.

Of course, she wasn't going to be there. She was avoiding me.

My emotions were back and forth, sparring invisible battles. One minute I was angry, wanting to prove I didn't need Mia in my life like she didn't need me. The next I was kicking myself. Friday, a wanker. Saturday? A bloody mess. My medication was back in full force, but this time was different. This time, my body didn't submit to the side effects like the pills wanted because my body didn't belong to the side effects. My body belonged to her.

Dr. Butala sat across from me in his barren office during our two-week check-up. "Mood swings?"

"Understatement."

"What else, Oliver?"

"I'm so angry, I fear I may lose it at any moment." My fingers ran through my hair as I adjusted in the small chair. "And I'm horny," I said with my hands in the air, "Why am I so horny all the time? It's dangerous, Butala." If I didn't get my dick into something soon, I'd detonate.

Butala moved his glasses up the bridge of his freckled nose and brought his pen back to the notepad. "You're on four different medications right now, one in which is supposed to stabilize your mood swings, not instigate them."

"What are you saying?"

"I'm adding to your medication."

"Will it help with my constant hard-on?"

"What makes you angry, could neutralize someone else completely. What makes you aroused could cause another unable to perform. Medication reacts differently to each person," Butala sighed and returned his black beady eyes to me, "It's trial and error, Oliver."

I slapped both hands over my thighs and looked up to the ceiling. "I don't like what I'm hearing. Why not just put me on the same regiment you had me on last year, yeah?"

"We did. It's not taking."

I leaned forward and slapped a hand over his desk. "Either make me feel nothing or everything!"

"I'm doing my best," Butala returned his hands to his keyboard in front of his computer, "This new treatment plan can take anywhere from two to four weeks, so don't expect immediate results. I'm sending your new prescription to the nurse's station. You'll start classes on Monday. If you notice any significant changes, let me know."

With a single head nod, I stood and walked out without answers or solutions. Chances were, I'd have classes with Mia starting Monday. Ready or not, I would be forced to face her.

I didn't have two to four weeks to right myself.

I needed to make things right with Mia this weekend.

SEVEN

"The cruel irony is
you are my forever
but not my right now."

OLIVER MASTERS

Mia

Saturday morning, I woke up with Ethan gone, and a note slid under my door. The torn, yellowed book page had been folded and refolded numerous times, having dozens of creases. Despite my brain, my heart opened it. "*We need to talk. Like old times, you know where to find me, -OM.*" Even his handwriting was familiar across the blank space of the page. I drew in a shaky breath, knowing what I should do, and what I was going to end up doing.

    Knowing damn well I was walking through doors of disappointment, the small ounce of hope simmering inside my heart convinced the rest of my doubt to quiet down. Without looking like I tried or put too much thought into it, I showed up in sweat pants, T-shirt, and my hair a mess on top of my head. Dean Lynch had asked for my clothing sizes after the gruesome prank and gifted me the basics. I never needed much.

As soon as the library doors closed behind me, the familiar maze brought back a wave of emotions. I hadn't been back here in months, only to retrieve the book to learn sign language. Since then, I couldn't bring myself to walk through that door. The library was suffocating, each step back to our spot, shelves closed in on me. I picked up my pace, keeping my eyes fixed ahead.

Ollie sat on the floor in his corner, and he lifted his head as soon as I entered our nook. We looked like twins in matching gray sweats and white tees. His brown hair poked out from under the infamous beanie he always wore whenever his life was in ruins. He never hid his mood; even his eyes screamed, *"I'm a fucking train wreck."*

He tilted his head, and I thought I saw the man I loved in those green eyes, but these days, I could never be sure. I needed to know if it was him. My sights set on his face, appreciating the prominent wave of his lips, and the small freckle that usually disappeared in the curve of his smile. He wasn't smiling now, but his face still managed to blow me away to places we both should have stayed.

He looked away, feeling insecure as I stood there in the heartbeats of silence. His cutting jawline flexed against the words we both wanted to say, but still trying to figure out how. The words of affirmation ran through my head as I moved closer, but he beat me to the punch.

"It didn't always look like this," he hardly whispered, but I heard every word.

I paused and crossed my arms, leaning into my hip as I waited for him to continue. Standing firm, but inside, all I wanted was just another second in his touch.

Ollie rose to his feet and dusted off his hands. "I never told you this before, but it took me two weeks to color coordinate these books. The first time I saw you reading in the mess hall, every spare second I had was in here, creating this space for you, trying to impress you." He chuckled nervously and ran his fingers along the spines of the books. The same fingers that used to run down my spine. "This space was never mine, Mia. I mean, yeah, I found it. I was here first. This used to be my safe haven. But I created this space for you to run away to, to feel safe because that's what you are to me. You're my safe place." He dropped his hand and looked back over at me. The lump in his throat moved as he swallowed. "To find out you never liked to read, I was the bloody fool all along."

I shifted on my foot, digging my nails into my flesh to ease the temptation to reach out and touch him. "Why am I here, Ollie?"

"You tell me."

"I can't help it."

"I can't either," he said, taking steps toward me. "I don't know what's happening to me. When I was gone and without you, I caved to the pills because the distance killed me. You have no idea what a mess I was off it. How I left things … I went mad in jail. Giving in was easier because I knew I couldn't be with you. Now that I'm back, every part of me is fighting against it. I'm so back and forth. I'm going crazy." He stood over me, us barely touching. I had to lift my chin to meet his gaze. "Does that make any sense?"

"You pushed me, Ollie … Right into Officer Scott."

"I know"—his hands tugged nervously on his shirt— "I was angry you denied me. I thought you gave up on us, and I took it out on you."

"You kissed Maddie, right in front of me," I choked out, averting my eyes so he didn't catch the pain lingering inside them. The image was on constant replay.

"God, I'm sorry," his hand touched my cheek, bringing my eyes back to him, "I can't believe I did that. Even while I was kissing her, my stomach was sick about it. But it wasn't me, Mia, you have to know that. I'm not myself."

His single, warming touch still managed to disentangle my tension. My shoulders dropped as I watched his gum peek from his parted lips. We stood so close, and I closed my eyes to breathe in his minted breath. When I opened them again, emerald, adoring eyes greeted me. "What do you want from me, Ollie?"

With his hands steadying himself over my shoulders, he briefly looked to the ceiling as if the words were written across the tiles. He always knew the right things to say, and when to say nothing at all. Yes, he silenced the world with his voice, but he was able to stop time with his silence, and every part of me hung on like a last breath.

When his head dropped back down to face me, tears pooled in the corners of his eyes, and that was when I knew for sure it was Ollie standing before me. "I want you to love me anyway," a single, lost tear trickled down his cheek, "Give me a year to get better, and I'll give you a lifetime."

My brows snapped together as my head dipped back out of his grasp. He couldn't be serious. "A year? You want me to put up with that for a year?"

"Mia, I'm going crazy. I can't lose you through this, but I can't control myself either. It's going to get worse, but I promise just one year. Give me a year. After Dolor, I'll get off the pills, and we never have to look back," Ollie's words scrambled everywhere, nothing like the slow and controlled tone I just had, already losing him. The struggle was evident in his eyes as they scanned my face, reading my reaction.

The only way I could get through the next year was not to watch him self-destruct. Knowing what we needed to do, a new level of ache flowed through my veins before attacking all vital organs. It already hurt merely thinking about it, and I knew the next words I was about to say would only double this pain inside me. But they were words that needed to be said to protect what we had. "I'll give you a year, but in the meantime, we can't talk—"

"No," Ollie immediately stated, shaking his head.

"You keep your distance and stay away from me."

"No, you can't do this..." both his hands gripped his beanie as he paced back and forth.

"I can't see you like this. You can't show up in my room. You can't sit with me in the mess hall. You can't mess with my head. You stay away for a year, and when we leave, I'll give you my life. But don't drag me down before then, Ollie. You may be able to climb your way out, but it took me eleven years to get here."

Ollie rushed in front of me. "Because of me!" he painfully said with a shaken finger pointed at his chest. "You beat me up for six months, and I accepted you at your absolute worst because I fucking love you, yet you won't do the same for me?"

Of course, I would do the same for him, I'd do anything for him. But I couldn't say that. If I agreed to sit back and allow him to treat me this way, for him to plant more images inside my head, ones I could never shake away, like kissing girls, pushing and pulling me in all directions, making snide comments, or worse ... I didn't know if I could ever recover from it. In the end, he would expect forgiveness while I withered away in his aftermath.

"That's not fair. I wasn't on meds messing with my head. You are."

"Let me get this straight. So, you're up here," Ollie said with a finger pointing up in the air, "and you forgot to take me with you," another tear fell down his face as his chin trembled, "You lost your bloody grip on me."

"I never lost my grip. You slipped!" It was my turn to cry, but my tears didn't come out as easily as the guy standing before me. Mine struggled, each one a painful remainder of the words he left me with seven months ago. "No matter what, as long as you stay away from me until we leave here, I'll still belong to you."

"This is ridiculous," Ollie wiped his face into his sleeve and drew in a deep breath, "I can't stay away from you."

"It's the only way this will work. What you did in the hallway broke me. Seeing you kiss Maddie killed me even more. I can't sit back and watch. There will be nothing left of me after the year is done. It's the only way, Ollie. You have to stay away from me."

Ollie's face twisted, unable to comprehend what I'd said. His green eyes strayed from mine, as if looking at me was too painful, and ran a palm down his face before turning his back to me. "Dammit, Mia," he managed to get out through each struggling breath. His palms hit the bookshelf as he leaned over and hung his head. "Are you so goddamn selfish, you don't care what you're doing to me right now?"

My head shook as I took a step back.

"What are you waiting for?" Ollie's palms hit the bookshelf before he straightened his posture. He spun around to face me and slapped himself in the chest. "Go on and finish me off!"

Tears streamed down my face. "What do you mean?"

"You just broke my fucking heart, and yet you're still standing there. The least you can do is grant me the favor of finishing me off by walking away because you know I can't so much as breathe without you. So, fucking leave!" He pointed toward the exit fixing bloodshot, challenging eyes on me. "Go!"

Everything inside me wanted to comfort him, but it would only undo the purpose of this. The only reason I'd pushed him away was because I was weak and scared. For over eleven years, I was dead. If his destruction brought me back to that place, I didn't know if either one of us could survive this year. In the process of protecting myself, I risked the chance of losing him. Knowing losing him was a possibility already had regret coursing through me.

I turned and ran through the maze back toward the entrance of the library on legs I could no longer feel beneath me.

Ollie's words from last year circled in my brain, *"as long as I don't stray too long or far, I always find my way back."* At the time, he had been talking about getting lost in the library, but I silently prayed the same would go for me.

Though after the pain I just caused him, I wasn't so sure I deserved his love at all.

Before I reached the door, a hand gripped my wrist and spun me around.

"Right now," Ollie breathlessly said, pulling me away from the door. "I'll stay away for a year, but I want you right now." His unforgiving hands grabbed my face, and his thumbs swept the tears staining my cheeks before he crashed his lips to mine.

Ollie

Mia wanted a year without me, but I was taking right now with her. A slow-burning rage filled me, and I needed to fill her to release it. Be inside her. Smother this anger with our connection. Subtle moans came from her throat, and I relished in it. Though we always fought for control, right now was my time, and she eventually surrendered to me, knowing it was what I needed.

I grabbed her plump, pouty lip between my teeth as I walked her backward into the desk. In one quick and precise swipe, I cleared the desk of all clutter—even the monitor fell over, but neither one of us cared as I lifted her off the floor and over the edge of the aged wood.

Mia's hands pulled off my beanie, and her nails dragged up my scalp, only stimulating my need for her, kissing her harder in a silent cry for connection. She let me undress her. Perfect, round breast bounced free. I reluctantly pulled away from our kiss to see her as my heart hammered inside its cage.

Unclothed and perfect, she sat before thousands of books we've run past, and I etched every detail of hers into my brain. Her hair, twisted with dark and light shades, fanned around her oval face. Ivory skin glowed against the colorful bindings, and big, golden-brown eyes lit up as she looked at me as if I were the only man worthy of this moment with her.

She leaned back on her hands while we both panted in unison from our taunting separation. My sight touched every inch of her skin, her desperate eyes watching me do it. "Why are you looking at me like that?" Mia asked. She tilted her head to the side with a small curve of her lips beside her tear-stained cheeks.

"It's been eight months, love, and you expect me to stay away for another ten. I need to hold on to right now for as long as possible." I slowly withdrew my shoes, jeans, and boxers as if we had no other place to be.

"And how do you suppose you're going to do that?"

After spreading her legs apart, mine buckled and, like a fiend, I was back on my knees. "We're taking our fucking time." My eyes drifted up her curves and back to hers. "I'm not going to make you remember me, Mia. I'm going to make it where you can't remember anything else."

Mia's small smile was enough to engulf me in a windstorm of feelings, bringing me back to where we were before.

Before our time apart.

Before the pills.

Before I turned into the colossal mind-fuck of a man.

A time where we existed.

My devotion and bond to this girl was unbreakable, and my kiss against her abdomen was a silent promise that I would violate every rule she placed against me. There was no way I could go another year. Our love was our breach, and it would go against every force of science because no pill could keep me away. I refused to allow it.

Gripping the insides of her thighs, I spread her wider as my knob pulsed below, blood rushing to every surface at the close proximity, though my desire to taste her was stronger. She was already wet for me, glistening as she pooled at the base, and so that spot was where I started. Treading my tongue up through her folds, I kept my eyes on her and waited for that small reaction I'd been dying to see.

Her eyes closed.

Her head fell back.

And her hips rolled into my mouth for more.

And I fucking took it.

Both of my thumbs spread her apart before I drank her in.

The sweet taste of Mia Rose revived me in more ways than one.

My tongue knew every detail, design, and feature and what made her break away against me. In no time, I had her legs shaking as I opened her up and inhaled her slowly. Her fingers gripped my hair, begging to be filled, but I could never get enough of her taste. Her legs clenched around me, and I lifted her off the desk, guiding her to the floor until she was sprawled out for me. Like an obsessed addict, I drove my tongue inside her to appease my appetite.

Her walls convulsed against my tongue as her heartbeat dropped to her core.

Kneeling between her legs, emotions built up inside of me, ready to break chains and move mountains. Holding back became an impossible task. I was defeated.

"Ollie…" she moaned in a plea, and it was all the motivation I needed to merge with her. I fell over her trembling body as her walls tightened, and wrapped around my aching dick—beating along to the rhythm of the orgasm I just gave to her. My fingers dug into her thighs to stop her movements. Otherwise, I would've busted inside her right then and there.

Tongues collided.

Her tiny fingers eagerly gripped my hair.

My hand grabbed her backside, and I lifted her body as I eased into her again and again and again, feeling every heavenly detail as she reeled in the climax against my knob. "Fucking perfection," I breathlessly panted in her ear.

"What is?"

"Us."

Her golden eyes captured mine. "I love you, Ollie."

Grasping my heart.

Breaking those chains.

Pushing those mountains.

"And I'm going to love you through this—"

My mouth silenced hers because my heart couldn't bear it, and I made love to her right there on the library floor. The only way I was able to get through the next half hour without coming was because of the fear of our disconnection. I held on by a single thread, making sure my hands and mouth kissed every inch of her skin. Together, we bled into one as I emptied myself inside the girl who was my forever but not my right now.

Because my *"right now"* had expired.

I pressed my face into her neck and cried.

Like a fucking pussy, I cried.

Still deep inside her with her arms wrapped around me, I shook in her grasp.

"You just have to hold on," she choked out.

EIGHT

"For a love everlasting,
make her roses out of paper.

                    For a love as poetic,
          make her roses out of literature.

                                And if you're lucky enough to find both,
                                      remind her every damn day."

                                                        OLIVER MASTERS

Mia

The September temperatures cooled the building as Jake and I walked through the hallway after class and back to our wing. Walking side by side, he rambled on about Brian breaking it off with him earlier in the summer, but my mind was on a different guy I hadn't spoken to in weeks.

So far, Ollie kept his promise. He hadn't shown up to my room or confronted me when our paths crossed. He had kept his distance, which only killed me even more. I'd said things I knew were for the best, but my heart held on to the tiny hope that I could be wrong, and I'd hoped this time, Ollie wouldn't listen.

"I'm ready to spread my wings." Jake stretched an arm out to the side.

"Your wings or your wiener?"

"You pervert!" he laughed and bumped my shoulder with his. "Do you know how hard it was to find a good source of protein on a mission trip? I couldn't wait to come back here."

"What's here?" Having Jake back made this situation with Ollie a little easier. I didn't bother telling Jake what happened between Ollie and me, but Jake was the perfect distraction.

"So, you promise you won't say anything?" Jake asked as we approached the stairs.

My eyes bugged out when I noticed both his tone and posture changed. "Oh, dear God, this has to be good."

Jake gripped my arm and pulled me against the wall out of ear-shot of any bystanders. "Promise me, Mia. You can't tell a soul." His lips disappeared while his eyes waited in eagerness.

"Fine, fine. I promise…"

He leaned into my ear. "Liam."

My eyes grew wider and my jaw dropped. "No way."

"Yes."

"No …"

"Yes!"

"Ew, Jake," I shoved him in the shoulder, "I've been with him!"

Jake's head jerked in all directions while hushing me. "I know!"

"He's a grunter!" I whisper-shouted.

"I know, I fucking love it!"

"Oh-my-God, I don't want to hear about it. Now I want to stick a pressure washer inside me."

Jake giggled, and we returned to our pace, descending the stairs. "You can't tell anyone. He hasn't come out yet, and I don't want to lose him."

"I get it. My lips are sealed."

Our feet touched the second floor, and we walked through the main corridor back to our wing when my gaze landed on Ollie walking toward us in the opposite direction.

And just like that, the smile on my face faded. Ollie's presence was a daily reminder that I'm without him. Words swirled on the tip of my tongue, all the things I wished I had the nerve to say: *I miss you. I love you. I'm sorry. I wish I was as strong as you. I don't deserve you. I wish I wasn't so selfish. Be patient with me, I'm still learning these things ...*

I tried to force my eyes to the ground, instead they stayed glued to his. Soft green eyes held onto mine as he ran a hand through his backward wave, taking longer strides toward me, ripping my heart to shreds.

And just like that, the two of us locked in slow motion as the rest of the world buzzed around us. My pace habitually slowed from Ollie's proximity. He pulled his hand from his pocket and grabbed mine from my side as we passed one another.

Time stopped. My heart stopped. For two seconds, even my brain stopped turning all the words I wanted to shout out to him. Ollie gave my hand a soft squeeze before he released something into my palm.

Then the moment was suddenly gone.

I turned back around. Ollie didn't.

In the palm of my hand was an origami rose from battered book paper, and my breath left me.

"What's that?" Jake asked, bringing me back to speed with the rest of the world.

My heart shook as I tried to find oxygen after reading the script in Ollie's handwriting across a petal—*you're my evermore.*

"A reminder," I whispered.

"Jett," someone announced, and I looked up from my hand to see Ethan approaching. "You have a visitor."

Jake and I exchanged glances.

After dropping my things off in my room, Ethan escorted me outside. Somber clouds kept the sun hidden, and after my eyes adjusted to the sunbeams seeping through the clouds, I saw my dad pacing back and forth beside a bench on the lawn, rubbing his hands together.

"Why is my dad here?" I wondered out loud, unsure if I wanted to know the answer. Did something happen to my step-mom, Diane? I looked over to Ethan, and he dropped his head.

"I'll give you time alone with him," Ethan said, gesturing with his hand. "I'll wait until you're finished to walk you back, alright?"

Nodding, I walked in my father's direction. The fierce wind blew my hair in my face, and I did nothing to keep it away as my arms wrapped around myself in an attempt to beat the cold. Delaying the inevitable, I slowed my pace. My revived heart beat faster with every step closer. Nerves set in. This was unexpected, and I didn't like the unexpected.

"You look good," my dad said as he took a seat at the bench and patted the space beside him. "How are you?"

I sat down and looked over the man, who I hadn't seen in over a year. The last time I'd seen those empty eyes were at the airport before he walked away from me. "What are you doing here?"

Yes, I'd changed, but our relationship hadn't. My father had given up on me, too many times to count. When others remembered family vacations or game nights around the dinner table as childhood memories, his abandonment would always be mine. Gray, unforgiving eyes met mine, but still looked past me.

"I spoke with David …"—My father paused and cleared his throat—"Dean Lynch. I spoke with Dean Lynch, and he said you're doing well here."

Twisting my neck back, Ethan stood before the door with his eyes trained on me, watching me like a hawk. I turned back to face my father. "I am."

"You lost more weight."

"My taste buds don't agree with the food here," I said casually with a shrug.

My father nodded once and looked out in front of him before returning his eyes to me. "Regardless, you still look good."

even when i'm gone

He didn't come all this way to check on me. Cutting the awkwardness with my tongue, I drew in a cutting breath and asked, "Why the sudden visit?"

My father drew in the same deep breath and folded his hands over his lap. "You know, Mia, I never wanted kids of my own. But the second I met your mother, I would have agreed to anything to be with her—"

"Cut to the chase."

His chest rose while his empty gray eyes looked up to the sky. "This is hard for me, so I need you to listen." His gaze flicked back over to me, waiting for understanding. I nodded, and he continued, "You were only two years old when I married your mom, and we agreed to keep this a secret, but I just can't anymore. I was never fit to be a father, and Jackie's not here anymore." His breath shredded. "She left me. She left you. It's not fair for either one of us."

My heart bottomed out while the rest of me hung on to every tingle of nerves. "Keep what a secret?"

"You're a smart girl. You can't tell me you've never questioned it."

"Questioned what?" My voice grew louder despite the blank expression on my face. "Stop bullshitting me and spit it out already."

"You're not my blood, Mia, and it's time that you know the truth."

An incredulous laugh belted from my lips, and my father snapped his furrowed brows together.

"You …" I paused and shook my head, "You came all this way to tell me that? You could have saved half a day of your life and a thousand bucks."

"Mia, stop this."

"No"—I stood— "a simple phone call would have sufficed."

"I'm not done talking with you. Don't you want to know the rest?"

I stretched my arms out to my sides. "Oh, please … tell me, Dad, or should I start calling you Bruce? I can't wait to hear this."

"You were never born in the United States, Mia. You were born here…in Surrey. Your mother took you back to the US after you were born, so you have dual citizenship. The reason I was able to convince the judge to get you into Dolor in the first place."

Another disbelieving laugh escaped me. I couldn't help it. It was all too much. "Okay, I've heard enough."

"I'm not done!"

"I am! Basically, what you're saying is, I'm not your daughter, and I'm not welcome back. How am I doing so far, *Dad*?"

"Don't say it like that. It's not what I meant."

"What exactly did you mean?"

"I was never cut out for this, but I did the best I could! Of course, you're welcome back at any time. I want you in my life, but I want you to want to be in my life too, all while knowing the whole truth. And the truth of the matter is, we both somehow ended up together, but we made it this far. Diane will come around. She just needs some time. She doesn't understand you and can be closed-minded by all this mental illness shit—"

"Mental *illness* shit? Fuck you!" And I left him standing there as I marched back to Ethan in front of the building. What my dad really was saying was I was his past, and he wanted to move on without me. Ethan stood about sixty yards away, but each step I took away from my dad didn't feel as if I was adding enough distance between us. My brain turned to mush, unable to sort my thoughts on how I felt, and tears never poured when I thought they would.

"You alright?" Ethan asked as he studied my face.

"I'm fine."

"No, you're not, Mia. I can see it on your face."

"Just take me back inside," my voice hitched. "Please."

My mask was slipping and trying to stay strong for this long turned into a struggle.

We walked back through the double doors of Dolor, and as soon as they closed behind us, Ethan grabbed my hand and tugged me through a side door on the right until we were out of sight. His long arms wrapped around my waist, pulling me in for a hug, and I didn't resist. I threw my arms around him, and as soon as my face hit his neck, I broke apart.

"He's an arsehole," Ethan said calmly, cradling me in his arms.

"How did you know?" I asked after pulling my head away and searching Ethan's eyes. "How did you know why he came?"

"I talked to him when he first arrived." Ethan pressed my head back into his neck while his other hand ran up my back as he fell back against the wall. His stubble grazed my cheek as he held me tighter. "The number of people who love you doesn't determine your worth. Remember that."

Through my dinner and shower routine, I stayed quiet as I tried to get a grip on everything that happened. The remainder of the night, I took my restlessness and anger out on my journal, writing everything out as if it were a punching bag. If I said I wasn't hurt, it would have been a lie.

The truth was, I was hurt because it was all a lie.

My entire life had been a lie.

Bruce was never my father, only an acting participant in my life because he loved my mom—not me. Never me. Probably the same reason why he blamed me for her death. Most likely why he never took the time to understand me. He never cared. Since Mom died, all I became was baggage. A fucking obligation.

The lead tip broke while writing out the last sentence, and I threw the pencil against the cement wall before leaning back into the chair. My gaze landed on the clock above the door to read that it was almost midnight.

I slipped out of my hoodie and sweatpants, and threw myself over the mattress.

Pain ripped through the skin of my back. I cried out and jerked my body against the bed, trying to get up, but the pain only sliced deeper, driving my screams. The one foot hanging off the bed couldn't find traction to the floor and my arms stayed pinned at my side as the burn in my back expanded with every sudden movement.

Afraid to move any further, I laid frozen as my screams turned into soft moans and tears fell from the corners of my eyes, unsure of what was happening to me. As long as I didn't move, I would be okay. I had to lay still.

Ethan barged into my room and rushed to my side with wild eyes. "Jett? What's wrong?"

Uttering a single word grew to be a challenge when all I could think about was the pain, and all I could do was let my silent tears flow freely.

"You're scaring me. Talk to me!" Ethan demanded again, his hands gripping my shoulders.

When I didn't speak, he pulled me up, and another scream clawed up my throat.

"What in the hell?" Ethan asked, examining my back. As quickly and carefully as he could, he picked me up off the mattress and carried me through the dark halls of Dolor to the nurse's station. His lips landed on my forehead as he tried to console my cries the entire way.

"Ethan," I tried to get out. "What's in my back?"

Ethan ignored my question as he muttered threats and curses under his breath. "I swear I'm going to kill whoever did this." He kicked the door open and laid me over my stomach in the first available bed as his footsteps frantically sounded all over the marble floor. "Rhonda!" The jarring pain simmered as if it lived inside me, and I laid as still as possible as I bit my cheeks to fight it off. Ethan's face appeared before me again. "Rhonda isn't working. What do you want me to do?"

"Make it stop!" I cried out. "Whatever it is, get it out of me!"

Ethan's face fell before he left my side. A series of bangs and shuffling sounded around me, and then he returned to my side with tweezers in his hand. Ethan pulled a chair next to the bed and took a seat. "It's glass. This is going to hurt."

My eyes went wide, and the second he removed the first piece of jagged glass from my hip, my eyes clamped shut as I screamed.

After Ethan removed the bigger pieces, he peeled my tank top from my back, taking smaller bits along with it. He tossed my blood-soaked top in the trash before he got started on the smaller pieces, which took hours through the night. At one point, I passed out from the pain.

"This is from lightbulbs," Ethan muttered to himself as he plucked small pieces from my shoulders, disposing of the contents in a nearby tray. The large fluorescents were turned off, leaving a spotlight over the place on my skin he was working on. He said he needed to see the glare from the glass, and it was better this way. "I think that's the last of it. I'm going to clean up the blood."

Still in shock and unable to speak, I only nodded.

A few moments later, Ethan returned with a wet towel. Starting at the nape of my neck, he patted the towel over my back, my bottom and down the backs of my thighs. Once finished, Ethan ran his hands over my back. "Tell me if you feel anything still in there."

His warm, callused hands smothered the harsh cold of the room as I remained naked and face down on the bed. I shook my head as he reluctantly ran his hands over my lower back and hips. "Here?"

"No."

"Go on and check the rest of yourself."

I reached behind me and swiped my bottom and the back of my thigh. Aside from the soreness and the multitude of cuts my fingers ran across, I didn't feel any more glass. I pulled myself up and sat at the edge of the bed before Ethan. "Thank you."

He dropped his head and took in a deep breath. We were both exhausted.

"I should've rang a bus and had you seen by a doctor. Bloody hell, Jett, I should've rang the police, but it's too late now." Ethan lifted his head and met my gaze. "You can't tell anyone I did that for you. I'll lose my job."

"I won't say anything."

"But I'm going to find out who did this."

"Thank you."

Ethan's eyes roamed over my breasts before they snapped back up. "Sorry," he mumbled and turned away. He jumped to his feet and dropped the tweezers in the tray. "Go take a shower right through there and I'll get you some clean clothes."

Warm blood trickled down my legs as I shuffled to the shower. I turned the knob and waited for it to heat up, thinking back to who the hell was screwing with me. Maddie had been here all summer long, quiet, and kept to herself, never bothering to even talk to me. There were several new students here, but the only person this prankster was targeting was me, and the only two people who I'd grown semi-close to over the last few weeks were Tyler and Jude. It had to be Jude. Tyler wasn't capable of something like this.

I stepped under the searing water as the temperature burned my cuts, and I bit the inside of my cheek from crying out. Ethan knocked before entering, and a brush of cold air cut through the steam. "I'm leaving clothes over the counter for you with a towel."

"Thanks," I think I said.

"Are you going to be okay?"

I lifted my head under the water to hide my tears. The last thing I wanted to do was cry again. Ethan saw me as a victim, and I hated being the victim. I hated how much everything affected me and made me feel so fucking weak. Now more than ever, I wished I couldn't feel anything again.

"Mia?"

"I'm fine," I rushed out. I didn't mean for it to come out harsh, but it was hard to speak at all without stumbling over my words.

"I know you by now. You're lying." The door closed. "This would rattle anyone. You need to quit acting like a badass and let me take care of you."

I laughed as I finished rinsing off the body wash. "A badass? You think I'm a badass? Because I swear you treat me like a victim, and I'm tired of feeling like a fucking baby."

"Right now, you are a victim!"—The shower curtain flew open with an angry Ethan on the other side— "I'm going to find out who this bastard is and take care of it. But you have to let me. You have to let me in and find out who's doing this."

I turned off the water as he grabbed the towel and handed it to me. "No offense, Ethan, but you make me feel like I'm something to pity, like a helpless girl who can't take care of herself. I need Ollie …" I let out a breath and wrapped the towel around me. "I miss him, Ethan. I wish it were him here. I wish he were the one to remind me it was going to be okay." If Ollie were here, he'd say, *'Are you mad, love? Good. Use it. Fight through it. We're in this together,'* or something beautiful along those lines. And it was true, Ollie and I used to be a team, whereas Ethan took care of my shit without me. "Where you remind me I'm weak, Ollie reminded me I wasn't alone."

Ethan's lips pressed together as he clenched his fist at his side. "Look around you. Do you see *Ollie* anywhere? Because I don't, and if you keep this up, you *will* be alone. Now, sit your arse down," he ordered, pointing to the chair. "I have to bandage up the bigger wounds. Unless of course, Ollie's going to magically appear and do that for you?"

I rolled my eyes and straddled the chair. "Dick," I muttered under my breath.

"Wanker," Ethan replied in amusement.

My head snapped back to see him.

Ethan didn't smile, though his eyes did. He pulled up a chair and sat behind me, balancing a first aid tin over his thigh. Carefully, he removed the towel and exposed my back. "Whoever did this got ahold of a case of lightbulbs and planted broken pieces into your mattress. Has anyone been in your room?"

I shook my head. "No. Not that I recall. I don't know. We were both busy when my dad showed up." It had been a long day. Ethan applied cream before wrapping my back in bandages. "You think any of these will scar?"

"Probably," he exhaled in concentration. "But it's up to you on how deep you let the scars in."

NINE

"There may be a storm inside my head, but never get between me and my heart. That is a battle you will lose every time."

OLIVER MASTERS

Ollie

"Get out of here, mate. We're not Romeo and Juliet." I laughed and chucked a pillow at Zeke from the bed as he sat on the floor of his dorm. To occupy my time and stay out of trouble, I spent the remainder of my days in Zeke's room. I figured Zeke could share the goods. The only dorm in all of Dolor to have a mini-fridge stocked with Schweppes and a telly.

He signed, *"Pam and Jim,"* and I threw my head back.

"It's more intense than Pam and Jim," I returned my attention to his telly as we watched re-runs of *The Office*. "This show is poisoning your brain. You need to read a book."

Zeke shook his head rapidly and pointed over at the telly, signing more with his hands.

"No, Zeke. Not Pam and Jim. Not Ross and Rachel. Not Romeo and Juliet."

Zeke jerked his head back and rolled his eyes.

"We're Ollie and Mia. Not some bloody love story or fairy tale. Those all have endings," I reiterated before finishing off the bottle. "Real love never dies." I hopped off his bed and retrieved another bottle from the fridge, my mind wandering to weeks ago when I cried after our lovemaking in the library.

Couldn't.

Believe.

It.

There I was, trying to give my girl something she couldn't live without—a reason to take back her words on being without me for a whole year, only to lose control with a heap of emotions. I blamed it on seven months without her. *Yeah, let's blame it on that.*

Tears reminded us we could feel.

Pain reminded us we were alive.

And I'd rather feel too much than feeling nothing at all.

But right now, all I could feel at the moment was my hard dick against my joggers as I imagined myself inside her. The moment Mia had told me she loved me before reaching the inescapable brink, it had been enough to push me over the edge. It's what our love did. But our climax was never the intended purpose—it was the result of what we shared.

Falling back over the bed, I adjusted my hard-on and asked, "Have you been watching over her?" Zeke didn't respond. The back of Zeke's curly head faced me as he sat before the telly on the floor. "Someone's messing with her. You think it's the new security guard?"

Zeke shook his head.

"Do you know who it is?"

Zeke shook his head.

"Do you like The Office?"

Zeke shook his head.

Bloody hell, he wasn't listening.

"Alright, mate. I'm leaving, and I'm taking one for the road." I reached into the fridge and grabbed another Schweppes. "See you tomorrow."

After the door closed behind me, Maddie's eyes trapped me in before her body did.

"Where ya off to in such a hurry?" she asked, taking the Schweppes from my hand and shaking the wisps of hair out of her eyes. I stepped around her, not in the mood for another pissing contest. "Did ya hear about your girl?"

My feet stopped before my brain fully registered. Turning around, I finally looked at Maddie like she wanted all along. But all I wanted was to know what the fuck she was talking about.

And all my dick wanted was to be inside something as it jerked at the closeness of a wet fanny. "What are you talking about?"

Maddie drew closer and fluttered her lashes. I froze as she lifted herself on her toes and scraped her teeth along my earlobe. "Rumor has it, while you're trapped in your room all hours of the night being a good 'ole boy, Officer Scott creeps into Mia's room and doesn't come out until the sun comes up." She pulled her head away. "Every night," she enunciated.

My mouth went dry, and I tried to swallow. "You're a liar."

"Ah, I wish I was." She shrugged. "Guess miss perfect isn't so perfect after all." My head heated. I flipped Maddie around and squished the side of her face into the cement. My eyes made their rounds, scanning the hall to make sure we were alone. The security guard must already be in the mess hall for the dinner rush. "Ironic, isn't it? You're all fucked up while Mia's getting fucked."

Clenching my jaw, I dug my fingers into the back of her neck as I leaned into her ear. "Leave her name out of your mouth."

Maddie's arse grazed the chub in my pants. I should have known this was all a ruse to get to me. I released her, and she turned around and replaced her arse with her hand. "I love it when ya wear these joggers,"—

her grip on me tightened, and my growing knob obeyed— "Let me take care of you."

"Fuck no," I seethed, just as Jude walked by. He flicked his eyes back in front of him, pretending he didn't see anything.

"C'mon, O," she whined, her hand doing me favors and my pelvis leaning into it—wanting it.

Fuck.

Mia.

Mia.

Mia.

"I can't. I have Mia. I love Mia."

Maddie walked backward, taking me with her until her back was against her door. My body, for some reason, wasn't resisting the way it should have. Instead, my hand turned the door handle, and in seconds, we were both inside.

"Ya, you keep telling yourself that." Maddie yanked both layers down until my anxious cock emerged. Paralyzed and in need of a release, I didn't stop her as she eagerly wrapped her lips around my aching dick, deep throating me like slapper who'd escaped from Hell. I wrapped my fingers through her hair, slammed my eyes shut, and pounded into her mouth. The girl gagged, unable to handle my size.

What should feel good, didn't.

What should be getting me off, wasn't.

"Undress," I ordered in a hurry before I changed my mind.

Maddie happily climbed to her feet and removed her clothes as I rubbed over my slick knob. I wanted to blame Dr. Butala for turning me into this. I wanted to blame Maddie for instigating this. But the only person I could blame was myself.

Images of Ethan creeping into Mia's room consumed me, the redheaded wanker climbing into bed next to her. Him touching her, comforting her, being everything I couldn't. I kicked off my shoes and jeans.

Maddie's skin was the color of milk, and her big breasts didn't match her thin frame.

"Condom?" I asked, not recognizing my own voice.

Shamefully, I looked down, hating myself. *God, I fucking hated myself.*

She retreated to her desk, bent over slightly, revealing a place I knew I shouldn't go, but my throbbing dick wasn't giving me much of a choice. Flashes of Scott kissing Mia compelled my feet forward. Picturing Scott touching Mia's skin caused me to push Maddie over the desk and thrust two fingers easily inside her.

Nothing like my love.

But my head didn't seem to care.

Maddie moaned as I fucked her with one hand, and I yanked the condom from her with my other. My knee spread her legs wider, and I continued my assault. "Tell no one, you understand?"

Maddie nodded. "Ya mean ya don't want me to tell your precious Mia?" I fisted her hair and yanked her head back, and the girl cried out, "I understand! I won't say anything."

I ripped the condom between my teeth and slid it over my pounding dick. Bending Maddie over, I ran my fingers back through her sex, finding her soaking wet. Like a slip 'n slide, my cock should've easily slid inside her, but before I could, my dick went soft.

What the fuck is wrong with me?

I rested my hands over the edge and tried to catch my breath. "This isn't going to work."

Maddie turned to face me, and my gaze fixed on her breasts as they bounced while she jumped up and sat at the edge of the desk. "It's the condom. Take it off."

I gritted my teeth. "Have you gone mad?"

Maddie pulled her knees up and dipped her finger inside her. I focused on what she was doing to herself. Her other hand gripped my cock. "Touch me, O."

"*Touch me, Ethan,*" Mia's voice sang in my head as I imagined Mia laying out for Ethan across her bed, her delicate fingers roaming over her body. I couldn't take it; the image hurt too much. Before, my imagination was my friend, but now it turned into my greatest enemy. I fought against the ache in my chest, and the burn behind my eyes as these dark thoughts devoured me whole.

Desperation led to regret, but at this point, I'd do anything to numb the pain—even if it were only temporary.

Pushing Maddie on her back, I pulled her thighs apart, concentrating on the way she played with herself. The girl gave me a front-row seat, and naturally, my dick grew. "Keep going," I coached her, listening to my arousal, but I was nothing but a coward. Her finger eased in and out of herself. "Yeah, just like that."

Each one of Maddie's cries brought even more images of Ethan screwing Mia. I rubbed the tip of my cock across her entrance while my fingers pierced her thighs, keeping her spread and sure to leave marks. Maddie said some things, I was sure, but my head was in a different place as I tried to thrust into her …

But I went soft again.

For the last, aggravating, time, I pulled away. Picking up Maddie's desk chair, I threw it against the wall and ran my hands through my hair. "I can't do this!" I grabbed my boxers and jeans off the floor and hastily got back into them. My first stop back to my dorm would be the bathroom to discard the only evidence of this colossal mistake.

"Nothing fucking happened," I warned Maddie, not bothering to look at her.

"You're right. Nothing happened, and nothing will ever happen until ya let Mia go."

What I wanted to do was choke her until she rendered unconscious and quiet, but that was the demons inside talking. I shook my head. "It will always be Mia."

"Funny, Ollie. You think it will always be you for her?"

I froze under the comment. It hit me like a freight train. The smell of fanny and regret filled my senses, reminding me where my fingers had been and knowing it would be the one thing to lose Mia forever.

What the fuck did I just do?

Mia

There were two people absent during lunch, and it stuck out like a flashing red light—Ollie and Maddie. I tried not to think of the worst-case scenario.

Really, I tried.

"Oh-my-god, Jude's coming over," Bria whispered, leaning over the table. "Act cool."

"I *am* cool," I countered, pretending Jude didn't make my skin crawl every time he was near. I believed he was the one behind the attacks against me, only I couldn't figure out the reason why.

"Care if we sit with you?" Jude asked as his hair swept over his shoulder with Gwen by his side. "It seems our table got lighter all of a sudden."

Jude eyed the empty seat between me and the window, and Bria immediately spoke up. "Here, you can sit next to me. That's Ollie's seat." Bria chuckled to herself. "For when Ollie comes back to his senses, of course."

"Yeah, I don't think Ollie is making good decisions right now." Jude laughed, and my face twisted when a sickness slid inside my stomach. Jude's smile disappeared as he took a seat beside Bria. "Ah, sorry about that. I didn't mean to—"

I waved my hand out in front of me to cut him off. "It's fine." I couldn't bother to hear anymore, whatever he meant by it. Last year, the idea wouldn't have crossed my mind, but seeing Ollie kiss Maddie right in front of me reminded me he was no longer the man I used to know. Now I could no longer be sure who he was at all.

The table got quiet as I spaced off into the *what ifs*, when suddenly a hand landed on my back causing tiny splinters of pain to course through me from my injuries. "I'm sure they're just talking," Tyler whispered, and I bit my lip to control the discomfort.

"Yeah, I'm not sure they're doing much talking the way Maddie's hand was on his junk," Jude said with a mouthful of food. Bria hushed Jude, shoving her shoulder into him. "What? The girl needs to know, no?"

It was all too much—finding out about my dad, the glass incident, and now this. My heart couldn't take anymore. I pushed out of my chair just as Jake stood. "Mia?"

"I'm okay," I forced out. "I'm going to get an early start on a shower and go to bed." Because of my promise to Ethan, I hadn't told anyone about the glass incident, or the fact I was up the entire night before as Ethan pulled both large and tiny bits of glass from my body.

I walked into the bathroom and there was only one other stall on and no security guard to watch over me. The only stall I ever used was unoccupied, and I turned it on before hanging my things inside. The steam swirled around me, making it even harder to breathe without Ollie and the thought of him with someone else.

Stepping under the water, I attempted to drown out the noise inside my head. The visions of what Ollie could be doing this very moment with Maddie reminded me that this was exactly the reason I needed him to stay away from me. Was I only pushing him into the arms of someone else?

I should've fought harder for him.

We should've stayed together.

It shouldn't be like this at all.

And if I were honest with myself, every breath without him was a blessing because it took that much effort to breathe, and I finally understood what he had meant.

As if I manifested him, it was Ollie who appeared before the mirror through the small opened slit of the shower curtain. His hair dripped over his naturally tanned skin, drops running through the details of his hard lines and faded tattoos. Black joggers hung low, and I snapped my attention back to his face when our eyes connected.

No matter how hard I tried, I couldn't look away.

Then, instead of flashes of him and Maddie, it was only us and the moments we shared in this very bathroom. The only sound between us was the beating shower against the tile and my shallow breath. Familiar green eyes penetrated me through the mirror's reflection.

Tears fell from my eyes and I was glad I was under the water to hide them. Though my vision grew blurry, I was too scared to blink to break this connection.

Ollie turned and walked toward me. His bare feet took a step into my stall and closed the curtain behind him, his eyes never leaving mine. It wasn't a primal look, but more of a look mixed with heartache and despair. Still clothed, he took another step toward me, and we were merely an inch apart. Ollie stood over me, both our chests unable to find a calm rhythm. Water drenched his joggers, but he seemed oblivious to the weight holding them down.

And I seemed oblivious to everything else around me.

There was so much we both wanted to say, but words could only make or break this moment, and neither one of us wanted to take the risk.

Each slow movement he made filled with hesitation, catching my reaction and relishing in the way it made him feel. His fingertips traced down the sides of my arms, and if it were the only touch I'd receive from him, it would be more than enough.

Ollie lowered his head and grazed his lips across mine, then pulled away to see me.

His green eyes laced with conflict, hopeless and hope-filled—only he could pull that off. Seconds passed us by in heartbeats hanging on by the movement of the other.

And I stood frozen with a conflict of my own, afraid of every damn decision, yet him taking each doubt away by every subtle touch. His closeness healed and tore me open with every anticipating second.

Ollie's hands ran through my wet hair as his breathing staggered. I looked up for the first time under the water to catch his expression. Water fell over his lashes and lips, and the muscles along his jawline tightened.

As if it were too much for him to bear, he pressed his forehead to mine, screwed his eyes shut, and his fingers gripped the back of my head.

He pulled me into him as his lips touched mine, hovering, pulling away, drawing near, and my hands shook from holding back for this long. Breathing turned into a song, our ultimate playlist in our sacred moments such as this. But even silence told stories, wants, needs, and we always shared the same melody.

The shape of his lips latched to mine, and a drawn-out breath of relief escaped through his nose. I grabbed hold of his waist to keep myself from falling as he breathed the one word that made time standstill.

"Mia …" His tone struggled in a wave of emotion. Ollie fell back against the tile, taking me with him. We kissed like it was our first and last time, happily trapped in an inescapable bond, tethered by lips.

And the water turned cold, but we were on fire, knowing damn well this moment would burn into us until we could be together again.

His tongue tangled with mine in a slow, soothing cadence, hitting every nerve, each stroke healing every ache. I sucked the water from his lips before returning to our dance of give and take. The taste of him sent a buzz through my bloodstream, making me dizzy and drunk on him.

I moved my hands over his waistband, tugging it down when he pulled back and shook his head against mine. He opened his mouth as if he was going to say something, but it closed just as quickly. Ollie licked the water from his lips and kissed me one last time before stepping around me and exiting the stall.

Motionless, I stood there, feeling empty and rejected.

Time passed, I didn't know for sure how long exactly. I left the shower and moved on auto-pilot. Dressing, drying, staring at myself in the mirror. Waves of people rushed around me as I brushed my teeth, unable to comprehend my own thoughts or the words of others—until Dean Lynch's voice came through the intercom.

"We are on lockdown until further notice. I repeat, this is Dean Lynch, and we are on lockdown until further notice. Stop whatever you are doing, and retreat to your dorm for a headcount."

"Alright, turn off your shower, you know the drill," a security guard called out after a single clap of the hand before he ushered people out the door.

Questions and theories buzzed through the hall until I reached my door.

It was nearly three in the morning when Ethan woke me. This time, he was already in bed behind me with arms clutched around my waist. I knew it was him by the way his stubble grazed my shoulder, and his warm breath hit my neck. Bodies tend to remember the familiar presence of another before having to see with your own eyes.

It was a sixth sense telling you when you should be scared and take action, and when you were safe in the arms of another. Everyone had it. Few chose to listen to it.

My sixth sense confirmed Ethan had always belonged in my life one way or another. I just didn't know what role he was supposed to play. Regardless, my mouth still opened and said, "Ollie," attached with a denied hope.

And as always, Ethan corrected me with a sigh, "Ethan. It's always Ethan."

"What happened tonight?" I asked without turning around.

Ethan let out a breath and dug his fingers into my waist.

I didn't feel guilty for the relationship we had, if anything, I was grateful for it. No one knew the depths and it was better that way. Around Ethan, I never had to identify what we had or put it into a box. He was a friend. He was my hero. He was everything when Ollie was gone. And he was everywhere when I needed him. He was an anchor when everything else turned to chaos.

But the sad part was, if it came down to Ethan and Ollie, I'd choose Ollie. Ethan understood this, too, yet he still held on, taking the time we both had until Ollie would come back around, allowing me to use him in ways I needed. Perhaps Ethan used me too.

We killed each other's loneliness.

"There was a suicide in a dorm room in second wing," Ethan said dryly. "Lynch wanted to make sure we had a headcount and clear the area for police presence."

I flipped around to face him, and he moved the stubborn hair from my face. "Did you see?"

Ethan nodded. "I don't want to talk about it anymore, alright?" It was my turn to nod, and Ethan turned his eyes away and looked to the ceiling, his brain working overtime.

Ethan had seen enough death. He should be numb to it all, but it still seemed to rupture him every time. Ethan turned back to face me, lips pressed together, world shaken up. "I need tonight," he whispered.

I'd never seen him like this, and I'd wondered if he was close to the person who took their own life. "What do you need from me?"

"I need nothing *from* you, Jett. I just need *you*."

"Okay."

We laid there in silence as he dug his face into the groove of my neck, every part of him on the edge of breaking but refusing to. I should have told him it was better just to let go—to cry because your heart can only be forgiving for so long.

Though this was Ethan we were talking about.

Ethan had a soul of stone and the heart of a grim reaper.

His fingers laced in mine as he pinned my back to his chest, squeezing his broken away.

Dr. Conway entered my second class of the day. Tyler sat beside me with her brow in the air as whispers bounced through the small classroom.

"Today is going to be a little different," Ms. Chandler announced, sending a nod in confirmation to Dr. Conway. "Everyone here is familiar with Dr. Conway, and today she's going to talk about bullying and suicide help and prevention."

Tyler turned to face me and whispered, "Every time someone commits suicide, they have to make it a big deal as if it were a contagious disease."

I shook my head and gave her the *keep-your-thoughts-to-yourself* eyes.

Dr. Conway cleared her throat, and Tyler and I snapped our heads forward.

"It's the people you would never expect, Tyler. Something that shouldn't be taken lightly," Dr. Conway stated before returning her attention to the rest of the class. Tyler's blonde hair fell around her shoulders as her eyes found the surface of her desk.

Dr. Conway went on to talk about what had happened the night before. Not in detail, of course, but how Haden was a confident young man with many friends. He had never been bullied, but the one to bully others. Internal struggle was invisible, and sometimes the easiest way to counteract the silent pain was to try and beat it into someone else. You would've never known what he had planned to do, and those were the types of people who were the most danger to themselves because there was no cry for help. But she still listed signs to look out for and how to go about reporting suspicious behavior.

Then there were people like Livy.

"Who's Livy?" Tyler asked in a hushed tone.

I pointed back to Dr. Conway, advising her to listen as I remembered the night Alicia told me the tale of Livy and Tommy last year.

Livy had walked through the doors of Dolor broken and confused, much like myself. Then found herself again through Thomas, like the way I did through Ollie.

Livy had been in love.

Livy had been happy.

Livy had planned on making it out of Dolor alive.

Except she didn't.

Livy and Tommy fell victim to the curse of Dolor.

"Livy took her life after months and months of being strong against people like Haden. Ironic how both were struggling with demons of their own, and if we only opened our eyes and hearts to one another, if only we listened, they would both still be here," Dr. Conway explained.

What Dr. Conway failed to mention was Livy had been gang-raped, which would be enough for some. She still held on until she became pregnant, then later lost her only source of continuance when Tommy had been taken to jail after he killed one of the rapists. Losing Tommy was her breaking point. Livy had been later found in her dorm room, hanging from the ceiling.

After she had stepped off the chair, I wondered what had gone through her head—If she'd regretted it. If flashes of the rapist and people who taunted her had entered her wounded mind. If she'd thought about Tommy, and what her decision would do to him.

Over a year had passed since Tommy's vengeance and Livy's death, but students still talked about them in whispers as if they were a myth or a spell you could cast onto another.

"We will hold a vigil tonight after dinner for Haden and Livy," Ms. Chandler finished up as Dr. Conway gathered her materials. "It is not mandatory, but we expect your respect at the very least."

After dinner, Tyler, Bria, and I walked side by side across the lawn toward the dimly lit lights in the center. The burnt orange sky bled across the starry canvas as night fell. Jude stood beside Liam, while Jake kept a distance on the other side of the circle—eyes wandering back and forth from the center to Liam.

Maddie giggled behind me as she walked up with Ollie by her side.

"That's annoying," Bria whispered beside me.

I shrugged and allowed the quietness to take over the moment.

A few students said words about Haden. No one said anything about Livy. No one knew Livy. My sights landed on Ethan, who stood off in the distance—caught in a daze and lost in another place, another time. His face was a mask, shielding his thoughts, saying nothing though his fingers wrapped around his belt, knuckles turning white.

"I'll be right back," I said quietly to the girls.

I slipped out of the circle unnoticed and stood beside Ethan. His attention remained forward, and we both looked down at the circle from the top of the hill. Grabbing his hand from his belt, I pulled our linked hands behind him, and he let out a long breath and closed his eyes.

We stood like that for the rest of the vigil—his lips parted, his breathing uneven, and my comfort hidden from the rest of the world. But it was what he needed.

The wind blew, flickering the candles the staff were holding.

Words were done being spoken, but the sudden quiet was the loudest. Ollie looked up with narrowed eyes and a pained expression at the two of us.

Then the clouds parted, and rain broke out.

The circle scattered as students ran up the hill toward the school, but Ethan and I were frozen in place, his hand squeezing mine from behind him, unwilling to let go.

"Let's get on with headcount," another security guard said as he approached, eyeing Ethan's demeanor.

Ethan released my hand and returned his eyes to the security guard, speaking up for the first time within the last twenty minutes. "I'm right behind you, Jerry."

Jerry gave me a nod under the falling sky before leaving as the rest of the students blew past us in a frenzy.

Ethan turned to look at me.

"You don't have to say anything, I know," I said. It was hard for him to admit when he needed someone, let alone say thank you. But with me, he never had to.

Ethan's eyes twitched away toward where the circle used to stand and back to me, "You have five minutes before you're back in your dorm room." My gaze landed where Ethan's gaze just left to see Ollie standing at the bottom of the hill with his back to us. "Five minutes, Jett."

It had been over a month now since Ollie and I had spoken, not counting our time in the shower because we hardly uttered two words.

I walked toward Ollie. He'd stripped off his hoodie and was down to his white tee which was soaked and clinging to his wet skin. His bird tattoos were visible as they crawled up his back from his side, and he hung his head as I approached. "Are you fucking him?" his tone clipped and his focus off in the distance.

"No," I immediately said and took a step out in front of him.

He lifted his passive gaze to me and tilted his head as he clutched his hoodie in his fist. "Are you lying to me?"

"No."

He let out an exhale and blinked raindrops away. "Are you okay?"

"I don't know … No … I don't think I am."

Ollie looked away and shook his head as a clap of thunder broke the silence. "I hate this," he stated, undisturbed by the weather around us. "Dammit, Mia … I fucked up bad. I did so—"

Silencing him, I grabbed his wrist. "Please, I don't want to know."

"I miss you," he said harshly. "I miss you so fucking much it hurts." His brows snapped together as he clenched his fist tighter. "Do you remember how we felt? Are you hurting from constantly thinking about me the way I am about you, or do you have someone else to ease it? Do I ever fucking cross your mind at all? Because I can't help but think I'm going through this alone."

I blinked the rain from my lashes as I looked at him.

"Fucking answer me!" Ollie demanded, causing me to wince. "Or do you enjoy torturing me?"

"You have no idea what I've been going through."

I turned to walk away when Ollie snatched my wrist and jerked in front of me.

"You have my blessing, Mia. You're set free, no point in waiting around for me anymore. Turns out, I'm just like my brother. I'll never be the person you once knew. That bloke you fancied so much, he's fucking gone."

His green eyes held a void I badly wanted to fill again. It wasn't my Ollie staring back at me. This side of darkness knew him well. So damn well, his demons were rejoicing to have him back and if I didn't stop now, his darkness would swallow me too.

TEN

*"Do not fear the hurt in their eyes.
Instead, fear when hurt fades to hollow.
For the difference between the two
is the heart."*

OLIVER MASTERS

Bria

"I'm so over this week," Bria whined. "Where's Tyler?"

A full week had passed since the vigil, and I looked around to see both Tyler and Jude missing from the mess hall. Immediately, my thoughts went to Tyler and her safety. "I don't know,"—I stood up from my chair— "I'll be right back. I'm going to check her room."

Bria nodded as Jake commented on a girl all over Liam at another table. As far as I knew, Bria didn't know about Jake and Liam's relationship. But that didn't stop Jake's inability to control his mouth. Bria's thoughts were somewhere else and didn't see much into it, anyway.

I walked through third wing and approached Tyler's door. Soft cries sounded, and my heart jumped into my throat as I pushed the door open. My eyes landed on Jude's bare ass as he thrust into Tyler from behind. "Oh-my-God," I mumbled as I immediately closed the door. With wide eyes and frozen feet, I stood on the other side of the door, trying to piece together and shut out the image I just witnessed. My hand still glued to the doorknob, Jude swung the door open from the other side and brushed past me.

"Mia, I'm so sorry. You weren't supposed to see that," Tyler said out of breath. I turned to face her through the opened door as she slipped a shirt over her head and shoved her legs through pajama pants. "Please, you can't tell Bria. She'll kill me."

Her blonde hair was in as much as a wreck as this situation she put me in. "Why can't I tell Bria?"

"Because," she huffed. "They're like a thing now."

"Tyler! Why would you do that to her?"

"I like him, and I haven't found anyone I've liked enough since the ... you know ... since I was forced. I'm done putting myself on the back burner and letting people walk all over me!"

"I can't deal with this right now," I rubbed my temples, "I came to check on you to make sure you were okay. I don't trust that guy, Ty. You shouldn't either."

"He's good, Mia. You have him all wrong. If you would just get to know him."

"No, I'm not wrong about this." How was I supposed to tell her that I believed it was him who had hurt me? Who had put glass in my mattress and into my back?

Her blank stare was stuck to mine. "Say you won't say anything. At least let me figure this out first. Then, I'll tell her myself."

"Fine." I threw my hands up in the air. "It's your funeral."

Unable to face anyone, I decided not to go back to the mess hall and retreated to my dorm instead, spilling my secrets into my only trusted friend—my journal.

Our weekly meeting of Woman Against Sexual Assault was awkward that evening. Tyler, Bria, two new girls, and I sat spaced out on the floor. The new girls helped deflect the big fat elephant in the room—the elephant being Tyler and Bria sitting across from one another and sleeping with the same guy.

My loyalties laid out before me. I glanced over at Bria, her listening intently to the small mouse-like teen with a voice to match, nodding in moments when she was supposed to, completely unaware of what was happening behind her back.

Then there was Tyler turned blonde-bombshell playboy model after losing a quick ten pounds in a month, gaze sailing back and forth between Bria and me with guilt hovering over her like a raincloud. I nudged my eyes over to Bria, instigating this was the safest place to spill her confession, but she only shook her head with wide eyes.

"... and now here I am. I know it was so long ago, and I should be over it by now," the new girl continued.

Bria interjected, hushing her. "No, that stays with you forever. The important thing is that you're here now." Bria crawled across the floor and offered the girl a hug.

"What about you? Can I hear your story?" the girl asked.

Bria glanced over at me before settling into a spot beside her. "My story isn't even mine; it's Mia's." Bria held her hand over her heart. "The wanker who raped me only did it because another bloke wanted to get to her. I was never the objective ... only an opportunity for distraction."

"Thank you, Bria," I clipped out, not wanting to hear that night all over again. Bria shot me a small smile to comfort me, but I didn't need comforting. What I needed was Tyler's confession to be out in the open because I didn't know how long I could hold on to this one for.

After our session, the girls branched off as Bria and I fell into step back to our wing. My mouth ran without admission, trying to keep the subject away from all things Jude and Tyler, only to talk about safe matters such as being sick of the cafeteria food and craving a taco and a mocha iced coffee when Bria stopped me in my tracks, placing a hand on my arm before we turned a corner. Her black bob grazed her shoulders as she turned her head around to make sure we were alone. "Want to know a secret?"

No. Fuck no. Absolutely not. No. Uh-uh.

"Sure," I said, my voice vacant and my teeth grinding.

Bria's lips quirked. "Jerry got me some ..." she pinched her forefinger and thumb together and brought it to her mouth, imitating a blunt.

My eyes bulged. "Jerry, the security guard?"

Bria nodded excitedly, hooking her arm into mine and ushered me forward around the corner. "I'll let you join me in the woods tomorrow, but only you." She faced forward but my eyes stayed on her, trusting she wouldn't lead me into a cement wall.

"How did you get Jerry to get you something like that?"

She shrugged as we stopped in front of her door, "I caught him banging one of the doctors while everyone was at dinner. A small threat can go a long way." A snort blew out before my head fell back into a silent cackle. "Mia!" Bria nudged me with her shoulder. "You can't say anything. Got it?"

"Okay ... okay. I got it." I quickly recovered, but my smile still lingered.

The next morning, I woke with Ethan snoring lightly beside me. I jerked my head out the window to see the sun shining blatantly through, meaning it was past seven. Frantically, I shook him until his eyes sprang open.

"Fuck," he jumped to his feet, looking around blindly for his clothes scattered across the floor, "Bloody hell, Jett." Black boxers clung around his waist and thighs. Bare-chested and beautiful, I couldn't help but admire the way his muscles moved under his untouched-by-ink skin. My gaze drifted across his chest, down his abdomen, to the morning wood stretching in his boxers. "Jett."

I hadn't noticed he stopped his movements to watch me ogle at him, and Ethan did nothing to hide his huge morning surprise as it stared right back at me. Instead, he planted two hands over his hipbones and leaned forward. "Jett ..." he said slowly.

I snapped my eyes back to his face. "W-w-why were you naked?"

"Oh, grow up." Ethan shook his head. "This isn't naked, and I had to get comfortable." He pulled a white tee over his head, and the hem draped over his boner like it was no big deal. "I can't sleep with clothes on."

To distract myself, I leaned over the edge of the mattress and snatched up his pants before throwing it at him and covering my eyes. "Put that away. You're going to hurt someone with that thing."

Ethan forced back a laugh, but a smirk did push through his features, and it was a rare moment that should have been documented. "Am I making you uncomfortable?"

"I think we just passed a boundary in our friendship."

"That boundary was pushed the moment you dropped your towel in the bathroom." One by one, he pushed his legs through his pants. "And the second you invited me into your bed." After securing his pants, he scooped up his uniform shirt and stood over me. His hand came over the top of my head and he ruffled my hair like a child. "Don't worry. I don't come in second for no one. It can never go where you're thinking."

"Never crossed my mind." *Until now, thanks to him.*

"Good."

"Good."

"See ya later, Jett," Ethan finally said with a thick voice full of something I couldn't put my finger on, and he slipped out the door without a trace.

I fell back against the mattress with anxious thoughts of where this was heading. Ethan said it could never go down that path, but now that path was coursing through my mind. Ethan was easy. He was secure. He was

119

everything Ollie wasn't right now. Ethan would be the right decision if I had a choice to decide at all.

But I didn't have a choice. Ollie took that away the moment he stepped into my life.

Instead of joining Bria in the woods, I opted for Movie Day in the recreation room, a place I hardly visited. I stood by the entryway, door ajar, and scanned for a familiar face in unfamiliar territory. The lights were low, and all eyes faced the television resting on a rolling cart like back in high school. Beanbag chairs sprawled out in front of the room, and an oversized couch sat in the back. Many had brought their pillows and blankets from their dorm rooms, and silent whispers and giggles played out under the subtle sounds of the crackling TV.

A security guard sat under the covered window with his feet kicked up and his hands stuffed into a chip bag, indulged in whatever was playing.

"Mia," a voice whispered, and my eyes filtered through the room when a small hand waved into the air. *Tyler*. A breath of relief spilled out of me as I made my way toward her near the back with Gwen curled next to her.

Tyler moved from the corner of the couch, and I slid beside her as Gwen greeted me. "What are we watching?" I asked.

"Two words: Dylan O'Brien," Gwen said through a sigh and a hand over her heart.

"Dylan?"

Gwen pointed in front of her just as a boy ran across the screen through two walls closing in on him.

"Ahh, gotcha."

"Crushing on blokes you know you can't have is so much easier than the real deal. They can't hurt you," she added casually with a shrug.

Tyler snorted a laugh. "They also can't please you."

"Eh, I always do a better job myself anyway," Gwen confessed before pursing her lips with an added head jerk. Tyler threw her head back, unable to fight her laughter when two kids sitting on a bean bag in front of us snapped their heads around, hushing us. Gwen flipped them off and turned back to face me. "Speaking of getting hurt, how are you holding up?"

I curled into the couch and drifted my gaze back to the TV, buying time and wondering which incident she was talking about. Did she somehow know about the glass incident? My father? "What do you mean?"

"The whole Maddie and Ollie thing. Figured it'd crush you, no? Unless of course, you have someone else now."

"I'm fine. A kiss doesn't bother me." Except that it did, but showing an inkling amount of weakness to anyone in this place put a target on your back, and I already had enough people gunning for me. Still, you couldn't show tears. You couldn't show emotion. If people found out your weaknesses, your secrets, they had weapons to use against you. And Ollie was the one weapon that could destroy me.

Gwen shook her head, her large breasts peeking from her low-cut shirt moving like Jell-O. "I'm not talking about the kiss. I'm talking about Ollie banging her." My heart plummeted to my stomach. My eyes slid to hers, and I had no control over my expression. "And if I have to hear one more time how he plays with her fanny like a bloody guitar, I swear I'm goi—

"Gwen!" Tyler screeched, head dipping away from Gwen and shoving her in the shoulder. "What the hell is wrong with you?"

Without a word, I'd managed to get back to my feet, and the rest of Tyler's words blurred behind me as I made my way to the door.

After everything I'd been through over the last month, nothing hurt worse than finding out Ollie wasted no time sticking his dick into someone else. Not just anyone else, but Maddie of all people. Even with him keeping his distance, he still had the power to burn me. But this wasn't the same burn we embraced before. This burn hurt like hell.

Each foot felt heavy as if tied down by cinder blocks as I trudged through the halls in hopes of coming in contact with him. The burn in my heart raced up my chest to my neck and behind my eyes. My head throbbed from holding in the rage and tears wanting to let go. I didn't have a plan, or what I would say, all I knew was I had to see him to confront him. Had he stooped so low, only to ruin our future entirely?

When I reached my wing, another origami rose waiting outside my door only fueled my fury toward him. Swiping up the reminder he had left me, I marched toward his door and pounded until the door opened and Ollie stood on the other side with wide eyes and disheveled hair.

"Mia?"

The burn spread to all my senses—behind my eyes, in my nose, to the back of my throat, and ultimately ringing in my ears. I slapped the rose against his bare tattooed chest with a shaking hand, and I kept my eyes locked on his as the rose fell to the floor.

"You bastard," I'd managed to say, and I wanted to hurt him and have him feel the same agony that brewed inside me.

"You know." Those two words came out as a statement instead of a question, and he hung his head in defeat.

"It's just me now. There is no *you and I* anymore. You and I were done the moment you quit fighting for us," each word stained by a love I once knew, but seeped out with every ounce of strength I managed to gather.

Call me a hypocrite. Call me selfish. Go on and hate me.

The thing was, Ollie had known what I'd needed to get me to this place. He'd, somehow, known the very thing I'd needed to break down my walls was by him pushing and pushing me and never letting go.

And I knew exactly what Ollie needed this very moment.

The only way to get Ollie back was to give him the girl without emotion. The girl without feelings. The fucking sociopath—the girl he fought so hard for once upon a time.

"I didn't mean those words at the vigil! I never stopped fighting!" Ollie's voice grew louder, "Listen, I'm sorry. I'm so fucking sorry, but I'm fighting. Every day is a constant battle, but I've never given up. Despite everything I said, I'm not giving up …"

Through Ollie's plea, I managed to close my eyes and turn off the lights. *It's only temporary*, I kept reminding myself. *Only for a little while.*

I mentally counted until the burn subsided and my heart maintained a steady rhythm.

Then I opened my eyes.

Ollie's words ran together before they came to a complete stop.

He looked at me.

I crossed my arms over my chest and looked down at our feet. "Pick it up."

"Mia?" Ollie's chest heaved and he snapped his brows together.

"The rose," I kicked the paper at our feet, "pick up the rose."

Ollie hesitantly bent down and scooped up the rose before returning his eyes to me. His expression remained confused as he tried to read me. But I'd turned unreachable. Hollow. I'd figured it out, and he could no longer hurt me with my mask on.

I had done this for him. It was the only way to get through to him.

"Now tear it up."

"No," he whispered. "Don't do this."

"Tear it up, Ollie!" I screamed, and Ollie slammed his eyes shut. My tone dripped with anger and my body shook in its wake, but I kept the lights off in my eyes. I had to keep them off. Slowly, Ollie tore the rose up as each piece floated to our feet. Once the last piece landed on my boot, I snapped my eyes back to him. "Now, say you're sorry."

"Mia, please. You're not making any sense." He reached out to me, but I took a step back.

"You love the word so much, what's the hold up now?"

He dropped his arms to the side. "I'm sorry!"

"Not to me, to the rose."

Ollie dropped his chin and stretched his arms out to the side. "I'm fucking sorry," he looked back up at me, "Better?"

I looked down; the rose still in pieces at our feet. With my foot, I kicked the pieces around. "Nope still broken. Looks like 'sorry' didn't do shit. That's me,"—I pointed to the pieces— "that's my fucking heart, and your apology isn't going to mend or heal your mistakes anymore. Your 'sorry' doesn't piece back what you've broken. And this time, it was us you broke. For good."

The realization hit him, and he dug both palms into his eyes as he took a step back. "Mia, you're wrong about this. You're so wrong … you don't understand," he fell to his knees, "I can fix this. I can fix us and … we're going to get through because we're supposed to be together …" Ollie continued to mumble through tears as he picked up the pieces at my feet. "I couldn't go through with it. Nothing would let me … I'm going to make this right."

I took a step back, and I finally had Ollie right where I wanted him—crawling on his knees, begging. His long fingers gripped my thighs, refusing to allow me to move as he dug his face into my legs, continuing to mumble incoherent promises and apologies.

"Stay in hell, Ollie." I jerked back, causing him to land on his palms. "You're nothing to me."

Power. Love was power. But by being dominated by love could bring out the best and the worst in people, a back and forth game of tag to make sure you weren't the one left powerless. I could mark that as my worst moment—purposely hurting the only person I ever loved just to prove a point. Yes, I wanted to hurt him, but only to bring him back.

This had to work.

With one foot in front of the other, I blinked my lights back on successfully.

Ollie called out my name. The burn returned and the tears finally fell from the corner of my eyes.

Come back to me, Ollie.

ELEVEN

> "When the night arrives,
> and all the stars have died,
> you are still not alone.
> I go through many phases
> but will never leave.
> When all is lost,
> wish upon me.
> –advice from the moon"
>
> OLIVER MASTERS

Ollie

"Why the fuck did I tear this up to begin with?" I mumbled to myself ... to Zeke ... to the heavens above ... to whoever would bloody listen. I kneeled on the floor over the edge of the mattress, sprawling the pieces out in front of me. The small and flimsy pieces slipped through my fingers as Mia had.

My brain, heart, and body were—for the hundredth bloody time—fighting against each other, yet she was the one slipping now.

I had to fix this. I needed to fix this.

I couldn't have her go back to the way she used to be.

"I gotta fix this, mate. I have to," I said, and Zeke tossed a small bottle over the mattress in front of me. *Glue?* I jerked my head in his direction, snatching the glue and holding it up between us. Controlling my breathing, I pushed my anger to the side, knowing he was only trying to help. "Where did you get this?"

Zeke shrugged and signed some words.

"I didn't know there was a craft room here." Turning back to face the broken pieces, I tried gluing two small bits together. Impatient for perfection, and only wanting to see it sitting together before me once more, I pressed them together between my thumb and forefinger, only to have them split into two soggy pieces and tearing upon pulling my fingers apart. "Bloody hell," I scoffed, swiping an arm across the mattress, shoving the scattered paper in all directions. I fell backward onto the floor and dropped my head in my hands. "She's right, mate. I don't think I can fix it this time."

A warm hand landed over my shoulder, and Zeke shook me. Glancing up, I met eyes with him as he signed, *You're Mia and Ollie. Never broken, only bent.*

I tapped the side of my head. "I'm not right in the head. I'm fucked up. I can't think straight, and I sure as hell can't trust myself anymore. I'm only making matters worse for her." Zeke's eyes fell before his hand did, giving up on me too. I parted my mouth, choking back words I wanted to say, but couldn't. They weren't words intended for Zeke's ears. They should be spewed in Maddie's.

Maddie.

Pushing up off the floor, I brushed past Zeke and out the door.

Love and hate existed on the same thin line. Love was dangerous. Hate was nasty. But just like love, hate controlled me—consumed me. Compelled me to do things I would never do sober, and right now, all I wanted to do was banish the blame by beating it into Maddie. My heart screamed to stop, but my body moved forward to no avail, with only one objective.

I dropped a single nod in the security guard's direction as I headed toward Maddie's door. Using one knuckle, I knocked and leaned into the door to listen for movement.

"She's not in there," a whiney voice broke out.

Jerking around, Gwen came to a stop before me. Spearing a shaken hand through my hair, I lifted my eyes from her chest. "Where is she?" Gwen crossed her arms, only pushing her chest higher as her breasts spilled out of her shirt. My eyes darted down the hall then back to her. "Don't make me ask twice."

"Oh yeah? Or what?" She laughed. *I damn near hit her.*

A woman.

Settling for option two, I closed the distance between us and leaned into her ear, spinning my finger around a lock of blonde hair, and pulled—hard. "Do you really want to find out?" I whispered, and Gwen bit her lip with discomfort, shaking her head. The guard's eyes fixated on us, waiting for something to go down—waiting for me to lose my shit. "Now I'm not in the fucking mood to play games. Where is she?"

"In the woods," she stuttered. "She's with Bria."

Dropping my finger, I took a step back. "Maddie's with Bria?" Chuckling incredulously, I grabbed her hand and yanked her down the hall. "Prove it."

Gwen didn't argue. Once I knew she wouldn't leave my side, I dropped her hand as we pushed our way through the double doors and outside under the cloud-covered sky. Long strides ahead, we made it halfway down the hill when Gwen stopped and pointed forward and into the woods. "See, she's right there. I'm not going with you."

I scanned the woods and turned back to Gwen, looking her up and down. "What don't I know?"

"Nothing," she barked, leaning into her hip and folding her arms over her chest, retreating. Cowering. "This is between you two. Leave me out of it."

She wasn't worth my time anymore. Brisk autumn air stirred around us, and I couldn't help but notice Gwen's nipples harden beneath her shirt as she looked around nervously. My knob pulsed to its own accord, and I wet my dry lips, hungry for a release that could never come because my heart was with Mia.

"Get out of here, Gwen." I turned back around and continued my walk down the hill. The grass faded to leaves. The forest grew thicker. The day's light around me dimmed from the branches overhead, darker and darker until I reached the girls.

Maddie had been my mistake, but girls with loose mouths should be punished. If anyone should have told Mia, it should've been me, and I had planned to tell her as soon as I deserved her again. Maddie stripped me of that option.

"Coming back for seconds?" Maddie chimed, causing past regrets to consume my memory—unwelcomed flashes of my fingers inside her, her toying with herself, me watching. But I didn't stop my pace, eating away the distance between us like a cancer.

"Do you have any idea what you've done?" Words flew out of me, and all I saw was blood-red. Bria took a step back with a wicked smirk stretching her face, and Maddie looked almost … scared? Maddie didn't get scared. "What lies have you told?"

Maddie's dark eyes darted toward where Bria stood, and I followed her gaze when Bria lifted her arms in the air. Patience completely diminished, and I slammed Maddie against the nearest tree and fear sprang in her eyes.

"You're scaring me," she choked out.

I tilted my head and leaned into her. "What's the matter? You've never been scared of me before." *Truth.* Maddie never once withered against me.

"I know you, Ollie. I know when to be scared and when not to, and right now you're fucking pissed, and I don't know why."

"What did you say to Mia?"

Her brows snapped together. "Mia?" confusion spilled out from her lips. She didn't get to say her name like that. She didn't get to say her name at all. "I haven't talked to that cow."

I slammed my palm against the tree, purposely avoiding her head and trying to control the demons inside before they became a permanent fixture inside me. I wanted to ruin her. I wanted her to disappear. Worst of all, I wanted to fade away because I couldn't live a life without Mia in it. I couldn't fathom it. "Who did you tell?"

"Does it matter?" She pushed me off her and straightened her shirt. "It's done, Ollie. You two are done, and that's not even the funny part."

"What are you talking about?"

"I'm not the one you should be angry with," Maddie hissed—returning to her normal self. Here she was, the Maddie I'd known well.

At the corner of my eye, Bria took a step forward and laid a hand on my arm. "Come on, let's go. She's not worth it." My nerves reached its limit, officially at capacity. I couldn't contain it anymore. I didn't know whether to scream, cry, drive my fist through a tree, or my dick into a pussy. There was only one girl that could make this all go away, and I wasn't looking at her. "I'll walk with you back to the building."

I pulled away from Bria's grasp and shoved my fists into my pockets. Clenching. Controlling. Containing. "No, I don't need your fucking pity." Turning to face Maddie, I fought back the evil wanting to backhand her. "Stay away from Mia, and stay away from me."

Sitting alone, I watched Mia from afar. I hid under a beanie and a hood, blindly swiveling my fork in whatever was on my tray with my attention on Mia like a vulture. My teeth hurt from constant grinding. With eyes fixed on her, I shoved my hand into my pocket and pulled out a piece of gum before popping it into my mouth.

She couldn't see me, but I could see her.

Her smile was gone.

She sat, staring at the table before her as the rest of them talked around her like she didn't matter. She was lost. She needed me. *I need you more. So much that it fucking hurts.* I was a shadow, the dark side. I was once the light casting shadows. Now I didn't know where this light was coming from that caused me to still ... simply exit.

Yes, I do.

That light was the constant reminder of what was waiting for me after this darkness would leave. It hung above me like a lamplight—the memory of us. Instead of standing in it, with my hand in hers, I was cast to the bottom as a black silhouette. A different shade. The shade of being without.

A place I never wanted to be.

My eyes never left hers as I plotted my next move until it hurt too much. Then I clenched my eyes closed, disconnecting what we had become and imagining what we used to be. Remembering Mia's touch, her sweet soothing voice, the vibrations of us in the same room, and the way she used to make me feel. I ignored the clinking of my rings against the edge of the table as my finger tapped nervously.

My eyes stung from the inability to shed a single tear since the moment she left me on my knees at my door. My heart was turning cold. I felt it spread to my bones. All the warmth, gone. Tighter, I screwed my eyes together. The clinking increased, the only sound now in my ears.

I couldn't even imagine her kiss anymore. I couldn't imagine up a single moment of us together. All I saw was the darkness.

And then I was transported, shifted to a time I never wanted to remember.

It's cold—too cold. The only warmth is me in this small closet. Though, if I take my hands off my ears to hug myself, I hear the cries. "O," I whisper through the pitch black. His outline is visible from the light that bleeds through the hole of the door—the hole an angry old man once punched through when he heard me cry. So, now I stay silent, as quiet as I can.

Oscar's breathing grows louder as his fingers wrap around his knob when I wish they were around me, keeping me warm. I try to look away, but I can't. He's on his knees, eyes watching over my mum. He's probably making sure she doesn't get hurt again, but it looks like he's hurting himself instead, the way his hand is moving angrily up and down. Maybe he has to go potty. He doesn't need to do that. It just comes out by itself. You just get the feeling.

"Come here," O whispers, one hand on his knob, the other waving me over. I don't want to move from this spot though. When I don't, his hand reaches behind my neck and forces me forward and pins me against the door. "Mum is getting fucked. Soon you'll be able to do that. Not to her, because that's gross, but you'll be able to fuck girls like a real man."

My eyes remain shut as I try to pull away, refusing to acknowledge the sin I know is before me. Oscar pinches my neck, the pain cuts through me, causing my eyes to pop open. Mum is leaning over the kitchen counter and I can't turn away, but my brain begs to turn it off—to make it stop.

My mum rocks harshly, slamming against the counter as he slams in from behind her, and her head falls back.

No, it didn't fall.

He yanked it.

The demon has his hands in her raven-black hair, as his hairy chest beats against her back.

"No," I breathe.

"Yes," O hisses. "Soon enough, I'll take over the business. You and me, brother. We can finally get out of this hole, have this fucking town and all the pussy eating out of the palm of our hands." I want to ask what he means, but I can't say more. Oscar's fingers dig into the back of my neck, the cold grips me, the cries from my mum slice through me, and what I see stains me. "But I'll call the shots, Oliver," he breathes, each word comes out harsh and uneven. "And if you ever touch one of my girls, I'll make you watch me beat into them until you'll want to tear your own eyes out. That's a promise, brother." Oscar slams me against the cold wall, and although it hurts, I'm just thankful I can't see mum anymore.

Oscar hits his palm against the doorframe as his body jerks forward until he turns to mush. With a small tilt of his head, his eyes pierce mine.

Evil. Dark. Wicked.

I grimace.

"Don't worry, Oliver. I'll find you a nice fanny. But never one of mine."

My eyes flew open to see Mia gone. Her entire table vanished. I scanned the mess hall as people retreated to their dorms.

I'd always remembered my past. Memories had always haunted me, feasted on me, but it had always been a constant reminder of the kind of man I refused to be. But since I'd been playing nice with the pills, the demons inside had different plans for my past. They used it to taunt me, to aggravate me, and to laugh at me.

Jerry appeared beside me. "Time to go."

Angrily, I pushed out of my chair, gathered my rubbish, and disposed of it in the can in passing. My thoughts lingered to its usual place—*Mia*.

Tension wrapped its fingers around my skull, digging its nails into my bones. Moving down the wing, I sensed Mia near. The buzz in my soul was unmistakable. My heart vibrated inside its cage the devil created, and my shameless dick ached to be inside her, to remind her.

Halfway down the hall, I stopped in my tracks and lifted my head until my eyes met hers. Pajama pants I'd never seen before laid low on her hips. I'd known every article of clothing she'd once owned. I didn't know anymore because I lived in a world without her.

Lost wet strands stuck to her neck along with the beads of water she failed to dry off as the rest of her hair piled carelessly on top of her head.

Mia's golden-brown eyes pinned me still, glowing and full of life.

She was perfectly fine, never slipped.

Perhaps she had always been fine without me.

Mia had me imprisoned in the heartache, and it hurt to look at her. The agony intensified, burrowing into the marrow of my bones. I wished I could rip them out.

Standing feet away, I took notice in the way her tiny hairs raised over her bare arms. My eyes roamed over her, inch by inch. Goosebumps coated her, and my eyes made the journey down to her bra-less chest, staring at me, taunting me like the bloody shadows.

She turned away, and I wanted her to stop this pain eating away at me—put me out of my misery. It was the least she could do.

She lost her bloody grip, yet I still loved her to the point I hated her.

And right now, I wanted to fuck her to show her how much.

Like when water was so cold, it burned.

Frostbite.

Mia

It wasn't just six hours ago I'd pushed Ollie away, yet he stood there staring at me like I was a snack—jaw tensing, fists clenching, nostrils flaring. Feral cat-like eyes nailed me in place. It only took one glimpse into his angry eyes to know I'd gotten to him.

I pushed my door open, and an inferno landed against my back, guiding me forward through my doorway. Familiar fingers gripped my sides eagerly, digging into the crevices of muscle and bone. A gasp rolled from my lips, and Ollie kicked the door closed behind us. All my belongings dropped to the floor. Recognizable lips brushed my earlobe as his tall frame pressed against me from behind, pinning me to the door.

Ollie—familiar, warm, safe. My heart hummed from his closeness. A heated breath raked over my cold skin, and the familiar minted aroma became a well-known passenger between us. Without a word, Ollie slid his fingers inside the band of my pajama bottoms and panties, pushing them down my thighs, scraping fingers over my skin.

"Ollie ..." The tears in my eyes blurred the scene around me, and my sex ignited, begging for a fix of him—to be touched and adored by him. Pushing him away would've been an impossible task.

His teeth scraped over my shoulder to the nape of my neck as his hard length rubbed against me. I reached behind me wanting to touch him, to feel my fingers in his messy hair, but he snatched my wrist and gathered both my hands in one of his, planting them over the door. His demeanor was off-kilter—needy and angry.

With one hand, he pushed against the middle of my back until my face flattened against the door. His grip tightened around my wrist, and his knee broke apart my legs. Defenseless and exposed, the fangs of desire sunk their teeth into me as my center pulsated to his tune. Ollie would never hurt me, and my heart needed to be refueled by him.

"I wanted to fuck her, but I couldn't," Ollie informed, his voice stiff and without emotion. "I physically couldn't because I'm a slave to you." A single finger slid through my sex, and I shivered. Ollie dropped his head over my shoulder, drawing in a breath. I tried to turn to look at him, but he withdrew his hand and pressed my face against the door again, pinning me in place.

Confusion seized me blind.

His palm returned to me, dragging through my dripping wet center, not focusing on pleasing me, but every movement he made was for himself—and again, I did nothing to stop him. I embraced him; the closeness of him, his touch, his ragged breath spilling over my skin. I embraced it all.

Fingers pushed inside me—stretching me, thrusting into me, fucking me.

"Tell me to stop," Ollie warned, his voice broken and troubled as he pumped in and out. When I didn't answer, he pulled me back against him before gripping my wrists tighter. He thrust into me harder—hungrier, and more demanding. "Dammit, Mia. Stop me!"

"No!" I screamed.

He released his grip from my wrists, and in a moment when I thought something snapped inside him, his cock emerged from his pants, grinding and rubbing between my crack—hard, solid, and untamed. Ollie embodied a wave of fury, clenching my hipbones, and dragging me from the door before slamming me against the desk.

Still, I wasn't scared, only worried for him … because this wasn't him. He'd never manhandled me. He'd never pushed me. He'd never fucked me. And everything screaming inside me knew it was exactly what he was about to do. For the first time, Ollie was going to fuck me. Before I had the chance to turn and face him, Ollie wrapped his fingers in my bun and pressed my face down.

As if I lost all will to move, I morphed into whatever he needed because I didn't want to say no. This time, I was his punching bag. With my chest pressed against the—now cleared—desk, legs spread wide, and my bottom in the air, I felt his fingers pull me apart as his swollen cock drove inside me. I chewed my lip to fight a sound from escaping as he continued his revenge on me.

Over and over, he pounded into me with a fist in my knotted hair, yanking my head back.

Over and over, his familiar pelvis slammed into me in an unfamiliar way as my eyes stayed fixed on the mattress where we used to make love.

Over and over, fingers digging, leaving marks deeper than the skin, until warm semen pumped inside me from his pulsing weapon.

Then everything stopped.

Silence.

Stillness.

He stayed pinned, deep inside me. His entire body trembled as he gasped for a steady breath. Time passed slow—too slow—as we both froze in the moment still connected. I never saw his face because he refused to let me see him like this. It was as if he faced me, he wouldn't have been able to go through with it, yet it still broke him because his body shook in regret.

Finally, he pulled out, and the warm liquid dripped down my thigh, but I still couldn't move. I couldn't speak. I gripped my eyelids shut, turning my teeth to the inside of my cheek.

Seconds passed, and the sound of my door closing behind him was the only indication his unsettling retribution was over.

The small hand lingered over the three as I waited for Ethan to come through the door. He should have been here by now. The one night I desperately needed to not feel alone, I was. I remembered the days when all I'd wanted was to be alone. I'd never needed anyone until I fell victim to love.

I wasn't angry with Ollie for what he did, if anything, he showed me a part of him, and I finally understood. Like a blanket, he wrapped me up in the hell—the place he couldn't break free from—to give me a morsel of the torture he faced daily. Each word he'd uttered, I'd felt the struggle inside him. Each time he'd gripped me tighter, it had been an unsaid cry for help. Each breath had been a scream. Every thrust had been a beg for mercy, and the only person who truly took the beating had been him.

I'd felt it.

Like a ghost walking the planes of the earth aimlessly, lost and confused, unheard and unseen, I'd felt Ollie's internal pain. And it was that same feeling that kept my eyes open in the slow passing hours of the night.

My eyes stayed open, heavy yet fighting, locked on the door across the room until the sun came up blazing through the window. The only sound was the rattling of the vent. My mind spun like a frantic racing hamster on a wheel. Round and round. The visit from my father. Ollie. The glass in my mattress. Ollie. The dead cat. Ollie. Focusing turned into an impossible action I couldn't grasp.

Then the unlocking of the wing sounded, reminding me I hadn't gotten a lick of sleep.

Usually, I would have jumped out of bed at the sound. I would have—should have—collected my belongings and head to the community bathroom before everyone else. But it was Saturday.

Saturdays used to be spent in the library with Ollie. Then they used to be spent with Zeke in the group therapy room on the piano. But now I didn't want to leave my bed as I lie awake, naked, and drained from my short trip to Ollie's hell.

My eyelids felt like two elephants were sitting on them, and I'd only closed them for, what felt like, a second when a pounding at my door had them snap back open to the clock above.

Nine.

Two hours had come and gone in the blink of an eye.

I'd fallen asleep.

I jumped out of bed, threw on my hoodie and sweatpants, and peeked my head through the door. Chaos broke out in the hall. Shouting was all around me. People scattered as papers littered the floor and painted the walls. White everywhere.

Ethan held a red-faced Bria back from Tyler.

Jerry had a guy in zip-ties faced against the wall.

Liam cowered in the corner as two members of his crew surrounded him.

Jake stomped toward me, eyes glossy, face wet, and chin shaking uncontrollably. "You promised!" he screamed, clutching a paper in his hand. "You said you wouldn't tell anyone!"

I snatched the paper out of Jake's hand, and my eyes eagerly scanned over its contents as my heartrate spiked. *My handwriting.* The papers were covered in my handwriting. Tears blurred my line of vision, dropping from my eyes and landing on the ink, smearing the words together. It only took the first sentence to know exactly what everyone else knew.

The pages from my diary corrupted the hallway, filled their minds, and fueled their aggression toward each other. Everyone's secrets had been spilled.

"No …" I breathed, turning my head at the scene around me. People screamed at each other, tears bled out, venom spewed, spit flew as if it all happened in slow motion. Turning, I headed toward my desk. I ransacked my room for the journal I'd spent two months writing in since Dr. Conway gave it to me.

For two months, the journal had been my best friend, kindly accepting every thought I had of everyone, allowing me to share everyone's deepest secrets so I didn't have to carry the burden on my own. My brain went haywire as I remembered every secret that passed from my fingers, through the pen, onto the paper. The same papers that someone plastered on display for everyone to see. "This can't be happening …"

Gone. My journal was gone.

Empty-handed, I stood in the middle of my room. Tyler appeared beside me, hurt evident in her eyes. "You selfish cow," her lips mouthed, but I couldn't hear her, her voice drowned out by the screaming in the hallway and the clouding of my brain. Pushing past her, I needed to get away. I ran, shoving people aside to find a way out.

To my left, Ollie stood posted-up in his doorway, shoulder resting against the frame. Empty green eyes locked on mine as his expression remained bleak and hollow. His lips parted, and for a second, my stupid mind believed he'd pull me into his arms, but instead, his eyes turned away from me.

Curse words swarmed in the air, all directed at me, and I continued forward until their comments faded behind.

In a daze, my hand pushed open the library door, and my feet walked through the same maze I'd traveled more than a dozen times before until my body curled into a ball in the only spot I could be alone and no one could find me. The same place Ollie created for me.

And it was there I closed my eyes and begged for sleep to take me away from this nightmare.

TWELVE

"Once upon a time, there was a girl with a black heart and a lost soul. She was unpredictable, impulsive, never allowed anyone close enough."

"Don't tell me you fell for her."

"I am ... falling, that is. No one tells you about the fall, how once it starts it never stops. But that's a story for another day, my friend."

"Go on."

"They said she wasn't capable of feeling, but the way she looked at me said otherwise. They said she was better off alone, but her kiss pleaded for me not to leave. They said I was wasting my time, but my heart begged to differ. They said she was the devil ..."

"And what did you say?"

"Even the devil was once an angel."

A chuckle comes from his throat. "How does the story end?"

"That's the beauty of it, mate. It doesn't. Love has no beginning and no ending, much like the fall no one warned me about. Love is unpredictable, impulsive, and doesn't allow anyone or anything close enough to threaten it, much like the girl I fall every day for. Her black heart was a shield and her lost soul had been searching—protecting herself from predators while wandering the earth for me. Perhaps God gave up on his angel too soon ..."

"You're questioning God now?"
"All I'm saying is, I would've given her an eternity plus a day past crestfallen."

OLIVER MASTERS

Ollie

"Come sit with us," Bria suggested, batting her lashes over me. My eyes landed on Mia tucked away in the corner. *How did it come to this, Mia?*

She sat at the opposite end of the mess hall—opposite of me—alone and abandoned. Nowadays, she didn't care about the way her hair looked or the clothes she wore. She drowned herself in that atrocious oversized hoodie that wasn't here last year—and not mine. It was new, along with this situation we found ourselves in.

"It won't be awkward anymore now that we bumped Mia from our table," Bria added.

I blinked my gaze to Bria. Head held high and lips pursed, she looked good, comfortable under her new, unsaid ranking at Dolor.

"Mia's table," I reminded her. "It was Mia's and Zeke's before any of you bothered to show Zeke an ounce of compassion." I tilted my head. "Or did you forget?"

A smirk tugged on the corner of her lip before a frown ate it up. Sighing, I leaned back in my chair and crossed my arms over my chest. "Looks to me you forgave Blondie fairly quickly." My head nudged in the direction of the new girl sitting beside Zeke. "Wonder why that is. Rumor says Jude's john bounced between the two of you and you had no idea."

"Jealous?" Bria asked, leaning over the table. Her shirt dipped, revealing her tiny bare breasts, B-cups, nipples the size of quarters but the color of pennies. I'd never been a boob-guy, but my knob tightened against my black jeans, and my mouth watered. I ran my palms across the surface of my jeans. Nope, never been a boob-guy, only a Mia-guy, but right now all I could think about was how I could fit one whole breast into my mouth. "What's the matter, Ollie?"

"Walk away," I commanded, eyes still fixed on the buffet laid out before of me. It was anyone's guess what Bria's intentions were, but here they were, mine for the taking.

Bria laughed and straightened her posture. "My invitation still stands."

Double. Fucking. Meaning.

Both a giant mistake.

"Did you get lost?" Dr. Butala asked as soon as I entered his office. A white noise machine sat on a small table beside the door, humming low, and I ignored him as I took a seat in the black chair across from his L-shaped desk. Extending my arm off to the side, I waited for him to take my vitals.

Dr. Butala pinched his lips together, rolled back in his seat, and opened his drawer. "Any changes since last week?" He shuffled around in the drawer, gathering medical equipment I didn't know the names of.

Since the night I'd fucked Mia in her room, I'd mellowed out. I wasn't angry anymore, didn't have mood swings or lash-outs, I was … just.

Just living.

Just breathing.

Just sleeping.

And just horny.

"Your ticking is gone."

My fog lifted, and my focus returned to him. "My what?"

He pulled up a chair beside me and wrapped the plastic around my bicep. "The bouncing of your knee. It's gone."

"Oh, yeah ... Would you look at that?" I hadn't even noticed. Had I finally found the calm? The eye of the storm. It was nice here. Like a cyclone, chaos circled me, but it couldn't touch me. I'd finally entered a place where I felt nothing at all. If only my brain could pass the message along to my throbbing dick.

Dr. Butala pumped the black bulb as the plastic clenched tighter around my arm. Words took a hiatus as he locked eyes on his watch.

Tick. Tick. Tick.

The beating in my arm labored against its constraint.

Then the ripping of the Velcro snapped me out of the zone.

"Vitals look great," he offered, returning to his chair behind his barrier. "I think we have you under the right dosage of medication and found a combination that works for you."

"Brilliant."

Tap. Tap. Tap. Dr. Butala entered notes into the computer. His brown eyes hid behind his glasses. "And the ... erections?" he asked low under the white noise, not bothering to return his gaze to me.

"All cured," I lied with my palms in the air.

His shoulders rolled back. "Good. I was beginning to think it was psychological."

I lifted a brow in the air. "Psychological?"

"Well, yes. The brain is very complex. I can do my best to balance the chemicals, but childhood trauma can't be undone. I'm going to make you an appointment with Dr. Conway."

"I'm good."

"It's not an option."

I shook my head and stood from the chair. "Sounds fantastic, mate."

"Great," he bit back with stone features. "Tomorrow it is. Be there at two."

I threw a thumb in the air before heading toward the door.

"And Oliver?" Pausing with my hand on the doorknob, I waited without turning to meet his gaze. "Don't be late."

Cracking open another can of Schweppes, I lay back over Zeke's mattress with my eyes glued to the back of his head and my ears pinned to the telly.

The poor kid had been hard at work piecing back together the destroyed origami rose. I'd told him it didn't matter anymore, but Zeke was determined to fix my mistakes.

I threw a pillow at the back of his head to get his attention. Zeke's head snapped back to face me with his brows knitted together. "Let it go, mate. Relax. Watch *The Office*," I suggested with my hand pointed toward the telly. Zeke shook his head and returned to the puzzle before him at his desk. "Your loss."

The Schweppes hit the back of my throat, bubbly and kindling the mint in my gum. Crazy to think just a year ago, I had planned to take the kid home with me.

Oscar had told me what happened. Said he'd overheard Zeke's story in the breakroom, and how Zeke had been here since he was no older than seven or eight, abandoned on Dolor property like an unwanted pet. Instantly, I took to the kid. Got to know him, learned his language. Zeke had a heart of gold, and an old soul mine related to. Somehow, we clicked. He didn't remember much of his past and made a home here.

I'd made a promise to Zeke. As soon as I'd graduate, I'd adopt him and show him what it should feel like to have a real home. We could find out together. An actual birthday. A real Christmas. A real family—a family consisting of Zeke and myself.

A family both of us wanted yet never had.

The only way to accomplish the adoption was to make sure I would be financially inclined upon our departure. Before the school year started last year, I had sent my work to an agent. The agent had stated she liked my style, signed with me, and dispersed my poetry to a handful of publishers. But by the time a publisher agreed on me, I had been arrested for the rape of Bria and had been thrown into solitary.

During my time in jail, the publisher had pursued our contract. A proper check had been mailed to the jail, and I'd decided to make a deal with Travis, my only friend from my seven months outside of Dolor. Since he was leaving before me at the time, I'd made him agree to staying away from the gang he had been associated with, the Links, if he'd work for me and become my assistant.

I trusted Travis, and he agreed.

The only thing left to do, other than leave here with a clean record, would be to find a roof for over our heads. Then, I would submit the paperwork for adoption for Zeke. Legally, I'd become his guardian. Zeke was excited about the idea and joked he would start calling me "Dad."

I'd told him it wouldn't be like that.

We were mates.

Mates to always have a home to go back to.

Amidst it all, Mia had come along, my little plot twist. She only fueled my desire of becoming someone important. I'd never wanted anything more than to make something of myself for her. Everything had been perfect. Mia and I had grown closer and closer the same time Mia and Zeke were growing closer. Mia had accepted Zeke with an open heart. The day the storm had passed over Dolor, and Mia held scared Zeke in her arms, it was as if everything had fallen into place. I'd always known, from the first day I met her, she was the one, but that single moment left me in awe of the way God moved his chess pieces across the board, making everything I'd ever wanted within reach.

The plans for Zeke and me had turned into Zeke, Mia, and me, and not once had I clued her in on my promise to Zeke, or this life I had been planning for the three of us. Mia still had no clue about any of this. Perhaps it was every artist's fear of rejection—from her, Zeke, the publishing house, the world—and the fear of failure.

This time, I was a failure.

I'd failed Mia.

I'd failed Zeke.

But here Zeke was, picking up the pieces I destroyed, trying to fix the same future I'd painted then ultimately gave up on. I should have told him, even if he could fix it, it wouldn't bring Mia back. It wouldn't bring me back. The rose would be broken, misplaced, and cracked. It would never be the same.

Even if I did reveal this dirty truth to Zeke, none of it would have mattered.

I knew him well.

He'd still be there, piecing the paper rose back together.

Poor kid.

I threw the can across the room, and it slid into the can beside his desk, scoring me three useless points. Zeke had made no progression with the paper rose, and he didn't bother to turn around and face me as I stood behind him. With one hand on his shoulder, I advised him I was leaving and slipped out of my new haven and walked through his wing back to my own.

It had only been a week since Mia's diary was revealed for the school to see. Also, a week since I fucked her for the first time. That night, I'd stayed up as the darkness preyed on my remorse. Grief had gnawed on me, and tears emptied from my eyes until the sun came up. It wasn't until I wasted away in my shame when the void took over, tired of crying, tired of fighting. The entire week, I'd distanced myself to the world around me, relishing in the quiet and going through the motions.

Even in the hall when the release of her journal had gone down, people turning against one another, claws coming out, havoc-wreaking, tears pouring, I just couldn't seem to care anymore. Mia had walked past me, my little explosion of hope, to see all mine had vanished. Perhaps on the outside to everyone else, it had, but my heart still jolted, reminding me it was broken by what was happening to her.

Because what happened to her happened to me.

The worst part of caring too much, of feeling too much, of having too much to give, was that eventually you drain from being too much for too long. My fucks to give had a number, and between the medication and my tank depleted, I'd finally landed in the center of the storm, out of gas. The place I remember so vividly, and it welcomed me with open arms.

But as I stood there, Mia rang in my ear like a tiny bell, unwilling to let me go completely.

Showering that night was a walk in the park. No one talked to me anymore besides Maddie and Bria—Maddie still wanting to jump my bones, and my bone not wanting to jump inside her. Whenever I found myself alone with her, she'd try, but it never led anywhere. The only girl my body seemed to want was Mia.

My john wouldn't even take to my own hand.

I stood under the warm shower with a palm against the tile.

The room hummed around me, every stall occupied.

My body was tense, needing to rid myself of the arousal that had been built up since last week. My aching knob stood out in front of me, heavy and angry, and every ounce of blood rushing to its surface. Grabbing it with one palm, it twitched in my hand, confused by the reminder of being in the soft tightness of Mia. I yanked on it, dragging my teeth against my bottom lip to fight off the hiss wanting to leave. My eyes screwed shut, and I selfishly remembered the way Mia felt, her warmth clenching around me, pounding, pulsing. A small groan left me as I fucked my hand, pretending to be inside her.

But it was no use.

"Dammit, Mia," I breathed, releasing my dick and slamming both my palms against the tile.

Despite the void, every part of me still belonged to her. My head knew it. My heart knew it. My soul knew it. Even my fucking cock knew it. How long would it take for every part to come to a mutual understanding there was no such thing as forever?

"Times up, Masters," Scott rang out, and my body went stiff.

After turning the water off, I swiftly ran the towel over my skin, slid on my boxers, and slipped out of the stall. A few people lingered as Scott impatiently stood beside the door. I'd never needed to compare myself to others, but I couldn't wrap my brain around this one.

Mia liked him, possibly even loved him, and I could learn to be okay with that. If he'd be the one to prevent her from flipping her bloody switch again, I'd pat the bloke on the back before my time ran out at Dolor.

But there were many layers to the bloke standing beside the wall with eyes locked on mine. There was no doubt in my mind, Scott had cruel intentions of being here. Secrets hid behind his façade.

I flipped on the faucet to brush my teeth when I found my reflection in the mirror.

Not me.

Mia.

She stepped out of her stall and stood there with a towel around her tiny figure. Our eyes linked and my hands hit the counter to hold myself up from the power she still had over me. Her coffee-colored eyes held strong, undisturbed by the distance between us. Her perfect lips parted, wanting to say something. *Just spit it out, love.* If I had to wrap my fingers around her jaw and exhume them myself ...

"Let's go," Scott barked.

Mia snapped her mouth shut and dropped her towel. She stood stripped and bared. My first instinct was to snatch her up in my arms and remove her from hungry eyes. But then my gaze landed on her fading injuries. Her flawless skin had taken a beating, and my soul went cold. Yellowed patches marked her thighs and hips, and my grip tightened around the edge of the sink as my eyes continued their journey back to her face. "Who did this to you?" I asked, each word pained by the view before me.

"You did."

No. I would never hurt you.

My head shook the nonsense away, and my eyes jerked in Scott's direction as he looked at Mia who stood between us. The piece of rubbish had the nerve to look at her while I was in the same fucking room.

I swooped up her towel, wrapped it around her, and pulled her into me. She didn't resist. Scott took a step toward me, and I held up a palm in his direction to stop him.

Mia shook in my grasp, and I couldn't tell if it was because she was cold or scared of me. I lowered my head into the crook of her neck. "Tell me I didn't do this," I whispered out of earshot. My entire being hung on her answer.

"It wasn't you," she cried softly into my chest. "You weren't yourself."

Her words devoured me, shredded me to nothing. Absolute nothing. Chest pains so intense blurred my vision, and I held on to her tighter, digging my head into her neck.

A fierce sting fought its way through, and I pinched the bridge of my nose to control it. "I'm done saying I'm sorry. I'm going to make this right," I quickly promised before I turned into a wreck in the bathroom. The words couldn't come out fast enough in the little time we had. "I'll show you. Please, wait for me. Just stay with me, Mia."

"Even when you're gone?"

I placed my hands over her face and pulled her away so I could see her as my eyes watered. *Fuck*, I was about to break. She still had belief in the two of us. Somehow, she understood me. My lips met her forehead, and I breathed in the scent of her and buried it into my memory. "Especially when I'm gone."

Releasing her, I pushed my legs through my sweats, grabbed my things, and walked away from her. I couldn't get out of there fast enough. Emotions shredded me like a wild beast, ripping me apart. And it fucking hurt. I stopped in front of Scott and clenched my fist from putting it through his skull. "Don't ever fucking look at her again," my sick pride warned him.

THIRTEEN

"My first mistake
was bringing flowers
to a gun show."

OLIVER MASTERS

Mia

"I can't believe it's already the beginning of October," Dr. Conway rejoiced with a smile on her face. "Halloween is right around the corner, my favorite holiday. Me and Mark sit at the end of our driveway and hand out candy every year. Seeing the little kids …" she continued to gush as my thoughts transported back to the bathroom where something had changed within Ollie.

Ollie was fighting. I'd heard it in his voice. I'd seen it in his eyes. I'd felt it radiating from him, and the way he held onto me. One look at me, and he'd broken free from his somberness, ready to whisk me away and pull me from this nightmare. My heart jumped at the thought of him coming back to me. Our love was something to fight for, and Ollie still fought with everything he had.

Words had been exchanged between Ollie and Ethan before Ollie dipped out of the bathroom days before. Words that had been conveniently soaked up by the distance. But whatever Ollie had said caused Ethan's demeanor to change when he appeared in my dorm room later that night.

Ethan had stripped down to his boxers and climbed in next to me. I hadn't even had a night terror, but still, he'd fused to me without so much as an explanation.

Ollie had gotten to him.

The same way Ollie always got to me.

We'd fallen asleep, and when I'd woken a few hours later, Ethan's hand had traveled down to my inner thighs, softly gripping as he mumbled in his sleep. His hard erection had pressed into the space between my legs. I had every reason to wake him up and pull away, starting with the most important reason: Ollie. But I couldn't.

I desired to be needed and wanted by Ethan in an unhealthy way that never made sense to me. So, I'd fallen back to sleep, allowing his hands to roam and length to stay as he repeated words in my ear I couldn't piece together.

Each night after that had been the same routine—Ethan and I not on speaking terms, but his hands on claiming terms. I'd fallen asleep in his warmth, pretending it was Ollie. It always had been easier to pretend, and Ethan continued to touch me in his sleep like he had something to prove.

"Every year we dress as Morticia and Gomez Addams from the Addams family. The newer generation of kids don't get it, but it's a hoot with the parents," Dr. Conway rambled on as my attention steered back to the boring conversation.

"Nice," I faked an interested voice, pretending I had been listening.

Dr. Conway shot me an all-knowing look and removed her pad of paper from her desk. Crossing her legs, she returned to her title as a doctor from a friend. "How are you coping with the visit from your father?"

"You mean the man who never was my father and lied to me for twenty years? I'm doing fabulous."

Her face fell. "A million questions must be running through your head."

"Not about him ..."—I turned my attention outside the window and followed the rain from the sky to the ground— "Honestly, I have so much going on right now, I haven't even had a second to stop and think how it affects me."

"You have every reason to feel hurt."

Hurt? I was hurt, not by the man who claimed to be my father then took it away from me, but at the friends who neglected me. Jake. Bria. Tyler. With one mistake of writing down their secrets in my journal that had been stolen from me, the three of them were quick to up and cut me off like it was easy for them.

October meant I had six more months until I was released, and I couldn't enable my attacker by showing I was hurt. They could display the pages of my journal all over Dolor, hide dead animals in my dorm, put glass into my mattress, but they would have to kill me before I submit to their pathetic games.

Still, a part of me believed it was Jude, the other part of me was leaning more towards a female. Guys would mutilate a cat. Girls would steal a diary and paint the walls with its contents. Am I dealing with two different people?

"Mia?"

"Yeah?" I responded automatically, snapping my eyes back to face Dr. Conway.

"Your dad ... how are you taking it all?"

Great, we were still on that subject. "Don't call him that."

Her brows pinched together as she slumped her shoulders. "What do you want to call him?"

"Bruce," I stated, and the word sounded so foreign rolling off my tongue. There was no room in my mind to think about Bruce, or who my actual father was. All I needed to do was survive the rest of my time sentenced here. Pushing it away seemed like a better plan until I could gain access to my records … and a computer. "I'm a dual citizen, you know. I could stay here in the UK."

"Is that what you want?" Dr. Conway asked, and I nodded, knowing it was the only thing I wanted since I left Pennsylvania. "I can help you make that happen, but you still have to return to the states to take care of some loose ends with the judge after your release. And you will need a plan after Dolor. Will you continue in school? Where will you live? Will you work? Dolor has a great release program—"

"Okay, okay …" I cut her off and dropped back into the warm leather. Too many questions, too fast. "I don't know. I need time to figure it out." A year ago, I never cared where I ended up, whether it be jail or six feet under. I called that progress.

"I'll help any way I can."

On my way back to my wing, I passed by Jake and Tyler. Slowing my pace, hope sparked inside, thinking today would be the day they'd speak to me. But they passed by with only a look of disgust to give.

Out of nowhere, Maddie appeared, trapping me in. "How was counseling?" she asked, chewing on a stick of gum. The mint smelled like Ollie's, and I instantly grew jealous.

"Go away, Maddie." Taking a side-step away from her, I tried to escape her bubble. Maddie took a step out in front of me, blocking my every move. "What the hell do you want?"

"I just wanted to thank you."

An ambiguous laugh sauntered between us. "Thank me for what?"

Long fingers pushed my hair off my shoulder before they skimmed along my face line. My arms were occupied with books, so instead, I wiggled out of Maddie's filthy grasp when she smirked. "For making it so easy for me. You were exactly who I thought you were, a cold-hearted slapper. It makes sense now why your mother killed herself."

My last straw blew from my grasp, and my books dropped to the floor. "You bitch!" I screamed out, hurling myself at her. I was only a few inches shorter than Maddie, but still managed to knock her backward to the ground and throw my fist into her face.

Maddie's eyes went wild, and she snatched my wrist as I straddled my legs around her. "Ya hit like a bloody girl, princess," she said through a laugh. "I'm surprised ya have what it takes to take the beating from Ollie, knowing how rough he likes it." My adrenaline overpowered her, and I threw my elbow into the side of her jaw.

Arms snaked around my stomach, swiftly pulling me off of Maddie, and my frantic gaze skimmed the hallway to see a crowd gathering around. Hands gripped my cheeks and directed my gaze. My eyes met two green ones as Ollie brushed the hair from my face. "It's not worth it, love." My breathing was erratic, yet his voice was calm. Soothing. I wanted to drink from the tranquility rolling from him. "That girl right there,"—he pointed over to Maddie still lying on the ground with her palm over her jaw— "She's not worth destroying your future for, alright?"

My Ollie.

"Breathe, Mia," he added, and I hadn't realized I wasn't. Returning my attention to Maddie, she looked almost scared. Ethan helped her up from behind while his eyes stayed fixed on Ollie and me. "Hey, look at me," Ollie whispered, and I faced him again. His eyes scanned over my face before he offered me a small smile. "Better?"

"Yeah." The one word was a struggle to get out, and it came out more like a sigh of relief. "Yeah," I said again with a convincing nod. Ollie's sudden appearance stunned me into submission, and I was scared for it to leave me.

He kissed the side of my head, before taking off in the blink of an eye. Ollie was gone.

"Alright, everyone break up and go back to your dorms," Ethan called out with a clap of his hands. "Jett, I need to see you."

And just like that, it was as if Ollie never appeared at all.

Ethan waited until it was only the two of us remaining in the hall. He stood on the opposite end, and when the last lingering soul dispersed around the corner, he took two long strides over to me. "Don't fucking do it, Jett. I know what you're thinking, but don't you dare start pushing me away because he's slowly coming back. He'll only bring you down with him."

"I never said anything."

"You didn't have to. I see it all over your face. He comes to your rescue once, and like quicksand, you literally sink into him. I saw what happened to my sister, and I'm not going to let that happen to you!"

"I'm not your sister, Ethan!"

"No fucking shit! You think I slept beside my sister every night? You think I touched my sister the way I touch you? Don't be fucking stupid." Ethan darted his gaze around and calmed himself before his eyes found mine again. "He's not right in the head. Meds or no meds, he's been messed up his whole life."

"I'm messed up, too, yet you still sink your hands on me like quicksand," I spat out. "Take your own goddamn advice." With that, I blew past him and never bothered to turn around when he called out for me.

Stupidly, I sat at my desk to write in my journal without remembering it was gone. Stolen. Vanished. Out in the world for all eyes to see. Slumping back in the chair, I threw my pencil at the wall, remembering times I used to throw my fist in it.

Again, progress.

Over the last few months, the walls in the room turned their back on me. Finally, I'd reached the point where I was itching to get out of here, even the walls whispered through the night, reminding me I was trapped—taunting me like this unknown prankster.

I ran my fingers through my messy brown hair when I heard sounds coming from outside. The clock above the door read midnight. Jumping from my chair, I rushed to the window to see two figures out in the distance. One was Ethan. I could pick his shadow out in a line-up. Ethan towered over the other man on the lawn. From Ethan's face, I could tell they were yelling back and forth at each other, but I couldn't decipher. Ethan faced the building. He stared right at me, but there was no way he could really see me, was there? The other man turned his face, and I recognized him instantly.

Dean Lynch.

Did he know Ethan crept into my room at night to calm my terrors? Was Ethan in trouble?

Dean Lynch marched away, leaving Ethan standing under the night starry sky on the lawn. The light from the moon reflected off him, and the red tint glowed from his hair. I would be lying if I said he wasn't beautiful, but looking at him didn't affect me the same way Ollie did.

Ollie had the ability to eradicate and piece me back together in one single breath, and with one look, he had the power to erase the world around us. I felt his words when he spoke, vibrations in the spaces between my bones. His love pumped through my veins, even when he was gone because we were bound together by something much bigger.

Ethan was beautiful, but Ollie was something else entirely.

My gaze followed Ethan's movements back inside the building, and after he disappeared, I crawled into the bed.

It seemed like an hour passed as I waited for him to walk through the door and sleep beside me, but he never showed. Slowly, my eyes closed, conceding to the exhaustion and preparing for a night terror to soon wake me.

Movements from behind stirred me back to life, and the familiar smell of Ethan's cologne filled my senses. He didn't wear it often, but whenever he'd come from his home, he smelled so distinct—like spices and woods. "I couldn't sleep," he spoke softly into my ear as he climbed in beside me. His bare chest warmed my back as his body fused to mine. "I tried to sleep in my own bed, but I couldn't sleep without you."

I pretended to be asleep, and Ethan sighed, believing my bluff. "I don't know why, Mia," he continued to say, "but you're the one good thing that's happened in my life since she passed and I'm not letting you go without a fight. Ollie may be your number one, but you're mine. And if you were awake right now, I'd never admit to it."

I lay still, quiet, keeping up with the charade. Ethan's hand slipped under my tank and flattened his palm against my bare stomach. "Like quicksand," he whispered, lips and stubble brushing across my back. "Mia..." his hand raised to my rib cage beneath my breast, "can I have one night with you?"

My eyes snapped open. I couldn't speak, think, or breathe, for that matter. The only thing I could do was pretend a light snore, feeling like a damn idiot.

Ethan exhaled, and I didn't know why, but I felt selfish at that moment. He'd been nothing but good to me, and I couldn't man-up and give myself to him for one much-deserved night. A single tear rolled down my cheek, and I'd realized this was the farthest point Ethan and me could ever reach. It could never go past this. I would never know what his lips would taste like, or what it felt like with him deep inside me because I didn't want to know.

Ollie was all that mattered. Rock-bottomed-messed-up-mind-fucked Ollie.

Ollie

"Oliver, you have a visitor," Jerry called out, tapping his hand against the door frame.

I gathered my things and sent a wicked smile over to Mr. Mahoney, and he shook his head at the front of the classroom. Mr. Mahoney didn't like students disappearing from his class and denied every request to use the restroom since the year had started.

Dolor had visiting hours posted outside campus walls on the gate and, I was sure, online. But if someone made the gruesome drive out here, Lynch had trouble turning away a family member.

People like us rarely got visitors.

If someone came, it was either because there was a death in the family, or an urgent matter that needed to be rectified face-to-face.

Having no family left, there was only one person it could be.

Jerry walked silently beside me as we made our way downstairs and toward the visitor room at the front of campus. "You have an hour," he stated, then opened the door and guided me in.

Standing beside a window was none other than Travis, my mate from my seven months in lock up.

"Ah, look what the cat dragged in," Travis said with a massive goofy smile on his face. Our hands shook before he pulled me in for a half hug, and I gave him a pat on the back.

"Good to see you, mate." I rested my hands on his shoulders and held him out at arm's length.

Travis was a good-looking chap with blond braids running along his scalp and a tattoo crawling up his neck. "Being a free-man looks good on you,"—I patted his stomach— "I see you picked up a few pounds. You've been eating proper, yeah?"

Travis pushed my hand away. "Wait until you're out of here. Six months and I'll be having a nice fucking filet waiting for you at your new house."

I took a step back and raised my brows in the air. "You found one?" Travis and I made a deal in jail. I'd take care of him, pay him as my assistant as long as he handled my finances. After I was transported back to Dolor, I'd sent him on a mission to find me the perfect house. Two bedrooms, a master bedroom with a bay window, and a beautiful view overlooking water. All Mia ever talked about when leaving here was putting her toes in the water, and I was going to make that happen. I'd give Travis the tools he needed to make the purchase, and he could live in the house until I left here. My weekly phone calls had been spent with the bank, setting up a separate bank account and making transfers for the purchase.

Despite how fucked I'd been in the head, my heart could never give up on my dream of a life with Mia and Zeke.

Making a deal with Travis was risky. He could have taken the money and run, but he wouldn't have. His only goal was to turn his life around for love. I'd never discussed Mia with him, but Summer was all he'd talked about.

And I knew from experience that love could change a man.

"Yeah, mate. It's all right here. Just needs your signature," Travis said with a ridiculous smile and a hand pointing over to a file lying on the table beside us. "Eighteen properties. Eighteen fucking properties me and Summer walked through to find *the one*, and I really hope you're not disappointed …"

I opened the file, and the first page that stared back at me was a cobblestone house, complete with a creek running through the front lawn. My heart pounded in my chest. "… it's not on the coast, but there's a garden and a lake in the back with a dock. As soon as I stepped foot on that dock, it had your name written all over it …" I continued to flip through the papers as he rambled on.

Fully furnished, the main bedroom looked like it had escaped from my mind and painted over the paper. A bay window took up one side of the wall, complete with a fireplace, and unwelcomed tears pooled at the corners of my eyes as my knee picked up a bounce under the table.

I closed the file and leaned back into the chair. Pinching the bridge of my nose, I fought the emotions threatening to consume me. It was all I ever wanted—a home. But what I never expected was for him to find *the* home. The same home I'd imagined for Mia and I so many times. I'd sent him on a ridiculous goose chase, believing the chances were slim to none. But he found it.

"Bloody hell, you don't like it …"

Running my hand over my face, I collected tears in one swift move. "No, mate. I fucking love it. It's perfect." Leaning forward, I opened the file again and fingered through the paperwork until I reached the contract. "I need a pen."

Mia talked highly of Dr. Conway. This was our first one-on-one session. I entered the small room, and my gaze touched over the posters, the window with the view of the front of campus, and the large brown couch, thinking how many times Mia had been in here.

"Do you prefer Oliver or Ollie?" Dr. Conway asked as she walked behind me and closed the door.

"Doesn't matter." My body sunk into the leather in the corner, and I stretched out my legs.

Dr. Conway took a seat in her office chair and turned to face me. "Oliver it is. I have a thing with nick-names, never liked them."

"Fair enough."

"Looks like Dr. Butala referred you to me. How are things going with the medication?"

"Quite frankly, I need to get off them. They're not working like they're supposed to, or not like they used to, anyway. This void is inside as if I'm missing something. I'm incomplete. They turn me into a hollow-horny-wanker, and I don't want to feel like this anymore. You understand what I'm saying?" The second I saw what I'd done to Mia, I'd realized none of this was worth it. When I'd told Butala to make me feel everything or nothing, I wasn't in my right frame of mind. I wanted to feel everything. Mia deserved everything.

Somehow, even on the pills, Mia still pushed her way through, only driving me to utter insanity. Our love pushed its way through. No amount or strength of pills could force me to surrender any longer. I needed to get off them completely.

"It says here you can be hot-headed without the meds," Dr. Conway pointed out, a question mark lingering at the end.

Leaning over, I dug my elbows into my knees. "I'm also kind, loving, and sincere without them. Doesn't that count for something?"

"You don't have much longer, Oliver. Six months and you graduate. You'll be a free man."

"I don't have six months." In only two months, I'd caused enough damage to push Mia to never speak to me again. Risking another six wasn't an option.

"What's this really about?"

Had I been talking to the fucking kitten on the wall this whole time? "I can't lose her."

"Who, Oliver?"

"Mia."

"What does Mia have to do with this?"

"Everything."

The small room went quiet as Dr. Conway's brown eyes bore into mine. "I want to try something."

"Anything."

"First, I need you to relax. Get comfortable and close your eyes." I sunk back into the leather chair and hesitantly closed my eyes. The sound of papers shuffling sounded around me and the slight gust of air blew over me from the AC vent. "We're going to do what's called mindful meditation. You don't have to speak. I only want you to listen to my voice."

Dr. Conway wasted no time and continued speaking in a soft voice as I tried my best to drown in this spot and lose myself from the world around me.

The only vision that came to my mind was Mia.

Big brown eyes. Hair the color of an oak tree—twisted shades of lights and darks. Her touch so delicate yet able to penetrate my soul. I sank deeper and deeper.

"Why are you smiling, love?" It couldn't be past six in the morning. The sun has yet to come up, but the light she's putting off warms my very soul. There's definitely a smile on her lips this very moment, and it's touching every inch of me, waking me, filling me—my heaven.

"How did you know I was smiling?" she asks in amusement.

"I can feel it." I can also feel her turn to face me as I lie on my side. Then her finger runs across my lashes as they do every morning to get me to open my eyes.

"Because I'm happy," she finally responds. It was my turn to smile, though with her it was hard not to. "Open your eyes, Ollie."

"No." The only time I have ever refused her. She knows I would give her anything, but opening my eyes? We're not ready for that yet.

"Why not?"

"If I open my eyes, it means you have to leave, and I'm not ready for you to go. When my eyes are closed, I get to pretend it's a Sunday morning and we have no place to be." A bigger smile spreads across my lips as an idea comes to mind. I have to show her. She has to see this world I created for us that one day I'd give her. "Go on, close your eyes."

"Why?"

"Just close them …" I insist as I trail my fingers up her side and rub her bare back. "Are they closed?"

Her giggle fills the room, and the sound is music to my ears. "Yes, Ollie. My eyes are closed."

"It's a Sunday morning, and I already made your coffee before sneaking back in bed with you. You smell it?"

"Mmhmm …"

"The whole day is ours, no work, no obligations … only you and I. The sun is coming up, Mia. You feel the warmth coming through our bay window and the darkness behind your eyelids slowly lifting? Do you feel it? The sun?"

"Yes, Ollie. I can feel it."

"We can take your coffee to the water and finish watching the sunrise, or we can lay in this bed all day. I have a few books on the shelf that I haven't read to you yet. Or, we can put on our trainers and walk along the boardwalk, hand in hand because that's what we do in the summer on a Sunday morning." I brush my fingers along her cheek. "What would you like to do today?"

"Mmm … all of it."

Flashes of Mia and I faded as new, unwelcomed ones, sprang from a place I never wanted to return.

"What did I say, brother?" Oscar asks. "Or need I remind you?" My arms yank against the rope tied tight around my wrists behind the chair. If I were older and stronger, I'd be able to bust from these ropes and save her. I'd be able to do something—anything. But I'm only twelve, scrawny and pathetic. Oscar reminds me every bloody day.

Jasmine lays naked across the bed, completely vulnerable, yet tame. She doesn't have to be constrained by rope or have tape over her mouth; Oscar's threats are enough to push her into submission. In Jasmine's eyes, she is his girlfriend. In Oscar's, she's his third victim. She never saw this fate coming, but I did. Keeping my distance became difficult when all I wanted to do was save her.

But she beat me to the punch.

Last night, she snuck out of Oscar's room and entered into mine, pleading for me to help her run away. *I tried Jasmine, I really tried.* Oscar found her kneeling beside my twin-sized mattress on the floor. This scene before me is my punishment.

"Whatever my dick slides into first is mine," he adds, lifting Jasmine from her starfish-position and onto all fours like a sack of potatoes. Jasmine's long black hair slides off her back and covers her face, and the hard smack against her arse causes my eyes to jerk away.

"Look, Oliver," Oscar demands.

I shake my head.

A loud cracking sound of his hand against her skin pinches my eyes together, and Oscar shouts once more, "Oliver!"

Reluctantly, I turn my head back to face him. I don't know much, but I know if I didn't, he'd find a way to force me. With his black hair gelled back, the devil in his eyes curses me as he stands next to Jasmine, who remains still on all fours. Her backside faces me as her head points toward the wall. Jasmine shouldn't be treated this way; she's not a fucking object.

Using both hands, he spreads her cheeks apart. "Did you stick your twelve-year-old knob in here?" he laughs, and my only reply is another jerk against the chair. Waves of emotion rush through me, and my fists clench together, unable to handle its crashing madness.

Rage.

I try to yell against the tape across my mouth, but nothing comes out.

"*Of course, you didn't. You wouldn't know what to do with a pussy if it sat on your face.*" *He chuckles again, and the simmering of my blood turns into a boil. "You see, Oliver. If they're dripping wet, they want it. You don't even have to ask." Oscar grabs a handful between her legs before his fingers disappear inside her. "And she's fucking soaked."*

With the same hand he just pulled out of her, he rips the tape off me and slaps me across the face. "You're fucking sick!" I scream.

Oscar throws his head back and jams his fingers back inside her, pumping harder than he should be. "You like that, pet?" he taunts Jasmine.

"Yes," Jasmine moans, completely dominated by him.

My eyes grow wide. "Tell him to stop!" I cry out.

Instead, Jasmine arches her back, and her fanny opened up for him. I pry my eyes away.

"See what I mean?" Oscar laughs and unbuttons his jeans.

"Jasmine, stop this!" I cry out again as Oscar takes out his bulge.

She doesn't speak another word when last night, all she did was beg for me to stop him and take her away. Oscar slams her face against the mattress as her arse raised high in the air. "I'll get you your own, brother. Never touch mine again."

Jasmine cries out, and my eyes slam shut.

My eyes jerked open as Dr. Conway stood over me with her hands on my shoulder. "Are you okay?" she asked, and I stumbled to my feet and stepped away from her. Worry hit her eyes. "Oliver, you need to sit down. You're pale."

"I'm fine." I looked around to catch my bearings.

"What did you see?" She asked, taking a step closer.

I held up a hand between us. "Stop."

She paused, and her face fell. "Do you want to talk about it?"

Shaking my head, I ran my fingers through my hair and took another step back. My stomach rolled, and my mouth watered, indicating it was only a matter of time before I was about to throw up. My eyes darted around the room for a safe place to hurl up my lunch. I launched forward as Dr. Conway backed away, and I reached for the trash can just in time.

Even on days I'd tried drinking my feelings away, I'd never thrown up. "I'm sorry," I mumbled, hanging my head over the can afterward. "I'll clean this up."

"Oliver, it's fine. I'll take care of it. Let me have Nurse Rhonda take a look at you. I can walk with you to the station."

"No." The last thing I needed was Rhonda getting involved. She could be overbearing at times. "Really, I'm alright." I tried to stand when my balance failed me. My hand caught her desk, and the other pinched the bridge of my nose.

"Alright, Mr. Hot-Shot. You're going to see Rhonda"—Dr. Conway picked up her phone— "I'm not taking no for an answer."

I gripped the desk and leaned over, annoyed with the situation I found myself in as Dr. Conway spoke over the phone.

Not too long after, none-other-than fucking Ethan Scott showed up at the door.

"Ethan, hi. Can you walk with Oliver to the nurse's station? Make sure he's checked out?" Conway asked as I rubbed over my temples.

Ethan dropped his chin in a nod before waving me out. "Let's go, O."

My knuckles turned white against the desk before I pushed off it. "Ollie," I corrected him in passing. "It's fucking Ollie."

"Po-tay-to, po-tah-toe."

I shook my head, and he fell in step at my side. Silently, we strolled through the halls until we entered strange territory. "I think you're lost, mate." Ethan's pace didn't slow beside me as he kept forward, turning another corner and down another hall. "Hey, man. This isn't the way," I tried again, but Ethan remained quiet, keeping his eyes out in front of him. One turn later, and we reached a dead end when I turned to face him. "Is this a bloody joke to you?"

Suddenly, he grabbed me by my shirt collar and slammed me against the concrete wall. Before I had a chance to react, his fist came across my face and a cracking bounced in my head. Ringing sounded in my ears, and I lost my balance before another blow to my stomach knocked the air from my lungs, taking me to the ground. "Get up you fucking pussy," Ethan barked.

My hand reached for my gut with one hand as I stumbled to my feet. Spitting out the blood pooling in my mouth, I fell back against the wall for support. We both knew this was about the bruises I'd left on Mia. "Give it to me," I offered with my fingers begging for more. "I won't even fight back. I deserve it. I fucking deserve it." There was no amount of pain he could inflict on me than what my heart was already doing. "Hit me!" I screamed.

His right-hook connected with my jaw and a jolt of pain shot through my skull. Another cracking sounded in my head, and I fought through it and caught my balance. Before I could right myself completely, another blow knocked air from my lungs, and I hurled over.

"Does it bother you, O?" he asked, and I straightened my posture. Blood poured from my lip as he gripped my hair in his fist. "Every night, it's my name she's screaming. Every night, it's my fucking hands all over her body. And every bloody night, I fuck her into morning." His fist made impact again, and my head jerked back against the concrete before I slid to the ground. My face swelled and my vision blurred, but I didn't have to see his face to know he was scared.

This wasn't about what I did to her.

This was about him gradually losing her.

"No," I struggled to get out, and a laugh blew past my lips. "Mia wouldn't fuck you."

"Yeah? What makes you so sure?"

I spat a mouthful of blood off to the side. Every bit of strength I had was wasted on holding myself upright. "You wouldn't be here if she was."

As if he answered a silent prayer, his boot came over my face, and all the lights went out.

FOURTEEN

*"I smiled,
temptation could try
to find a way in,
but no hand can touch
the places I've been."*

OLIVER MASTERS

Mia

When Saturday morning came along, I didn't waste time hurrying over to Zeke's, excited for the chance to play the piano and for a little human interaction with someone who didn't completely hate me.

Last night during dinner, Zeke had looked back at me in confusion as I'd sat in the far corner. It had been a while since we spoke, and I made a mental note to myself to pick up our Saturday piano session in the group therapy room to mend our time apart. Seeing him sitting at my old table last night as the rest of them talked blindly around him, not showing him an ounce of attention, had stirred an agitated snake awake inside me. Countless times, I'd thought of removing him and taking him over to my new, longer table, but Zeke thrived on routine. And as routine would have it, that had been the table he ate at.

I missed Zeke. It was hard not to, given he had become my first friend upon arrival and the only one who stayed by my side through everything.

So, here I was.

Zeke cracked the door and stuck his brown-curly head through.

"Piano date?" I asked with a hopeful smile. He looked to the ground and shook his head. I tried to see past him, but he blocked my view. "Zeke? What are you hiding from me?"

His eyes darted around frantically before he dropped his shoulders and closed the door in my face.

I knocked again, three frustrating times, but there was no answer.

Was he upset with me? Had the prankster taken him away from me, too?

The weekend passed with no sign of Zeke, Ethan, or Ollie. My world shrunk to the population of one: me.

It was lonely here.

Monday morning, Ethan stood at the back wall during breakfast, as usual, fidgeting in place with his hands behind his back. We hadn't spoken two words to one another since he confronted me in the hallway after the Maddie altercation, and he never bothered to show his face when day fell to night, and my terrors came to life. Over the last three nights, I'd woken alone and afraid.

I wanted Ethan, but not in the way I desperately needed Ollie.

Even in Ollie's absence, he ran freely through my veins, his love circulated, pumping to a crimson song stuck on repeat. A continuous reminder. Every part of me belonged to Ollie, and there was nothing I could do about it. My eyes searched for him in every room I entered, and in every person I came across. No matter how hard I tried to shake him, how hard I tried to stay away, even in Ollie's absence, he had a hold on me.

I hadn't seen him since he pulled me off Maddie, and I grew worried as a thousand worst-case-scenarios crossed my mind. The fear of losing him again crawled over me like a million spiders, using my weakness to spin their webs.

Entering class, Tyler averted her gaze as I took my usual seat beside her. Though Tyler had been caught fucking Jude behind Bria's back, it had been me they pushed away, only making them grow closer. They even moved our *WASA* counseling session into another room so I'd show up alone and confused and looking like an idiot. It had been me who'd put the entire group together, and the prankster took that away from me, too.

"Tyler, this is ludicrous," I whispered over to her before class started. "You can't seriously be pissed for something *you* did." Tyler exhaled, crossing her legs under the table, and flipped her blonde hair over her shoulder. "I didn't fucking tell everyone!"

Nothing.

Giving up, I slumped back in my chair as Ms. Chandler spoke up from her desk and advised everyone to complete the lessons on the board in silence. She was the kind of teacher who avoided interaction, more of a babysitter watching over us as we taught ourselves.

Once class was over, I debated on following Tyler out and giving it one more shot, but as soon as we exited, she fell into the arms of Bria. Two pairs of eyes shot bullets in my direction before they turned and walked away.

Fucking females.

"Trouble in paradise?" Maddie's voice sang, falling into step at my side.

"You got a nice bruise I see," I smiled over at her, "need one on the other side to match?"

"Ah, shut up."

I probably shouldn't, but I had to know if she'd seen Ollie. I grabbed Maddie's arm and pulled her to a stop at my side. "Have you seen Ollie? I haven't seen him in a couple of days, and I'm getting worried."

Maddie looked past me and nudged her head. "Ya, he's right there."

I turned my head, and my heart leaped when my eyes landed on his silhouette. In black jeans, a black hoodie, and the hood pulled high over his head, Ollie walked through the hall with his head down and eyes hidden from me.

Relief smothered my worries, and I moved in his direction without a second thought—only needing to look into his eyes and know he was okay.

"Ollie," I whispered, stepping out in front of him. He paused and lifted his head. Jaded green eyes met mine. But the sight before me only threw accelerant over the previously smothered worries, reviving my fears. Cut, swollen, and bruised, Ollie stared down at me utterly gutted.

My fingers reached for his face, and his hand caught my wrist. My eyes watered, and the lump in his throat bobbed before he slowly grabbed the back of my hand and brought it to his face. Ollie's eyes squeezed shut as if it pained for me to touch him. "I'm alright, love."

"Who did this to you?" Seeing him this way destroyed me. When I had been too busy protecting myself, I'd left Ollie behind. I understood his resentment toward me and the pain in his eyes. We both made mistakes, and I wished now more than ever, I could've taken every nasty word I'd said back.

We were supposed to be in this together.

Ollie kissed the inside of my palm before darting his eyes around. "Get to second block before you get into trouble. It's about to start."

"Please, talk to me."

Maddie passed by, and Ollie dropped my hand between us. "Get to class, Mia," he muttered through an exhale, then walked away from me.

The mess hall stayed eerily quiet. The thick cold air swarmed through the unsaid tension, and I darted my eyes around, just like everyone else, knowing something was about to hit the fan at any moment.

"Come with me," a voice said in my ear.

I twisted my neck back to catch a glimpse of short black hair rolling over my shoulder. My gaze darted over to my old table to see Tyler and Jake staring in Bria's and my direction. She had weeks to come and talk to me, why now? "Miss me?"

"Hardly."

My ass stayed put and my eyes locked on Ollie's, who fixed his attention on me from across the room. The slight shake of his head was subtle, but I caught it. A fire set ablaze in his two emerald gems beneath his hood, warning me. "Are you ready to put this nonsense behind us?" I asked.

Bria snorted. "Stand up, and let's go."

Rolling my head back, I stood. Bria linked her hand in mine, and I looked back to Ollie. His lips set in a hard line, jaw flexing, and hands ready to push off the edge of the table to stand. "What is this about?" I asked low, not wanting to draw attention. Security detail had gone rogue, and Tyler rose from my old table the same time as Jude stood from another, both following us out while Bria ignored me.

Side by side, Bria led me down Jude's wing and through his door. Once we were both inside, she released my hand and plopped down over his mattress.

"What are we doing here?" I was losing patience. Tyler and Jude walk through the door, and Tyler's eyes refused to meet mine as she took a seat on the mattress. Standing tall and on a mission, Jude stepped toward me until my back hit the wall. "Get away from me," I gritted out.

Jude smiled and dropped his hands on both sides of me. I pushed against his chest, but he didn't budge. He leaned one forearm over the wall, and his face came an inch from mine while his other hand fished for something from his pocket. "You know what snitches get ya, don't you?"

Pale blue eyes bounced between mine. My heart bounced, but I didn't dare show an ounce of fear on the outside. Jude dropped his mouth to my ear, and he inhaled a deep, sickening breath. My muscles went stiff as he dragged an object along the sliver of bare skin of my abdomen. "Now say you're sorry to your friends."

"Fuck you," I spat, yanking my head to the side. Tyler and Bria watched us from the mattress in anticipation. Is this why they brought me here? For a fucking apology?

A smirk stretched across his face when he placed a cigarette behind his ear. His fingers wrapped around my chin, forcing my eyes on his. "C'mon, Mia. It's not that difficult."

"I didn't do shit." I pushed him off me, and he took a step back and held his arms out in the air. My chest heaved as I dragged my gaze between all three of them.

Then they all burst out laughing.

"You should have seen your face!" Bria struggled to get out through her fit and shoved Tyler in the back. "Ah, that was totally worth it, yeah?"

"You suck,"—I pointed at her— "I'm leaving." I turned to walk back toward the door, and Jude jumped out in front of me.

"Aye, not so fast." He tilted his head and dropped his chin to face me. "You still owe your girls over there, and I'm kind enough to give you two options."

"Yeah? And what's that?"

Jude's smile reached his eyes when he turned his focus over my shoulder to Bria and Tyler. "Become one of mine, or don't."

"One of yours?"

"You see, Tyler and Bria came to an understanding. I can protect you, too, Mia. And from the looks of it, you need some protecting."

"I don't need anything from you."

"Because of Ollie, right? If you haven't noticed, Ollie can't even protect himself."

Bria, I could understand agreeing to something like this, but Tyler? She wasn't the type. I looked her over, and she still couldn't look at me directly. "Is this what you want, Ty?"

Her head snapped to Jude before turning back to face me. "I have two years here."

Shaking my head, I faced Jude again, scanning him over. "What happens if I don't?"

"Easy," he smirked. "Bria and Ty are off-limits. But I promise it won't be long before you come running back to me with your fucking tail between your legs." He gripped my hip and shifted his pelvis across my abdomen as his tongue slid along his bottom lip. "And trust me when I say, I take care of my girls."

I forced my body from flinching. Jude wanted to see me squirm, and I refused to grant him that small victory. "I can take care of myself." With that, I freed myself from his grasp and left, wondering if Tyler knew exactly what she had gotten herself into. You'd see these kinds of things in a prison, not here at Dolor, and I wondered how the rest of the students were going to take to it. Sure, relationships were forbidden, but this was something straight out of Prison Break.

The cold towel was like ice against my hot skin, and I wanted it to touch every inch of me. It started at my hairline, and over my face until the towel pressed against my lips. Cries echoed, and I couldn't tell what was real anymore. The chill swept along my neck and my shoulders, and I shivered but wanted to dive into it and drown myself in the cold.

My brain protested, half of me held hostage in the nightmare, and the other half of me stuck in the darkness behind my stubborn eyelids. The cries somehow stopped, and I couldn't fully gain consciousness, as if my soul left my body and watched me from above. My limbs were heavy and too tired to move. Trapped.

A dark figure loomed over me, but I feared more from the state of paralysis I found myself in. Low hushing chanted in my ear followed by, "I'm right here." My head knew it was Ethan, but my heart so desperately wanted it to be Ollie, and the part trapped in the stage of sleep couldn't respond either way. The bed moved as the figure climbed in bed beside me.

My eyes finally opened and I instantly calmed, fusing to Ethan, thankful to be released from whatever hell I was slipping from. Ethan moved the hair clinging to my cheek as I turned to face him. "What was it about?" he asked, referring to my terror.

"I can't remember. I can never remember." I glanced up and found his blue eyes. They no longer held the electric I'd grown accustomed to. His static had faded, and he ran a palm down his face as if he read my mind. Inching away, I asked, "Where have you been the last couple of nights?"

He looked away, but slid that same hand over my hip and dragged me until my chest pressed against his, right where he needed me. "Things I had to take care of."

"Right," I said, dragging out the "I."

"You're shaking."

"No, Scott," I said through an exhale and flit my eyes to him. "That's you." One other time I'd seen him like this—shattered—and it was when Haden had taken his own life. "You okay?"

"Let's not talk, alright?"

"Why even come?"

"Do you want me to leave? Because I'll go. Just say the words."

Panic rose. I shook my head and grasped him tighter. Afraid to face the night on my own, I'd become attached to Ethan and the way he saved me from the terrors. Deep down, I wasn't ready to let go. But I had to. The only way to get Ollie back was to let this charade with Ethan go. It had been going on long enough.

Biting my lip, I looked down as Ethan's muscles twitched against me. He knew too. We couldn't keep doing this. It wasn't fair to anyone.

Ethan lifted my chin. "One more night."

"And then we're on our own?"

"And then we're on our own."

And we lay there as I stared into bright blue eyes until my lids grew heavy, surrendering to the depths of his ocean, knowing I was safe in his arms from terrors and the hell begging to suck me back in.

It wasn't the sun that woke me, because it was still dark in my dorm.

What woke me was Ethan's hand inside my panties and his warm mouth over my breast. My body arched and my eyes snapped open to see red wild hair and shoulders flexing in the dark. My tank had been lifted up to my neck, and eager fingers slid my panties to the side and rolled over my clit. A desperate moan vibrated from within me, responding to a touch I'd been craving for so long.

"Ollie," I instinctively whispered as my body begged for more of what he was giving to me.

"No, Mia, It's Ethan," his voice thick and course, and his hard-on strained against his boxers, "and that is the last time you will ever call me by his name."

Wet lips traveled up the center of my chest, across my collarbone and over my neck as he moved on top of me.

I didn't want him to stop, and my hips matched every movement of his, wanting the same thing. But something inside me was screaming.

Inside, I felt sick.

But, still, I couldn't find the will to stop.

Ethan slid my panties off and pulled my legs apart, exposing me fully against the cold night air and his deep blue eyes. I watched as his eyes strayed and his hands roamed over my body. "You have no idea how long I've wanted to be with you," Ethan whispered, then lowered himself on top of me until his forehead touched mine. His large erection pushed through the hole of his boxers and kneaded over my clit through every hungry grind.

Ethan's lips brushed mine, and I turned my head to the side to avoid his kiss. "This is entrapment. It's not fair," I tried to get out, but I still couldn't control my hips as his cock slid through my center teasingly. "We can't do this."

"We're already doing this." His fingers traveled down, and he dipped a finger inside me. My hips involuntarily rocked against each satisfying thrust. "You want this too, just let it happen, Mia," Ethan breathed into my ear.

My head snapped forward. It was the first time he had said my name since we met. "It can't go further than this."

"Kiss me," he argued. I shook my head, and Ethan growled, picking up his pace. He added another finger as his hard shaft grazed through my wetness and crashed against my needy clit each time. Every brush of his lips against my neck, every thrust of his hand, every knead of his cock pushed my body closer despite the hard fight within my soul.

Ethan's lips inched closer to mine, and again, I shifted my head, causing his lips to graze my cheek. Frustrated, he picked himself off me.

Both our chests rose and fell at different rhythms, and I expected him to push off me and leave. But he didn't. Ethan stood at the end of the mattress and withdrew his boxers entirely. Perfect skin glowed against the small sliver of the moons light, revealing abs sculpted by God. Pure. Faultless. Untouched by ink and a needle. Dark blue eyes blazed in the night, boring into mine with a silent plea as he gripped my ass and dragged me to the foot of the bed.

With two hands, Ethan guided my legs open and lapped his greedy tongue from bottom to top, and my hips helplessly curled into his mouth, begging for it. His stubble grazed the insides of my thighs, and his tongue darted out over my clit before moving back down. My body shook against him, unwilling to pull away. "You're so fucking sweet," he moaned. "Come for me, Mia."

Ethan pushed two fingers inside, and my walls gripped around them, completely willing. Teeth scraped against my clit, and I slammed my eyes shut to imagine green eyes, brown hair, and inked skin before I finally climbed back up to the place I'd been trying so hard to reach. But right before I busted, Ethan completely stopped, taking everything away.

The sound of a condom wrapper tearing ripped an ache in my heart. Ethan stood and pressed his thick condom-covered cock against my entrance while his hand moved over my clit, rolling the knot of nerves between two fingers. "Your move, Jett," he challenged, and my heart pounded out of my chest.

Kissing him was out of the question. Fucking him was out of the question. He managed to take advantage of me while my guard was down, and though my body cried for release, my mind stayed fucked in this teased turmoil. Ethan's hands moved over my hips, and he jerked his hips forward, him and the tip of his cock testing me.

I lowered my hips, and his shaft slid back through my soaked center, and Ethan frowned but didn't stop his movements. "Let me get inside you."

Shaking my head, the burn erupted behind my eyes as my chest tightened and I tried to catch a steady breath. I snapped my legs closed and rubbed my hands over my face, fighting the tears threatening to pour.

Then there was no fucking use.

My confused body shook as the hot tears spilled from my eyes.

"I'm so sorry," I cried out. "I love him."

"Yeah, I fucking got that." Ethan bent over and picked up his boxers, shoving his legs back through. "What the hell was I thinking?" He laughed, but hurt laced each breath that followed.

"You don't understand."

"You're right about that. I don't. It's fucking cool. I'll be alright … but you?"—He shook his head before pulling his shirt over his head— "Oliver Masters will be the cause of your undoing. It's in his fucking blood. I read his bloody file. He doesn't know any different, ruins everything he touches. And you, Jett … you'll be just another fucking tally."

"You don't know what you're talking about," I said through gritted teeth.

He snatched his pants off the desk chair and shrugged a shoulder as he chuckled. "Yeah, okay. I'm a bloody liar." He stood over me fully clothed as I laid over my mattress completely naked and body shaking. His eyes roamed over me. "Tell me this, yeah? When was the last time he made you feel like that? When was the last time he touched you like I do? Tell me, Mia. Help me understand! When was the last fucking time he gave you pleasure over pain?"

I jolted upright until both feet hit on the marble. My hands pushed against Ethan's flexed chest once, but he didn't budge. "Get out!"

"Careful, Jett,"—Ethan took a step back— "You're pushing away the only person left who gives a damn about you."

"I said, get out!"

Ethan opened the door and something on the ground caught his eye. He bent down and swiped it up with his back to me as I scanned the room for a shirt. When he turned around, I'd just gotten the plain white tee over my head when he tossed the object at me.

After catching it mid-air, I opened my hand, and my heart plummeted when my eyes fell upon the origami rose, imperfectly pieced back together. My eyes glossed over, and my chin trembled. The tips of my fingers filtered through its leaves when Ollie's handwriting appeared.

There are cracks, but now the light can shine through.

FIFTEEN

> "Call me a criminal,
> killing her heartache
> with unsteady hands and
> lips shaped like a knife."
>
> OLIVER MASTERS

Ollie

Over the last weekend, I'd slummed it with Zeke.
Hid from the world.
Hid from Mia.

I'd taken over Zeke's project of "fixing Ollie and Mia" by gluing the origami rose back together, but only after Zeke had experienced a nervous breakdown over it. That final time I'd made the attempt, the pieces had fallen back into place with ease. Perhaps time was all that had been needed, or the right frame of mind. Either way, I wasn't going down anymore without a fight.

Mia and I was something worth fighting for. We were written in the stars. That's the thing about love. Once it touched you, it didn't go away. It was laced in every breath. It was embedded in your skin. It seeped deep into your soul and lived forever, and you spent your entire life feeding that single heavenly feeling afraid it would leave at some point.

But love never leaves you. It only hides behind every temporary emotion until you deserve to be embraced by it again. And bloody hell, Mia deserved it.

Dr. Conway held the answers. Every day this week, I'd shown up in her office, even on days I didn't have an appointment. We'd practiced meditation. We'd practiced control. She'd brought me back through the most traumatic situations, and I'd learned how to face it and let it go.

Today was no different.

"You should take a break, Oliver. You're going to overexert yourself," she said as soon as I walked through her door during lunch.

I sank into the couch and dropped my head back. "No, this is working. I'm ready."

"You have group therapy in a few hours."

My eyes opened to see a white ceiling, and I smoothed my hand over my bouncing knee. "If I have to live one more second in this hell, just kill me now."

"Don't talk like that," Conway muttered.

I lifted my head off the couch to face her. "Like what? You have no clue the constant battle I deal with every bloody day. The back and forth—the numb, the pain. I feel like I don't know myself anymore." Leaning forward, I dug my elbows into my knees. "Even on the meds, every whisper is a scream. Every dig is a blow. Every look is a blame. Every smile makes me high," I grit out. "A female so much as breathes on me, my dick gets excited—*excuse my fucking language*. Everything that made me happy is missing, and everything that sucks the life out of me surrounds me. I'm tired of being one way or the other, feeling everything and nothing. One second I want to kiss her. The next I want to strangle her. Do you catch my drift?"

Rage spilled out of me, and Conway met my gaze, refusing to look away. She understood exactly what I'd said.

"I've been doing research," she started to say.

I collapsed back into the seat and stretched out my legs in front of me. "Research, yeah? And how is your research going to help me?"

"Explain to me, when are you most calm? Without the medication."

My brow spiked in the air, and I studied her features. Conway's big brown eyes stared down at me in all seriousness. "I'm calm when I'm alone ... when I'm writing ... when she's safe and happy. I'm calm when Zeke's lip lifts into that stupid half-smile." I couldn't help but grin thinking about it.

Conway matched my smile. "And when you're angry? What pisses you off?"

"Being played, used as a pawn in a game. They think I'm a fucking fool, as if I don't know what's up their sleeve, but I see it in their eyes. Too many people in Dolor have a dodgy agenda, and it's overcrowded. A dark cloud hovers over this place, and I can't seem to escape it. It's stifling."

"They?" she asked.

"What?"

"You said 'they.' Who are you talking about?"

"Everyone!" I jabbed.

Conway lowered her head and smiled.

I cocked my head. "What?"

She pulled out a sticky note and clicked her pen. "I'm going to write down a book I want you to try and find at the library when you leave here. Hopefully, we have it. If not, let me know. I can order it,"—she handed me over the bright yellow paper— "I think it's important you look at all avenues."

I scanned the paper. *Emotional Sensitivity and Intensity*. "You think I'm misdiagnosed?"

"No, I never said misdiagnosed. There is science, Oliver, but then there is spirituality. I think it's important for you to look at *all* avenues," she reiterated with a wink. "Look up hyper-empathic, too. You may find you can relate."

"And in the meantime?"

Conway exhaled and crossed her legs. "In the meantime, I want you to avoid all situations and confrontations from negative people. If that means isolating yourself, very well. Only until you understand and learn to identify and control your emotions. Don't put yourself in a situation that you know will set you off or be around those who are negative. That negative tension rubs off on you a whole lot deeper than most."

Dropping my chin, I smiled. Finally, there was a light at the end of this long spiraling tunnel.

"Because you are hyper-sensitive, the medication also affects you more intense than others," Conway continued, "I don't know how much leeway I have in lowering your dosage or getting you off it entirely, but in my honest opinion, you shouldn't be on it. This medication isn't going to help, it's only going to hinder. Let me see if I can make a few phone calls. Until then, try to stay out of trouble."

"I understand. Thank you." I meant every word.

"And Oliver?" Looking back up, she leaned over and grabbed my gaze. "If you don't walk out of here with Mia, know there are other fish in the sea."

In an instant, my smile faded. "You don't get it. Mia is the sea."

"It's crazy, mate. This book explains me to a T." I flipped another page over and scanned over the words. The book she had recommended wasn't in the library, but I did find another regarding emotional intensity. "Know despair, but also beauty and rapture? Check. Experience emotions at an unparalleled level of depth and complexity? Check. Constant overflow of both negative and positive feelings? Check. Strong emotional connection with certain people? Fucking check." *Mia*. I tapped the page with the back of my hand. "I can get through this without the pills, my friend. I only need to identify what I can physically and mentally handle."

Zeke smiled.

I grinned and jumped to my feet. "I can't wait any longer. I have to go find Mia before group therapy."

If vultures hadn't been surrounding us, I'd show her how I truly felt back in the hall when she had confronted me. I'd wanted to hold her, to kiss her. All I had wanted to do was grab her by the hand and runaway with her. I'd seen the look in her eyes. In an instant, she had forgotten everything I'd done and looked my demons square in the eyes and accepted every side I'd been so scared to show her—all in one look.

My entire body vibrated under the single thought of her.

I missed that fucking feeling.

Zeke ran to the door and stretched his arms out, shaking his head. I rolled my head back. "Step aside, mate." His hands moved vigorously, and it became hard to keep up with his movements. "I'm good,"—I raised my palm in the air, showing steady hands— "I won't even touch her. Just want to see her."

Mia

"Mia?"

I snapped my attention to my left. "hmm?"

"Progress?" Arty repeated with raised brows.

"Oh, right …" The only progress I'd made this week was the continuous loss of relationships. Why did Ethan have to push things to the next level? Why couldn't he keep things the way they were? Everything had been fine with us. "I don't know. None."

In the last half hour, I'd managed to avoid all eye contact with Ollie. If our eyes locked, his force would break all barriers, revealing the regret and shame hiding within them from what had happened with Ethan. And his eyes were on me this very moment, calling me, screaming for me, begging for me to see him.

I feel you, Ollie.

A tingle in my bones.

"There's got to be something," Arty pushed.

"Pass."

"Setbacks?" Ollie asked, announcing himself in the room. He needed me to acknowledge him sitting across from me, but I clamped my mouth shut and kept my eyes facing the marble.

A few snickers echoed throughout the circle, yet Ollie's shift in his chair was the loudest. He lowered his hand and snapped his finger, calling for my attention, but I refused and bit my lip to fight the shame from spilling from my eyes.

The rest of group therapy carried on in the same manner, me staring at the ground and biting the inside of my cheek. Once Arty dismissed us, I jumped up and blew past the circle to make it out the door first and down the stairs.

I hadn't made it past the third-floor bathroom when I was yanked back by my belt loop and pulled through a door. I kept my head down and fixed my eyes on Ollie's black Vans as the tears pooled at the corner of my eyes. He stood before me, fists clenched at his sides, already preparing for the worst. Heat emitted from him and his breathing stopped.

Then his fingers stretched out as he let out a long exhale.

"Dammit, Mia. Look at me." I snapped my head up and faced the music. A fire burned in his eyes, and his nostrils flared. Then as if that one look sedated him, Ollie's shoulders dropped beneath his black hoodie, and he leaned into me, his body remembering me. Calm. Relieved. Revived. Hopeful green eyes examined mine, and he wet his busted lip. "It's going to be okay."

"How do you know?"

"I just do."

"Ollie, I—"

"No, Mia. I don't care to know the details," he cut in, all-knowingly.

"But—"

"It doesn't matter."

"I have to get it out!" I'd erupt if I didn't. It had only been nine hours since Ethan left my room this morning, but that meant nine hours consumed with shame.

He raised his brows and lifted his chin. "Did you fuck him?"

"No, but—"

"Did you kiss him?"

"No, Ollie."

His head tilted and his eyes narrowed. "Are you confused?"

Never. "No!"

"Then it doesn't fucking matter."

"How could you say that?"

"Because you have no idea what it's like to fall in love with you. I'm not stupid, he's in love with you, and he'd be a bloody fool not to try something." He looked off for a moment before his eyes hit mine again. "Let it go, love. Guilt looks horrible on you. It doesn't match the color of your eyes."

An unavoidable smile played on my lips.

His mouth lifted in the corner as he slowly blinked. "Ah, there she is."

"You going to tell me what happened to your face?"

He shook his head. "Doesn't matter."

"Does anything matter to you?"

Ollie's hand lifted and pointed at my chest. He held his finger there for a moment before turning his finger to his own, his chest steadily rising against it.

My eyes darted from his chest to his face. *You and I.* All barricades lifted from his green eyes, exposing himself entirely to me. Unsure of how long this moment would last, I gripped the black hood framing his face and yanked him down.

Mouths crashed, pulses kicked, and feelings flowed between our sacred moment. Weakness pulled me under, but Ollie lifted me, wrapping fingers around the back of my head to keep me with him—keep me grounded from floating in what always came of us. Rapture. My lips screamed that I missed him while his screamed to remember him.

To remember us.

As if I could ever forget.

His tongue pushed through the cracks, an injection straight to the heart. A moan rattled inside his chest, and he dropped his forearms on both sides of me against the wall, caging me in.

Our tempo morphed from eager and hungry to slow and sensual, linked by mouths and hearts permanently engraved in each other's names.

I kissed the corners of his lips, his injuries, and our noses brushed, then he dropped his forehead to mine. My chest ached, and I couldn't catch my breath, already grieving the absence of this and knowing I'd soon be without him all over again.

"You don't have to be afraid, love," he whispered, and I squeezed my eyes closed to ease the burn. "I know you're hurting, but we're going to get through this." I lifted off the wall and sank inside his arms, stuffing my face into his hoodie to breathe him in. Ollie kissed the top of my head and pulled me away just enough to see me. "Together this time. You and I."

The alarm for lock-down blared through the intercom before Dean Lynch's voice echoed throughout Dolor as I walked back to my dorm in a hurry. Once my feet landed on my wing, bodies disappeared behind doors before they locked behind them.

I scanned the hall for security. Nothing.

A girl blew past me.

"What happened?" I called out.

She shrugged her shoulders before receding inside her dorm.

When I entered my room, Ethan's back was to me as he stared out my window. His shoulder blades moved beneath his shirt as he tightened his arms across his chest. "Where were you?" he asked, then turned to face me with a blank expression.

"Group therapy," I deadpanned, closing the door behind me and dropping my shoulders.

Ethan's gaze slid to the clock above my door and back down to me. "Group therapy ended thirty minutes ago."

"What's it to you?"

Ethan walked toward me. "Let's go."

"Go where?" I asked, taking a step back.

"Lynch wants to see you." He opened the door and nudged his head for me to follow. When I didn't budge, he dropped his chin and narrowed his eyes. "We can do this the easy way or the hard way. Your choice."

"Is this because I denied you?"

Ethan let out an incredulous chuckle and swiped a palm over his face. "Now, Jett," he growled. "This is serious."

I crossed my arms over my chest, and after three seconds of locked eyes, I stepped forward and pushed past him just as Ollie reached his door, coming back from the moment we shared only moments ago.

Ollie's hand froze over his doorknob just as Ethan closed my door behind me four rooms down. Green eyes dragged from Ethan to me, and I could see his jaw tense from where I stood. Ethan pressed his chest into my back and grabbed my arm. "Come on," Ethan urged.

Ollie's lip twitched, and his arm flexed, and I shook my head.

Don't, Ollie. He's not worth it.

I yanked my arm from Ethan and started forward. My gaze fixed in front of me. The tension in the hall stretched around us like a rubber band ready to snap at any moment. Though I couldn't see Ethan's face, I felt every rush of emotion coming from Ollie to my left as we passed by. His eyes on the two of us replaced my blood with lava. The thoughts going through his mind somehow ripped me open from where he stood rigid. Ollie was ready to launch at any moment.

We made it around the corner, but the pressure didn't let off my shoulders. Ethan remained quiet the entire way to the Dean's office, down the stairs, and through the cold building. He paused when we reached

Lynch's door and turned me around to face him. "Relax, Jett. Just be honest."

My brows pinched together, and Ethan used his knuckle to knock on the door.

Lynch welcomed us in and advised me to take a seat. Ethan stayed by the door, back straight, arms crossed over his chest, gaze looking out the window into the dawn of October. Lynch's red velvet curtains laid open, overlooking the side of the building, the Looncy Bin visible.

"Where did you rush off to yesterday during dinner?" Lynch cut to the chase. I snapped my eyes forward. The shade around his eyes seemed dark, making his brown eyes look lighter.

My brain filtered through yesterday's events.

Bria. Tyler. Jude.

"I had to use the restroom." I shrugged, having no idea where he was going with this. Lynch leaned back in his rolling chair, and he rested his elbow over the arm of his chair, propping up his chin. His eyebrows pulled together as his eyes locked on mine, searching for answers—nerves set in. My mouth went dry.

"Don't lie to me, Mia," his eyes slipped to Ethan behind me before falling back on mine.

"This is ridiculous. I didn't do anything." The words came out faster before I could think.

"Ridiculous? You could have really hurt someone with your clever stunt. Not to mention cost Rhonda her job."

"What are you talking about?"

Lynch released his fist and held up a key. "This was found in your room."

I twisted back to face Ethan, but his focus remained out the window. Returning my attention to Lynch, I jumped to my feet. "I don't even know what that is!"

"Looks like a key to me," he scoffed, examining the object between his fingers. He leaned forward and slapped it over the top of his desk. "The key to Rhonda's medicine cabinet, found in your bloody room!"

"Well, I didn't take it! I have no idea how it got in my room!"

"A freshman is in the hospital. I have to find someone to replace Rhonda's job. What I want to know is, why? Why do you feel the need to take others down with you to prove a point?"

"You can't seriously believe I had something to do with this," my head spun, "Ethan, tell him I didn't do this!"

Ethan opened his mouth, but Lynch quickly interjected, "I've done all I can to keep you here in this program, but this is out of my control."

"Someone's messing with me! You know someone's been out to get me. I didn't do it!" My nails dug into the palms of my hands, trying to wake myself up because there was no other explanation as to why this could be happening. "Ethan, tell him!"

"Where were you yesterday during dinner?" Ethan asked, taking a step forward.

"Bria pulled me aside, and we went to Jude's. They were pissed and confronted me, but that was it! I swear to God, I wouldn't have fucked with people's medication."

"Not even to try and switch Oliver's?" Ethan questioned, but it came out more like an accusation. "You know, to get him off his medication? Switching it with something else?"

I fell back in the chair and dropped my head in my hands. "This can't be happening." I lifted my head with tears in my eyes to face Lynch who waved Ethan forward. "You're going to kick me to the curb now? Just like Bruce!" I stood back up and put my hands behind my back. "Innocent until proven guilty. Something we respect back in the states. You should fucking try it," I spat out, waiting for Ethan to put me into cuffs.

"Relax, Mia. You're being sent to solitary until we can do more investigating. I'm not giving up on you just yet," Lynch said with a tap over his desk.

Ethan's eyes filled with relief, but his mouth set into a hard line. "This isn't going to take well with authorities," he said through clenched teeth.

"Mia is under my supervision. They'd have to force my hand before I let her walk out of here until a thorough investigation is completed."

"Your call, boss." Ethan dropped his chin and released a held breath.

"I don't get it. You were so quick to point the finger at me," I said.

"You're right. You deserve to be heard. Let's hope your story sticks." Lynch tossed his head to the side. "Solitary, Scott. No visitors."

Ethan's hand landed on my shoulder to guide me out.

"Scott," Lynch called out.

Ethan and I turned back at the same time.

"I know," Ethan stated, answering an unasked question. Ethan pushed me forward, opened the door, and led me to confinement.

For how long? I had no idea.

SIXTEEN

*"You're not broken,
only bent to perfection."*

OLIVER MASTERS

Ollie

"Where the fuck is she?" I asked, slamming the red-headed wanker against the cement wall. My patience completely depleted after Mia's been M.I.A. for the second day in a row. "Last time I laid eyes on her, she left with you. Where did you take her?"

"You're a lucky bastard. I should drag your arse out of here," Scott snapped, pushing against my chest. "Now calm the fuck down, yeah?" Scott fixed his shirt as he scanned the empty hall.

My stomach churned, threatening to reveal the fact I'd been chucking up my pills since my last visit to Dr. Conway. I closed my hands into fists to bite back the honest tremors.

Something wasn't right. I'd shown up to the nurse's station to see Rhonda gone and a new nurse handing me over my cup with a chipper smile on her face, and my love unseen and unheard of in two days.

"I want her out just as bad as you," Scott admitted, evening out his hushed tone. His fingers flew to his temples.

"Out of where? Where is she? Psych?"

"Confinement."

"What the hell for?"

"You're kidding, right? Have you been so fucked in the head,"—he pushed against my temple with his pointer finger— "you have no idea what she's been through."

I slapped his hand away and pushed past him. "I have to go to her."

Scott grabbed my arm, but quickly released it as a student walked past from lunch. "It's more complicated than that. You can't just show up in solitary and demand to see her. You want her out? Find out who threw a spanner in the works. Find out who put the newbie in the hospital. Someone," he lowered his tone, "someone stole Rhonda's key, switched pills, and planted the key in Mia's room."

"Did you happen to start with who opened their mouth on where this said key was? Ace, Scott, I thought *you* were the fucking cop."

"Dead end," he replied dryly.

"Right," I shook my head. "Give me the name."

"Fuck off."

I shoved him against the wall, my nerves ticking, body shaking, this wanker under my last nerve. "This isn't a contest, she's no prize to be won." I wrapped my fingers around his neck and pinned him with a glare. The prick scratched at my hands. "Give me the bloody name."

Ethan gasped, surprised by my strength, but it was the adrenaline pumping, giving me the ability to take a guy the same height, same muscle, but unequally matched with his experience and training. It was the thought of Mia. Her being alone in confinement, a place I visited too many times to know she'd been alone, trapped, in the four walls I previously helped her escape from. Before, I'd let the bloke beat me because I deserved it, this time it was Mia who had been stomped on, and she didn't deserve any of this.

"Jude," Ethan fought out. I released him, and his eyes turned red.

"You're going to take me to her."

"Like hell I will."

"You think Lynch would take kindly to his security guard's slumming it with his patients? I'm not a fool. I know whose bed you sneak into each night, and how frustrated it makes you that it's all that will ever happen. Tonight, you're taking me to see her or I'll be in the dean's office first thing in the morning."

"I could ruin you."

I dusted off the front of his shirt. "I'm already fucking ruined."

The clock struck midnight, and I'd been in this same position for almost four hours now, sitting at the edge of my mattress waiting on Scott to unlock my door. The single door click meant everything. It meant I had been right all along, and Scott, for the past, I didn't know how long, had been lying beside Mia while she slept through the night—feeling her touch, smelling her scent, watching her dream.

But it also meant I'd get to see her.

The kiss we'd shared was everything. It had been confirmation Mia still believed in us, a silent promise. It was the one thing I held onto to know for certain she'd never cross that line with anyone else. Though what if I was wrong? If she had, I'd be able to forgive her. Because just as much as she was all-consuming, she was imperfect and honest—the representation of love. Consuming. Imperfect. Honest.

The door clicked, and I sprang to my feet, unsure whether I was pleased or not with the outcome. Scott stood on the other side with a blank stare.

I gave one hard look at the bloke who shared moments with Mia that were meant for me. Moments I'd given him on a silver platter because of my stupidity. I couldn't blame him. I would have done the same. If anyone understood what falling in love with her was like, it would be me.

Scott stared back, the muscles in his face tightened in the dark. "She loves me, but she's in love with you."

I smirked despite the jealousy clouding my heart. "I could've told you that."

"How are you so bloody certain you're it for her."

"You're asking me to explain the impossible, like taste a feeling or hear a touch. When we're together, I just fucking know."

"One night. That's it."

"Just take me to her."

With one hand, Scott held the door open to let me pass.

He led the way one step in front of me through the dark hallways. Only one bulb lit the end of each turn. He snuck me past wing three, distracting security detail in the process. Once I reached the stairs, I hung back to wait for him and swiped my hands through my hair.

I'd done this same escape last year, Oscar leading me out and across Dolor grounds to check on Mia in the looney bin. I'd never told him her name, afraid he'd find a way to meddle or use her against me. Oscar had a way with words and a knack for control. Keeping the two hidden from each other had been the best decision. Little did I know, they'd already met in more ways than one.

"We're clear," Ethan whispered, appearing from around the corner. I lifted off the wall, adjusted my sweats, and followed him down.

Once we reached the basement, he turned and held up a palm. "Stay here."

I dropped my chin as he took off behind the steel door. Nerves set in as my body grew closer to hers, every part of me pulling in her direction like it always did, but forcing myself to stand still.

The sound of a door shutting echoed through the chamber, and seconds later, the steel door opened, and Scott ushered me through. "Had to convince the guy to take over my wing tonight. I'll be out here, but you have to be back in your dorm by sunrise."

"I understand."

Scott walked me through the hall until we reached another door, and we stood in front of it. Soft cries came from inside, and I jerked my head in his direction. "Somethings wrong."

"This is how it always starts. It's a nightmare."

"A nightmare?"

Scott paused with a key in the doorknob to meet my eyes. "It gets worse. She's had them ever since the day you left. Imagine having to listen to it every bloody night."

"You've been helping her?" I asked, surprised.

"Trying."

The cries turned into screams, and my focus bounced from Ethan to his keys. "Get me in there."

Ethan snapped his eyes back to the doorknob and jiggled the key to get the door opened. I busted through and ran to her side.

In the dark, cold room, her small frame shook, drenched and hot with her hands into a fist. "Mia," I whispered, brushing my hand over her hair. I looked back to Scott to see him gone and the door ajar. "Wake up, my love. Open your eyes."

Every scream from her lips grabbed my own emotions and shook them harshly. I dropped my head into my hand and clenched my eyes when I felt a hand over my shoulder. I glanced up to see Scott standing over me with a towel in his hand. Snatching it from his grasp, I turned back to Mia and smoothed it over her glistening forehead. "Mia, open your eyes for me."

"Ollie?" She cried out.

My heart clenched, and a breath left me at the mention of my name. "Yeah, love. It's me. I'm here." Her eyes slowly blinked open, and the color shifted from a black to a golden brown instantly. "It's alright."

She scanned the room as her body shakes turned into a shiver. "Where am I?"

I looked around, and then looked at her, grinning. "Where do you want to be?"

When her eyes met mine again, a weak smile flashed across her face. "How did you get here?"

"Funny story," I tilted my head, "Your boyfriend let me in."

Her smile vanished, brows pinched together. "That's not funny."

"Why didn't you tell me about this?"

"You had enough going on. I didn't want to burden you with nightmares."

"That's nonsense." I withdrew my hoodie and sat over the mattress beside her. "No matter what, you can always talk to me. You know better than that." After stretching out my legs, I pulled her up and over me so her head could lay in my lap. My fingers slipped under her shirt and I ran them down her back. Scrapes and marks protruded beneath my fingers, and I lifted her tank and leaned in to get a closer look. "What in the hell…"

"It's nothing," Mia's voice broke and pulled away from my grasp.

It wasn't nothing. My touch knew every detail of her skin. Those had been scars. Fresh scars. Ones I'd never touched before. "Take off your shirt," I demanded with a rattled tone as I silently prayed I had been wrong. *Please, God, tell me I'm wrong.*

Mia faced me with humiliation in her eyes, and I tried to control my emotions from spilling out. "Mia," I urged, and for a moment, she hesitated, but then sat up and took off her shirt. The room was dark, and she turned her back toward me. I tilted her enough to hit the red blinking light coming from the corner of the room when I noticed scars covering her. "What the fuck happened?" She hung her head, and my stomach twisted into knots. "Mia? How the hell did this happen? Who did this to you?"

Mia's lips trembled, and she lifted her head to the ceiling, trying to curb all weakness.

I picked her up and slid her into my lap, facing me. Her legs wrapped around me while her arms unwrapped from over her chest. I yanked my shirt off and pulled her against me, needing to be close without barriers.

Mia released an exhale into my neck, and her fingers scratched at the back of my head. "I'm not okay," she cried. "I'm not. I can't do it anymore …"

"Listen to me," I pulled her head away to look at me, "I'm done listening to your stupid ideas about keeping us apart. We were not meant to be apart. Do you understand that?" Mia bit her trembling lip, and I grabbed her chin. "Anything that happens to you, happens to me. Every blow, every setback, every burn, every bloody beating. You are not alone in this. You hurt, I hurt. You're in pain, I'm in pain. Whatever you go through, I feel it because you're a part of me. We're in this together."

Mia's fingers gripped my sides, and I moved the hair from her face. "I'm not a hundred percent. I'm getting there, but this time, if I slip, if I fuck up again, I need you to fight for me. Don't ever let me go that easily again." Tears gathered in her eyes as she looked away, and I grabbed her gaze with mine, forcing her to see me. "Promise me, Mia."

She drew in a shaky breath, as her tangled hair fell from around her shoulder. "Promise."

Gathering her hair in one hand, I pinned her against me. Chest to chest. Heart to heart. Beats and breaths in sync and perfectly matched. Together was all we needed, and I was confident we could survive in the arms of each other forever, never needing anything else; not food or water, only shelter in one another. Never even needing fucking sex. Just this—bodies fused, becoming one like they were meant to.

We stayed that way, blended and unsure of where her body started, and mine ended. She spent the rest of the night explaining to me the past nine months, and everything she'd gone through. In certain parts, I had to stop her to ease the ache in my chest. And in others, I couldn't contain my excitement when she had explained that she had dual citizenship.

This new information changed my plan entirely.

"Do you know who your biological father is?" I asked.

She shook her head. "Not like it matters."

"Do you want to know?"

"No."

"Very well." I flashed her a small smile. "Who am I supposed to ask for permission to marry you?"

"Me."

I let out a chuckle and kissed her lovely lips. "I missed you every damn day, love. Even on days I wasn't myself, a big, empty hole was inside me." I crossed my hand over my heart. "You were missing." Mia's lips turned up in the corners, and she shook her head embarrassingly. "I missed that fucking smile, too." Her lips parted as she breathed out a laugh. "Yeah, missed that bloody laugh as well."

Our eyes locked, and her laughter dissolved. "I didn't do this, Ollie. I didn't. I wouldn't."

I held her face in my hands. "I know. I'm working on it. I'm going to get you out if I have to break you out of here myself, alright?"

She nodded and curled into my lap, laying her head into the curve of my neck. Her hard, pink nipples grazed along my chest as I inched my fingers down the sides of her arms and over her back. My knob relaxed in my joggers, not needing anything more than this fucking moment.

Mia fell asleep against me, not one stir of movement, and I hadn't felt this complete, relieved, and refreshed in a long time. This time, I kept my eyes open and ran my palm over every surface of her back, over and over again, touching every wound, silently thanking my God for keeping these wounds at the surface and not piercing her soul. Keeping her light, that we worked so hard to find, stay intact and untouched by this fucking prankster that I was now determined to find.

A single knock at the door came too soon, and I dropped my head back against the wall.

With my love in my arms, I leaned to my left to swipe my shirt off the floor. "Mia," I whispered, lifting her dead weight off my chest and pushing her head through the hole of my shirt.

"Stay with me," she mumbled, pulling her arms through.

My white tee engulfed her, falling over her breasts. I wrapped an arm around her back and laid her across the mattress. "I never left," I whispered into her ear and kissed her forehead. "Now close your eyes, love."

I rose to my feet and watched her curl into a ball before drifting back to sleep—*my angel*. Doctors saw imperfections, a mental illness, but all I saw was strength: a powerful mind and the ability to protect the rest of herself from it when needed.

People who couldn't fathom or understand one's complexity, blamed it on a sickness. The people who couldn't put you in a specific box, shied away. And the people who couldn't open their hearts to those who were different from them, undermined.

But where they saw flaws, I saw blessings.

That beautiful mind of hers kept her strong—kept her a fighter.

After adjusting my waistband, I pulled my hoodie over my head, crouched down beside her, and kissed her one last time before heading out.

Scott waited outside the door, leaning against the wall with his arms crossed. He dropped his chin to his chest and lifted off the wall before I followed behind him in silence.

SEVENTEEN

*"I suffer from the heart of a saint
with the hands of a sinner."*

OLIVER MASTERS

Ollie

Half the day went by smooth. I kept my mouth closed, ears opened, determination rolling, and operation *"get Mia out"* in full focus. Once she returned without a dent in her record, I'd move on to phase two: find the bloody prankster, as Mia liked to call him. Prankster seemed juvenile for the shit he'd put her through.

Scott and I had come to an understanding. He'd have my back, but once the job was complete, I never wanted to see or hear about him and Mia together again.

I'd never been the jealous type, utterly confident in what Mia and I shared, but that still didn't mean I liked seeing or hearing about it. I'd never keep Mia from someone she loved or grew close to. Finding someone who accepted and understood you entirely was rare, and forcing the ones you love, to sever those kinds of relationships, only hurt your own.

If I were honest with myself, she never belonged to me. She belonged to this world, and the only way to truly love her was to love her unselfishly. Otherwise, I wouldn't have loved her at all.

Jude walked through the door during lunch, and I tilted my focus to Scott who stood off by the entrance of the mess hall. Scott offered a faint nod, and I rose from my chair, abandoning my uneaten tray.

Before Jude reached the lunch line, I made it across the room and wrapped my hand around the back of his neck, steering him away.

"Outside," I ordered. Jude tried to pull his head from my grasp, and my grip tightened, forcing his weak arse forward. "No one's going to help you."

Jude nodded and walked ahead of me. I looked back at Scott, who glanced at his wristwatch. Five-or-so minutes was all I had to get this bloke to talk.

On our way out, Bria and the new girl, who I kept forgetting the name of, stopped in front of us.

"Go on, eat. I'll be there in a minute," Jude immediately said to the girls.

They both looked over at me then back at Jude. "We don't eat without you," Bria whined, and I craned my head in Jude's direction, looking for an explanation on what she meant by that.

"You are today," he said through an exhale and annoyance in his tone. "You can eat one fucking meal without me."

Bria rolled her eyes as the blonde studied me, and finally, they both stepped to the side Jude and I pushed through the double doors to outside, unattended.

"What's this about?" Jude asked, pulling a cigarette and lighter from his pocket as soon as our feet touched grass. He had the nerve to bring it to his mouth and light it as if my presence was a waste of his time. I ripped the cigarette from his mouth, split it in half, and shoved him against the side of the building. Jude's eyes went wide, and he tried to push me back but failed. "You have a problem, just say so! You can have Bria, she's a loose cannon, anyway."

"Bria? I'm here about Mia, remember Mia?"

A smirk crossed his face. "Ah, Mia, yeah?" And before another thought could cross his mind, I wiped that smirk off his face with my fist to his jaw. Jude's neck twisted before his body did, but I grabbed his shirt and slammed him back against the wall.

"Does this look like a bloody game to you? I'm in no mood, you piece of shit. Start talking."

"You got it bad for her I see." He pushed me off him and held up a hand. "I haven't touched the girl. Well … no … I take that back. Perhaps I touched her,"—he brought his thumb and pointer finger in the air, hardly touching them together— "but only a little."

In a hot flash, rage erupted, and my angry fist punched his gut, knocking the air from his lungs. Jude keeled over with a hand over his stomach.

Violence wasn't usually my first attempt at conversation, but this bloke had tested my patience, and I had none left. "You told detail where to find a key." I clenched his shirt in my fist and pulled him upright. "How'd you know about a key?"

Jude looked past me and sucked in a defeated breath. "A note, alright?"

"A note?"

He pushed his hand into the pocket of the black jeans painted on him and pulled out a folded piece of paper before shoving it into my chest. "A bloody note."

"Where did you get this from?" I asked as I opened it, and my eyes swiftly skimmed over the tattered paper. The letter was simple: *Tell Lynch the key is in Mia's dorm or everyone will know*. "Know what? What are you hiding?" I narrowed my eyes.

"I found it in my dorm," he dabbed his hand over his mouth, blood dripping over his already swelling lip. "That's all you need to know."

"Not good enough." I stepped closer, securing him still with a warning glare.

He jerked his head to the side, whipping his black hair off his shoulder. "It doesn't concern you."

"If it concerns Mia, it concerns me. You weaseled your way into this mess over some threat you *will* tell me about."

Jude laughed and looked off. "I get it now. You love her." He shook his head swiped a loose strand behind his ear. "Let me tell you something about love … love only leads to disappointment. Take my advice and run. Nothing good comes of it. Find yourself a couple cows, take the fanny, and shut off your feelings because love only ends in one way: excruciating pain." He slid down the building until his arse hit the ground and retrieved another fag from his pocket. "It's not worth it," he added.

I should've seen it before. Dropping my hands over my hipbones, I glanced down at the bloke who unraveled before my eyes. "Why are you here, Jude?"

He smiled, took a drag between his fingers, and dropped his head back. "You wouldn't understand," he muttered as smoke seeped from between his lips.

"Try me."

He glanced up and winced from the sun. "I fucked up," he shrugged, flicking the ash between his bent knees, "pissed and coming back from a do, totaled the car, barely made it out alive. The worst part about it? I did make it out alive. I wish I didn't. Wish I could trade places with her. I'd give up everything to bring her back, even my own life."

"Fuck," I exhaled and threaded my fingers through my hair. "I'm sorry, mate."

Jude hung his head. "Sorrys are for when people don't have anything else to say but have a need to fill the awkward space. Rather you'd say nothing at all."

"You're right." *I almost felt bad for punching him. Almost.* "You made a mistake. You're paying your price. No reason to punish yourself more.

God knows you're going through hell. You think she'd like what you're doing to yourself right now?"

"Fuck you. Don't talk like you know her."

I nodded and looked around. "I know she didn't die so you could pound into some pussy, wallow in your sorrows, and treat girls like they're property."

He stood and pulled the fag from his lips. "Easy for you to say, yeah?"

"It is easy. Plain and fucking simple."

"And if it were Mia?"

"I wouldn't have been so goddamn stupid in the first place."

"You're a real charmer, you know that?" He blew out smoke and dropped his head back against the wall. "We should've left it with 'sorry.'"

I held up the note in my hand. "I'm keeping this."

Jude waved his hand before bringing the fag back to his lips, and I turned to walk back inside. The chap was harmless. A complete and utter wreck, but harmless. This had been his way of dealing with the grief of his love's death. A death he had caused.

A pit formed in my stomach at the thought of losing Mia because of something I'd done, and Jude's grief rubbed off on me, growing this sickness inside me until it became unmanageable. Before reaching the doors back into Dolor, I posted up against the stone wall to catch my bearings from the dizzy spell taking over. I pinched my eyes together and drew in a deep breath, and counted to three. My emotional intensity was in full swing. The pills were officially out of my system.

Scott waited inside the building beside the doors. "And?" He asked as I walked by.

"Dead end."

"Like I said," Scott scoffed from behind as he walked down the hall behind me. "Where you headed?"

"I'm going to see Lynch."

"Masters!" Scott called out.

I ignored him and continued my stride toward the stairs.

203

Scott yanked me by the arm and spun me around. "You think he's going to sit back and 'hear you out?' Have you lost your bloody mind?"

"Get off me," I cautioned, eyeing his hand on my bicep. Scott released me and I turned my attention down the hall. "I have nothing left to lose, and I'm not letting her spend another night in the hole for something she didn't do." I continued forward. My only goal was to get Mia out of there. Scott followed close behind, his loud boots against the floor reminded me with every step. "You don't have to babysit, Scott. I believe I can make it to Lynch's in one piece."

"You need an escort," he muttered behind me. "Plus, I wouldn't miss this show for anything."

I didn't bother knocking and pushed through Lynch's door. The lights in his office were dimmed, curtains closed, and the chap snapped from his desk, startled.

"Have a nice nap?" I asked, and dropped in the chair across from him.

Lynch sprung to his feet, his attention jumped from me to Scott with surprised brown eyes. "What do you think you're doing?"

"Mia's being set up," I pulled the note from my pocket and tossed it over his desk, "she doesn't belong in there."

His eyes dropped to the note before returning to me. A single exhale left him as he fixed his shirt and retook his chair. "I was wondering how long it would take before you showed up here. If my calculations are correct, you're a day late," he sneered.

"Fuck your calculations. Release her!" I snapped, running on thin ice and desperation. At the corner of my eye, Scott took a step forward, and Lynch held up a palm in the air to stop him. "We both know she's a target in a bloody game, and Jude only a pawn. I'm sure there's another one out there who planted the key. The only way to draw this arsehole out is to get Mia back in her dorm."

As soon as the words left my mouth, I wanted to suck them right back in. I hadn't thought this through. Mia was safe in solitary. No one could touch her there. But what if Lynch was forced to hand her over to authorities?

"She'll be on twenty-four-hour watch," Scott added. I didn't bother turning to face him, kept my sights fixed on Lynch and took notice in the changing expression crossing his face. The thought of Scott tailing Mia twenty-four-fucking-seven wasn't on my bucket list, but it was the only way. My knee bounced from the new plan unraveling, and I pressed my palm over it, trying to keep my emotions in check.

It'd been too long since Lynch spoke, but then finally ... "And you'll be the one to watch her?" he asked, looking past me to Scott.

I turned in my chair for the first time and Scott looked to me then back at Lynch. "No, sir. Not me."

My brows raised. "What do you mean, not you? You already fancy the girl, may as well watch her, yeah?"

Scott narrowed his eyes. "I have a duty to uphold. Ten patients to look after. I don't have time to be Jett's personal bodyguard."

"Duty?" I asked in disbelief and stood. "If you were watching her in the first place, none of this would've happened. The dead cat in her room, the glass in her mattress ... all of it could've been avoided if you did your bloody job," I turned to Lynch, "You know about that right? While you were sound asleep, Mia fell over her mattress only to be sliced open by planted glass. Her entire back scarred!" I turned back to Scott, "Where were you then?"

"What is he talking about?" Lynch asked Scott.

Scott took long strides toward me and jabbed a finger against his heaving chest. "I carried her! And for four hours I pulled out each piece of glass, one by one—"

"Enough!" Lynch slammed a fist over his desk and his name plate bounced to the floor. Scott took a step back, and red burned in his eyes. Eventually, this would have come to a head. "I hired you to look after her!" Lynch shouted.

Those words grabbed me, and I slid my eyes back to Lynch. *Look after her?* "You mean watch her, right? Because if I didn't say so myself, it sounds like you fucking care about her. Which I know isn't true. In everyone's eyes, Mia is the spawn of Satan, here to cause destruction and stir the pot, or at least it's how she's treated."

"You know what I meant," Lynch corrected.

"No, I don't know." My temples pounded from it all. "All I know is, Mia is getting out, and I'll look after her. I don't trust anyone."

Lynch laughed and fell into his chair. "This is great. The blind leading the blind," he said through a humorless chuckle. "I've been working here too bloody long. Accounting keeps sounding better and better."

I flexed my jaw and leaned into his desk. "This funny to you?" my arms picked up a shake, and I closed my hands into a fist. "Release her, or so help me God, the next person to be investigated is you."

"Masters," Scott stated and placed a hand on my shoulder.

"No fuck that," I shook him off, "this whole place is a fucking joke."

"This place is the only reason you're not in jail, and Mia not in some mental institution in the states," Lynch reminded me. "I'll release her, but threaten me like that again, I'll make sure your next home is the inside of a jail cell." A few beats of silence and heavy breathing passed before Lynch turned his attention over to Scott. "You will be watching her, Ethan. One mistake by either one of them, they'll both be sent away for good on Oliver's account."

"What about the police?" Scott asked through gritted teeth.

Lynch picked up the note and dropped it into his desk drawer. "I'll do my job, you do yours,"—he slammed his drawer shut— "Now get out of my office."

As soon as Scott and I exited and the door closed behind us, he stopped me in the hall. "That was an ace move," he took a step closer, "but if you cock-up my plans here, I won't hesitate to take you out."

"The only person you're taking out is Mia from confinement. Then I'll be the one to look after her. I don't trust you, and you sliding into her fucking bed at night because of her night terrors days are over. Next time, you come get me."

even when i'm gone

The office door opened, and Lynch poked his head through, eyes bouncing between the standoff in the hallway. "Did you skip your meds after lunch today, Masters?"

I had forgotten the charade I had to keep up with. "I'll go now."

Trusting Ethan's next moves were to the basement, I shoved my hands in my pockets and took off.

The new nurse had her back turned toward me at her desk when I arrived, flipping through paperwork clipped on a clipboard, and I dropped my shoulder against the wall and cleared my throat. The nurse turned in her chair and looked up at me. Blonde hair, brown roots, and bright red lipstick greeted me. Then she smiled, and her teeth glowed against the red shade. The nurse was young, and I wondered what she was doing in a place like this.

Her eyes dropped to my knob in my joggers, and I shifted in place. "My pills."

The nurse's gaze jumped back to my face, and her smile faded. "Oh, right. Oliver Masters?"

I raised my arms out at my sides. "In the flesh."

"Are you going to give me trouble?"

"No, ma'am. Had more important things to take care of," I explained. She raised a brow, and my eyes flitted to the badge hanging from her neck. *Saunders*. She uncrossed her legs, her skirt rising in the process, and sweat split at my hairline.

I turned my gaze away. "Let's get on with it. I haven't got all day."

Nurse Saunders stood and walked to her medicine cart. Only a few cups sat over the top tier. "I'm sorry to hear about Rhonda. The lady you had yesterday was a fill-in, but I'll be the permanent nurse." She bent over, and I dropped my head back to face the ceiling. Saunders turned and took a step toward me. "You can call me Poppy."

I dropped my chin, and our eyes met. "Thanks, Saunders."

"Need water?"

"Nope." I tipped the cup back and forced them down, squeezed the cup in my fist and threw it in the trash before leaving.

"See you tomorrow," she called out before I slipped past the door and headed straight for the loo. I wasted no time to get this poison out of me before it entered my system.

Mia

"What are you doing here?" I asked, eyeing Ethan suspiciously from the corner of the room. My knees pressed harder against me inside Ollie's white tee. The shirt still smelled like him. The smell of the ocean. The smell of freedom.

"Masters can be pretty convincing. Now let's go," Ethan mumbled and waved me out. I pushed up to my feet and took a step off the mattress. *Lynch was letting me go? Just like that?* I narrowed my eyes in Ethan's direction, wondering what the catch was, and Ethan's shoulders sank. "What is it?"

"Under what conditions?" I asked.

He raised a brow. "No conditions."

"Nothing?" I let out a disbelieving laugh. "What's changed?"

"Like I said …" Ethan took a step forward and held out his hand, "Your bloke is convincing. Now let's go."

I relaxed my arms at my sides and followed him out. "I need to shower," I stated in passing.

Ethan walked me back to my room to collect my things to shower before dinner started. We hadn't talked about what happened between us, or what didn't get to happen. Ethan was hurt; I saw it in his eyes. The rejection transmitted from him, a flashing yellow light.

The community bathroom was empty. Ethan stayed back against the door as I undressed, stepped under the water, and took my time.

The warm water felt incredible as I hadn't showered in days.

"You want to talk about what happened?" Ethan asked, startling me. His voice came from right outside the curtain. "I don't want things to be weird between us."

"Things aren't weird. You're the one making them weird," I pointed out.

"I see it now. I didn't before, but I get it."

I turned the water off and grabbed my towel. "Get what?"

"This thing between you and Masters. Hell, I haven't even seen the two of you together, but I don't have to. Every word Masters speaks, every look in his eyes, every time he takes a bloody breath …"—Ethan exhaled— "It's all you, Mia. All I hear, see, and feel is you. You're mixed in him, and if you dropped dead, I wouldn't be surprised if Master's heart gave up along with yours. It's fucking weird, Jett, and hard to explain." He paused, and I'd been standing wrapped in the towel, dripping wet and stunned by his words. "Fuck, I sound like—"

"He got to you," I finally said.

"Huh?"

I opened the curtain, and Ethan dropped his head to the side to face me as he rolled his shoulder against the tile beside my stall. "Ollie has that effect on people. He makes you believe in the impossible."

"I barely talked to him."

"That's the thing with Ollie … you don't even have to speak to him. You just have to know him."

"He pisses me off," Ethan muttered, and we both shared a laugh. "You think I'll ever find someone like that?"

I raised a brow. "Like Ollie?"

Ethan rolled his eyes and lifted off the tile, turning to face me fully. "No. Someone who makes me feel the same way Masters feels about you."

My gaze drifted. Before, I didn't believe in any of this at all, it was crazy to think how much had changed in the year and a half I'd been here. "Yeah, I do."

"It's a shame it couldn't have been you."

"Trust me. When you do find her, you'll be thanking me."

Out of solitary, freshly showered, and stomach rumbling, Ethan and I walked together to the mess hall. We stopped at the entryway, and I scanned over the crowd. Bria and Tyler sat on both sides of Jude at my old table with Jake kicked to the end. All eyes found me, and though Bria forced her gaze away, Jake held mine, and a small glimmer appeared in his eyes before it instantly dulled. My gaze made its journey, stopping at Maddie and Gwen, and Maddie held up her fist and flipped me off.

The old me would've returned the favor. Instead, I did nothing and my eyes carried on with their journey across the room.

I felt him before my eyes found him. He was somewhere in the room, and my entire body hummed to his wavelengths. I didn't have butterflies in my stomach. No. This feeling was a couple dozen phoenix's rising from their ashes.

And then my eyes found him. Ollie sat leaned over with his head in his hands and his hood pulled over his head, facing an uneaten tray. My feet moved as my brain disciplined me—reminding me about the repercussions of getting hurt, and a million words ran through my head as I continued forward, finding words to say. Which Ollie did we have today?

I laid a hand over his shoulder, and the tension released from him in that single touch and his shoulders dropped.

"Mia," Ollie uttered through a breath. His right hand crossed over him and grabbed my wrist, pulling me over his lap to straddle him. Long arms wrapped around me while his head dug into the crevice of my neck, drawing and breathing me in.

We sat like that for I didn't know how long. I felt their stares on us, but Ollie didn't move, and I didn't pull away from him. The only movements were his hands slipping under my shirt, needing skin to skin contact.

Then he lifted his head, and his nose grazed along my jaw with eyes still closed and holding on to wherever he wanted to be in his beautiful head—a perfect paradise. His lips lingered over mine, releasing long breaths.

"Open your eyes," I whispered.

Ollie shook his head. "Not yet."

The dreamer grabbed my mouth with his and sank into it.

A damn perfect paradise.

And Ollie was back. My Ollie. Full-force, empowered and rejuvenated. He held our kiss, never took more than what he needed, and this simple connection was enough to relax him as he breathed out through his nose. His lips brushed against mine as he released our kiss, and his eyes opened, staring back at me.

Last night, all we'd talked about was me, and I had no idea how he'd been coping, what struggles he'd been facing. Suddenly, I wanted to know everything. "You have to tell me how to help you. I don't know how to do this," I whispered.

"One day at a time, love." Ollie's eyes beamed. "We're both figuring it out. Just know I never meant to hurt you. My heart was always in the right place, but my mind wasn't doing the right thing."

"What about the medication?"

A burst of laughter from afar didn't snag his attention. Eyes, hand, and focus remained solely on me as he leaned over and dragged a nearby chair closer. "Sit, you need to eat." I slid from his lap and fell back into the chair before he pushed his tray in front of me. "I've been off the medication for three days now. It's easier this time." Ollie dropped an elbow over the table, turning in his chair to face me and gripped my thigh with his other hand. "I'm alright. Eat, love."

"No shakes?" I asked, taking a bite of the mashed potatoes.

Ollie held out his hand, showing me. "Well, not from the withdrawal." He flashed a half-smile, and his eyes studied mine. "I'm okay. Swear to it. Now tell me whose pot you pissed in. Who do you believe is fucking with you?"

"Jude."

Ollie's head shook. "No, Jude's not capable of it."

"How do you know."

"I just do."

I took another bite and scanned the room. "Then, I have no idea." A few beats passed as Ollie's fingers wrapped around my thigh. "What if I go to jail over this?"

"I won't let that happen!"

"You're not above the law, Ollie. You can't control my fate."

"Hey, look at me." I dropped the fork and turned to face him. "Remember I told you to believe in us?"—I nodded— "Don't hold back on me now, we're almost there. I may not be above the law, but us? Together, we're a fucking perfect storm."

"A notion that even science can't grasp."

He smiled, leaned in, and kissed my temple. "There's no doubt in my mind we can get through this, alright? And if the law fails us, if this place fucking fails us, don't think for one second I wouldn't have you out of here and across the world before the order for your arrest is even in motion."

A shadow loomed over us, and I looked up to see Maddie and Gwen hovering. I paused mid-chew as her eyes darted between us. Turning to face Ollie, he squeezed my leg under the table and captured my gaze, holding it hostage.

"This is cute," Maddie sneered. "And the saint fell in love with the sociopath, but it's anyone's guess who is who in this story. Truly, I'm shocked. She forgave you faster than I thought she would." Maddie lifted on her toes before dropping back down. "Those same fingers touching your leg were the same fingers buried inside me not too long ago." I flinched, and Ollie's jaw tensed, but his eyes stayed on me, not bothering to look her way and keeping me with him. "Does it bother you, Mia?" she continued, prying for a reaction. "I tasted him. Sucked his—"

"You good, love? Ready to get out of here?" Ollie asked as he jumped to his feet. He wrapped my hand in his, and I nodded, standing with him. My heart hit so fast or not at all and the back of my eyes burned from the resistance.

"He'll be back. It's only a matter of time before he falls off the rails again," Maddie said through a laugh.

Ollie pushed through the double doors and led us outside. Though we walked in silence, the regret and disgust punished his stride and darkened his mood. When we reached a clearing in the woods, Ollie sat over the ground and fell back until his head hit the ground. His hands flew over his face as he tried to catch his breath.

In an instant, his whole demeanor changed, and I couldn't help but feel for him. Ollie always knew the right words to say, but at this moment, I couldn't find any to make him feel better. His hands folded behind his head as he looked up at me with tortured eyes. "I'm a liar, a coward, and a hypocrite."

"No, you're not."

"She has no right putting that image in your head."

"It's Maddie. I can handle Maddie."

"Fuck Maddie. Can *you* handle what happened?"

I took a seat beside him, and his green eyes followed, taking notice in the distance between us and where my hands fell at my sides. His jaw ticked, waiting for a reply and disliking the space. "It doesn't matter," I finally said, and the truth was, it didn't. Both Ollie and I had made mistakes.

Ollie caved and waved me over. "Come here." I inched over, and once I was within reach, his arm snaked around my stomach as he pulled me over him until my head hit his chest. The tips of his fingers traced over my arm as he stared up into the darkening sky. "I haven't been able to write a bloody thing since the day I was thrown in confinement. But now I have these words swimming inside me, making my head spin."

"What is it you need to write about?"

Ollie shook his head and thread his fingers through my hair, sights still in the sky, perfectly content now. "Moments like this."

"And tell me, Ollie, what exactly would you write in this very moment?"

He dropped his chin to look at me. "I'd write about your lips," his thumb grazed over my bottom lip, "and how they were made perfectly with mine in mind. I'd write about those brown eyes of yours, and how they were created to hold my reflection. And your touch ... how you don't understand the power a single brush of your finger has over me. But what's truly remarkable is when the world attempts to pull me under, you arrest my heart, and the rest of me could slip away, but it wouldn't matter. Still, it would beat. Steady. Solid. Secure." He looked up to the sky again watching the trees sway in the October dawn. "Something like that. But it reads better on paper, yeah?"

I shook my head. "I prefer to hear you say it."

"Really?" He pulled me over him until our bodies aligned, and my forearms dropped to the ground on each side of his head. "Why's that?"

"Because you have a lovely voice, and I don't think you fully comprehend the impact it causes. Or maybe I'm biased, and it only affects me."

Ollie smiled, his eyes beamed, and my heart tightened. "Can I touch you?" His brain bounced like an evenly matched tennis game and never in one place for too long. His internal conflict took me by surprise when it flowed through his cautious touch over my sides. "Or do you need time?" It took me a moment to realize he had been referring to what just happened back in the mess hall with Maddie.

"I don't need time, Ollie. When it comes to you, time is not something I want to waste."

Ollie smiled and wrapped his hands in my hair. "I saw your face, love. She got inside your head. You have every right to be upset, and you don't have to pretend to be strong around me. Alright? It's okay if you need time."

Side-stepping the topic, I fell over to the side of him and thread my fingers in his, staring at the same sky. "You think anyone would notice if we slept out here tonight?"

"Scott would notice, and we wouldn't be able to get back in once the doors are locked. But I'll tell you what,"—he lifted our linked hands and pointed in the sky— "Same time next year, we'll be sleeping under that same moon, probably a different strand of stars."

"What day is today?" I asked.

"The tenth."

"So, October tenth two thousand twenty. Ten-ten-twenty-twenty." I closed my eyes to make a mental note.

"Ten-ten-twenty-twenty," Ollie repeated. "*Fuck*, sounds good. I love it." He turned his head and rested his forehead to my temple. "Come on, love. We have to head back."

Ollie lifted off before pulling me to my feet, and we ran our way back to the campus as the date chanted in my mind. Plans. A future.

Ten-ten-twenty-twenty.

EIGHTEEN

"Kiss her crazy and love her insane."

OLIVER MASTERS

Ollie

"Mia's a psycho," Liam shouted in the hall. "Bitch almost killed that freshman. She doesn't deserve to be here."

My head snapped behind me to see Liam talking to some random bloke, Mia and me not much farther away, capable of hearing every word rolling off his malicious tongue. The air around me changed, and like a predator watching its prey, my eyes zeroed in on him as my body shifted closer to Mia, protecting her from the ugliness.

It was Halloween, the day of the dead. As much as I'd like to teach him a lesson, it wouldn't have done any good. He was just as scared as the next person, projecting fear onto those who were easy targets.

The prankster had easily walked into Mia's dorm and stolen her journal, managing to broadcast everyone's secrets over the walls, including Liam's sexual orientation. The issue was never the fact that everyone was now aware. The issue was Liam's inability to accept his own heart's preference.

He was ashamed, and that made me only pity him.

Didn't he know? Love was attracted to the soul inside, blind to everything else. No one had an option—no choice in the fucking matter. Love had no guilt, fear, or negatives—only pure in form, attacking the organs, embedding itself deep, hungry, to thrive and grow. Shamelessly, love had no barriers or rules, and the real tragedy was the resistance from the close-minded.

One day, love would conquer fear. *It's only a matter of time, Liam.*

I grabbed her empty hand and held it to my chest. "Block it out. Liam's just embarrassed," I whispered with my mouth dropped to her ear. Turning my eyes from Liam to Mia, her chest filled with air before she let out a long breath and nodded with her eyes fixed out in front of her. I moved around to face her, pinning her still and towering over her fragile frame. Her brown eyes lifted until they hit mine as her naturally wavy hair fell around her face. "Hey, if you're a psycho, then I'll love you insane."

Mia chuckled and dropped her head. "I don't think anyone understands us."

"No one understands us? Good. Sounds like we're finally making history then," I stated. She smiled, and my stiff muscles relaxed under her spell. "I want to kiss you right now."

Mia's eyes drifted around us, and her cheeks tinted rosy. "What kind of kiss? Are you talking about a light kiss?" her eyes turned back to me, challenging me, and her lashes lowered along with her voice, "or the insane, mad, crazy kind?"

Those words hit me in the chest, and the only way to ease the ache were that lip she was now biting. I snatched the books from her arms and pulled her down the hallway, pushing through Liam and the crowd forming between classes.

After we turned the corner, we reached an empty hall. The books dropped from my arms as Mia fell back against the cement, and I could hear her breathing. I ran my thumb over that bottom lip before I grabbed it with my mouth and kissed her crazy.

Her chest hummed against mine as I held her up with my hands and consumed her everything—her taste, her scent, her nostalgic soul mine connected with. The ache was now long gone, and my tongue pushed through the part in her lips. I sank, all of me going under, and I never wanted to be pulled out from the depths of Mia ...

"Uh-hmm," a low grunt sounded behind us. My forehead dropped to Mia's, and her eyes shifted behind me. She let out a small chuckle and straightened her posture the same time I hesitantly pulled away. "Next block starts in a minute, what are you two doing over here?" Jerry asked.

All it had taken was one person outside our bubble to remind us of where we were.

Sure, we were adults, but stripped of our freedom and deprived of our identity by the hands of medication and means of brainwash—an attempt to reset us like a broken toy.

Six more months left. Six bloody months. I'd gone seven months behind bars without Mia, another six in this hell hole seemed unmanageable. But when my eyes latched onto hers, belief that it would all be worth it erased every doubt.

The house I'd set up for us came forth in my head—the life waiting outside the iron gates. Mia and I, and if everything worked out according to plan, Zeke too.

Without removing my eyes from Mia, my mouth opened. "I'm kissing this beautiful creature, my friend." I landed my lips on a smiling Mia once more. "Ready?"

Mia nodded, and her hair fell over her face, hiding that shit-eating grin.

It took a lot of convincing, but I'd managed to transfer Zeke over to my table in the mess hall. When Zeke's schedule was interrupted, he'd lashed out. But I couldn't stand back and watch him being ignored as Bria, the blonde, and Jake talked around him.

My family—*my everything*—belonged together.

Between the commotion, I hadn't been able to discuss my plans with Mia about Zeke. *Hell*, Mia and I had never confirmed plans, only the fact that I'd steal her away, wherever she would be, once we left here. Little did she know, I had a house ready for the three of us. With news of her dual citizenship, it took a massive weight off my shoulder.

Things were falling together.

I moved my hand over Mia's thigh to get her attention. "I'm working on becoming Zeke's guardian," I blurted, airing out plans and hoping the news wouldn't close her off.

Her lovely lips turned up in the corners, and her hand covered over mine on her thigh. I closed my eyes and released a breath. "Is that even possible?" she asked low, matching my tone.

I dropped my chin. "My mate on the outside has been doing some research. Once my record is clean, I can adopt. I'm over-age," I nudged my head in Zeke's direction, "Look at him. He may not be my brother by blood, but he's my brother by bond, and I'm not leaving him behind."

If anyone understood my love for the kid, it was Mia.

"You're amazing," she said through a sigh. "I know whatever it takes, you'll find a way to make it happen."

I could breathe again. "You're alright with this?" I had to make sure.

"Am I alright with you getting Zeke out of here? Hell yes."

"It would be the three of us," I clarified, putting things into perspective. "It would always be you and I, love, but Zeke would finally have a life. A chance at something he deserves."

"Like I said," she squeezed my hand, leaned in closer, and I held my breath, "Hell. Yes."

Those soft lips merely touched over mine, and I closed off all senses to feel every sensation they stirred as small bumps rushed over the surface of my skin. When my eyes opened again, Mia's contagious smile greeted me, and my stupid smile returned.

I looked back over to Zeke who watched us from across the table, and the clock at the back wall came into focus. "Dammit," I breathed out. "I have my phone call for the week in ten minutes." I kissed the side of her head before standing to my feet. Ethan was posted at his usual place, and I looked down at Mia and ran my palm over her head to lift her focus back to me. "You gonna be alright?"

"Yes. Quit worrying so much." The volume in the mess hall spiked, and my head snapped up to see a punch thrown in Liam's direction. Ethan sprang to action, pulling the kid off him and Mia's hand landed over mine. "Go, Ollie. I have a session with Conway, anyway."

"Yeah, alright," I mumbled and pointed the finger at Zeke, "Look after her."

Zeke signed, *always*.

I rushed down the stairs, the halls empty, and made it to the closed chamber in time. A guard sat right outside the door with a clipboard. "Name?" he asked, not bothering to look up from his small desk.

"You know my name, fuck-face."

Jinx lifted his head and grinned. "Ollie, my man," he stood and lazily shook my hand, "feels like I haven't seen you in a minute."

"It's been a week." I laughed. "Got what I asked for?"

Jinx was an interesting character. A big fella with missing teeth, but a heart I wished people could see. He knew of my brother and despised him. It had taken some time for him to see that I was nothing like Oscar.

"You owe me hot-shot," he pulled the gum pack from his pocket and tossed it over to me.

I looked over the already opened package to see two missing. "Send my bill to my new address. I'll take care of you." For a while, Travis had mailed me cash until the cash started disappearing. I had to fuel my gum addiction a new way without the funds. Jinx was my only option.

"You're on fire on *The Amazon*, brother. Just looked you up a few days ago. You're in stores and online. People are buzzing."

"It's not *'The Amazon,'* mate, just *Amazon*," I shook my head, "Thanks, means a lot, but it's only a start. My first publication. Something small. I'll be able to do better once I get out of here."

Jinx chuckled, flashing his missing teeth. "Damn, brother. You don't take compliments well. Don't be so hard on yourself, yeah? People are eating that tosh up like it's candy. Everyone on the outside is dying to know who Oliver Masters is. Soon enough you'll have so much fanny, you won't need to recycle."

I popped a piece of gum in my mouth and smiled over at him. His remarks were innocent, something every bloke would say or want to hear.

Mia and me hadn't made love since the beginning of the school year, our quick fuck not counting in the least bit. She'd mentioned she already forgave and looked past the whole Maddie situation, but she needed to know what I did was unacceptable. I had to earn the chance to be intimate with her again. My choice. "You know I'm not into it. I'll pass them over to you, big man." I patted him on the shoulder before pushing through the door, charging for the phone.

Jinx's laugh bounced through the closing door. "My man!"

I lifted the phone off its receiver and brought it to my ear, thinking about Jinx's words. People were talking about my poetry; my words were out there in the world while I was isolated in here. The irony laughable, but my vision still blurred from my eyes glossing over.

And then it hit me …

I'd touched hundreds of souls.

After punching Travis's number into the receiver, I pinched the bridge of my nose to fight back the waves threatening to crash.

"You're a fucking legend," Travis greeted.

My hand found the wall as I leaned into it, my legs growing weak. "What are the stats looking like?" I managed to get out. "Hundreds?"

"No, Ollie. Thousands! They want to do merchandise. I told them no merch until you're released, but they're getting antsy. They want to get it out now while people are talking and schedule a signing."

"You know I can't do anything for another six months. They know where I'm at." I didn't intend for all this to happen. All I wanted was to make a little money for the house—for Mia. Get enough funds together to travel and collect people's stories from around the world. "Go ahead and approve the merchandise. You have the okay from me. But, don't go overboard."

"Alright, alright. I have you, my friend."

There was a deep sigh on both ends of the phone.

"How you holding up," he asked. "You sound different."

Travis had never heard or seen me at my normal self, and I was surprised he'd noticed as soon as he did. "Things are good. Can't say much, calls recorded, but I'm exactly where I want to be." Off the pills, no withdrawal, with Mia.

"You sound happy … you sound good. Summer wants to paint the walls at the cottage. She understands it isn't ours, but she's excited for you. Wants to help out any way she can, you know?"

A thousand questions went through my head, starting with if Mia liked to paint, and what color Mia would choose. This was her house as much as it was mine, though Travis did not know that. "What color are the walls now?"

"A rubbish orange. It has to go."

"Paint everything white. Brighten the place up, alright?" Mia would decide once she stepped foot in her new home. As long as she was standing beside me when I walked through the door, I could care less what color the bloody walls were.

The door closed behind me as Travis agreed into the phone. Lifting off the wall, I turned my head to see Maddie pick up the phone beside me. "I have to go. I'll ring you next week."

"Just to be clear, yes on—"

I hung up the phone before Travis could finish his sentence. The last thing I needed was for Maddie to listen in on my conversation. "What are you doing here?" My eyes slid to the window to see Jinx relaxed in his chair. "This isn't your scheduled time."

"Had it changed." She took a step closer, and I took a step back. "Why ya so jumpy?" she asked, and I shook my head and trudged past her. Nothing good ever came from Maddie and me in the same room alone together, and as if I spoke too soon, her arm slithered around my waist to stop me. I pulled back and turned to face her, my face reddening, my jaw clenching. "See? So jumpy."

Sinister thoughts crossed my mind, a thousand things I could say to belittle or hurt her, but Maddie's eyes shifted, and I saw a desperation inside that I'd never noticed before.

But I couldn't put a finger on why she was so desperate.

She didn't look like she wanted this—any of this.

The four walls around us inched closer as I studied her. "What do you want with me?" I finally asked, getting to the bottom of her intentions. Her forehead creased and arms folded over her chest as if she was hiding from the question. "Maddie?"

Maddie's gaze dropped to the floor, and she dragged in a breath.

When she looked back up, her features twisted into the rat I'd always seen her as.

"Come on, let's get out of here and talk in my room. Mia's with Conway."

"You know Mia's schedule now?" I raised a brow. "What do you know her schedule for?" Maddie looked away again, a sign she was thinking of a lie, and I was already over this. "This is your last warning. Stay away."

I passed her for the second time with long strides straight for the door, slamming it behind me. "All good, mate." I held up my hands, and Jinx shook his head.

I must have fallen asleep in my dorm, because the next thing I knew, there was a knock on my door, waking me and bringing me to my feet. "I told you to stay away," I groaned while opening the door.

Then I was face to face with my love—Mia.

Her eyes went wide, and she took a step back.

223

"Dammit, Mia. I'm sorry."

"You didn't show up for dinner, I was worried,"—she raised a brow—"Maybe I should come back another time?"

"No, no, no," my arm snaked around her waist, and I pulled her into me, "Don't go." I inhaled her, and her scent instantly brought me back from whatever nightmare I got sucked into.

Before I had a chance to close the door, an ear-piercing scream rang through the wing.

I peeked my head through the door, and a girl ran from the bathroom near the end of the corridor.

"What's going on?" Mia asked, turning to see outside the door.

I shook my head. "I'm not sure," I turned my attention back to Mia, "Stay here. Don't leave this room."

She nodded, and I took off down the hall.

The girl shook on the floor against the wall as she stifled her cries with her hands.

"What happened?" I asked as people formed a circle around us.

The girl pointed her thumb back toward the bathroom, unable to speak anything coherent. I pushed open the bathroom door, and I froze.

Hanging from the ceiling with a makeshift noose around the neck was Chad. Face blue, eyes wide open, and feet dangling. My stomach rolled, and I took a step back when someone caught my balance. I snapped my head around to see Scott standing behind me with his hand on my shoulder.

I fisted his shirt. "Where were you?" I screamed and threw him against the wall. His eyes darted back and forth between Chad and me. "You're supposed to be watching them! Where the hell were you? How could you let this happen?"

"Calm down. I was—"

"You were what?" I shoved him into the wall again as tears pricked my eyes. "This place is filled with people ready to take their own lives. You're supposed to be looking out for them!"

Scott shoved his palms into my chest. "I can't be everywhere at all times! Now calm the fuck down, I have to call this in."

He put his palms up before reaching for the radio on his belt, and I ran my nervous hands through my hair as Mia's voice sounded through the cracked door. "Ollie?"

"No, Mia," I struggled to say, choking on emotion and took long strides to stop her. "You can't come in here." Slipping through the door, I blocked anyone from entering. I flew my hands over my face and dragged them back through my hair. Fighting. Battling. Struggling. A constant brawl raged inside me. The image of what was on the other side of the door seared into my mind. I curled my arm over my face, and Mia enveloped me immediately. Her warm hand slipped up the front of my shirt and to my chest as she held me close. My heart slammed against her hand, and I dropped my head over her shoulder.

"I can't handle it," I whispered as the sickness stirred inside me and a burn punctured my eyes. "It's too much."

"Let's go back to your room," she whispered.

I moved my head side to side against her. "Not until the police get here."

She never asked questions, only stood with me, trying to comfort me the only way she knew how, and it was more than enough. When I'd reached the point of finally being able to breathe normally, I pulled the hood over my head and locked eyes on her. She'd always been that one person to quiet the turmoil seething in my heart when the surroundings got to be too much.

She was my center. My home.

NINETEEN

"You're a thief in the night,
robbing my gaze,
swiping my hand,
stripping my breath,
cheating the odds,
stealing my heart,
and I don't mind."

OLIVER MASTERS

Mia

It took a little over two weeks to find our rhythm after the death of Chad, a boy I'd never known personally. Ollie hadn't known him well either, but he explained the impact of Chad's death on him. He'd said seeing Chad hit him like an atomic bomb of one hundred grieving people. Even Chad himself, feeling the emotions of his last moments closing in on him, and Ollie's heart unable to contain it. I didn't fully understand it myself, but the look in his eyes was that of a million broken hearts. The single moment had utterly drained him, and for a week Ollie ran on empty. It had been heart-wrenching to witness, how someone else's pain could physically affect him in the way it did.

It was a cold mid-November afternoon, and I sat in Conway's office wrapped in Ollie's oversized hoodie. His familiar scent fought against the bitter winter and Conway's unwanted opinion.

"You are capable of so much more than to skip out on college," Dr. Conway said through a shake of her head, and spun in her chair to face her desk. My teeth sunk into the plastic end of the hoodie string and I rolled my eyes. "You're a genius. And you're throwing it all away. Why?"

"I don't have to explain myself," I mumbled, annoyed with the conversation. My head was overflowing with current events—*the prankster, Bruce, Ollie, Ethan*—leaving no room to think about the future. At one point, I was sure I'd been destined to help victims of sexual assault, but the prankster had taken that away from me the second he revealed my journal and showed everyone I couldn't be trusted. Maybe I was never cut out for it.

Empathy had never been my strong suit, so perhaps he did me a favor.

Conway narrowed her eyes, reading my body language because she couldn't understand the words coming out of my mouth. "Do me a favor, Mia. Take a walk around campus tomorrow. By yourself. Fresh air and no distraction. Give your future an hour of your time to think this through before you make a drastic decision. It deserves that much, okay?"

The string fell from my mouth. "Okay."

Sales trick *one-oh-one*: leave the question ending in *"Okay?" "All right?"* or *"Sounds good?"* and nine times out of ten your audience would reply with a positive response, automatically agreeing to whatever they said without thinking it through. A trick of the mind.

She got me.

Fuck.

I quickly came to terms with it and stood from the couch.

"See you next week," Conway said through a knowing smile as I headed for the door. "Oh, and Mia?" Resting my palm over the door frame, I turned to face her. "I still cook for Thanksgiving. I'll bring leftovers, and we can have a mini Thanksgiving during our session Thanksgiving Day, sound good?"

"Sounds good."

Shit. She got me again.

I chuckled to myself. "You're good, Dr. Conway," I called out while walking away.

"I know," she reminded me from behind.

It was difficult to dislike Dr. Conway. Since day one, she'd grown on me. Even when I'd thought I doubted her and couldn't trust her, she'd proved she truly cared, being the only acting parental figure who pushed my limits and had been there every step of the way. I was going to miss her.

On my way back to fourth wing, Jake, Tyler, and Bria blew past me with cringed expressions. Well, except for Jake. His eyes betrayed his disgusted look, and I knew he missed me. But around Tyler and Bria, he wouldn't dare defy his loyalty. I had to get him alone and talk to him.

I knocked on Ollie's door before opening and found him asleep in his bed with a book sprawled out over his stomach. Gently, I lifted the book and set it aside before melting beside him. Ollie hummed, wrapping his arms around me, burrowing his head into my neck.

I dove my hand under his shirt and trailed my fingers over the surface of his warm skin.

"Conway give you the third degree again?" he asked, his breath brushing my neck.

Goosebumps flared, and I leaned into him with a small laugh. "Always."

"She's right, you know ..."—his arm pulled me closer— "You can become anything you want, and you choose to do nothing. It's a waste if you ask me."

"Wonderful. You too?"

Ollie pulled away and opened his sleepy eyes. "No. Conway has different reasons, then I do. Me? I believe everyone is sent to earth with a purpose." He wiped a hand over his eyes. "What interests you, love?"

"I'm not so sure anymore."

"Your body tells you every day of what you're meant for. Any time you get goosebumps, never ignore them. Your body reminds you to take notice in case your brain doesn't get the message."

"So, I'm meant for you? I wonder what major that falls under."

His smile grew. "Give me your hand." I lifted from under the thin sheet and held it out in front of me. Ollie's hand disappeared from my waist. His fingertips touched mine and continued to trace down the length of my palm. Shivers rushed through me, and Ollie smiled. "You feel that?" I bit my lip and nodded. His fingers continued, merely brushing over mine, but the faintness alone sent the small hairs standing straight. "It will feel like this, and you will know it's what you're meant for. Don't ever question it."

"Is that how you feel about writing?"

Ollie's fingers laced through mine and he brought our hands close to his chest. "Yes. I feel that way when I write, and I feel that way when you're near. Even when the demons take me, my soul always remembers." His lips landed over my forehead, and he lingered there for a moment before he pulled away. "but you never felt that way about playing the piano, have you?"

I shook my head. "How did you know?"

"Because if you did, you'd be playing all the time."

"I guess I'm just not cut out for this life."

"Or maybe you need to see things from a different perspective." Ollie's boyish grin returned, and his mischievous eyes bounced between mine. "I got you something. It's under the bed." I opened my mouth to speak, but my tongue wouldn't work. "Go on." He nudged his head.

I flipped the other way, reached under the bed, and waved my hand around until it grabbed hold of something. When I pulled it out, I laid back and took a look at it.

A camera.

And not your average camera.

A machine of some sort I had no idea how to use. "Ollie?"

"Another perspective, love. It may help you see the world a little differently."

I sat up and crawled over him, pulling the camera over my face to look through the lens. "Nope. You're just as beautiful, but I prefer the real thing. And how in the world did you find this?"

Ollie's hands clutched my hips, and his eyes beamed up at me. "You're smiling. You like it."

"How, Ollie?"

"I asked a friend." His head tilted into his shrug. "It doesn't matter. Come here, let's take our first picture, yeah?" His fingers dug into my hips, and I curled over, severely ticklish and falling on top of him. Ollie grabbed the camera from my hands and held it above our heads, snapping the picture before I had a chance to be ready for it.

When I looked back up, the film came from the top and Ollie dropped the camera beside him on the mattress and held the picture over us. We both looked up, waiting. "You didn't let me get ready."

"Ready? You mean a fake smile? No. I had to get the real one." He fanned the film, and the picture came into focus. "You see there?" The picture showed my head over Ollie's chest with a cheesy smile plastered on my face as he looked down on me. "Breathtaking."

"Black and white?"

He shook his head. "There's enough color between us, don't you think?"

"Yeah," I said through an exhale as I looked up in awe at the first photo we'd ever taken.

"I'm keeping this one." He stuffed the picture under his pillow and turned to face me. "The rest is yours. Take as many pictures as you want, I have a box of film at your disposal. See if you can find inspiration somewhere."

After taking a few more pictures, reading a few chapters, and spending the afternoon being lazy in bed like we always seemed to love, Ollie and I walked through the mess hall together and headed straight for the dinner line.

We carried on with our routine, saying goodbye to Zeke and headed for the bathroom early before the rush. The silent battle to see who could brush their teeth the longest was in full effect, and we both spit into the sink at the same time. I hopped up over the sink and took a seat as he turned the water on, both of us moving in sync.

Slowly, students made their way into the bathroom as I sat facing Ollie's shower stall.

Ethan appeared beside the wall. His expression exhausted and locked eyes with mine. We hadn't spoken much since I left solitary, and I wondered where he slept or if he slept at all anymore.

"We need to talk," Jake said, appearing out of nowhere.

I glanced back at Ollie's stall. "What is there to talk about? You completely shut me out over something you know I didn't do."

"I know. I'm starting to realize that now. Bria is a fucking bitch. I can't stand her anymore."

"Let me get this straight …" I snapped my head in his direction. "You and Bria are going through some girly tiff, and now you have no one? Your sudden need to want to talk is beginning to make more sense."

Jake rolled his eyes and leaned into the counter. "Don't be like that. I miss you, okay? I know you didn't mean for that to happen. I know someone is messing with you and has been since the year started. But, come on, Mia. You wrote my secrets down in a journal. Those weren't yours to write. They were mine. Now Liam won't even talk to me." He crossed his arms over his chest and looked out in front of him. "Not only did I lose Liam, but I lost you, too."

I dropped my chin to my chest and crossed my legs that had been dangling off the counter. "We're cool. Let's forget it happened."

"Thank fuck," Jake muttered through an exhale. "This whole polygamist relationship those three have going is downright disgusting. Jude is a nice guy, don't get me wrong, but having to watch the three of them smash grosses me the fuck out."

"You got a mouth on you now." I chuckled, and Ollie opened the curtain, stepping out of the stall in nothing but his boxers and a towel in his hands.

Ollie's eyes slid between Jake and me. "Everything good now?"

"Was this your doing?" I asked with a raised brow.

"No ... not at all." He walked up to the sink beside me with a smile that didn't match his words.

"I was the one who went to Ollie. I had to know where we stood," Jake said in a hurry.

"It's fine. I'm glad you did. I missed you too." I waved Jake over and wrapped my arms around him. "And I'm sorry about Liam, but he'll come around." Ollie and Jake shook hands, and my attention drifted over to two girls eyeing Ollie. I leaned over and snatched his clean pair of joggers and threw it into Ollie's chest. "Get dressed."

Ollie let out a small laugh and looked past Jake to see two freshmen ready to devour him. His green eyes hit mine as he raised a brow and pushed his legs into his joggers.

"They want to lick you all over," Jake sang, "and over again."

If anyone was licking him all over, it would be me. Ollie and I hadn't had sex since he'd fucked me and left me hanging in my dorm room. We'd had numerous opportunities, but Ollie had said he wasn't ready for lovemaking yet.

And Ollie could take all the time he needed. I'd wait for as long as it took.

Ollie shook his head and took a step forward, filling the space between my knees. "Never allow it to bother you," he whispered.

"I don't like the fantasies probably running through their heads right now," I confessed.

Ollie's eyes darted between mine, and his fingers gripped my waist while his other hand grabbed at the nape of my neck. Wet lips and a rush of mint slammed into me, and Ollie kissed me slowly, brushing his tongue against mine and sending flurries through a hot summer day. *Fire and ice.* His hand moved to the base of my neck and up to my jawline before he pulled away. "There," he licked his lips, "That should ruin their fantasies."

He winked, and I playfully shoved him off me as we shared a laugh.

Jake whistled. "Bloody hell, you two didn't miss a beat,"—He fanned his face with his hand— "Pretty sure the entire room felt that one."

My cheeks heated and Ollie pulled his shirt over his head before pulling me off the counter and landing a kiss over my head.

Things were finally going back to normal.

Ollie

My lashes parted to see Scott standing over me in the dark with his arms crossed over his chest, and I jumped up from my bed. "Jesus Christ, Scott," I muttered.

"It's Mia."

My feet landed on the cold hard ground, and I shoved past him, heading straight to Mia's dorm. It was annoying how Scott wouldn't just let her sleep with me at night. Instead, he'd come and wake me only on nights Mia got sucked into the terrors. I'd rather her not get sucked in at all and sleep beside me where she belonged. The weight of Dolor was growing heavier by the second. Only five fucking months left until release day.

The door closed behind me, and Mia laid drenched in a cold sweat. Wayward strands stuck to the side of her face as she moved back and forth, crying in her sleep. I pulled the sheet up to see her in her usual white tank and panties—her skin glistening and her lips trembling. "Ollie," she called out through her terror with her eyes screwed tight.

"Mia, you have to wake up." I pushed the strands from her face and swiftly rolled her over to the side as I continued to chant her name.

Mia's lashes fluttered, then her eyes opened meeting mine. "Ollie?"

"I'm right here."

"I couldn't reach you," she uttered.

My eyebrows pulled together. "What do you mean?"

"I heard you. I heard your voice. But I couldn't see or touch you. You were talking to me in my head. It was dark. I was falling really, really fast and everything was closing in on top of me. Like being buried. I couldn't breathe."

"It's gone now."

"It's the same dream over and over. And I'm stuck, and I can't get out!" Tears sprang in her worried eyes, and fear had her in its death-grip as her body shook. It had been the first time she was able to remember. But now it all made sense.

My love's brilliant mind played tricks on her, forcing her back to the girl she used to be—the girl who lacked emotion and was numb to it all. And it was all my fault.

"Look at me." Her eyes snapped to mine, and I grabbed her hand and placed it over my chest. "You feel that? This is real. Whatever's got a hold of you in here," I tapped her head, "it's working really hard to turn that fucking switch again. But I have a hold on you too, and I'm never letting go."

She let out a substantial and extended breath, the anxiety leaving along with it before she curled into me. I dragged my fingers through her hair, knowing it wouldn't be long before the shithead Scott came in to pull me back to my room. "Don't go," she whispered through the darkness. "I don't want you to go. Not tonight."

The last bloody thing I wanted right now was to leave her. She finally remembered, and knowing Mia, she'd be up all night without an ounce of sleep, replaying her terror over and over again. "I'll be right back. Let me go talk to the wanker."

Back on my feet, I walked to the door and poked my head through. "I'm staying."

Scott's brows dipped. "No."

"She fucking remembers. I'm not leaving her alone. I'm staying."

Scott pulled me from the door and slammed me against the wall. The sound echoed down the dark hallway, and I pushed him off me. "You're going to ruin everything," he seethed.

"Ruin what? Give it up, Scott. It will never happen between the two of you."

Scott turned his head down the hall and chuckled under his breath. "That's not what I'm fucking talking about."

"What is it then?"

The red-head took a step back and silence fell between us.

"Just go then," he stated with his arms in the air. "This is on you two."

Without wasting another second away from her, the door closed behind me, and I slipped out of my clothes, went back to her side, and peeled off her tank. I hooked my fingers at the sides of her panties, taking those off too.

Both completely stripped bare, her breasts pressed against my chest and we pieced back together— heart to heart, limbs entangled— with my throbbing knob against her heat. "Go to sleep now," I whispered as my fingers kneaded along the muscles of her back. "I have you."

Her breathing steadied as my fingers moved along her thigh and pulled her leg over mine, massaging and annihilating all the fear built up inside her, until finally, she drifted back to sleep.

TWENTY

"Make love to her like you mean it."

OLIVER MASTERS

Mia

I'd kidnapped Ollie and Zeke and escaped to the group therapy room to get away from the dark cloud that always hovered over the school. It had been months since I'd played the piano, and for once, both Ollie and Zeke needed a lighter day. The sun decided to show its beautiful rays, but the lawn was littered with students.

Ollie and I had both learned that crowds affected him emotionally as well, so this space had been the perfect answer. It was fascinating, learning about this beautiful man. He gave and gave, but all everyone else ever did was take from him—most without them ever knowing.

I looked up from the piano and caught Zeke staring back at me in awe. He loved music. He sat relaxed, big brown eyes remained fixed on me, and I flashed him a small smile as my fingers danced fluently across the keys, speaking in a way he connected with. Music had no language barriers.

My gaze switched to Ollie as my fingers took on a new melody, a song I'd heard once before, but had never fully understood the meaning before until now.

Now? It hit me in the gut, flamed my heart, and ignited my soul.

Firestone.

Ollie sat in the black folding chair by the window with his notepad in his lap, pen in hand, and feet propped over another chair. The hood had disappeared, and his messy brown hair lacked ruling, strands falling into his eyes. His focus coasted over his paper to me, and our eyes connected. My heart rate slowed to heavy and hard single hits. My chest held despite my fingers having a mind of their own. His fingers relaxed, and the pen he had been holding fell over his notepad. Beats of the moment, of the song, played out our sacred moment.

Ollie's expression calmed, but his eyes were haunting and all-expressive.

I let out a breath, my brain finally kicking back in, and I flashed him a smile and shook my head. Ollie dropped his head, but the closed-lipped smile appeared before he looked back up and his smile grew, his eyes drifting from Zeke and back to me.

He felt the impact too.

Zeke rose to his feet and walked toward me as I finished up the last chords of Firestone. Reluctantly, he eyed the space beside me. I inched over, making space for him and pat the area with my palm. "I'll teach you."

Zeke wasn't deaf, only a mute, and this was the first time he was interested in learning. I'd asked him numerous times over the summer, but his only response before was a rapid head shake and a wave of his hand.

With two fingers, I played a simple pattern on the left side of the keys, hoping he'd repeat on the right. Zeke floated his two pointer fingers over the keys. As soon as the second finger pressed down, the wrong key sounded, and he snatched his hand away.

"It's fine. I mess up all the time." Straightening my posture, I drew in a deep breath, forcing him to copy, and repeated the same pattern over the keys.

Zeke copied my movements, completing the pattern the second time with ease, but missing in rhythm. I'd come to realize there were two types of musicians in this world—those who could play by ear, and those who played by instruction. Zeke was an instruction learner, and there was absolutely nothing wrong with that. As long as the heart, passion, and drive was there, the flow would come with time.

"Okay, we're going to play a song. You keep doing that pattern and don't stop. I'm going to play the second part over here," I informed as Zeke continued. I glanced up toward Ollie who sat relaxed in his chair with eyes hooked on the two of us. Ollie's smile beamed, his eyes glowing, and I returned my attention back to Zeke before playing the second part of the song.

Zeke stayed focus, facing the keys with his fingers straight, keeping up with the rhythm. My new string of notes didn't disturb him.

"Yes!" I encouraged, continuing the first song I ever learned on the piano. I'd never thought Zeke would get to this point. It was a giant step for him, and I couldn't wipe the smile off my face as I watched him concentrating hard on the song I'd taught him.

After three more repetitions, I'd slowed, seeing if he could match my pace.

He did, and together we came to a stop.

Zeke turned to face me with a finger pressed firmly on the key with a glowing smile over his innocent features.

I wanted to hug him, or at the very least pat him on the shoulder so he'd understand the monumental moment we'd shared—the beginning of something new we'd uncovered. But I couldn't risk it, unsure of his reaction with me touching him. The smile across his face was enough to know he understood.

"You did it, mate," Ollie stated, grabbing both of our attention as he stepped in front of the piano. His palms hit the top of the piano as he leaned over. "Now get out of here." He nudged his head toward the door with a permanent smile. "I need to be alone with my love." Brown curls bounced as Zeke glanced back at me, his smile uncertain, and his eyes darted. "Go on. It's alright."

Zeke scurried out, and Ollie kept eyes locked on mine until the door closed. The single sound influenced his feet forward.

Ollie moved around the piano, then threw his leg over the bench, straddling to face me. "Ollie," I whispered. The closeness between us seized every word from my brain.

"Play again for me," he requested, hardly above a whisper. "Firestone." Ollie's smile took hold of me and his dimples deepened. It seemed like forever since I'd seen them. "Play," he encouraged again, looking off and his face beamed. Green eyes flitted back to mine, and he tilted his head. "Please."

I let out a breath and returned my eyes in front of me, unsure how I was going to play now when all my hands wanted to do was leave the keys and be on him.

I gathered all self-control, and my shaken fingers trailed over the keys to the beginning of the song. Ollie's eyes anchored me, becoming the gravity holding us together in our bubble as my heart fluttered in my chest. I knew if my eyes chanced a look at him, I wouldn't be able to keep up with the song. So, my gaze remained fixed out in front of me while I reminded myself to breathe.

The sun filtered through the opened blinds of the large window across the shadowy room. Halfway through the chorus, Ollie's hand moved over mine to stop the song and pulled me up from the chair. The room fell silent, his arms wrapped around my shoulders to pull me against him, and he closed his eyes.

"Where are you always escaping to?" I asked, lifting my head and holding on to his hips.

Ollie smoothed his hands over my hair and opened his eyes. "You. Your music. Us. We deserve better than to be in this place, wouldn't you say?" His eyes scanned the room before returning to me. "You hear that, Mia?" I shook my head, and Ollie closed his eyes. "Firestone," he said through an exhale. He swayed us slowly back and forth with a song in his head and us dancing somewhere other than a poorly lit room of a reformatory school. "Where do you want to go, love?"

I smiled. "All the way."

Ollie's pulse in his neck kicked. Green eyes transformed right before me, turning into a lighter shade. Defenseless. Naked. Vulnerable. He wet his lips and dropped his gaze to my mouth, and our movements came to a standstill. His fingers smoothed over my hair, dropping my head back in their wake to face him.

He lowered his head and grabbed my lip between his while his hands grazed up my neck and cupped my head. His touch, his lips, his mint taste—it all sedated and quenched me at once. The room spun as he pulled away and rested his forehead to mine to keep us in place.

And suddenly I was picked up at the thighs and walked over to the base of the piano, and left standing there. Ollie jogged across the room and locked the door, and on his way back, he took long strides as his erection strained against his joggers. He gripped his eager hard-on and stopped in his tracks. Taking a step back, he studied me as I grew needy.

"Ollie, come here." I took a step forward.

He shook his head. "Just stand right there, love. I just want to look at you."

With his eyes on me, my skin heated.

He let out a long exhale and took the few steps toward me and lifted me over the piano.

The amount of restraint he contained remained a mystery when all I needed was to be connected with him again. It was no secret we both remembered the way he'd fucked me, and the regret coursed through his actions and stained his soul.

"I'm afraid," he confessed in my ear while his hips leaned between my legs. "I'm going to fall apart."

Ollie had explained once before how our sex made him feel. When we collided, the moment shook him to the core, licked his wounds, and the wave of emotions he experienced was colossal—my Ollie.

The first time we'd ever made love, after going through all of that, I'd closed him off in his most vulnerable state. The second time, he'd broken down in the bathroom in the shower stall. It had taken time for Ollie to build up enough trust with me to know I wasn't going anywhere. And then he had slipped, and we had to start over. When we made love in the library, he'd cried in my arms. Then after that, fucked me in my dorm. Ollie had every right to feel afraid.

"Fall apart so we can fall in place, together," I reassured him.

His eyes snatched mine as he ran his hands up my thighs. I kicked off my shoes. He yanked off my jeans. I tugged down his pants. He removed his shirt before my own. I unlatched my bra, and It had all happened so fast until our bodies crashed.

Then we slowed.

Lips made with precision traced my jawline as my center ached, but Ollie took his time while his arousal pressed against me. His hands grabbed my bottom, pulling me to the edge. Every touch and kiss remained gentle, slow, and long-lasting, drifting down my neck and to my breasts.

My back curved into him as he blessed both of my nipples before moving down. Though I was ready, he'd always took his time and tasted every surface. His hand pushed me backward until my back met the cold piano. My breath hitched when his warm lips kissed over my pelvis, sensual and heavy. My heart lost control when his hands wrapped around my sex and massaged me apart. My hips curled into his mouth when deep full strokes of his tongue trudged through my center before his lips covered my clit.

Gentle thrusts of his tongue drove me mad and closer, and my breath held as he pulled away. His arm snaked around my back as he lifted me until I was against him, needing the closeness as his thick head pressed against my entrance. I wrapped my arm around his neck, and his fingertips crept along the sensitive skin, down my arm and side, before gripping my thigh.

Our eyes latched onto one another, and then he drove himself inside me.

It wasn't until we were connected entirely did our mouths fall in line. Ollie's tongue slipped inside as he kissed me unhurriedly, grinding so slow and torturously while his thumb pressed firmly over my clit.

Ollie fell apart. I fell apart.

But we fell together.

Hard.

"I love you," his voice shook through our kiss, and his hand wrapped around the back of my head to keep me together from turning into liquid. "Consuming, timeless, unselfish, love. I'd loved you in my darkest hour when I wasn't myself, and I'll love you in every lifetime after this." My body shook under his utter honesty—never holding back, leaving himself exposed in such a raw state.

"Ollie ..." I started to say.

"I know, Mia," he stopped me, unable to contain my response. "I know."

And our mouths slammed once more, and his cock throbbed against my walls. His palms landed over my thighs, and his fingers dragged across my skin as he came closer. I wrapped my legs around him as he stroked deeply inside me and my sex clenched around him on edge, ready to break—a perfect rapture bursting at the seams.

It wasn't until I let go when he chased my climax and held our kiss. Our bodies slick against one another and are hearts on fire, Ollie reached that holy feeling, and a single tear rolled down his cheek.

"Marry me, Mia," he said breathlessly. "I had it all planned out, but what better time than right now? Look at us. Stripped down as one. Bare and bound to one another, just made sweet love. Bloody hell, I'm still going, and I can't believe I'm able to speak right now … fuck … marry me."

"Yes."

"I'd been certain since my heart found yours, and I thought the moment had to be perfect. But this is so perfect—"

"Ollie," I let out a small laugh, "I said yes."

"Yeah?"

I nodded.

He grabbed my head and pulled me toward him for another kiss, smiles never leaving either one of us.

"Mia, I'm literally shaking," Ollie said through a laugh and pulled my hand to his heart. "Fuck. I can't imagine anyone as happy as you just made me right now." He let out a heavy and shaky exhale.

Sunday morning, I awoke with a smile and Ollie by my side. Ollie had convinced Ethan to let him sleep in my dorm, and relief set in knowing I'd never have to sleep through a night terror alone again.

Hopefully.

But if there was one thing I'd learned, anything could change like a flip of a switch … No pun intended.

"You don't need a shower," Ollie groaned, voice thick and husky and eyes still closed. "You smell amazing."

A light laugh left me. "You don't have to come. I'll be fine. Just go back to sleep, and I'll be right back." The sun hadn't come out yet—the dorm in complete darkness—and I gathered my things into my arms. He knew I preferred morning showers, and on most days, he'd join me. But we had been celebrating through the night, and he was exhausted from not getting any sleep the night before.

The hallway was empty. Ethan must have had the night off at home. I padded down the dark hall and toward the bathroom. Mindlessly, I went through my morning routine, flipped the light switch, turned on the shower, and stared at my own reflection, looking for changes.

I was someone's fiancé, and not just anyone's. I was Ollie's. My face smiled back at me, and I dropped my chin before pushing off the counter, remembering the days I'd never imagined getting married to anyone and how the most significant changes were happening inside of me.

After two minutes of being under the shower, the entire bathroom went into complete darkness.

"Hello?" I called out.

The only sound in return was the shower pouring overhead.

I reached my hand out in front of me, unable to see anything.

Then a loud smash pierced the room as the sound of glass falling to the floor followed close behind.

My entire body froze until a second mirror broke. I curled in the corner of the shower stall, wanting to scream, but nothing could escape me.

All I saw was darkness around me.

All I heard was the crunching of glass under footsteps.

Then the sound of my curtain against its rod whipped through the eeriness.

Two gloved hands grabbed me from the corner and yanked me from the stall.

I fought against them but was unable to get a solid grip. I reached out to grab their face, but it was covered. I tried to find hair to pull, but a hood was over their head. My bare feet slid along the glass, and jagged edges sliced through my skin. Water dripped from my hair, falling to the floor, and mixed with blood and glass.

The figure pushed me back across the floor; my healing wounds broke once again. Fear gripped me as I fought against them, crying out for help. I screamed until my throat burned and all the air left my lungs. Hands yanked my ankles, pulling me through the glass until something hard struck my head.

I went limp for a moment when all I wanted to do was fight. I had no control over my limbs. A hand fisted my wet hair and dragged me across the slick floor until my back was against a wall. They said nothing as tears rolled down my cheeks. My cries came out as whispered pleas, and I was afraid to move. Each time I tried to lift myself against the tile, the pain of the glass cut deeper.

And then they took a piece of glass to my thigh. It burned, and I screamed out from the excruciating pain until another blow to the head silenced me.

"Please, Jude," I begged. "Please stop this."

The silent figure moved the glass up to my center, and before they could slice another part of me, I pushed them onto their back. I tried to stand to run, but they were faster.

My head slammed back against the tile, and I spiraled through the blackness.

Cold air surrounded me as I floated. A light beamed overhead behind my eyelids, merely warming me, though not completely. For a split second, it was beautiful—until my consciousness kicked back, and the pain replaced the peace.

Death would've been easier, but the agony in Ollie's cries never would've made it worth it. "Mia! Someone fucking talk to me!" he screamed out. My eyes shot open to see a crowd of unfamiliar faces staring straight ahead. I tried to get up when someone pushed my shoulders back down. Ethan appeared out of nowhere, taking my hand into his at my side as I was wheeled across Dolor grounds. Ollie's frantic voice drifted through the morning chill. I couldn't see his face, but the sound of his voice caused what was left of my soul to rip into fragments, small enough to be carried away by the wind.

"She's losing too much blood," one of them said. Big brown eyes peered down at me. "You have to stay with us, darling. You have to stay awake."

"Ethan, go with her," another male's voice stated as Ethan's face expressed nothing to my left, his hand gripping mine tightly, showing more than his eyes could say.

"Get off me!" Ollie screamed. "Mia!"

The doors to the ambulance closed. I opened my mouth to speak, but my throat was thick, and my brain cloudy.

Ethan pulled my hand over his lap as he took a seat, eyes locked on mine, jaw tensing.

TWENTY-ONE

"Let's runaway with freedom in our eyes,
to a place measured in rapture,
and clocks a sign of the times.
We could chase the moon, outrun the sun.
No cages to keep us hostage, only bound by love.
Let's catch fire and dance in the wind.
Forget this fucking place,
let's just ...
r u n a w a y ..."

OLIVER MASTERS

Ollie

My heart hit rock bottom, and my chest caved. A shattered cry ripped through my throat as I fought against the two who held me back from her.

Jerry and Jinx finally released me as the ambulance rolled away, and I charged toward Lynch whose stance faced the descending bus with Mia inside.

"Lynch!" I shoved him from behind with both hands. "You have to let me go!" Lynch stumbled forward but refused to turn around and face me. Seconds later, Jerry and Jinx's hands wrapped around my biceps to keep me back. "Look at me, you sorry fuck!"

Lynch turned around slowly, his face pale and eyes reeked of guilt.

We stared at one another.

My vision clouded and my chest heaved. A scorching ache lived inside, making it difficult to breathe. "You have to let me go to her," I pleaded, and snatched my arms from the two blokes. Taking a step forward, a blast of November morning wind swirled around us, and I should have been cold—no shirt, no shoes—only the joggers with Mia's blood soaked through and smeared over my skin. "Please," I begged. "She's my fiancé."

My blood-covered hands shook at my sides as I stood there waiting. Every second felt like an eternity in these tears. If I had to wait any longer for a response, I was scared of what I could be capable of doing to him, to all of them, to get to her. Demented thoughts tangled its dirty fingers inside me, wanting to break me.

But Lynch was afraid to speak. He was too afraid to do anything, hadn't bloody moved at all. Paralyzed. "You care about her," I managed to get out. "You fucking care about her!"

Lynch's wide brown eyes locked on mine, and all I saw in them was Mia.

Suddenly, it hit me.

All at once, everything became clear, and I shook my head. "No, that can't be right …" I mumbled to myself, pushing my fingers through my hair and down my face. I had to be losing it.

"Not another word," Lynch said through gritted teeth. "Go get dressed. Five minutes. You're coming with me."

I turned to Jerry. He was about the same build, only a few inches taller. "Give me your shirt and shoes."

Jerry laughed and took a step back. "Bugger off."

"Here," Jinx said as he worked on the buttons of his uniform. "I'm a big guy, but I don't think you care." His uniform dropped to the ground, and he peeled off his under shirt and tossed it over to me. Next went his shoes.

"Thanks, mate. You're a good man, I owe you one," I said, sliding the second shoe on then turned to Lynch. "Let's go."

Lynch never cuffed me, and the ride to the hospital was tormenting. Visions of Mia lying on the floor covered in glass and blood filtered through my mind on non-stop replay.

She hadn't left longer than ten minutes before a sickness crept inside me, and I'd known something hadn't been right. Oxygen had been sucked from the space around me, and walking to the community bathroom turned into a struggle in itself. All my senses had known the worst, but my heart hung on to the glimmer of hope as I'd pushed that door open.

And there she had been, my little explosion of hope.

It was as if a part of me left my body, running to her as the rest of me, the weak part, stood fucking frozen and unable to comprehend the scene laid out before me. I remembered crying out before my feet registered, treading through the glass, only caring about getting to her.

At this moment, I still didn't feel the glass embedded in my feet.

The only thing I felt was the ache in my chest.

I looked out before me in a daze as the city passed us by. Closing my eyes became impossible when it was all I wanted to do. The fog of fear trapped me.

"Oliver?" Lynch's tone came out harsh and loud, pulling me out of the daze. I didn't bother meeting his gaze as he whipped through winding roads to the hospital. "How did you know?"

It didn't matter.

Lynch exhaled and rubbed his palm over his balding head before returning it over the wheel, and his thumb tapped to whatever mantra repeated in his head. "She can't know. You can't tell her," he continued.

I remained silent for a moment, neither confirming or denying I'd keep his secret. I'd do whatever was best for Mia.

"Your eyes," my voice came out low and quiet. "She has your eyes."

My lips sucked in, and I was finally able to close my own eyes.

Mia had to be okay. She had to be okay.

"We're here," Lynch stated and the car whipped into a space in the car park. Before the gear moved to park, I was already out and running to the entrance. Nothing moved fast enough. Even the air and blood pumping through me couldn't keep up with my racing thoughts and stride.

"Mia Rose Jett." My bloody hands trembled over the desk as the receptionist looked up in horror. "What room?"

"Sir, you need to si—"

My fist slammed against the desk. "What room?"

People walked all around me. The energy from the crowd ricocheted off me, not able to touch me. Nothing could touch me.

"Are you family?" she asked with a raise of her testing brow.

The sudden hand on my shoulder was Lynch's as he took over the conversation. "Jett is a patient of mine. I need an update on her status."

My jaw tensed, and I shrugged his arm off me and broke out into a run through the double swinging doors. My eyes hit every inch of the place as I walked in circles, gripping my hair and my eyes burning from trying to keep it together for Mia. She had to be okay.

"Mia Jett?" I asked as a nurse passed by with her head down, and I stepped out in front of her. "Please, what room?"

Her attention landed on me. Her gaze roamed over me, studying me and judging me, then turned to her clipboard in her hands. "Umm ... Jett? Uh ... Mia, Mia, Mia ... Ah there," she looked back at me. She's in the OR. You can wait with the officer in the waiting area until she's released."

Her finger pointed behind me, and I turned my head back to see Scott behind a glass wall in a closed-off room down the hall, pacing in circles.

I looked back in front of me, and the girl disappeared.

"Bloody hell," Scott's words rushed out as soon as I made my way inside the far too tiny room, not nearly big enough to hold the tension and worry spilling out from the both of us. "How the fuck did you get here?"

Ignoring him, I took a seat and pushed my elbows into my knees to control the bouncing, rubbing my palms up and down my face. "How was she? In the ambulance? Have you heard anything?" I asked, lifting my head to meet his eyes just as Lynch walked through.

Everyone's gaze made the journey around the room before falling back on me. I jumped to my feet and gripped the ends of my hair to avoid finding their way to flesh, drywall, or glass. "How the fuck is she?"

Scott looked to Lynch again. "She passed out in the bus, lost too much blood," Scott shook his head with a tremor in his voice, "It's not looking good."

"She'll make it." *She had to.*

"And how are you so sure of everything? Mr. Glass-Half-Full, everything honky-dory," tears pricked his eyes, "And why is he here?" Scott turned to Lynch. "Why the fuck did you bring him? You will risk everything—"

"He knows," Lynch interrupted.

It turned quiet after that.

I couldn't sit still. The smell of the emergency department did nothing to ease the sickness eating away inside as I wordlessly prayed to any god who would listen to take care of my love. Every doctor, nurse, and worker who had walked by, I'd asked the same bloody question, and the only answer I'd received was the same: *"Her doctor will come to talk to the family as soon as they can."*

Milliseconds turned to minutes. Minutes turned to hours. I'd walked over every inch of the small room, sat in every chair, touched every surface of the glass wall. I'd prayed, cursed, and replayed that moment in my head over and over, condemning myself for letting her out of my sight.

"Mia?" A doctor announced, walking through the electric sliding door with her information in the palms of his hands.

I was the first to appear before him as the other two surrounded me. "She's okay?"

"She pulled through," the doctor said and exhales let go like a domino effect between the three of us. "Now …" his eyes darted between the three of us, "Who's family?"

"I am," Lynch and I said in unison. "I need to see her," I added through gritted teeth.

"She's being transferred to a room now, but the pain meds have her out cold at the moment. She probably won't wake for another hour or so. In the meantime, I have a few officers coming to take statements."

"Of course," Lynch breathed, dropping his tense shoulders and relief visible in his expression. Me? Not yet. Not until I saw her with my own eyes.

"What room?" I demanded.

The doctor looked up from Mia's file. "Excuse me?"

"What room is she in?"

For the first time, the doctor examined my wardrobe. His eyes fell to Jinx's shoes on my feet, up to the blood smeared across my arms, then down the front of the white tee hanging loosely around me.

I cleared my throat.

"It's best you stay here for the police to take your statement."

I narrowed my eyes and took a step forward. "I'm not doing shit until I see Mia."

"Oliver," Lynch warned with a hand over my shoulder. "What room?" he asked the doctor from behind me.

"Nine-sixty-four."

My shoulder bumped the doctors as I moved past him and jogged down the hall. The numbers beside each door declined, falling into the eight-hundreds, and I whipped around to run back the other way. Each step felt like a thousand-pound weight had been anchored around each ankle, not able to get there fast enough.

I'd reached the room and didn't slow down until I was face to face with Mia.

Tangled hair. Perfect lips. Twelve freckles.

My hand eagerly laced in hers by her side, and it was cold to the touch. Though the monitor showed a steady heartbeat, I dropped my head over her chest, needing to be reassured. The steady rhythm allowed me to breathe, and the moment that one long breath escaped, so did the tears. I held them for far too long, imprisoned and undeserving to relieve my heavy heart. "I'm so sorry …" I cried, kissing her cheek, her temple, her forehead, her nose. My thumb smoothed across her forehead. "Open your eyes, love. I need to see your eyes."

"Oh, she'll be out for a while," a nasally voice said, closing in from behind. I didn't bother turning around, knowing the casual tone could only come from someone who dealt with situations like this on an everyday basis. My entire being stayed focused on Mia, taking notice in the way her lashes fluttered under a dream coursing through her beautiful mind.

"How is her condition?" I finally asked now that I was able to feel, breathe, see Mia.

"Who are you to her?" the brave nurse asked, appearing at Mia's other side and looked over the information from the monitor. I gave her a hard look, trying to decide for myself how to answer. What answer would be good enough to reveal information? "Let me guess …" she continued, "boyfriend?" I turned my gaze back to Mia, emotions having a tight grip around my throat, and the burn returned behind my eyes. "She's in good hands," she finally said, trying to relieve the noticeable pressure.

I sucked in a breath and wet my lip. "Her condition?"

"Stable." The nurse's eyes wandered to the blood smeared over my ink. "You found her," she concluded with a nod. "You know, she's lucky you found her when you did. She could have easily bled out. You did the right thing by stopping the blood flow."

Air blew out of my nose as I shook my head, rubbing my thumb over Mia's.

"She could wake up soon. I'll be back in about an hour to check on her."

The nurse left as Lynch and Scott appeared in the doorway.

"I'm not leaving," I said without turning back to face them. "I have to be here when Mia wakes."

"The police are waiting for your statement," Lynch said as he drew nearer.

"Bring them in then. I'm not leaving her side."

Two sets of footsteps sounded. My eyes stayed locked on Mia.

The impatient click of a pen sounded.

Click. Click. Click.

I dragged a nearby chair closer to Mia's bedside, pulled her hand into my lap, and faced the men in uniform as my knee bounced.

"Name?" the older officer asked.

"Oliver Masters."

"Mr. Masters, can you tell us the events of this morning leading up to the time you found Ms. Jett."

My teeth clenched. "Mia always takes a shower as soon as the doors unlock at six. I felt something was off—"

"You felt?"

"Yes. I felt," I annunciated. I looked over at Mia, still sleeping soundlessly beside me. I squeezed her hand, pushing and pulling strength between us. "I went to check on her and …" My head dropped back, and I needed a second, "And the lights were out with the water still running. I flipped on the lights and found her."

"Was there anyone else in the bathroom?"

"No. She was alone." *I should have been there.*

"How would you describe your and Mia's relationship?"

I kept my eyes trained on the officer asking the question, but four sets of eyes burned a hole into me as both officers tried figuring me out, profiling me. "This is ridiculous. I could never hurt her. I *love* her."

"You attend Dolor Reformatory, for what crime?"

"Is this about me, or Mia?"

"It's a simple question."

"It's an irrelevant question." I looked over at Scott. "Did you ask him?" I asked with a head nudge. "Where were you when Mia was attacked?"

"We've already questioned Officer Scott," the officer stated, redirecting focus back onto me. "Have you ever physically hurt Mia?"

"Fuck no," I shook my head, unable to believe this was happening. "I would never fucking hurt her."

"It was reported Mia had bruises?"

My eyes jerked to Scott for the second time as my jaw clenched, a headache building.

"Ollie," Mia suddenly spoke at my side.

Jumping to my feet, I scanned over her. "I'm right here." Mia's eyes flitted open, and I used my hand as a shield over her eyes so she could adjust to the light. "Hi, love."

"Hi," she whispered.

Again, that single word engulfed me then broke me into a million pieces like it did every other time. I dropped my head into her neck, and her fingers combed through my hair.

I pulled away, and my blurry vision found her beautiful face. Mia's tiny hand brushed over my wet cheek, and she smiled. But then the smile faded, and she pinched her eyes together as pain carved into her features.

"Mia, if you're up for it, we'd like to ask you some questions," the officer stated.

I dropped my chin into my chest. "No. No more bloody questions."

Her hand squeezed mine and a misery-filled moan shot up her throat. "Ollie, it hurts."

My chin hit my shoulder as I looked back at the officers. "You two need to leave."

The controller for the bed fumbled in my hands before I pressed the button numerous times, ringing the nurse as their heavy boots descended from the room. Scott and Lynch walked outside the door to join them. Their small talk not so small, but the only thing I could focus on was freeing Mia from the pain. "I'm so sorry," I repeated over and over, wishing I could trade places with her. Wishing I had a way to make the pain disappear. I'd never felt so helpless and useless in my bloody life.

The same nurse returned and shot something into her IV.

"Don't go," Mia said to me, her brown eyes sliding between mine.

Shaking my head, I grabbed her hand and sucked in a breath. "I'm right here. I'm not going anywhere."

Seconds later, she was out.

TWENTY-TWO

*"There's a thin line between a win and loss,
the line being how you respond to it."*

OLIVER MASTERS

Mia

I threw my head back onto the pillow. "I didn't like that one."

Ollie looked up from the last chapter with a smirk. "And why not?"

I'd been at the hospital for four days now, and Lynch brought Ollie during each visit. Today was my last day here, and I'd talked to the cops this morning, told them what I knew. Also, confirmed Ollie had nothing to do with it.

The stab wound to my right thigh scraped an artery. After an operation, a blood transfusion, and the four days of being looked after, I was given the okay to head back to Dolor. The doctor had said I should have a full recovery, just needed to be on the lookout for infection.

"You know why," I said through an exhale. It wasn't the fact I didn't like unhappily ever after's in books, but it was because of this particular story. "It's stupid. If they are soulmates, why can't they be together?"

Ollie chuckled, dug his elbow into the mattress at my side, and dropped his head into the palm of his hand. "Do you believe in soulmates, Mia?" His brow quirked up, and his smile deepened. "Because from your reaction, it sounds like this book got to you, yeah?"

"In the story," I made clear, "If they were soulmates, then they should be together. Isn't it … like … a law or something?"

"There are no laws in love. In this particular story, they were not meant to be together in this lifetime. Their sole purpose in this story was self-discovery. To accomplish a journey apart from each other and grow as individuals. When the time is right, possibly even lifetimes away, they will reunite and become one again for eternity. But first, they have to find themselves."

"They were lost."

"Yes, but only because they aren't together."

"You're confusing me."

Ollie made a fist with his hand. "Think of it like this. When we're created, we're a single entity, all inside the infinite light. Most call the infinite light, 'God,' yeah?"

"Yup."

"Okay, so the spark is the first time the soul splits from the infinite light," Ollie's fist changed into his pointer and middle finger crossed together, "A soul on a mission to seek experience outside of the infinite light. Then, to continue its growth, this single spark divided into two," he uncrossed his fingers, "The birth of soulmates, each wanting to explore human delight.

"This process is in need to heal the planet. To keep the infinite light's creation thriving and alive. We live on for many lifetimes, growing as individuals, providing balance and peace. Once we're done with our journey, we must equally be filled, each having done our individual work. It is only then we can merge once again with our soulmate. When we do, the combined energy heals the earth, offering completion on the way back to the infinite light to spend eternity together as one again."

"Why can't soulmates go on the journey together?"

"When the souls are together, in their minds, they are already complete, not needing anything other than one another. When they are separated, a part of them is missing, which forces them to continue to learn and grow without knowing the reasons why. They must first know pain and heartache, learn to overcome trials and tribulations. Grow strong apart so they can be even stronger together once reunited."

He spoke passionately about this. I was unsure if this was something he believed in, or if he was retelling the story of *A Thousand Years Apart*. "If this is all true, then there is no way we are soulmates."

"Why do you say that?"

"Because ..." we were both broken before we found each other. We weren't complete, healed, or *filled*, as Ollie called it. "I was a mess before you came along. And I'm pretty sure I'm still a little fucked up."

"You're missing the point, love. It's not about seeking perfection. There is no way one soul will ever reach perfection without the other. It's about finding the best version of yourself, and perhaps we met sooner to push each other in the right direction because, as I said, love also has no laws. It's not a coincidence we're here."

"Will Harry and Nora get their happily ever after?" I asked, returning to the characters in the story.

Ollie returned his attention to the hardcover book laying over the mattress between us. "Harry and Nora knew it wasn't their time. They met, the instant connection undeniable. There is no question they're soulmates, but they gained what they needed in the little time they had together to be reminded and push each other to complete their journeys so one day they can live happily ever after."

"Moral of the story, not all books will have a happily ever after."

Ollie shook his head. "The story is about doing what's best for the one you love. Harry had a purpose in this lifetime. Despite what Harry wanted, Nora would have only held him back from accomplishing it. She knew this and understood the only way to love him, was to love him unselfishly."

"You're all set to go," Lynch stated as he walked into the room with a wheelchair. I rolled my eyes as Lynch parked it at the end of the bed. "It's necessary, Miss Jett. Unless you'd like to walk all the way to the car."

"You don't want to overdo it, love," Ollie added as he stood and tucked the book under his arm.

He held out his other hand as I moved to the edge of the hospital bed. "I got it."

Ollie chuckled and gestured over to the chair with a raised brow. "Alright. Have at it."

Both of my sock-covered feet hit the ground, and my right leg buckled, sending me hopping on my left foot and using the bed for support. "So bloody stubborn," Ollie muttered with a shake of the head.

I fell into the wheelchair and lifted my feet onto the pegs with a smirk on my face. "Now which one of you is wheeling me out of here?"

Two weeks had passed, and I'd made a full recovery. In the mess hall, the students of Dolor had come around and shown forgiveness toward me, but everyone remained on high alert, knowing there was a predator within the walls of the school.

It was December. The air was crisp, and we were days away before the staff would leave for holiday. Though, this year was different.

This year, security remained in full force.

"Trust no one, love," Ollie had reminded me each time we parted ways. Ollie didn't trust Ethan, and he never had to say it. I saw the way Ollie took notice in Ethan's every movement in every room we stepped foot in.

Ollie and I disagreed on very little, but we were on two different pages of the same book when it came down to Ethan. When Ollie had a feeling, usually his hunches were correct, but I was sure Ethan would never hurt me.

On the last day of classes before holiday, I dropped my completed essay inside the bin over Ms. Chandler's desk before taking my seat beside Tyler. I pulled my arms through the sleeves of the hoodie and stretched out my numbing leg.

"All healed up?" Tyler asked.

"Yeah, got the stitches removed yesterday by the new nurse. My leg still cramps up from time to time, but I think maybe it's all in my head."

"Understandable. Your body's been through the wringer. You got a proper scar?"

I turned in my chair and showed her my thigh. "This big," I said, using my thumb and pointer and pressed both fingers against my black jeans.

"It'll fade."

"I'm not worried about it." At this point, I was a walking scar. Down to nothing, I'd looked like I'd been put through a wood chipper.

Ms. Chandler advised the class to complete the lessons on the board and work quietly, and as soon as she sat in her desk and pulled out her phone, light chatter picked up around the room. Ms. Chandler never cared, as long as she wasn't bothered.

"You can come tomorrow," Tyler continued in a low whisper after she scooted her desk closer and her blonde hair rolled off her shoulders shielding her face. "The woods. We got a bottle." Her brows wiggled, and her smile turned wicked. Bria had been a bad influence on her. "Bring Ollie, too."

"I don't know ... I'll talk to him." I'd finally regained their forgiveness. Although, Bria's I was still working on, but at least they were talking to me again.

"It'll be fine. We're all cool. Bria was the one who wanted me to invite you."

I raised a brow. "No shit?" Maybe I didn't have to work as hard as I thought.

"Seriously."

"Whose all going?"

"Bria, Jake, umm ... Gwen and maybe Maddie, I'm not sure."

261

An involuntary groan left me.

"Maddie isn't so bad once you accept the fact she's an attention whore," Tyler explained.

"Yeah, Okay." Ollie would smash the idea ten-fold, but if I were going, he'd go.

Tyler's grin beamed back at me before she faced forward again, returning to the lesson at hand.

There were no bells at Dolor. The teachers dismissed us, and once Ms. Chandler did, we collected our things and bee-lined for the door—Tyler not straying far from my side.

"You still in a three-way-relationship?" I asked, caring too much about the two girls who had quickly shoved me to the side when things turned for the worst. Perhaps Sociopath Mia had turned into a softy. After everything the two girls had been through, the last thing I wanted for them was heartache. Another rip into their already fragile organ.

At the corner of my eye, her expression froze as she contemplated her next words. "I know what you're thinking, but it's not what it looks like."

I placed a hand over her arm to stop her mid-stride, and Tyler turned to face me with water in her eyes. "Explain it to me then," I insisted. Tyler's gaze bounced around as a herd of students walked passed us in the hallway. "Has he hurt you?"

Tyler's eyes returned to mine and the expression defrosted. "God no, Mia. It's just that … Oh, fuck, I don't know. I think—"

"Ty! What are you doing?" Bria interrupted, linking an arm in Tyler's. "Jude's waiting for us." It took a moment for Bria to acknowledge my presence and Tyler shook the moment away, forcing a faux smile. "You healing up okay?" Bria asked me with a frown. "Heard you put up quite a struggle, yeah? Could've been a lot worse."

I threw my hand in the air. "You know me. I don't go down without a fight."

"That's right," Ollie's voice rang behind me in my ear. He pressed a kiss over the top of my head before pinning himself against my back, and

I dropped my chin to my chest to conceal the effect he had over me. "You ready?"

I nodded as Bria shifted in place before saying, "You both coming tomorrow?"

"No," Ollie said the same time I released, "Yes."

"Maybe," Ollie caved.

"We'll be there," I confirmed, not meaning to defy him. I needed this. I needed to make right with these people and show them that I wasn't someone to distrust. Leaving Dolor with no bad blood was the least I could do—starting with this rather stupid get-together.

Bria flashed a pleased smile and moved her eyes to Ollie who stood tall behind me. "Tomorrow after breakfast then."

The bitter December temperatures bit through my thin black jeans as Ollie and I walked down the hill and toward the woods. Leaves crunched beneath my combat boots while Ollie blew hot air into our linked hands. "It's so frustrating for what they did to you." Ollie shook his head and continued, "Nothing good can come out of everyone being together. Nothing good ever comes out of it."

We reached the bottom of the hill, and before we walked into unknown territory, I turned to face him. Ollie shivered under his black hoodie, wearing matching black jeans, a beanie, and the hood pulled over his head. The tip of his nose red against his natural bronze skin and his cheeks flushed from the sting of chill in the air. "Have I changed your mind, love?" He asked with a hope-filled stare.

I shook my head. "You taught me to see the good in everyone. That everyone deserves a second chance."

"Yeah, well, I'm a hypocrite among other things."

"What other things?"

"A man in love, and someone who will go against everything he believes in to make sure his fiancé is safe."

"They can't hurt me."

"Someone already did, Mia. Who says the very person who fucking stabbed you isn't one of the people waiting for you in the woods this very moment? Gaining more ammunition to take you out?"

"Then let's call this detective work."

Ollie cracked a smile and threw his arm around my shoulder. "Then no drinking on the job."

"Deal."

Everyone had sprinkled around the broken tree limb. The group of outcasts passed around a faceless bottle, laughing, when we showed up. Bria and Jude stood secluded in deep conversation against the tall stone wall that kept us inside this hell. Tyler swung her legs off the broken tree with the bottle to her lips, chugging before passing it below to a giggling Maddie, and Jake and Gwen laid in a pile of leaves throwing twigs at one another.

Maddie's lazy and hungry eyes landed on Ollie, and she pushed the bottle out in front of her with a slow-rising smirk. "Oliver fucking Masters…or should I say, Oliver *who-can't-fuck* Masters." She threw her head back while laughing, and it bounced off the tree.

"Someone clearly had too much to drink, yeah?" Ollie snatched the bottle from her hand and looked around the littered area. A graveyard of drunken bottles collected over many Friday's I'd missed.

"I'm sorry, Mia," Maddie slurred, eyes sliding to me as she stumbled to her feet.

Uneasiness washed through me, and my fidgeting hands hid inside the pocket of the hoodie. "For?"

"I'm sorry you fell for a guy who can't get it up."

Ollie's head snapped in my direction to catch my reaction, but I stood undisturbed, having no earthly idea where this was coming from. My mouth went dry, and I dragged my nail against my wrist inside my pocket to fight the fact I was on the outside now looking in. I knew something had happened between the two of them, but never cared to know the details. Ollie had offered to tell me at one time, but I didn't want to hear it before.

And I especially didn't want to hear it now.

"Alright, we're leaving," Ollie interrupted my thoughts by placing a hand over my shoulder. Always the protector.

Tyler kicked Maddie with her Vans. "Maddie's just jealous you only have a hard-on for Mia." She paused when Jake giggled. "Stay, please. She'll eventually pass out."

"Yes, stay Ollie. It's been forever," Bria announced with Jude on her tail and a new bottle in her hand, and I'd wondered where the alcohol was coming from now. "Relax. Like old times." With her free hand, Bria grabbed Ollie and pulled him off to the side and sat him down as if he were a disobedient child.

Ollie declined the bottle and kept his attention trained on me.

"Just to make things clear," I started to say, building the nerve to finish the sentence I'd started. "We're all good, right?"

Silence settled, and I held my breath.

I should have never come. It was hard, the constant change within myself. For over ten years, it had only been me—never having to worry about other's feelings, only depending on me and looking out for myself. It had been easier that way.

Then Ollie had found me.

And then he'd left me, leaving me as a brand new person.

After Ollie, I'd made friends; got on a routine.

Now? I scanned the faceless bodies staring back at me. I no longer recognized these people I used to call my friends. My posture wavered, the uneasiness creeping up my legs, attacking all my limbs. It shouldn't feel like this. Life was too short to be standing here next to them, feeling as if I was staring down the barrel of a gun.

"Mia," Ollie called out low, and all my senses immediately recognized his voice. His light eyes from below looked up at me, calling upon me. A single look managed to grasp my soul and empty every worry I possessed. "Ready now?"

Dropping my chin in a single nod, Ollie stood, and together we walked away.

It hadn't taken me long to realize it wasn't worth it. Each step away from them felt lighter. What should have made me feel weak made me feel stronger.

Walking away made me stronger.

Ollie squeezed my hand. He didn't have to say anything. Maybe I wasn't cut out to be a social butterfly. People became who they surrounded themselves with, and I decided losing a piece of my identity wasn't worth it.

TWENTY-THREE

*"Give me a love so intoxicating,
I never suffer a hangover."*

OLIVER MASTERS

Ollie

Ever since Mia had been sleeping with me, she hadn't experienced another night terror. If only I had known what she had been dealing with, maybe it wouldn't have taken me so long to find my way back to her.

The way her body fit perfectly against me brought a morning smile to my lips. I didn't have to open my eyes to know she was awake, too. It still blew my mind how early she woke, but the girl loved her bloody naps later in the day.

My stubborn eyes remained closed, making this small moment with her safe in my arms last for as long as possible. Mia's faint breathing kissed my chest as my fingers wandered over her hips and her thighs.

And what came next was what I looked forward to every morning.

Mia's dainty finger fanned over my lashes, begging them to open, and I felt the essence of the smile I knew she was wearing this very moment.

"Merry Christmas," Mia whispered, and that same dainty finger traced over my nose, across my lips, and over my chest.

Crazy. A year from now we would be spending our Christmas in the home I'd prepared for us. She still didn't know, and the restraint in telling her took every ounce of strength.

It was still dark, most likely close to six in the morning.

Her finger swirled over the pattern of ink in the middle of my chest, and I hummed in the power she had over me—a surge flowing from her fingertip igniting through my entire body.

"Where are you now, Ollie?"

My grin was an answer in its own, but in case she didn't know … "With you."

"What are we doing?" Her velvet tone was playful.

I wrapped my hands in her messy long hair and pressed my forehead to hers, inhaling her natural jasmine scent and etched the outline of her lips with mine. "Whatever the hell we want."

And what came next was the product of her and I.

Every whisper, penetrating.

Every kiss against my skin, electrifying.

Every touch, ecstasy.

And moments without, a tragedy.

The effects of feeling too much, but with Mia, it wasn't just too much. It was everything all at once. At times, I had to pause to reel back the emotion from spilling over, but Mia wanted to see, feel, taste, and be a part of me and every intimate moment we shared. Together, we were untouchable to anyone and anything—pain, misery, loneliness. Not even death could pierce through our barrier. The whole world could be crumbling beneath us, waves crashing into us, the sun falling toward us at an impossible rate, and it would all be okay because we had each other.

Hearts hammering, blood roaring, and feelings aflame, we let go.

And the lingering smile upon her lips afterward was the reminder of how terrified and relieved I was that we had made it this far. Terrified because we weren't one hundred percent in the clear yet, but relieved we had right now.

She held her hand over my cheek as I pinned myself inside her, still trembling from the never-ending emotion and the ecstasy we'd climbed. I laid my hand over hers and kissed the inside of her palm before moving her hand over my heart. "Calm me down, love."

Laying my head over her chest, Mia ran her fingers through my sweaty hair, and my eyes closed again as she pulled me back to solid ground.

"You cannot throw this far, mate."

"Fuck you," Jake squealed through a chuckle as I took another step forward. "No, back ten more steps." He gestured with his hand.

I walked backward five, Jake tossed the football, and it landed ten feet in front of me.

H threw his arms in the air. "You have to go to the ball. It's not going to come to you." Jake had been looking forward to Mia's Christmas football tradition since it had been disrupted last year.

Shaking my head, I swiped the ball from the lawn and glanced back at Mia, who sat with legs crossed off to the side, dilly-dallying with the camera I had surprised her with. She wore ripped blue jeans, sex-hair pulled up messily over her head, and my oversized hoodie that read, *"Poetic,"* enveloping her tiny figure. The hoodie had been the first article I'd approved in my store Travis managed while I was gone.

Mia had no idea.

I picked up into a light jog toward her. "What are you doing, love?" I crouched down, and my eyes roamed over her scrunched up face as she toyed with some buttons on the camera. "That thing kicking your arse?"

Her brown eyes shot up at me, and she pushed me over into the grass. The camera flashed, and her laugh knocked me down again. "Perfect," she exhaled as the film emerged.

I rolled to my side and kicked a knee up, admiring the collection of photos lying across the grass. "What are these?"

"Nothing," Mia fanned the picture in the cold air, "just messing around."

I picked up one of the photos, seeing a side of myself I'd never noticed. I'd just caught the ball in mid-laugh. Only the side of my face was visible as I stood hunched over. Another photo of a partial Jake throwing the ball, and one of Zeke's curls blowing over his smile from a different day. "What are you talking about? These are really good."

"You think so?" her tone lifted.

Nodding, I scanned over each picture. "Wait, is this my arse?" I snatched it, taking a closer look. "You took a picture of my arse?" The room in the photo was dark, but sure enough, that was my white crack peeking from the top of the sheet lying as I lay in bed facing the wall.

I dropped my elbow into the grass and looked up at her, surely grinning like a fucking kid.

Mia snatched the photo out of my hand. "It's beautiful." She admired her picture and tilted her head. "It's amazing, isn't it?"

My brows pinched together. "My arse?"

Mia chuckled. "Well, yes, that too." Her laughter calmed but the smile remained as a permanent fixture on the photo. "I see this, and I feel everything I felt when I took it." Her cheeks turned pink and she dropped her head for a moment. "We didn't even have sex. We only laid in bed naked all night playing This or That, remember? I asked you for either breakfast for the rest of your life or all meals except breakfast. You chose breakfast all day every day, saying, and I quote, *'Our dates will consist of flipping pancakes at three a.m., sipping caffeine in our knickers and—*

"Dancing to The Beatles," I finished with a matching smile.

"In case we never make it out of here together, I wanted to always remember that vision you gave me. This picture does that for me."

Her hand fit perfectly in mine. "We're almost there." A cold wind blew wildly between us, sending Mia's defying strands against her face as she continued to look over her work with stars in her eyes.

"You feel it, don't you?"

She looked up from the photos. "Feel what?"

No doubt in my mind, this right here was her calling. "I see it in your eyes. The way you talk about photography. You're lighting up, Mia. You're really into it?"

"Yeah," she blew out through her lips, and her smile reemerged. "You knew. How?"

I lifted my shoulder.

Mia blushed. I gripped her thigh. Then a shadow hovered over us.

A whistle blew out of Jake's lips as he crouched down behind Mia. "Fuck me," he breathed. Mia dropped her head back, and I snatched the photo from her hand.

"Get out of here, mate. You've seen my arse before. This isn't new." It was true. Before Mia, I'd walked around numerous times in the bathroom and during midnight parties in my dorm wearing absolutely nothing. Since Mia came along, I'd shown respect for her by remembering to put pants on.

"Still gets me every time." Jake waggled his brows.

"You and me both," Mia agreed. Her eyes fell back on mine. "Ollie, are you blushing?"

"No." I dropped my head to the side and covered my face.

Mia was under the impression the prankster hadn't made a move since she returned from the hospital, but they had. Scott and Lynch were the only two people who knew she'd moved into my room at night. Occasionally, I stopped in her dorm to check things out, and a few days ago, I'd found a vague letter slipped under her door. *It isn't over*, it read in chicken scratch. The only reason I hadn't told her about it was because her holiday shouldn't have been spent in fear.

"I have a feeling they're waiting around for the perfect opportunity," I said low to Scott beside me against the wall of the mess hall. "No one can touch her when I'm around. And I'm always fucking around."

We only talked when necessary, feeding him updates for him to pass along to Lynch. If there was a way I could go to Lynch myself without Scott, I would, but someone had to keep an eye out for Mia.

My attention was locked on her across the room as she talked to Zeke in fluent sign language. Mia knew the kid could hear her, but she still refused to use her voice, saying it was the only way she was going to learn. Her hair framed her delicate face as her hands moved smoothly in front of her.

"I'll let Lynch know," Scott murmured and crumbled the paper in his hand before stuffing it in his pocket. "Have you told her about Lynch yet?"

I ran my hand through my hair and gripped the ends. How was I supposed to drop a bomb like that at a time like this? "I'll tell her when I know her head is in the right space."

"Lynch should be the one, yeah?"

Yeah, he should have. Then I'd found out, and deciding to hoard the secret from my fiancé was wrong on so many levels. "He had over a bloody year to tell her. What makes you think he's going to speak up now?" I folded my arms across my chest, speaking directly to Scott but my eyes watching Mia. Always. "Now that I know, I'll be the one to tell her. It has to come from me." Honestly, I was fucking scared. Knowing Mia, if she only knew I'd known this entire time, it would give her every reason not to trust me.

I'm doing this for you, love.

Pushing off the wall, I said, "Get that over to Lynch, and I'll keep you updated."

Jake had joined the table, teary-eyed and upset. He sat beside Mia, the two of them facing each other as Mia consoled him. "I can't get him alone. I miss him, and I know he misses me too," Jake said low as I pulled out a chair and took a seat.

Conversation halted, and all eyes landed on me.

"Don't stop on my account," I insisted.

"Ollie is the best person to ask for advice." Mia smiled. "He'll know."

Encouraging the challenge, I motioned with both hands to give it to me.

Jake turned toward me. "He's always around people. It's like he's making himself untouchable to me. But I see the way he looks at me."

"Liam?"

"Yeah," he sighed, "I never felt this way about anyone. We really had something. Then the whole school found out. Now he's avoiding me, his feelings ... shit, I know he feels the same way."

"I get that you miss him, mate. Truly, I understand one-hundred-percent what it's like to miss someone, but the bloke is clearly confused and still trying to wrap his mind around it all."

"I'm afraid the more time that passes, the less of a chance we'll ever get back together."

My fingers laced through Mia's and I pulled our hands into my lap, my thumb drawing invisible circles over hers as I listened intently. "You love him?"

Jake sucked in his lips and flicked his eyes to where Liam sat. Casually, I dropped my chin over my shoulder and took a look at the same bloke who not only kissed my girl but fucked her, too. A time when Mia had been confused herself and tried everything to push away the feelings she had toward me. I shifted my eyes back to my girl beside me. We'd come a long way. She'd come a long way. All she'd needed was someone to show her how to tear down the four walls, one by one. She'd grown accustomed to those fucking walls. Probably had hung pictures and painted them with her own bloodshed from the scared eight-year-old girl hiding inside.

Liam's eyes found Jake's. For only half a second, but it was there. I saw it. I felt it. A helplessness. A plead. An *"I miss you,"* screaming back at him over the sound of a breaking heart. "I fancy a bloke who smashes into fanny to fuck the feelings away," Jake finally stated with misty eyes. "No offense, Mia."

Mia held her free hand out in front of her. "None taken."

"Look at me." I leaned forward. "Four months and we're all out of here. Four months and Liam will go back home and have every reason and tool available to push you away altogether, conforming to society and fitting into a perfect box they created. Take my advice and go after him now. Don't wait until the last minute." I fell back into the chair. "No better time than right now. The only time that's guaranteed. You want him alone? I'll get you alone with him … but the rest is up to you, my friend."

If I hadn't caught the small moment exchanged, I would have told him to give the man space to figure it out, making my life a hell-of-a-lot easier. However, my heart was too fucking big to dismiss the obvious. Liam and Jake needed saving.

It was New Year's Eve. This very day last year haunted me every night, eyes wide open depriving me of sleep. I had every intention of drowning that night with new memories. But before I could spend midnight watching fireworks, I had to talk to Liam.

The ache in my chest didn't hold a candle to the weight in my heart as Mia and Scott walked side by side down the stairs. Her golden-brown eyes glanced back up at me under the baseball cap as I leaned over the railing. The wink and smirk on her face lifted the weight, but the ache would remain. It always did whenever we were apart. Once the two disappeared, I set forth on my mission to find Liam while Jake waited in the group therapy room for him.

My feet touched over every inch of Dolor, only to find Liam waltzing casually out of a closet zipping up his jeans. Gwen appeared behind him, wiping the aftermath from her lips with her shirt stretched and hanging from her shoulder. Jake didn't deserve this. "Liam, we need to talk."

Liam and Gwen paused wide-eyed.

"You can go," I directed to Gwen, jerking my head down the hall. "This isn't a conversation you want to be a part of." Gwen fixed her bra strap before taking off down the hall.

"What's this about?" Liam pulled his blond hair back into a pony.

"You're fucking kidding me, yeah?" I pushed him in the chest. "Blow jobs in the closet? Have you stooped this low only to prove a point? And to who? No one else is here!" My plan wasn't to confront him, only to take him to Jake. Knowing Jake was waiting this very moment to speak with him, only to find Liam busy getting his knob sucked off blew my fucking mind.

Liam ran a palm down his face with an incredulous smile. "Mia not doing it for ya anymore, mate? Have at it," he held up a palm toward a descending Gwen, "but I promise you won't find a girl as favorable as Mia. And I know …" he straightened his back and puffed out his chest. "Be thankful for your first-class fanny while I'm sticking it in commercial."

I was stuck between pounding his face in and choosing to understand. I relaxed my balled-up fists and released an exhale. "Let's go."

"Despite what you heard, Masters, I don't play for the same team."

My next action was very unlike me, but I couldn't not do something. I slapped the kid.

Not punch. I'd slapped him. No mark. No evidence. A bitch slap to the face for acting like a pussy. Liam and me faced off as he held his cheek.

"That was for Mia. And despite what I heard, I'm not here for anything other than to take you to someone who you don't deserve. Get your head out of your arse, your dick out of every female hole, and open your fucking eyes," I gritted out through clenched teeth. "You're in love with a fucking man, and the only two people you're hurting in the process is Jake and yourself."

Time was measured by every slow blink of Liam's eyes. He dropped his head and tilted his gaze down the hall. "Where is he?"

After dropping off the lovebird, I ran downstairs to meet Jinx while Scott had Mia.

Jinx posted in his usual spot with headphones in, bumping his head with his eyes closed. I swiped the buds from his ears, and his eyes bounced open. His toothless smile beamed as he unplugged the buds and handed over the phone. "The girl has taste," he said through a belly laugh. "No idea what she's doing with you."

"Ha! Nice one, mate." I pocketed Mia's phone. "Can I make a quick call?" I'd asked Jinx to get a hold of Mia's phone so I could surprise her tonight with the music she'd been dying to listen to, but since I was here…

"Yeah, man," Jinx waved me away, "Make it quick."

I pat him on the back of the shoulder as I passed through the door.

Mia's mobile burned a hole in my pocket as I picked up the phone from the receiver to ring Travis. He answered on the third ring, and I leaned back against the wall and withdrew her phone, twirling it in my hand. This was her life before me. Her music and photos, items worthy of capturing to either listen or see time and time again—an inside of what made Mia Rose tick.

"House is all painted. It looks clean, mate. Bright. Just like you wanted it."

"Thanks, man. How's Summer?"

"Pregnant! Eight weeks, we just found out last week … so now we're nine weeks. Can you believe it? I'm going to be a dad."

Smiling, I nodded though he couldn't see. "Congrats, mate. You deserve it. You deserve it all."

"Four more months until you're out, and with the income I'm getting in from you, we can start looking for our own place soon. I can't do much, but it's a start. I should be out just in time for when you get home."

"It will all fall into place. No rush. You're going to be a dad, Summer a mum. You have family now. Save as much as you can in the next four months, and I'll do whatever I can to help. But, Travis. Don't fuck this up. Stay away from your old boys, the Links. You don't need their money. You understand what I'm saying?" The last thing Travis needed was to fall back into his old ways, get mixed with the same crew who'd brought him down the last time.

"Yeah, I understand. I'm not going to mess this up."

I let out an exhale. "You're marrying her, yeah?"

"I want to. But, damn, I don't want Summer to think I'm only proposing now that she's pregnant."

"Ask her, Travis."

"Now?"

"No, you lazy twit, get it all set up. Something special."

"Yeah, yeah … I'll think of something."

"How's the hoodie coming along?"

"Can't keep it in stock. You're doing good, mate. Who knew a fucking word would sell out."

"It's not the word—it's the meaning."

Travis's laugh came through the phone. "Listen, I'm not going to try and understand it. As long as it's selling, yeah?"

"Yeah, you're doing good." Jinx tapped over the glass with his knuckle. "Look, I have to go. I'll ring you Thursday."

"Sounds good! Happy new year, brother."

"Happy New Year."

I hung up and stuffed Mia's mobile back in my pocket before pushing through the door. "Thanks again, mate."

Jinx closed his eyes with a single nod. "Anytime."

TWENTY-FOUR

"When the sun dies and darkness bleeds,
she's the black sheep I'm counting;
A loose cannon; another's regret.
A what-if, and repeated mistake.
She dances for no one and howls with the wolves.
A moon child with the spirit of a mood ring.
She's my all-time love."

OLIVER MASTERS

Mia

"You're into this photography thing now?" Ethan asked as we passed the same bench my father sat when he'd confessed the truth.

Bruce, my father, had said I was welcome home after my time here, but he could no longer live under the weight of a lie. But did he ever truly love me? Or had I turned into an obligation? Maybe I'd been my mother's baggage all along. It had been the reason he could no longer look at me, seeing as I looked just like her. Aside from her hazel eyes, I was the spitting image of my mother.

"Shouldn't you be with your family? You know, celebrating the holidays like everyone else?" I snapped another picture of him. I'd only seen Ethan in uniform or boxers. Never had I seen him dressed in a leather jacket, white tee, and destroyed jeans.

Ethan's head fell to the side, giving me that all-knowing look.

"Hold it," I demanded, and snapped another picture just as Ethan reached for the camera. Just in time, I hid it behind my back. "It's not me, I swear, but the camera wants to fuck you."

"Yeah, and I'll fuck up the camera if you take another photo."

"Don't like your picture taken?"

Ethan scratched his stubble. "Nope."

We paused when we reached our tree, and Ethan fell back over the grass and looked up at me. "And to answer your question, it was only my sister and me. My mum has Alzheimer's and lives in a home. Dad died from a heart attack shortly after she was diagnosed. Olivia was the only family I had left."

I plopped down beside him and laid back. Since I'd known Ethan, he'd never opened up about his family. I'd pried and tried to wiggle my way in without anything in return, until now. And I took full advantage of right now, soaking up as much as he'd give me. "Isn't your mom young to be in a home?"

"Nah, she had me at forty-three. She's pushing seventy."

"You visit her often?"

Ethan folded his hands behind his head. "It's hard. She looks at me and has no clue who I am. I guess the only good thing about Alzheimer's is the fact the death of her daughter can't touch her." *Damn.* "I have you, Jett. You're my family." He turned on his side to face me and lifted his head into his palm. "The reason I'm telling you all this is because even though Masters is back, nothing changes between us. I can accept Masters. I'll welcome the tosser with open arms if that's the man you decide to spend the rest of your life with, but not a bloody thing changes between you and me. If I knew for one second the bloke couldn't take care of you, if he didn't ... love you more than I love you, he'd already be gone."

A lump lodged in my throat. My gaze remained out in front of me, my eyes watching a cloud move across the sky as Ethan's words repeated over and over in my head.

"Yeah, I said it," Ethan fell back against the grass, "and I know you love me, too, but never in the way you love him, and I'm all right with that. I've come to terms with it. One day, my time will come, and when I do find the one, this thing between us remains the same. You. Are. My. Family."

Ethan's fingers found mine in the grass, and I closed my eyes. "Why are you telling me this now? Why do I feel like this is a goodbye or something bad is about to happen?"

"After you graduate, I'm leaving the country. I have to disappear for a while. I'm tired of this place, the people, fucking everything. Being here only reminds me of my sister, and I thought I could do it. I really did." He squeezed my hand and pulled me close, snaking his arm around my neck. It had been forever since we'd been this close, and it was comforting. When everything changed around me, Ethan and his loyalty to me stayed. "You're the reason I've pulled through. For twenty years, people gave up or walked out on you, and just because I'm disappearing doesn't mean a bloody thing. You'll have a way to contact me."

"Where are you going?"

"No idea."

"Don't forget about me, Ethan."

"Never."

"Pinky swear?" Unfolding our linked hands, I held up my pinky in front of us into the cloudy blue sky.

Ethan's chest raised, filling his lungs completely before he finally said, "Yeah, Jett," his hand came up and linked his pinky with mine, "I swear."

Sure, our relationship was unconventional. It never had and never would fit into a mold. One thing I knew for sure? We found each other while searching for ourselves.

Time left us, and we decided it was time to go inside when the winter air grew angrier. The cold stung Ethan's face, blotches matching his blood-red hair. He pulled me up to my feet before we walked back toward the prison. Ollie sat over a bench near the entrance with his back to us and head hung between his shoulders. The muscles in his shoulders strained against his hoodie.

Side by side, Ethan dropped his mouth down to my ear. "Last chance, you sure he's the one?"

My eyes flicked over to Ethan, meeting his electric blue eyes and a smug grin. I smacked him in the stomach and returned my attention to Ollie, who was now standing with his hands shoved into his pockets, staring at us from afar. A familiar flame ignited within me, warming me in the bitter cold. Ollie's gaze filled me up and called upon me, the kind of connection that branded into your bones. With the camera dangling from my wrist, I broke out into a jog, and a smile broke out on Ollie's face. My feet ate away at the distance—space never belonged between us.

Distance, demons, fate, time ... eat your fucking heart out.

Ollie caught me mid-air as I wrapped my legs around his waist. A laugh came up from his chest and fell into the crook of my neck. His arm secured me in place while his other hand rested under my thigh, and he pulled his head away to meet my eyes. "Ready for our date?"

I nodded, my feet finding solid ground again. "Why were you waiting here? In the cold?"

Ollie's arm swung around my shoulder and pulled me to his side as Ethan walked up. "I was downstairs. Saw you two through the window but didn't want to intrude." Ollie offered his hand to Ethan. "Thanks, mate."

Ethan shook it, and my heart warmed at the sight of the most important people in my life falling in sync. The smile on my face was easy.

An understanding took possession of all previous tension, and the realization hit me.

I'd soon walk out of Dolor unchained, in love, with a safety net to break my every fall.

After dinner and bathroom routine, Ollie and I reached his door, and he paused with a hand over the doorknob. "The night is ours. You're safe. No one's coming in, no one's leaving. Tonight is our New Year's. We'll pretend this is our first of many, alright?"

No question, that single night still taunted me whenever I'd battle my nights alone, reminding me of my past. The defenseless little girl I'd pushed away for over ten years had been saved and put to rest, only to rise from the ashes because of that one damn night—New Years of last year. The ghost of New Year's past. I never needed to hear Ollie's reassurance, but he still gave it without a second thought.

"Let's do this," I said through an exhale. His lips landed on my temple before opening the door.

Somehow, Ollie snagged cheap red wine and music. Not just any music. My music. For hours we drank, danced, laughed, played Magic 8 phone, and claimed the night.

We had fifteen minutes until midnight, and I swayed to *Bloodstream* by Stateless. The heat from the liquor persuaded my flow as Ollie soaked me in from the floor below. Hypnotized, eyes hungry and heavy, his dimples kissed his cheeks as he sat shirtless in his joggers against the mattress. The blankets and pillows had been transferred to the ground, and I twirled with the bottle of wine in my hand in my black bra and sweatpants falling low on my hips. My air-dried hair swung around me as the room spun in circles.

Intoxicated and free, I closed my eyes to take in the way his eyes on me made me feel.

Alive.

"Come dance with me," I insisted, slowly blinking. Ollie lazily rubbed his hand over his chest and down his inked stomach before climbing to his feet. Within arm's reach, he pulled the bottle from my hand and brought it to his lips. The lump moved as he swallowed, and he set the bottle over the desk. Wet lips glistened, and his eyes grew needy. He closed the unwelcomed distance and traced his fingertips up the length of my arm.

"I don't know which I like better," he said slowly, fingers tracing over my collarbone. "Watching you lose yourself on your own or being a part of it." He continued slowly, "Do you have any idea what you do to me, love?" I shook my head, and Ollie tilted his head. "All night, I struggle to remain still. The way your wild heart beats to your savage spirit, and it should be a sin to stain such beauty with my bare hands. But still …" his fingers trickled down the center of my chest, "I can't help it." His eyes moved from what his hand was doing against my heaving chest to my lips. "You see my dilemma?"

Ollie the poet had emerged from the alcohol. Words moved effortlessly, tone steady and slow, suffocating and resuscitating—a reviving poison spewing from lips made by God. His fingers moved over the surface of my bare stomach before he slid his palm down to my waist. With the song set to repeat, he set the phone over his desk with his other hand, and our foreheads connected, and together we danced.

Ollie's eyes bounced between mine, and he wet his lips. Goosebumps flared over my skin despite the warmth radiating from his blazing skin. We danced until a minute before the fireworks were set to go off before we rushed to the window. I waited, my gaze fixed out into the darkness with him beside me, hand in hand.

In my peripheral, I felt the weight of his stare. "Watch Ollie," I tapped on the window.

"I am."

And the fireworks went off, lighting up the entire sky. Colors bled together—blues, purples, whites, reds—colors of hope, and shapes of a new year. Ollie squeezed my hand, and I turned to face him. "Close your eyes, love," he said.

"Where are we going?"

"Under the stars."

Then his lips grabbed hold of mine before his hands reached the nape of my neck. Ollie took me there, under the stars—under the fireworks. He kissed me into color with taste buds mixed with mint and red wine. We sank into each other before my greed took over. My tongue pushed through his swollen lips wanting to enter *his* bloodstream, and a soft moan came up from his throat.

Slow. Dramatic. Torturous.

The three heart-hammering ingredients that made up Oliver Masters and the way he moved. The straps of my bra rolled off my shoulders by the tips of his fingers. His hands moved leisurely over the thin fabric, thumbs brushing my hardened nipples, as his mouth made its journey down my neck and across my collarbone.

Drunk and messy, I couldn't stand still as he pulled down the rest of the bra. My breasts hit the cold air, and he took both into his hands before his tongue swirled around, sending a heatwave through me. I fell back against the window and dropped my head back as Ollie sank to his knees. A firework display exploded behind me and inside me. My fingers moved through his unruly hair to keep myself from falling.

He yanked my bottoms down, my insides swam freely, and Ollie dragged his tongue through my sex, gathering the wetness. My heartbeat dropped to my clit, and he pulled it between his teeth gently before taking all of me into his mouth. He pulled my leg over his shoulder for more access, and my legs shook. Trying to hold myself together became an impossible task.

Intoxicated or not, Ollie had no boundaries when it came to pleasing me. His palms grabbed my bottom, guiding me to grind against lips. I wanted to cry out, but my chest held as a surge entered the same time his tongue did. My hands clenched to fists in his hair. My legs gave out, completely dependent on him, holding me together as he built the climax higher and higher. "Ollie," I cried out in warning. He only moved his hands around his punishing mouth, pinning me open to take all of me in.

Ollie indulged in my orgasm, draining me completely until he stood back to his feet. His swollen lips glistened and turned into a lazy smile. "You alright, love?"

Heat flowed up my neck and to my cheeks, and I covered my face with my hands. In a single move, Ollie picked me up, and I wrapped my legs around him. My wet sex slid down his pelvis, my core still reeling.

Ollie's erection strained against his joggers. "Where do you want me to make love to you?" his lips lingered over mine. "I fancy the view right here, but it's your call, love."

"Here," I whispered, and I kissed his wet lips, tasting myself on him. He pinned me against the wall and dropped his sweats, his hard shaft bounced against my bottom, and he pulled away to see me. Green cautious eyes seared into me, his lips twitched, and I inched back to move his shaft through my core. "I got you."

Three words to remind him it was okay to let go.

Ollie's palm hit the window before he thrust himself inside me. He released a breath and closed his eyes, and for a brief moment, we stilled connected as one. I touched his face, bringing him back. The grind that came after sent us both in a sweet craze. We chased each other into multiple highs. Lips and tongues moved over every surface, and hands satisfied every touch.

Somewhere along the ride, we ended on the floor in the heap of pillows and blankets as music dripped from the small speaker of my phone. We made love into all hours of the night and until the sun came up. The spell of the night overcame our hangover, and an acoustic guitar from a folk song penetrated the air around our heated and slick limbs.

"Knock-knock," Ollie whispered, twirling a lock of mine between his fingers.

I laid over him, and a tired smile played on my lips. "Who's there?"

"Olive."

"Olive who?" I asked, tracing my finger over the tattoo on his chest.

"Olive you."

As I pulled away from his chest, Ollie dropped his eyes down to see me with a boyish grin.

Naked and laced in each other, we fell asleep to the soothing music into the first day of the new year.

Ollie

"Have you been skipping your meds?"

My knee bounced under his scrutiny. Did I feel guilty? Not in the least bit. But the weight of Dr. Butala's eyes felt like the entire campus of Dolor sitting on my chest. I'd like to call myself an honest man ... but only when I was free of the beast who raged inside me.

The pills. The past. Oscar.

Fuck you, Oscar.

"No," I lied, and that bloody lie infiltrated through me to the tips of my fingers as I drummed them against my knee.

What I didn't think was at all possible, Dr. Butala narrowed his eyes, increasing the weight. I could hardly breathe. The lie I'd just told hovered like a dark cloud above me with two huge arrows pointing at my head, blinking *"Liar."* My entire body defied what my heart and soul was doing, but my mouth had a mind of its own.

If he knew, he'd apply force, and there was no way in hell I'd ever go back to what I was before. Mia and I only had four months left before we were out of here. Ending up in the psych ward until then wasn't a part of the plan. Protecting her was.

"Has your arousal balanced?" he asked impassively.

My arousal. I pressed my lips together while Butala struggled to remain serious. My erections only rose at the simplest thought of Mia. Even on the fucking pills, she had been the only one my heart and knob both agreed on. Silently, I thanked my dick for not getting me into too much trouble during the dark time. "My arousal is doing just fine."

"Good." He typed a few more notes on his keyboard before he finally looked up at me. "Dr. Conway will be back tomorrow. I think it's a good idea to pick up counseling sessions once a week until the end of the school year."

My palm ran down my face. It only meant once a week that Mia would be left alone with Scott. I may have trusted Scott to keep her from harm, but that was the only thing I trusted him with. Scott was in love with her, and if I were him, I'd never stop trying. Anyone would be a fool to give up a feeling once it touched them, and Mia didn't only touch me, she flowed through me. "Is it mandatory?"

Butala jabbed his pointer finger into his mouse with a single click. "Yes, Masters."

"Then I suppose I don't have a choice." I gripped the arms of the chair before I stood, itching to get back to her. "Next week, same time, yeah?"

Butala studied me. "Yes, Oliver. Next week."

He wasn't stupid. He knew I wasn't taking the bloody medication. I only needed him not to push the topic until I breathed the air on the other side of the wall.

I stopped at the loo for a leak before meeting Mia in the common room. Classes hadn't started back up yet, and to keep the restless from throwing themselves into trouble, movies played on repeat.

Moaning sounded a few stalls away, and I rolled my head back at the distastefulness of fucking next to a bloody toilet.

"Fuck, yes …" a whiney voice hissed, and I slammed my eyes shut, focusing on the job at hand—quite literally.

"Ollie," the girl sang, and my eyes sprang open.

"What the fuck did you just call me?" a bloke asked.

I shook off my knob and zipped my pants, unsure of what to do with myself.

"Oh, just go with it," she breathed.

The sound of flesh slapping together bounced off the stalls. Over and over. The girl cried my name. The bloke grunted, and I stood frozen.

"Ollie," she whispers with tears in her eyes. "It's alright."

"No," I seethe through gritted teeth, shaking my head. It isn't right. What he wants me to do isn't right. I look up at Oscar, who stands beside me.

"You will, brother. I got her just for you. She'll comply." Oscar's palm hit my nauseated stomach with a condom inside. "Should fit your fourteen-year-old knob, yeah? Get him going, darlin'. It's time for Lil' O to enter manhood."

I freeze, eyes set out in front of me but looking at absolutely nothing as the older girl unzips my pants and Oscar has a tight grip at the back of my neck.

She can't be much older. Oscar likes them young, and apparently, she was picked and primed for me. Platinum blonde hair. Ice blue eyes. Fake nails. Fake lashes.

If I had to guess, I'd say she's seventeen or eighteen.

Any boy my age would jump at the idea of losing his virginity to an older girl with a beautiful face and pristine body. Not me. "But I'm saving myself."

Oscar throws his head back, a menacing laugh escaping. "What for?"

I shrug, unsure exactly. I've never been the one to have to prove something to anyone. I've never had to prove myself to Oscar, and I read enough books to know that the action about to take place shouldn't be done lightly, especially with an audience. "When the time is right, I suppose."

Oscar sends a nod of approval to the girl who he calls "Lacey," and Lacey pulls down my pants and boxers.

"He's blessed," she declares.

"Runs in the family," Oscar mutters and slaps her arse. "Get on with it."

Oscar plops down over a chair against the wall behind me, rubbing over his knob as the girl rubs over me. It is wrong, and I want to hate myself for how my body reacts to her.

A few minutes pass and Oscar's frustrated breathing mixes with the sound of the girl blowing me. Yeah, I'm hard, but can't reach the fucking point. She snatches the condom and rolls it over my aching dick. I look back over to Oscar in a desperate plea as he clutches his junk in his hand. "Fuck her, you coward. No one's leaving this room until you become one of us."

I know how to fuck. I've watched Mum bang blokes, and Oscar beat into fanny so many times before. I just don't want to. Not like this. Not here. Not now. Not with her.

Lacey turns her back to me and bends over. Her fanny splits open, offering whatever I want. I could leave, get my arse beat and be back here again tomorrow.

Or I could take it.

One last look at Oscar, the dirty fucking scumbag only pumps his hand over his knob harder. "Fuck her, brother," he barks. "Now!"

"Is this what you want?" I ask Lacey, her face pressed into the mattress and arse ready to take a beating. She nods, and rage blows through me like a tornado. Oscar wants to create someone just like him. I spat on my hand and grabbed a handful of her fanny and my dick responds. "You sure?"

"Yes, Ollie …" she cries out, and it doesn't take long before I turn into the monster sitting behind me.

"Yes, Ollie …" My name pulled me from my memory. I had to get out of there.

The swinging door slammed against the wall as I pushed through. I couldn't think. I couldn't breathe. I should've asked the girl why the hell it was my name she was screaming, but all I wanted was to get out of there as quickly as possible in search of oxygen—in search of Mia.

TWENTY-FIVE

> "Perhaps the most
> dangerous man,
> is a man in love."
>
> OLIVER MASTERS

Mia

Ethan dialed up the volume on the TV to drown out the chatter in the room before he fell back into the desk chair beside me. My legs kicked up on the wobbly desk, and I shoved my hand inside a bag of Lays. The fluorescent bulbs were out. The only light was the sliver streaming through the blinds and Die Hard playing at the front of the room on a rolling cart.

"Christmas movie or not a Christmas movie?" Ethan asked, snatching the bag of chips from my hands.

"Hey!" I screeched, but his fingers had already pulled out a chip, and I proceeded to suck off the tips of mine. "Christmas movie … definitely."

"Agreed." He nodded.

The phone on the wall rang, and Ethan bounced back to his feet and tossed the bag in my lap. My eyes followed him over to the phone beside the door. Ethan was back in his black uniform, belt snug around his hips and red hair fixed wildly over his head. Moments after answering, his gaze shot over to me before turning to face the wall, nodding in agreement to whoever was on the other end of the line.

Ethan hung up, walked behind the TV, and leaned over the desk to whisper to me, "That was Lynch's assistant. There's a call for you downstairs."

"I don't know who it could be."

"Maybe your dad wishing you a Merry Christmas?"

A laugh came out in the form of a rush of air. "He's a few weeks too late."

"So, you're not going?"

I shook my head, pulling my thumb between my lips.

"Something could be wrong, Jett. He rarely calls. Maybe it's important."

My hand fell from my mouth, and Ethan pressed me with that *just-talk-to-him* look. I groaned and slapped my palms against the wooden desk as I rose to my feet. "Fine. Are you coming with me?"

"Can't," he jabbed a thumb behind him, indicating his duty to Dolor.

"Ollie will be mad," I sang.

Ethan dropped his head to the side and raised a brow. "Masters will survive."

I walked down the lifeless halls. The sound of my combat boots against the marble mirrored the creepiness, and though I was fully clothed in my black jeans and Ollie's black *"poetic"* hoodie, the building put off enough resentment to turn this hell cold.

My pace quickened, and before I made it to the stairwell, a force grabbed my hood from behind, choking me and thrashing me backward. My nails dug into the skin of whoever had grabbed me, but they didn't stop yanking until I was thrown into a dark closet.

The door slammed, and all that surrounded me was the dark.

When fear should have reared its nasty head, all I found was anger. Hesitantly, I reached my arms out in front of me for the doorknob. "Let me out!" I screamed, beating against the door.

I screamed until my voice went hoarse, I pounded my fist until my arm grew weak, I kicked until my legs gave out, and then I sank to the floor. Regardless if my eyes were open or closed, it was still dark. It no longer mattered. So, I left them closed and waited for someone to realize I'd gone missing.

It shouldn't be too much longer. Still, I kept my eyes closed, relishing in having the choice to see darkness under my own admission, not because I was locked in a closet. My blood simmered though I was freezing and my imagination ran wild. Many times, my brain played tricks on me, believing I'd heard my name being called. My foot tapped against the door to signal where I was.

Ethan should've come with me.

Ollie would be pissed that he didn't. He'd flip this school upside down until I fell from this closet. Not too much longer, and he'd find me. I curled in the corner, my knees pressed against my chest with my head dropped between them. I only needed to stay calm for a little while longer.

Then the lock clicked.

Or had I imagined it?

I crawled forward, pushing my hand out in front of me until I felt the cold metal of the doorknob. Sure enough, the knob twisted open, and the door creaked open.

Light entered, and I dropped my head in relief when my eyes moved across the floor. A note laid over the dusty marble. I sat back on my knees and held it out in front of me. It read, *That's what it feels like.*

"Mia!" Ollie's voice echoed through the hall. Sitting frozen with the note clasped between my fingers, he appeared in front of me. "What the hell happened?" Ollie pushed my hair back as he scanned over my face. "You alright?"

Ollie pulled me off the ground, and I nodded. "Yeah," I think I said, offering the letter to him. He took the note from my hand and read over it. His chest raised heavily and worry struck in his green eyes when they hit mine.

He was angry.

I was scared.

He was shaking in fury.

I was shaking in fear.

"What do we do?" I finally asked, my throat swollen.

"I'm over this shit. I'm so over it. *Fuck.* I'm taking down this son of a bitch," Ollie licked his lip and tore his eyes away from me and down the hall, "right after I go wring Scott's fucking neck." Ollie grabbed my hand, leading me down the hallway back to the common room, stride not letting up.

He was right and wrong at the same time.

I wasn't Ethan's responsibility. I was no one's responsibility.

"Ollie, it's not his fault." I squeezed his hand, trying to slow him down. "Stop and listen to me!"

He spun and towered over me, nostrils flaring. "He had one job, Mia. One." Noticing his tight grip on my hand, he quickly released before turning around and taking off with fists clenched at his sides. I ran after him, calling out his name.

Ollie only saw red—*Ethan* red.

I yanked on his arm from behind, but there was no stopping *one-tracked-mind* Ollie.

"Forget it, Ollie. Please. I'm begging you. Let it go!"

Ollie's hand landed on the doorknob, and he was quickly inside and across the room by the time I pushed through behind him. "Everyone out!" he shouted, his face red and sweat dotting his hairline. People stayed glued to their seats, leaning forward and eager for the real show that was about to start. Ethan had already jumped to his feet, his eyes darting around, taking in the scene around. "Get the fuck out!" Ollie ordered again, and that time, people scrambled.

I stepped in front of Ollie, covering his fists with my hands. "Please, don't do this."

"Get out, Mia."

"Look at me! This isn't going to end well!"

Ollie picked me up and carried me out the door before setting me on my feet. "Jake, don't let her out of your sight!" Ollie yelled over my shoulder before closing the door.

"Don't you dare do this!" I screamed through the small window, throwing my fists into the door.

Ollie's hollowed eyes fixated on me, and the door lock clicked. "Close your eyes, Mia." Then he turned his back to me and took long strides toward Ethan. Ethan circled the desk, trying to talk sense into Ollie, but Ollie swiftly moved around it. Ollie's daunting voice shook the walls before he picked up the desk as if it were a feather pillow and threw it across the room. The veins in his neck bulged as adrenaline pumped through emotional and fierce flesh.

Ethan held up his hands, taking a step back, but Ollie moved swiftly and launched his fist into his skull. The ear-splitting sound pierced through the door.

I screamed out, tears spilled from the corner of my eyes, and I fell to the floor along with the rest of me. People smashed into me, trying to get a view of the action inside, but all I could do was press my palms against my ears to drown out the sounds and move along the wall to get out of the way.

Time passed, and eventually people scattered. A wave of cold air brushed passed me, and I shivered against it. The door opened, but I was too scared to look up and face the music. Ollie's Chuck Taylor's appeared beside me. Then Ethan's boots came into view for a mere moment. I lifted my head to see the two shaking hands before Ethan turned and walked away before I had a chance to see his face.

"Mia," Ollie pressed, his hand landing over my shoulder. "Look at me."

"Leave her alone. She obviously doesn't want to talk to you," Jake muttered, and I had no idea he'd hung around for this long. I didn't have to look up to know he was standing across from me at the opposite side of the hall.

Ollie slid down the wall beside me. The heat and familiarity emitting from him comforted me, but I was too mad to accept it. "I'm not going anywhere, Mia. I'll sit here all night if I have to," Ollie said to me.

Sure enough, Ollie sat beside me. I didn't know who else was around anymore. I was too stubborn to lift my head and check. A few students walked by, but no one talked.

"Well this is fun and all, but I'm going to head out," Jake mumbled, and his footfalls faded down the hall.

Ollie and I sat in silence. I didn't know how much time had passed. I didn't know where the hell Ethan had gone or if he was still here. I didn't know anything anymore. The only thing I was sure of, I was fucking mad.

"I love you, Mia," Ollie whispered, bumping his leg next to mine.

"That was selfish. You're selfish."

Ollie blew out air. "Selfish, yeah?"

"Yeah," I breathed into the hoodie. "And dangerous."

I felt his mind racing at the speed of light. Somehow, his thoughts touched me and sifted through me. The need to wring out his worry made my fingers twitch inside my sleeve. He had just pounded into Ethan's head for no good reason. A reason that was all my fault. This had been all my fault, and the two people I loved were stewing in the aftermath.

"Selfish," he repeated with a shake of his head. He stretched out his legs in front of him and stuffed his hands into his pockets. "You know, I remembered seeing this movie ... I can't remember the bloody name of it and to be honest, I might've imagined it, but I'll never forget what the girl said ... something along the lines of you can't be both selfish and in love. Humans are created to love themselves first and foremost, the reason we can't physically harm ourselves with our bare hands. You'll never be able to break skin using your own teeth or scratch beyond the surface enough to draw blood. And the ones who do are considered dangerous—insane even."

Tilting my head, I laid it across my folded arms to face him. Blood seeped down his busted eyebrow, but I didn't say anything. He'd probably deserved it, and I wondered how bad Ethan looked.

Ollie put his thumb between his teeth and clenched his eyes, his brows knitted together in determination. I lifted my head as my breath held in my chest. "What are you doing?" It finally dawned on me, and I tried pushing his arm away, but Ollie leaned away, shielding himself with his other arm.

When he pulled his thumb away, blood pumped from the broken skin. My eyes bulged from their sockets, darting back and forth. Ollie straightened his posture and shook his head. "The most dangerous man is a man in love," he faced me, eyes wild and calm concurrently, "because I'd tear off my own flesh before someone hurts you … and if I'd do that to myself, imagine what I'd do to someone else."

I stared at him, his adoring green eyes staring back at me. Ollie's arm hung over his knee, his palm face-up as blood dripped over the marble. "Don't ever do that again," I seethed, and grabbed his thumb and wrapped it into the sleeve of my hoodie. "You're insane."

He smiled. "I'm in love," he corrected, and his head fell back against the wall. "Are you still mad at me?"

An incredulous smile rose to my lips, and I wiped my eyes with the back of my free hand. "Yeah. I'm still mad at you."

Together, we climbed back to our feet. Ollie grabbed my hand in his and sucked off his bleeding thumb. "Hey, Mia?"

"Yeah?"

"Don't ever try what I just did. It fucking hurts."

"Good." I laughed and shoved my shoulder into his arm.

My gaze burned holes into the side of Jude's face before it traced over his temple, his prominent nose, and long hair. Before, I had been a scared little bitch. But that was before.

My fear had since turned to anger.

Ollie's fingers dug into my thigh, attempting to absorb the rage rolling through me. "Baby, eat," he said.

Ollie had rarely called me that. He was desperate.

A security guard from confinement, who I nicknamed Yeti, stood in Ethan's usual place. Typically, we didn't see guards from other areas very often. Not nearly long enough to know their names, and many of them refuse to offer giving it, but Yeti wasn't much older than me with blonde wavy hair and crystal blue eyes. No facial hair, average height. The kind of guy who probably had girls following him around in high school, or whatever they called it here, and didn't have a dream to follow after that. Yeti rocked a dad bod, I was still unsure if he had the kid to match, working for a dangerous school on minimum wage. The Yeti nickname came from the silver Yeti cup he carried around, probably laced in liquor from the way he swayed against the wall.

Yeti would be the perfect victim, so easy for me to get access to his set of keys.

"I need to get into Lynch's office," I rasped out, a plan formulating in my head. "I need access to files to learn my enemy." Ollie drummed his forefinger and thumb against my thigh before pulling his hand away and scratching over his chest. My comment made him nervous, but I was going to do this with or without him. "I need to get my hands on a set of guard's keys."

Ollie's palm ran down his face, looking over every inch of the mess hall before turning his piercing emerald gems to me. I'd just threatened his plan of laying low and walking out of here together. One idea, and I'd threatened our future.

It's not my fault, Ollie. I'm just playing the same game.

"Got it all figured out, yeah?" Ollie asked.

I set my lips in a hard line.

"Dammit, Mia,"—Ollie slammed his fist into the table, making both Zeke and I jump— "Four bloody months. Until then, the only thing you're doing is eating, sleeping, and enjoying every fucking night with me." Easy for him to say. He hadn't beeen the one trapped in a dark enclosed room for over an hour. And even so, he was quick to take it out on the wrong person. "You have to trust me on this."

I lifted my chin and hit my gaze back on Jude. *That's what it feels like.* The words from the note repeated over and over, and I wondered what he meant by that.

Ollie's hand grabbed my face, turning my attention to him. "Promise me ... you're going to let me take care of it." His eyes prayed, and his jaw clenched. "Say it, Mia. Promise me."

"I promise." I bit the inside of my cheek to feel the sting of my lie. Looking into his eyes doing it felt like a blade to the throat. Ollie's lips landed on my forehead, and my eyes closed.

He held his lips there for a moment before pulling away. "Don't ever fucking lie to me again." Ollie pushed his chair out, and like the very gentleman he was and couldn't defy, he pushed his chair back in. "I need to take a walk." And he took off to the food line.

Ollie wouldn't leave this room, or any room I was in.

Zeke pounded his fist against the table, grabbing my attention from Ollie's back.

Mia and Ollie. Forever, Zeke signed adamantly. *Not Pam and Jim. Not Ross and Rachel. Not Romeo and Juliet. Mia and Ollie. Go after him.*

"No, he needs space," I reassured, too lazy to use sign language at the moment. "Just a misunderstanding."

He needs you, Zeke added.

"He has me, Zeke. Forever. He's not angry with me. He's angry at a faceless douchebag, and he wants to fix this problem but doesn't even know where to begin. Ollie's stuck between morals and destruction. Calm and a storm. Love and hate. He's stuck in the middle—everything he's so certain about being questioned." My eyes dragged until they hit faded tattoos and messy brown hair. The man my soul was promised to posted up on a wall, staring at me from across the room with his hand gripping the back of his neck and his leg propped. "In his beautiful mind, Ollie is carrying the burden of a thousand lost souls yet has the heart of a thousand angels. That's exactly why I can't let him do this for me. I lied because I can take this person down without so much as a scratch at my conscious. Ollie walked away because he knows it too."

TWENTY-SIX

*"Sometimes all we need
is someone who will
sit in the dark with us."*

OLIVER MASTERS

Mia

Ms. Chandler sat with her cell phone in front of her face, popping gum in her mouth and smiling at the phone as she was probably sexting. I'd finished my lesson approximately twenty minutes ago and had another twenty minutes to sit here and listen to her soft giggle and pop of the gum.

"Did you hear what happened in the Looney Bin last night?" Tyler whispered. "Another suicide. Told you … contagious. Spreads like wildfire."

It didn't make sense. That made three suicides in one school year. Highly unlikely. "How did you hear about this?"

Tyler shrugged. She'd changed so much since the year started. From the looks of it, twenty or so pounds fell off her. Her blonde hair, which was usually down and hiding her face, was up in a high ponytail. She lost two buttons on her Dolor shirt, showing cleavage. She was confident. Good for her, but at what cost?

Pop.

Tyler groaned. "If I hear that one more time, I'm going to scream …" Her eyes seared into Ms. Chandler as she continued to whine, and my brain went to a place where math, statistics, and suicide lived. Suicide shouldn't be associated with math, but unfortunately, we lived in a world where everything was measured in numbers.

In my world, both Ethan and Ollie seemed emotionally and physically affected by it.

I'd only seen Ethan in passing once since the beating, and it was all I'd needed to confirm Ollie had released wrath on his face. After the beating, they'd both shook hands and went their separate ways. Ethan's healing cheekbone looked like a July sunset in Pennsylvania. His lip had a cut, and his eye was still swollen, even after a week. When I'd thought he would have been mad at me, he wasn't.

I'd learned you didn't have to be feared to be respected. No one feared Ollie, yet most people respected him. *"If people fear you, you will be ten feet tall amongst enemies. If people love you, you will be a hundred feet tall among loyal defenders,"* Ollie had once said. People gave you respect if you gave them a reason to, and the day Ollie's fist blasted into Ethan's skull, Ollie had given everyone a lesson on what would happen if you turned your back on the people you were supposed to stand beside.

A spanking had been what it was.

Ethan walked into the classroom, and his eyes hit mine before steering toward Ms. Chandler at the front of the class.

"Officer Scott, what a surprise," she cooed, fucking Ethan with her mascara-clumped lashes and pursing her pink lips. It was no shock to anyone Ethan had the body of a god and the chiseled features of one of

Picasso's portraits. But only I knew what he felt like curled up in his arms in the middle of the night as he whispered the terrors away.

"Jett, let's go," Ethan called, ignoring the way Chandler made a fool of herself as she propped her elbow over the table and leaned forward to display the dip of her shirt. I smiled to myself as I collected my things and waved a hand at Tyler.

We walked one room over, and Ethan hurriedly closed the door and turned to me. His mask vanished and was back to the Ethan I'd known very well. "I need you," he quietly said. "One night. I need one night. I'm not doing so well. I'm so sorry for leaving you alone. I should've never done that. But, please, Jett. Tell Masters you're sleeping in your room tonight. Tell him whatever you need to, but I'm telling you, I fucking need you so bad right now. I'm going to bloody break. I can't handle it," Ethan continued to ramble.

"Okay," I nodded and grabbed his hand. Ethan never admitted to needing me before. I'd always assumed he needed me, but it had been the first time I'd heard him say those words. Whatever had him so worked up, I needed to be there for him.

Ethan let out a breath. "What are you going to tell Masters?"

"The truth. You're my family, and my family needs me right now. But I also need you to do something for me."

"What?"

"I need to break into Lynch's office."

"What the fuck for?"

"Files. I need to look at the student files. Ollie can't know."

Ethan let out a disbelieving laugh. "Let me get this straight, you'll be honest about lying next to me at night, but lie about breaking into Lynch's office? Have you told him I've touched all over you? Does Masters understand you're mine as much as his?"

"That's the difference between you and Ollie. To Ollie, I'm no one's property."

Ethan scratched his cheek. "I didn't mean it like that, and you know it." A moment of silence drifted between the two of us, then Ethan's rare smile slowly appeared. "So, we have a deal then?"

"This isn't a deal. There are no deals between us. I need to know you'll be there when I need you, and you know I'll always help you," I explained.

"Fine."

"Fine."

And just like that, we were back to our old selves.

"See you tonight?" Ethan asked, his rare smile relaxed.

"Yeah," I wrapped my arms around his waist, "I'll see you tonight."

He kissed my forehead before we exited, and like clockwork, Ollie waited outside the classroom, only this time, Maddie stood in front of him in a heated conversation. His eyes found mine, and he straightened his back when he noticed Ethan behind me.

"Come on, love," Ollie muttered, swinging an arm over my shoulder.

Maddie threw her arms in the air, bothered in the way he was leaving things. "That's it, ya?"

Absentmindedly, Ollie continued his stride with me at his side. "What was that about?" I asked him.

"A bloke we used to know, the summer before you arrived, hung himself in the Looney Bin. I hadn't seen him since that summer, but Maddie grew close to him during her visit in psych. She was just trying to talk to me, saying he wouldn't do something like that." His words were too casual. When Ollie talked about death, he spoke using his heart. These words weren't coming from the Ollie I knew.

"Ollie," I paused, moving my hand over his chest, "you can talk to me about it ... If something is bothering you."

"The only thing that bothers me is the way people talk about suicide and how it affected *them*. Are we so self-centered, that even in death, we selfishly cry for our losses, not once taking a second to think how much torture and pain the soul went through before deciding to end their life? It's sickening ... the silent cry for help no one responds to when the person needed it most. There's never an action, only a reaction on this bloody earth. The moment someone speaks up about their internal pain, they're shoved onto meds, counseling, and hospitals," Ollie tapped his head vigorously, "because we don't fit into their box and we're fucking weak and lazy, yeah? How about alone and misunderstood!"

He took in a deep breath and stretched out his fingers at his side. "Alone, and the world shunned them to their darkness. And the world cries selfishly at their wake because the victim decided to find peace when everyone else tossed them into quicksand during a sandstorm. The world stands over their grave, spitting words like selfish ... and 'what about their family and friends?' and we're back to square one, thinking about how the death of the victim affects *us*, not thinking about how the pain affected them before they died."

"Are you saying it's okay to take your own life?"

"No, Mia," he calmed and pulled my hand to his chest, "I'm saying if we showed more compassion and understanding, threw away the molds, boxes, and social status, it would never have to lead to that in the first place." His eyes locked on mine, and the wheels turned in his head. "Now tell me, what did Scott want?"

"Time. He's going through something and needs me tonight."

"Is there something I should know about?"

"Ethan has no one, Ollie ... except for me. I don't exactly know what has him so messed up right now, but he's only acted like this whenever a suicide had gone down. I'm sure seeing the bodies and taking the reports is enough to break anyone." If anyone could understand, Ollie would.

Ollie nodded at my side, and we picked up in a walk. "Ace, Scott. A fucking guilt trip," he mumbled to no one and turned to face me. "I'm not your bloody owner, love. You do as you wish. You want to spend the night with another man? Go ahead, I'm not angry about it. I trust you. Will I be waiting for your return? Abso-*fucking*-lutely. Will I get you off before you go? Hell. Yes. I refuse to allow you to run off with Scott needy and without my cum inside you."

My eyes bulged. "Ollie!"

During lunch, Lynch made an announcement over the intercom about another vigil held for a total of four lives stolen from Dolor.

Zeke tapped his finger on the table to get our attention. *I miss Livy*, he signed.

Tell us about her, Ollie signed back before grabbing my hand and falling back into his chair, keeping his attention on Zeke.

Strawberry blonde hair, Zeke's lip twitched as his hands moved, *Sweet, funny, Tommy and Livy. Big blue eyes. She was nice to me but didn't take no for an answer, like Mia.*

"She sounds like a nice girl. Someone hard to forget," I said through a chuckle.

Tommy loved her. She said it was Tommy's baby, Zeke signed. His hands dropped down, and we all waited to see what would come next—but nothing. That was where Zeke wanted to end his story. He picked up a roll and bit into it.

Ollie snapped his finger, bringing Zeke's eyes back to him. "Livy and her baby are living in your heart. Once a soul touches you, it's a part of you forever. Find comfort in that."

Zeke's eyes snapped wide, and the roll dropped over his tray. *What about Tommy? He was good. He didn't deserve what happened to him. Tommy's alone in a prison cell. Tommy was nice to me. My brother. Tommy is my brother.*

A tear rolled down Zeke's cheek, and I froze under his confession.

"No," Ollie shook his head and pulled up his hands, signing and speaking eagerly. "Blood or spirit?"

Zeke's eyes went frantic, and he pushed his tray forward angrily.

Ollie pounded his fist over the table to collect his attention. "Blood or spirit, Zeke?"

Zeke's hands moved fluidly yet violently.

I looked over to Ollie whose expression transformed with each movement of Zeke's hands. "I can't keep up. What is he saying?"

"How is he your brother? Why haven't you told me this?" Ollie said through gritted teeth.

My eyes snapped back to Zeke, whose hands and features were hot, brown curly hair bouncing as he moved. *"He came for me. He fell in love. Now he's locked away, and I'm stuck here forever. I can't help him. He needs me, and I can't help him. I couldn't save Livy. I was supposed to look after her. I was supposed to protect her. He said, don't tell anyone I'm his brother, or they would come after me next."*

"Bloody, hell." Ollie rubbed over his forehead. "You can trust me. I'm your family," Ollie insisted. "We're family. I'm your brother, too … in spirit. When we leave here, I promise to do everything in my power to free Tommy. Do you understand?"

Zeke nodded. Zeke understood, but the ability for me to catch up seemed impossible.

Later that evening, Ollie and I walked down the hill toward the vigil. Red, yellow, and orange painted across the sky as the sun simmered. The crowd forming the circle wasn't nearly as large as the last one. People had lost interest in caring for others.

Ethan stood in the same place. His hands hid behind his back, and we exchanged nods.

Ollie stood behind me. The mere touch of his fingertips against mine reminded me he was always within reach. The circle was silent, but Ollie's emotions shouted within him, illuminating like the sunset above. He dropped his forehead to the back of my head, whispering a prayer to himself. His words persuaded my eyes to close. His words wrapped a bubble around us, protecting us from the outside world. His words were the cause of the shortage of breath and my flickering pulse.

Ollie prayed for Zeke. He prayed for souls, for the lost and confused, and the selfish. Ollie prayed for love to prevail, hindsight to come forth, and the close-minded to blur their lines. He prayed for Ethan, for me, for himself. Everyone Ollie's eyes came across, and each person who hadn't had the opportunity to meet him has been prayed for.

He lifted his forehead from mine and sealed his prayer with a kiss to the back of my head. I scanned the circle. Bodies relaxed and tears subsided, and Ollie threaded his fingers into mine. "Let's go, love."

Our feet landed on the last step of the stairs as we retreated back to our dorm. "What do you believe in?" I asked.

"I believe in a lot of things." Ollie smiled. "You'll have to be more specific."

"Did you go to church? You know, before Dolor?"

Our pace was slow as we climbed the stairs, falling back behind the crowd.

"Why would I need to go to church? A building is manmade. I'm the creation of God. Our body is the closest thing we have to the eternal light, not a bloody building. I have the power to pray when and where I want. God hears me no matter where I am. No one can take that away from me. But a building? A building can be destroyed, knocked down, or turned into a McDonalds if the city permits it."

"You believe in God," I concluded with a nod.

Ollie licked his lips. "Remember the story *A Thousand Years Apart*? The one I read to you at the hospital?"

"Yeah. Something about an eternal light."

Ollie nodded. "That's one of many I believe in, but what about you, love? Are you going to tell me a story on how God failed you? Or are you going to tell me a story on how our creator gave you strength to get through?"

Suddenly, I felt ashamed. "I don't know what to believe."

Ollie and I reached the top of the stairs when he stopped and faced me. "If you believe in nothing, then that is what you live for. And living for nothing is a waste, wouldn't you say?"

"I hope our children take after you."

We fell back into step. "How many?" Ollie searched with a smile.

"Well let's see, how many croissants have you surprised me with?"

"Two, but I want three, so I owe you one."

Everyone seemed to be lost in a daze in the community bathroom. A place where Jake usually sang, Bria normally whined, and chatter usually filled the background noise. The only sound tonight was the water, the curtain swinging back and forth against the rod, and toilets flushing. Students moved at the same pace as the rising humidity.

It was the same place I'd first met Ollie. Our first *"Hi"* and smiles had happened in this very room—among other things: glances, a handshake, broken mirrors, attachment, stolen moments, sweet love, Christmas kisses, laughs, and tears. This bathroom held every pivotal moment in our relationship.

The tiny opening in the shower stall Ollie occupied revealed the shape of him. The dip at his lower back and his cute ass. He turned under the water, and his tattooed birds flew across the surface of his skin. Only half of him showed, and my eyes traveled over every crevice of his chest, stomach, and prominent lines leading to places I'd visited, and which I was lucky to have for the rest of my life.

This man was my fiancé.

He chose me, and I'd said it before, and I would say it again and again...I would never fucking understand it.

Ollie tilted his head, and green eyes peered back at me from the small opening. He motioned me over with the come-hither finger. My cheeks heated. I jumped down off the counter and made my way toward him before pushing my head through the curtain.

"Are you watching me, love?" Ollie whispered, his hand washing over the length of him.

I just showered, and I was wet all over again.

My gaze roamed over him. Yes, I was, and I'd gladly watch him shower, dress, sleep, eat, make love to me, everything. "Are you okay with that?" I asked, and I bit the inside of my cheek, fighting the urge to touch his skin.

"I need your eyes on me, you know this," a grin spread across his face as he turned his back to me to rinse off, "Just wanted to make sure." *Tease.*

Ollie turned off the water, and I threw him his towel, and he rubbed it over his hair. "You sure Scott needs you?"

The way his half hard-on stood and my core thumped second-guessed my entire night. "I can't talk to you like this," I breathed and closed the curtain shut. Ollie laughed while my back hit the tile, and I crossed my arms, waiting for him to come out.

We rushed out of the bathroom and down the hall, laughing until we made it behind closed doors and inside our little heaven we created. Mouths crashed as Ollie stripped off my clothes in a frenzy. "Mia, I'm not playing around," he muttered between kisses, "We're making sweet love, and you're staying with me until I fall asleep."

I nodded, and our lips collided once more.

Over and over and over again.

It took forever for Ollie to fall asleep. He refused to unlatch from me and to be honest, I didn't want him to. But Ethan needed me.

I slipped away from Ollie's hold and found my clothes in the dark. My need to kiss him outweighed the chance of him waking up and begging me not to go. "I love you," I whispered before pulling away. Ollie didn't stir. He never did. Sound asleep on his side, Ollie's arm crossed over the mattress where my body should have been.

The black hoodie engulfed me, but it was warm, and it was Ollie's. It read, "*Poetic*." Somehow, he had gotten another one and said this one was mine now.

Once the door closed lightly behind me, I turned my attention down the hall to where Ethan waited.

"Took you long enough." Ethan fell into a walk in my direction.

Together, we walked silently through the creepy campus until we got to Lynch's office. Ethan grabbed the ring from his belt and sifted through the keys. "Only the student files," he coached me while jiggling the door open. "That's it."

"Aye, aye, Captain."

The door creaked open, and if Ethan weren't here, I'd swear I still wouldn't be the only one in the room. Yes, I was the girl who believed ghosts were real, but I'd never been afraid of them. There were darker things in this world to be scared of, much more wicked than a spirit—something that could physically touch you.

"Jett?" Ethan interrupted my thoughts. My eyes snapped over to him, standing behind the desk with a flashlight in his hand. "Let's get this over with."

"Right." I walked around the desk and crouched down in front of him. "Flashlight?" I held out my hand.

Ethan exhaled behind me and dropped it into my hand. I put the sucker between my teeth, and filtered through the files. "Whas oos las aai?"

"What?" He chuckled.

I pulled the flashlight out of my mouth. "What's Jude's last name?"

"Hell if I know."

My fingers touched over every passing manila folder. Every familiar name I came across, I pulled out and handed it over to Ethan behind me. Madilyn. Brianna. Tyler. My finger touched over Oliver Masters and there was a skip in my heart.

I trust Ollie, and seeing his file would be wrong, I chanted over and over in my head. Sucking in my lips, I flipped past until my eyes landed on Jake, then Jude. "Jackpot."

"Why do you need all these?" Ethan asked after I crawled back to my feet.

"Because everyone is a suspect." I grabbed the folders from him and fell back into Lynch's leather desk chair. Ethan pulled the other chair up beside me, and we got to work.

"What exactly am I looking for?" Ethan asked as I handed him his first file.

"Anything that screams stalker, stabber, or cat mutilator."

"You do realize where we are?"

My eyes slid to him, and his attention was consumed by the papers and the long night ahead of us.

Lingering too long in Jake's file, an hour passed without so much as a hint in the right direction. After learning about his asshole father and criticizing mom, the only realization that hit me was the fact I may turn into a serial killer when I'd leave here. "This is pointless."

"No, I think I got something." Ethan leaned over, and I shone the flashlight over the file. "Jude's in for murder."

"Knew it." I pulled the file from his hand and took a closer look. My eyes scanned over the details of the car crash Jude had been involved in. My hands shook and my eyes burned at what I was seeing. "For driving while intoxicated …" My hand flew to my mouth, and I closed my eyes. "He killed his girlfriend, Ethan." I shoved the papers to his lap. "I think I'm going to throw up."

"Seriously?"

I curled over and rested my head between my legs. "Could you imagine?" I shook my head. "Shit, Ollie called it. He knew Jude couldn't do something like that. I was so wrong about him."

"Jett, don't feel sorry for that wanker."

"I do, I can't help it. It could have easily been anyone. I can't tell you how many times I drove while drunk off my ass, not once thinking about anyone else. Anything could have happened, Ethan. I was so fucking stupid. No wonder Jude acts like that. He's punishing himself. Holy shit, he's turned off his switch …" I continued to ramble with my head between my legs and tears on the verge of falling.

Ethan's hand landed over my back. "Listen, I'd love to make you feel better, but we don't have time for this. Pull yourself together."

Taking in a deep breath, I straightened my back. Jude couldn't be the prankster. "You're right," I wiped my eye, "give me the next file."

Ethan dropped the next one in my lap, which read Madilyn Wyser— also known as Maddie. I skimmed my finger over her description. Black hair? "Should say brown hair …" I mumbled to myself. "They even got the height wrong, stupid wankers,"—Ethan chuckled at my side— "Birth mom deceased in childbirth, father gave her up for adoption. Foster home to foster home ..." I continued to ramble. "Whoa, listen to this." I elbowed Ethan. "Mixed delusional disorder ... see notes for more," my finger ran down the page before turning to the next, "Here we go, Madilyn is high functioning individual suffering from mixed delusional disorder: erotomanic, grandiose, and jealous ... stalking, obsessive behavior, extreme sense of self-worth, and power ... Madilyn scored higher than me in testing."

My eyes bounced from the paper to Ethan. "Not to have a big fucking head, but I'm brilliant. I've never met anyone who scored higher than me."

"Looks like you've met your match." Ethan gripped my shoulder. "Now, focus."

"Right." I dropped my head forward and threw my palms in the air. "It has to be her. This is the perfect cocktail to create a prankster. What if she's in love with Ollie and believes Ollie is in love with her too? What if this is some delusion she has in her head, and I'm the one obstacle standing in her way?"

Ethan flipped the folder closed in his lap. "It's a start, but I don't understand what everyone sees in him."

I narrowed my eyes at him. "Do you really want to know?"

"Nope," he shoved the folder back in the drawer, "but we finally have a lead."

Finally.

Months of pranks, and it had been Maddie all along.

"That's what it feels like," I whispered as Ethan and I walked back to my wing at nearly four in the morning.

Ethan paused in the middle of the hall. "What's that?"

"That's what the note said after she shoved me in the closet, *'That's what it feels like.'* What did she mean? Like being alone?"

Ethan raised a brow and shook his head. "I don't know, Jett, but it's late. You need to rest. You should go back to Ollie."

"But you were looking forward to hanging out," I pointed out. This entire time Ethan had rushed me to finish, and now we were standing in the middle of the hallway, and he decided it was too late?

"Who are we kidding? You don't belong with me or anyone else for that matter. You should be with Masters. Go back to him. It's fine. Maybe I got what I needed from this time we did get to spend together."

"You sure?" I asked, begging to hear the three-letter word. As much as I loved being around Ethan, all I wanted to do was sink beside Ollie, close my eyes, and allow sleep to take me.

"Yeah," he grabbed my hand, "I'll see you in a little while." He squeezed my hand and forced a smile.

We said our goodbyes before I entered Ollie's room. It was dark, and he hadn't moved, still in the same place I'd left him. His chaotic brown hair stuck up as he laid on his side. Peeling off my hoodie, boots, and jeans, I admired his slightly parted lips as he slept lost in a dream, most likely thinking about us under the stars or strolling down the boardwalk. My lips broke out into a smile, and I sank in the bed beside him.

He nuzzled his head into my neck and dragged in a breath, moaning on exhale. "I missed you," his throaty words and pillow-lips buzzed across my ear.

Ollie pinned me against his warm skin, and in no time, we drifted together.

TWENTY-SEVEN

"Does it make me selfish that
I make you smile for my
own damn benefit?"

OLIVER MASTERS

Ollie

When Mia's brown eyes captured mine, time stood still, yet her smile pushed the clock to race against my unpredictable heart. The distance between us calculated in steps and the number of breaths I should have taken, but couldn't. Thirty feet tall and worthy of her, my days had been spent focusing on fucking standing because at any given moment, my knees could cave and slam into the earth.

This. The hold Mia had. Every moment measured in the way she controlled time, determined distance, and had full possession of me. And the beauty of it all? She had no fucking clue. Or maybe she had, the reason she put me out of my misery with her lips.

even when i'm gone

I was a goner for life.

"What do you think?" Mia held up a literary rose, rolling the stem between her two fingers against her cheek with a proud smile. The twinkle in her eyes burned so brightly it was almost too painful to look directly at her.

I swallowed and cleared my throat. "Perfect."

Mia bounced out of the chair in the mess hall beside Zeke, strolled casually around the table, and curled into my lap. My fingers instantly found their way to the bare and warm skin beneath her shirt at her waist. "Two more months," she whispered.

Two more months.

My hand moved up her thigh. I dropped my forehead to her shoulder and inhaled the moment to keep her flowing in me far after we would separate.

Zeke pounded against the table. I tilted my head to see him without removing my head from her. He signed, *Mia and Ollie, forever.*

"Evermore," I confirmed. Looking up, I caught her breathtaking smile and squeezed her thigh before returning my gaze to Zeke, the old soul, who was appreciating the connection before him. The child inside him beamed back. He reminded me of myself at that age of fifteen, a helpless romantic, thriving on hope and belief. *The Office, Friends,* and even *Romeo and Juliet,* Zeke measured his days in the love that surrounded him. The reason for his progressions and will to wake up each morning.

"I have to go to my appointment," Mia sighed, and her eyes dragged from the clock to me.

A full hour until I'd be back to get her. I wished following her around like a bodyguard wasn't necessary, but it was. At least until we found the prankster, and even after that, I'd still probably be following her around.

My hour was spent making a phone call to Travis, swiping up the new pack of gum waiting for me by the phone, and grabbing a book from the library. Travis had said they wanted more from me—more of me. I had nothing to give at the moment. The stress piled on top of each other. Between keeping Mia safe, keeping the outside world and the publisher happy, and battling my inner demons, breaking at any moment became my new reality. I was a saint who'd been stripped of his wings—my mortality in constant war against my soul. The rumble roared within, and each second away from her was scary as hell.

Forty minutes.

I popped a new stick into my mouth to appease my sore jaw.

Deciding to go back to the dorm was the best option. Being around a crowd drained me of my sanity. Especially this crowd. Their emotions, their tensions, their anxieties, I felt it all. My body soaked it up, and if I didn't have Mia to secure me, to hold me down, their fury slowly ate away the peace.

The only reason I hadn't told her the details of my past was because she had far too much on her plate. I should have told her. She was the only one I could talk to. She was the only one who understood me and knew how to calm my nerves. But again, her plate was full with a side of obstacles.

Mia knew about Oscar and my mum. She knew the kind of life I lived, and I was confident when I would disclose the details of the things Oscar made me do, Mia would forgive me.

I'd stained my skin with the brotherhood tattoo. No matter how hard I had tried to cover it up or hide it, it was always there. If I could rip off my arm and throw it to the wolves, I would. The brotherhood tattoo covered by scissors was a constant reminder; Oscar would always be a part of me. No matter how long or often Mia swam inside, flowing through my veins, Oscar and I shared the same tainted blood.

I'd only drifted for what felt like half a second, and when I opened my eyes, Bria stood beside my bed staring down at me. Was I still dreaming?

Sitting up, I pinched the bridge of my nose and slowly blinked my eyes back to life.

She stood there, raven black hair and porcelain skin.

"What are you doing?" I asked, my voice hoarse and groggy. I pumped my fist against my chest and cleared my throat. "Bria," I tried again and shook my head awake. "You can't be here." Bria only smiled down at me and stood there in a top revealing her pale midriff and thin black, stretchy pants. She had no shoes on, and her eyes glazed over. "Are you all right?"

"I don't feel so good," she finally said, and plopped down on the bed beside me. "Jude broke up with me. He picked Tyler over me ... Where's Mia? I came to talk to Mia," she fell back against the bed where Mia usually rested her head.

I inched my way to the back of the wall and pulled my knees up. "Mia's with Conway." I turned my gaze to the clock. "She'll be back in thirty minutes."

A tear rolled down Bria's cheek, and she pulled her hands over her face. I'd never once seen Bria cry, especially over a bloke. "It'll be okay." I gripped her shoulder. "He's a wanker, anyway."

"You think so?" She sat up and wiped her arm across her eyes.

Quite frankly, no. I didn't think Jude was a wanker, but I nodded anyway. She'd caught me off guard and I'd say anything to make her feel better and leave.

Jude was still grieving the loss of his girlfriend, and by the look he always had in his eyes, she was the love of his life. His actions were wrong, but I understood them.

Bria curled into my side, and I wrapped my arm around her.

"I miss hanging out with you." Bria's words muffled by my hoodie. "I feel like I never see you anymore. We never hang out. We used to be close. You used to be this badass without a care in the world. I missed that about you."

"That wasn't me." That was the arsehole on meds, allowing the darkness to take control. Bria swung her leg over my lap and snaked her arms around me, tears flowing into my chest. I sat confused and frozen. "Come on." I tried to pull her up, but she held me tighter. "Let's take a walk, yeah? You can walk with me to get Mia."

Bria shook her head. "I just need a hug, Ollie," she cried. "You give the best hugs."

My head spun, and all I could think about was Mia and how the hell I was supposed to get out of this mess. Keeping my hands at my sides, I looked up to the ceiling, waiting for her cries to dissipate, then Bria rolled her hips against me.

My knob jerked in my joggers, warning me.

I wanted to throw her off me, but the paralysis gripped every muscle and limb.

"Oh, Ollie," Bria cried again, her bony hip grinding against me, and the sound of my name hit me like a punch to the brain.

The bathroom. It had been Bria crying out my name.

Another hip grind, and I looked down between us to see her wetness seep through the thin material of her pants. She had no knickers on. The flashback of my first time with Lacey ripped through me, digging out the caged beast raging inside with every utter of my name from Bria's lips.

"Stop," I warned through gritted teeth. "Fucking stop."

One more fucking grind was all it took, and I shoved her off the bed. Her back slammed against the floor, and she looked up, shocked and disoriented. "What the hell was that for?" Bria massaged the back of her head.

"I warned you. Don't fucking come near me."

"Is this about Mia?"

My brows raised and I bounced to my feet, freeing myself of the joggers she ruined. "You're impossible." I swiped up a fresh pair of pants and shoved my legs through. "You tried taking advantage of me—*again*. Mia's not here to tear your arse off me this time, but I have enough willpower to say no." I shook my head, remembering the time Bria almost had her way with me last year after I'd stupidly drunk too much.

"What do you mean *again*? You think that's what happened? You think I tried taking advantage of you?" Bria laughed and looked around the room. "You remember, yeah? The long nights after Isaac, Alicia, and Maddie left, it was just you and me. We fucked, Ollie. You fucked me hard. You never said no to me before. What happened that night with Mia was only a misunderstanding."

All the color drained from my face. "You and me," I pointed my finger back and forth between us, "we never fucked."

Bria laughed and looked me up and down. "Wow. Congratulations, Ollie." Bria clapped her hands together. "You're the most screwed up person at Dolor ..." Her words ran together thereafter as I stood in a daze, trying to recall ever sticking it in her. "Don't worry, I accept who you are, regardless of your erection problem. But we can fix that."

With my contaminated joggers clutched in my fist, I took a step back, adding distance between us. "My dick was never the problem." I shoved my hand through my hair and peered down at her. "I want you out by the time I come back."

The entire way to Conway's, I ransacked through every memory of the summer before Mia arrived. Regardless if it had happened or not, it was a time before Mia. If it had happened, Mia wouldn't care. This wouldn't bother her. We'd been through worse.

But there was no way I'd been with her.

Was there?

Did I?

Bria got into my head, and I couldn't piece that bloody summer together—couldn't hear myself think anymore. I'd been pissed or messed up on pills half the time, then the other half spent in confinement. My pace quickened, and sweat rolled down my hairline. My eyes darted to every clock I walked passed.

Time—measured in the number of steps from my soul to hers, the number of words I'd have to get out before she had a chance to part her lips, and the seconds spent in silence that followed. She was too bloody far.

Five minutes.

I rounded the corner and collided with her.

"Ollie," Mia breathed out and pulled away from me. Her hypnotizing eyes examined mine and drove around my features as her hands grabbed hold of my hoodie.

Oxygen rushed down my throat, and the fresh air filled my lungs. I could breathe. "I think I fucked Bria," I blurted into the unnecessary space between us.

Mia's brows raised and her muscles twitched in my hold. "You think?"

"She came in my room when I was sleeping, jumped my john, got her shit on my sweats ..." I shook my head, "She said we used to fuck." Mia's eyes widened, and nothing had been coming out right. "I think I need Conway." I grabbed her hand and started for the doctor's door.

"Whoa," Mia yanked my arm, pulling me backward until my eyes were back on her. "You need to slow down." Her hand landed on my chest, and my eyes blinked rapidly. "Let's go talk."

"Dammit, Mia. Don't you see? I'm going mad!"

Five.

Four.

Three ...

Her fingers dipped beneath my hoodie, and her warm palm covered my chest and expanded throughout the rest of my body. Hitting me like a drag of nicotine, my muscles relaxed instantly. Amazing, really, my reaction to her. With closed eyes, my head dropped back, and I let out a steady breath against her subtle touch.

"I'm with you," she said a notch above a whisper, and I could have sworn she was a sorceress because this was nothing short of magic. Pure fucking magic. The heaviness lifted, and I pulled my head back to face her as my heart matched the beat of the subtle pulse in her fingers.

"Mia," I said in a gathered breath. "We need to talk. I can't hold everything in any longer. At any moment, I'll explode."

It hadn't taken long for Bria to poison our room. The rubbish smell. The thoughts. The cries still echoing from inside my brain to the concrete walls. I stripped the bed, bundled the sheets, and threw them right outside the door.

"Is all this really necessary?" Mia asked with her arms crossed. The heat of her stare followed my every move.

"I still feel her on my skin. I feel everything." I turned to her. "You. You were everywhere. Now she is." Refocusing on the task before me, I picked up the same pillow Bria laid her head across. "I hate it, Mia. I don't like the way she makes me feel."

The sound of the door closed, and I whipped my head back around to see Mia had left.

I pulled open the door and ran down the hall to catch up with her. "Where are you going?"

She turned to face me. Her brown hair fanned around her face, and a smile spread across her tender lips. "We need a little spring cleaning anyway. Come on." She twirled back around. "Lucky for you, I know where the cleaning supplies are."

An hour was spent drowning in bleach and the dirty confessions of my past. I told Mia about my time in the closet, the things I'd seen, losing my virginity, Oscar—everything. She took her anger out on the floors until I resumed the explanation of what happened with Bria.

Oscar had turned me into him, and for years I treated women like cattle. "You're just as much a victim as they were," she reminded me with a towel over her shoulder.

Another hour passed, and we propped the door open to air out the strong stench of cleaner, the worries of my past blowing out into the hall along with it. Our deep conversation turned light, and smiles broke on both our faces. We joked, I tickled her, she used her towel like a whip on my arse, and Mia's giggles didn't let up while cleaning out my desk, going through every drawer and scrap paper I'd written across. She laughed lightly to herself as I pulled a new sheet over the mattress. "You're high," I said through a laugh and shook my head.

"On life," she corrected, pointing at me with the spray bottle in one hand and my notebook in the other. A few people slowed as they crossed our room, sneaking a peek to see what we were up to. "This is too good to sit in a desk drawer," she said, fingering through my notes. "Like, so good." Her eyes peered up at me, and I sat over the mattress with a wide grin. "Why are you looking at me like that?"

"I did something." *Vague*. I had done a big thing, but I had done it all for us. I'd published my work. I'd bought us a home. I'd become something of myself because of her constant reminder I wasn't ordinary. I was someone. Her someone. Each moment with her stitched back on another feather of my wings, and once we'd leave Dolor, together we'd fly.

"Something other than having your ex-girlfriend rubbing her scent all over my fiancé?"

Hearing her refer to me as her fiancé touched my smile, heart, and knob. She knew better. "Ex" and "girlfriend" were never words tied to Bria's name. "Your fiancé?" I asked teasingly, both of us knowing damn well everything I was, belonged to the girl staring back at me from the desk chair with my poetry in the palm of her hand, but the way she'd called me her fiancé sent me into a breathless puddle of mess.

"My fiancé," she repeated matter-of-factly. The spray bottle and my journal left her hands before she stood and walked over to me. I leaned back on my elbows, and my eyes drifted over her every angle, twitching like a fiend to see where her next steps would lead her.

As long as it involved her on top of me, me on top of her, or us pinned to one another, I'd be cured of this craze swimming inside.

Mia stopped between my knees. Her finger rested under my chin as she tilted my head up to meet her eyes and my heart jumped into my throat. "I'm past the whole jealous part. Now? I'm just pissed," Mia whispered.

"What are you going to do about it, love?" We were so close, all my senses filled with Mia, overpowering the bleach and the incident that happened hours before. Mia was all around me, dancing through me again, tickling every nerve, pumping every organ. My knob tensed with anticipation.

She dropped her hand, and my heart stopped. "Where are you going?"

My eyes landed on her cute little arse as she pulled the door closed, and my breathing labored as she pulled off the hoodie made for her. Mia's smile illuminated the room, throwing the dullness of Dolor into color.

Her tiny fingers landed over my pants, sliding them down, and I lifted my bottom to allow her access. A gust of wind smacked against my stretched dick, begging to feel her warmth. Still, I stayed quiet as anticipation controlled my every breath.

"Dammit, Mia," I moaned from my throat as she pushed her hands over my pelvic muscles. Pre-cum spilled unapologetically, and Mia traced her bottom lip over my tip. "Fuck, this is going to be embarrassingly quick."

"Talk to me, Ollie," Mia rasped out before wrapping her wet lips around me taking me slow.

I wanted to tell her that there were over two hundred thousand words in the English dictionary. *Two hundred thousand.* Easily, I strung words together in the journal with her in mind on a day to day basis, but not one word came close to the single utter of my name rolling off her tongue and how it swallowed me whole.

"Ollie," she whispered again, and just like that, she seized my existence and reigned over me.

"I ... I ... I can't," I breathlessly said as her tongue stroked the sensitive skin underneath. As much as I wanted to watch the way she took care of me, my head fell back, and I closed my eyes. My tip hit the back of her throat, and all at once, the blood rushed to one place. My muscles strained, veins popped, and in half a second, I made a rash decision.

My hands fisted her jeans, and I ripped them off before yanking her knickers to the side. I grabbed the back of her thighs, picked her weightless body up, and slammed inside her. Mia's warm, tight flesh consumed me, and I pulsed, spilling every fucking ounce into her with shaky hands entangled in her hair.

"Sorry," I finally breathed once the waves crashed and dissolved into the beach of her and me. Mia's wet lips grazed my jawline, and my knob jerked inside her.

My girl laughed lightly and kissed my dimple. "You say sorry like it's a bad thing."

"The things your lips do to me," I ran my thumb over her bottom lip, "trust me it's enough, but nothing—and I mean absolutely nothing—compares to the way I feel when we're connected like this."

Mia's lips parted, and I dove into her mouth as my thumb fell over her little nub beneath her soaked cotton knickers. Her heavenly grind erased the hell of this place, and I was certain I could live inside the gates within her for eternity without needing a bloody thing.

Mia cried out, and I swallowed every testimony.

She shook, I anchored her.

She broke apart inside my arms, and I held all her pieces together.

Utterly stripped, unarmed, and exposed, the unity of us was a beautiful thing, and there was only one word to describe it.

Poetic.

TWENTY-EIGHT

"Perhaps you were here to remind everyone that angels are real,
in the shape of humanity and the color of grace.
And for a brief moment in time,
we all sang the same song."

OLIVER MASTERS

Mia

I t was February 29th.

Leap day, and a Saturday, nonetheless.

The sun still rose despite it being the coldest day of the year, streaming through the window and hardly able to warm my face. The light appeared behind my lids, demanding my lashes to part, but I'd learned it was okay to keep them closed a little while longer to soak it all in.

"You feel that?" Ollie asked into my hair. Warm hands attempted to blanket the chill as they ran up my arm and down my side.

"Mmhmm," I hummed, speaking of something else entirely.

"The sun is out, love. You slept through the entire night to wake up to a new day. One we don't deserve." His lips brushed across my shoulder. "What will you do with it?"

I flipped in his arms, my eyes disobedient to the sun but caving to his voice. Ollie intertwined his legs with mine with his eyes still closed. His dimple deepened beside his all-knowing grin. I wanted to crawl inside his brain and roll around in whatever place he imagined for us. Leaning away from him, I stretched my arm under the mattress to grab my camera. A rush of cold air came between us, and I snapped a picture, capturing his essence in a black and white polaroid that held more emotion than anything in color could portray. He was all shades of beautiful.

It was February 29th. Leap day.

Ollie, Zeke, and I sat around our table during breakfast.

Zeke's hair was curlier, bouncier than usual. His brown eyes glowed from across the table. The rare and saintly moments caught in Zeke's smile could light the darkest night. Ollie grinned right back at him, chewing the breakfast in his mouth and sent him a wink. Peace washed over the three of us.

Two and a half more months and we would all finally be set free.

Ollie would accomplish what Tommy couldn't, and rescue Zeke from this place.

I want to hear you play, Zeke signed to me.

"I'll play for you." I smiled.

Zeke had come so far since I'd first arrived. I remembered the times he'd only stare from across the table as I'd blurted every thought crossing my mind—mostly about Ollie and how he managed to piss me off, but it had been only because I couldn't grasp the fireworks and symphonies colliding inside me whenever Ollie was near. Zeke had been a part of every step of our journey, becoming the silent rock holding our two pieces together.

It was time for Zeke to write his own love story.

Ollie leaned over the table and took another bite before dropping his fork and breaking off into a silent conversation with Zeke. Ethan stood alert at his post against the wall with his hands clasped to his belt. His face was expressionless but wholly healed from the altercation weeks ago. Ever since we had found out about Maddie's condition, Ethan kept a close eye on her, watching her every move.

Coincidently, nothing more happened with the prankster.

My gaze moved over to Jake, who now sat at a different table with Liam, Tyler, Jude, and Bria. Liam and Jake indulged in small talk inside their bubble, and my heart fluttered at the smile expanding across Jake's thin lips. Jude's hand clutched firmly to Tyler's beneath the table as Tyler and Bria joked about something I was too far away to hear.

It was small, the glare Bria shot over to me, and if Ollie never told me what had happened between the two of them in our room, I would have missed it.

I was back and forth on whether or not I should confront her about the advance she made at Ollie. I wanted to punish her. All I needed was two minutes alone with her.

Then, my eyes landed on Maddie. She and Gwen sat alone, eating in silence in the middle of the mess hall between my table and Bria's. Maddie shook her bangs from her eyes before she took a bite, nodding as Gwen waved her hands animatedly in the air. Maddie's eyes fixed on the tray before her, tuning the girl out, I was sure.

Ollie had no idea the dirt Ethan and I had dug up on Maddie.

At this point, I had no reason to hide it from him any longer other than the shame for invading my friend's privacy—Jake's, Bria's, and Tyler's. Though, I was desperate.

And desperation made for bad decisions.

It was February 29th.

Leap day.

The keys of the piano felt like ice against my fingers as they danced with the notes to Ollie's current favorite: *Firestone*.

Awe struck in Zeke's eyes as he sat still in the black chair by the window with Ollie by his side. Ollie's fingers moved fluently across the pages of his journal under the sun, glances stolen between us. I inhaled the chilly air through my nose, and it felt like spearmint coating my throat and lungs when the door to the group therapy room swung open.

Bria stood there, examining the room with a raging fire in her eyes.

My fingers froze over the keys. My eyes darted back and forth to Ollie and Zeke by the window. Ollie flinched, sending a panic inside me.

"Keep playing, *love*. It sounds beautiful," Bria snarled, closing the door behind her. The click of the lock bounced, and she turned to face us. "Hey, Ollie," Bria smirked, but her stride closed in on me. Ollie stood, Zeke's eyes bulged, and I jerked my eyes in her direction.

"What are you doing here?" I asked nervously as she circled me.

"Bria," Ollie warned, and before he could make it to me, the edge of a sharp blade pressed against my windpipe.

"Sit down, Ollie, or I'll cut the bitch in two."

My eyes fixed on Ollie, afraid to move—afraid to blink. The lightning crashed behind my eyes and my vision clouded, but even my tears were too afraid to fall. Ollie's light eyes bottomed out, fear zeroing in, and the change happened almost immediately. He inched forward, his palms out in front of him, begging with scrambled words and a broken tone.

The sharp tip of the cold blade pierced my skin. It burned, and warm blood trickled down the length of my neck. I sank my teeth into my lip to fight my body from trembling or moving at all.

"N-n-n-no," Ollie stammered with bloodshot eyes. "Please, don't do this, Bria. God, I'm fucking begging you."

I wanted to speak, but it was hard to get any words out when you couldn't breathe. Shock took complete possession of me, and I sat stunned and watched as Ollie broke apart from ten feet away.

His words sounded distant, and his movements seemed lost in slow motion. Time lagged, and I squeezed my eyes closed to wait for the inevitable.

"Sit down, darling." Her tone was calm. Too calm. Bria's hair brushed against my cheek as she leaned over. "I've been waiting a long time for this."

"For what?" Ollie shouted, then quickly lowered his tone. "What did she ever do to you? Bria, you can walk away. Right now, we'll never speak of this. Please! *Fuck*. Don't do this!"

"Madilyn," Bria deadpanned. "My name is Madilyn and if I have to hear you call me that name one more time …"

"I don't understand," Ollie's voice shook, grasping his hair with tears falling from his red eyes. "But we can go talk. Let her go. We'll sort this out."

"No, I think Mia deserves to know the truth before I finally get rid of her," the girl said close to my ear. My eyes sprang open to see Ollie take two steps forward when she yanked my head back and dug the blade into my throat. "You want to test me? She'll be gone by the time you get here, Ollie. I wouldn't suggest taking another step."

Ollie stopped in his tracks, and his hands shook at his sides.

"I wanted a clean break, too—a fresh start," she began. "Brianna, the girl you've come to know as Maddie, the two of us got close at the institution before we arrived. Really close. The plan was brilliant. I'd have a new identity. The bitch did whatever I said, actually followed through with it and switched our folders, switched our bloody identities, before we arrived. I had her eating out of the palm of my hand," the girl blew out a menacing laugh. I turned my eyes to her, the girl I thought I knew—the girl whose black short hair grazed my cheek and I had called Bria for almost two years. She was fucking Madilyn—she was Maddie. She had been the one with the delusional disorder this entire time. "Can you believe she actually fell in love with me?

"But when we arrived, things between you and me just clicked. Brianna got jealous and decided to go out of her way to fuck you before I could, Ollie. All this just to spite me. Big mistake. So just like she went out of her way to have you, I went out of my way to have the cow removed and tossed into the Looney Bin. You were always mine, Ollie. You were never hers. You still *are* mine! I'll never forget that night we made love. It's all I can think about. You know it, too. Or at least until this one came along. Not only did Mia steal you from me ... no, she went as far as calling me a rapist! Can you believe that, Ollie? Like I'd have to rape you, you fucked anything that walked." The blade applied more pressure against my throat, and my eyes strained from the pressure. "I mean, I was just about to have you back, and she had to come along and fuck it all up, didn't she? Then Mia had *me* raped! Talk about a fucking hypocrite, ya? Remember that, Mia? Watching Isaac take advantage of me?" she seethed in my ear.

"It wasn't Mia's fault," Ollie rushed out.

"The hell it wasn't! When you left, I learned everything *Mia*. I learned how she talked, how she moved. I wanted to know what it was about her that made you tick, why you chose her and not me! Turns out, she's nothing more than a shallow whore." Her knee cap rammed into my spine, and my head bounced backward, and she fisted my hair. I winced, and Ollie jumped forward. "Come closer, please Ollie. I dare you. I so dare you."

Ollie gripped his hair, his jaw working overtime as tears fell fast from his battered eyes. "Don't think I won't kill you, Bria. Or Maddie. Whatever the fuck your name is. I swear to God I'll fucking kill you."

"Oh hush, I'm not done with my story yet." Madilyn laughed. "You were gone, and I was on my way to becoming this girl you always wanted. Then I overheard Lynch talking about your return. I had to make my move, get this one out of the picture for good. So many times, I almost had her. Even tossed Brianna straight into your arms to keep you occupied and away from Mia. Can you believe that? I let Brianna fuck you, keep you satisfied until we could be together. That's how much I love you, Ollie."

"You need help," Ollie gritted out with red in his eyes. "Let me help you. You're sick."

"Yeah, well love makes you do crazy things." Madilyn grabbed my arm and pulled me off the bench, leading me to a chair with the blade held firmly at my throat. The misery consuming Ollie hurt more than the knife or thought of death. I wanted to hold him, tell him that it was going to be okay. I wanted to wipe his tears and be there for him. "Any last words?"

"You trust me, love?" Ollie asked me, trying to maintain a steady voice, but it was laced with all emotion. I sucked in my lips and nodded. His lips trembled. "Close your eyes, real tight." Another tear fell down his red cheek, and he looked up before his eyes hit mine again. "Don't open them, no matter what."

I screwed my eyes closed, holding them real tight until the stars appeared. The stars turned into white shapes—triangles, spheres, moving and transforming. I envisioned Ollie and me dancing, the fireworks, the library. I fought to replay our stolen moments as the tip of the blade punctured my skin. Hot tears spilled from the corners, but I was no longer afraid. Voices sounded around me as my head spun, and the sharp blade disappeared from my throat and was replaced by Ollie's warm hand, granting permission for me to breathe again.

A gasp echoed.

And then a thump sounded.

My eyes slammed tighter.

And I was picked up from the chair and warmth wrapped around me.

A marine breeze filled my senses. Freedom. Ollie.

"Mia, look at me," he cried. My eyes blinked open, and I was face to face with a wrecked man. "I'm so sorry," he repeated over and over.

I turned my head, my body still shaking to see Madilyn on the floor with a knife lodged into her side.

I returned my gaze to Ollie. "I don't…"

He kissed me—my cheeks. My nose. My eyes. My neck. Ollie's hands moved over my face, and that was when I saw the reflection in his eyes.

His eyes moved past me to behind me. His emerald gems grew in size and was replaced once again by panic. Zeke's shriek pierced my eardrums, and Ollie shoved me to the side just as Zeke jumped between Madilyn and where I stood seconds before.

Time sped. Before Ollie could do anything, Madilyn had removed the blade from her side, and drove it into Zeke's stomach. The actions that followed raced at the speed of light. Ollie launched forward, an anguished yet hostile scream erupted from his chest like fire. Frozen in place, I struggled to take in what was happening. All I could do was watch as Ollie withdrew a pencil from his back pocket and plunge it deep into Maddie's neck. All I could hear was the thump as she hit the floor, followed by a second thump as Ollie collapsed. Blood ran down the length of his arm, smearing on the marble floor as he shuffled toward Zeke, frantically screaming his name in defeat and bottomless heartbreak, over and over.

I must have screamed. I didn't hear it, but I felt it in my throat. Everything seemed to go hazy, my heart now steadying to a slow but unsteady beat, a beat that could only be matched to broken pieces of my world falling apart all around me.

It was February 29th.

Leap day.

I froze with my arms wrapped firmly around my knees curled into a ball as Ollie's agonizing cries boomed around me. One hand fisted Zeke's shirt and the other pressed against Zeke's wound, trying to stop the blood from flowing. But it still did. I couldn't move. Ollie's soul crumbled before me, and I was useless. Shock took me over. Even tears froze mid-fall down my cheek.

Zeke coughed, and his head tilted as blood spilled from the corner of his mouth.

"You have to stay with me, brother," Ollie cried, frantically pushing down on Zeke's stomach. "Hang in there." Zeke's eyes slid to mine, and peace filled the dark circles of them. Calm in the storm, succumbing to his fate. He'd lost the will to fight, finally wanting to be set free.

Only once before had I watched someone's soul slip away. My uncle had fear and shock in his eyes as if he hadn't expected it. Our eyes had locked until he was gone, and even then, I had sat frozen, staring back at the lifeless glaze in the hollow pupils.

Zeke accepted his fate with open arms. He wasn't scared. He wasn't afraid. The peace inside him was calm and quiet, but the devastation surrounding him was unwilling to let him go.

Then his calmness slid back to Ollie.

A silent understanding passed between them, and still, I couldn't move.

Zeke tried to lift his hands, and Ollie took them both and held them to his chest.

"I did it. I saved her," Zeke whispered through a cough.

"Yeah, you did, my friend." Ollie broke and forced a small smile over his wet face for him.

"Mia, and Ollie, forever," Zeke finally whispered with a hoarse throat. His eyes blinked closed as blood spread through his shirt.

"No, no, no, no, stay with me," Ollie's head snapped in my direction. "Go, Mia! Get help!" The words seemed so far away, yet right in my ear. Until Ollie's hands clutched my face and demanded me to see him—to hear him. "He needs you ... I need you. Look at me! I need you to fucking hear me, Mia! Go find help!"

TWENTY-NINE

> "The only way to cheat death
> is by creating a love that
> will live forever."
>
> OLIVER MASTERS

Mia

It was March 2nd.

The clouds laid sad and heavy above us. I sat with my hands folded nervously in my lap and Tyler at my side. Lynch just gave a speech moments before at a makeshift podium seated at the top of the steps of Dolor. It looked like any other day, dark skies, black wardrobe, and whispers spreading in the small group of people who had come.

But it wasn't any other day.

It was the day of Zeke's funeral.

The sound of tires against gravel hit the driveway before rolling through the iron gates and the murmurs dissolved instantly. I craned my neck to see a white van come to a complete stop behind us. When my eyes landed on Stanley stepping out of the van and sliding the back door, I jumped to my feet and looked up at Ollie who stood beside Lynch at the top of the stairs.

Ollie didn't meet my gaze. His eyes fixed ahead.

I turned back, and a guy stepped out in a blue jumpsuit. The rattling of cuffs persuaded the whispers to start again around me.

"Holy hell …"

"Oh-my-god"

"Who is that?"

"… it's Tommy."

Tommy darted his eyes around before dropping his head to the ground when both feet hit the concrete. Loose brown curls piled high on his head but short around the sides. His face had intricate lines—strong jawline, sharp nose, and high cheekbones. All eyes watched as he took the last chair in the back row. Lynch cleared his throat, calling everyone's attention to the front. "Oliver would like to say a few words. We will have a moment of silence, and then it's back inside. Madilyn Wyser's memorial service is being held in her home town, but we will hold a moment of silence for her over the green tomorrow."

I looked back over my shoulder at Zeke's brother, who lifted his head at the same time. Our eyes locked. He held my gaze, dark eyes staring at me through the courtyard. Flashbacks of all the times Zeke stared at me from across the table in the mess hall raced through my mind. The color of red outlined his penetrating stare, yet a calmness swept through us and over me. I offered a small smile, and Tommy narrowed his dark eyes. His expression froze for a beat before the muscles in his face relaxed. An ache pricked behind my eyes and the air caught in my chest.

"I've written many words in my lifetime, well over a million, I'm sure," Ollie paused and gripped the podium at the front. His head dropped down, his knuckles turned white, and complete silence fell over everyone at the sound of his voice. "But what I'm about to say … it would never be enough. I could say some words, fill this silence with poetry, but the truth is, words could never describe the impact Zeke had on this earth, because with Zeke, you just feel it. Zeke was a friend, a fighter, a listener, a cheerleader," his eyes hit Tommy in the back, "a brother." Ollie exhaled and turned his eyes to the sky. "But most of all," he dropped his head down and found me, "Zeke was a lover.

"Love … the light in his mornings and the motivation to keep him from succumbing to the darkest of days. Zeke believed in fairy tales, in sparks, and happily ever after's, but he also believed in the honest, chaotic, and hardest kind of love. Zeke saw it before I had a chance to blink. And in times when I had nothing left to give and the thought of giving up was pulling at me from every direction, Zeke was there, eyes focused, fingers restless, putting all the bloody pieces back together.

"Zeke *is* love. He is a reminder that no matter how difficult it gets, no matter how often you're tested or what obstacles are thrown, love is always worth fighting for," Ollie sucked in a breath and ran a palm down his face, "and dying for."

"Zeke should not be remembered in tears. Zeke would want us to remember him in smiles, in laughs, and in every joyous moment we find ourselves in, because it's there, in those rare moments, when he is all around us."

He lifted his hands and signed the rest, *Love you, brother. Evermore.*

I dropped my head back, and a single raindrop landed on my cheek, and I closed my eyes.

The clouds parted, and rain fell over us. No one moved. No one spoke. Ollie took a step back from the podium and faced the sky. Tears mixed with rain streamed down my face, and I fought the urge to blink. Ollie pushed his hair back and pressed his palms to his eyes. He'd just spoken words of holding it together when all his body wanted to do was fall apart.

I jumped to my feet and rushed toward him, clothes completely soaked and feet not moving nearly as fast as I'd liked. When I reached him, I wrapped my arms around his waist and pressed my head into his chest.

Ollie held me tighter, his head fell into my neck and fisted the back of my sweatshirt.

We didn't say anything. We only stood under the rain until Ollie's breathing calmed and we shivered in the cold. When I removed my head from his chest and looked around, everyone else had already parted ways, Tommy included.

Ollie linked our hands together, and we walked back inside the doors of Dolor.

"That was beautiful," I whispered to Ollie. Dry and warm, we faced each other in bed. He had been quiet the past couple of days, and I wondered if there was a part of him that blamed me for Zeke's death as well. Not only had Ollie watched his best friend die, but he also killed Madilyn.

We'd hardly seen each other afterward. As soon as I'd left to get help, Ollie and I were separated and questioned in different rooms for almost an entire day. I had been released first and had waited for him all night last night. When he had finally entered the dorm at close to midnight, he'd stripped down and sunk in the bed beside me, silently holding on to me for dear life.

The funeral was the first time I'd heard him speak since Zeke's death.

Ollie nodded. "No words will ever amount to what he's given to me in return."

"He looked up to you. He loved you so much, and would have given you the world."

"That's the thing, Mia. He gave me the fucking world, and I'm looking right at her. I couldn't react quick enough. It could've so easily been you," Ollie's breathing shook, and he grabbed the side of my head and looked me in the eyes. "He did this for us. He did this so I wouldn't spend my days drowning in tears and heartache. So, I refuse to cry. He deserves more than fucking tears. He deserves every smile I put on your face for the rest of my life. He deserves all the laughter, the stolen kisses, the lifetime of feels, the sleepless nights of conversations ... He deserves for us to *live*."

The real Brianna, a girl we had all known as Maddie, had switched lives with a girl who only used her love and loyalty as a pawn in a larger game. Everyone had been a pawn in her game that only resulted in death.

Because Madilyn had switched files with Brianna, Madilyn never got the help she needed with her delusional disorder. The real tragedy was ... Zeke's death could've been avoided. From the very beginning, Madilyn had been under the impression Ollie and she were in love. To this day, Ollie still swore up and down he'd never been intimate with her, but those days when he'd lost himself were a blur. Madilyn had been waiting on the sidelines ever since, formulating her plan to get him back.

"We're getting together for one last rendezvous in the woods as like a farewell ..." Tyler whispered after Dr. Conway took over a discussion in Ms. Chandlers classroom. A little over two weeks had passed since the funeral, but the chatter hadn't dimmed. Tyler and Jude had another year here. Ollie, Jake, and I were leaving. I wondered how next year would go for her and Jude. They were unofficially official. Of course, Jake advised her of the curse of Dolor love, and to downplay the relationship, and keep the sweet moments to a minimum. "Jake and Liam said they'd go. You think Ollie would be down?"

"Yeah, he would." Despite everything that had happened, Ollie was in good spirits. At any moment, I feared he'd crash, but Ollie did exactly what he said he was going to do. He smiled.

"I'm sure as hell going to miss you. I wish I could go back and change things ... trust in the right people, ya know?" Tyler admitted.

"When you get out, come find me. I'll be here. I'm only going back to the states to clear my name, and I'm flying right back. I'm staying in the UK."

"Seriously?"

I nodded. "Yeah, I still can't believe it either."

Ms. Chandler walked around the classroom and collected textbooks off the corners of our desks, permitting us to leave once she'd passed by. Tyler and I stood together. "Ya moving in with Ollie? Where? It's not like you guys have a place after you leave here, no?"

Too many questions too fast. I shoved my hands into the back pockets of my jeans and dropped my head, wishing I'd wore my hair down to hide the fact I had no idea what the future held. I supposed I'd have to look for a job. I never had a job before. Maybe I'd work as a waitress while Ollie worked on his poetry. We could get a small apartment somewhere. Did they have apartments here?

"I heard they have a program after Dolor. They get you set up in a place as a transition back into the real world. I mean," Tyler shrugged as we stepped out into the hall, "you already qualify. A work program, too. They have a work program." I kept quiet, feeling empty without having to carry my textbooks but my head heavy with new burdens I had no time to consider.

We'd made it a few feet away from the classroom, and Tyler paused at our usual spot to wait for Ollie. "I'll figure it out," I sighed and fidgeted with the hem of Ollie's shirt I wore. "I always figure it out."

"What's up with that anyway?" Tyler asked. She fell back against the wall and looked down at the word printed across my chest. "Poetic," she said slowly. "What does it even mean?"

"It's Ollie's," I pulled the loose shirt away from my chest and looked down. "I'm starting to think he's obsessed with this brand. Or word. Can't be sure. He does write poetry, you know."

"He's a poetic?"

I arched a brow. "You mean a poet?"

"Okay, so he's a poet who writes poetry, and I'm guessing poetic is the, what? Adjective to this whole clusterfuck?"

I laughed. "Something like that."

"I don't get it," Tyler shook her head.

The presence behind me was unmistakable, and like a magnetic force field, Ollie and I leaned into one another. His warmth surrounded me. His minted breath hit the tip of my ear.

"Tyler," Ollie greeted.

"Oliver." She nodded.

"You see what just happened?" he asked her.

Tyler lifted off the wall. "Huh?"

"I hadn't touched her, yet she drifted to me as if her body recognized mine was near. We are on the same wavelength. Same rhythm. This," Ollie danced a finger across the nape of my neck, "This is the meaning of poetic."

"Oh." Tyler sighed, blushing. "I bet he's poetic in bed." She wiggled her brows at me, and I dropped my head into my hand.

A giggle tickled my throat.

"Why are you laughing?" Ollie asked. He sat up with his bare back against the wall and notebook in his lap, tapping the end of his pencil over the paper.

"Oh, nothing."

I returned to my paper in front of me at the desk and jotted another word. Another laugh threatened to come up, and I pinched my lips together to force it back down, but it was no use. A cackle escaped, and I leaned forward in my chair.

"What is it? What are you doing over there?" Ollie pried with a curious smile.

A happy tear fell. "Okay, don't make fun," I warned, pointing my pencil at him.

"You want to point wood at each other?" Ollie lifted a brow. "Mine's bigger."

My jaw dropped, and I threw my pencil at him, and Ollie's eyes followed the pencil flying clear across the room, but nowhere near hitting him. "Ace move, but I'm over here." Ollie smiled. "Tell me. Why are you laughing."

"I wrote you a poem," I said with a shrug.

"You wrote me a poem," he repeated, amused.

"Yes, but it's really bad."

Ollie dropped his pencil and relaxed against the wall. "Let's hear it."

"No way."

Ollie lowered his chin and gave me those daydream eyes of his. "Please. No one has written me a poem before."

"There's a reason why no one but you should write a poem."

"I won't laugh. Promise."

"Fine." I pumped my fist against my chest and cleared my throat.

> *"Roses are black*
> *The skies are clear.*
> *I get wet when you are near.*
> *You're the crack to my butt*
> *The whiskey to my drunk.*
> *How did I snag such a handsome hunk?"*

My eyes lifted off my paper, and I waited for his reaction.

Ollie sucked in his lips and nodded once.

I tilted my head. "Say something."

"Mia," he choked, then paused to control his lips. His dimples pierced his cheeks. "I don't even know what to say."

"Wow, Ollie has no words."

"Utterly gobsmacked," he agreed with an upside-down smile, partial chuckles blowing through his pressed lips.

"What did you write?"

Ollie held up a finger. "I'm going to need a minute, love." I watched him as he stretched his legs out, adjusted himself, and rested his head against the concrete wall. He looked down, and my eyes followed to the erection in his sweats. "Are you wet right now?" he asked with a tilt of his head and his brow in the air. A grin expanded across his lips. "Because even though that poem was terrible, I can't shake how wet you get when I'm near."

I lifted a shoulder. "Maybe."

"Come here," he nudged his head.

Standing, I walked over to the mattress until my knees hit the edge. The only two items covering me were my white panties and the Poetic shirt. Ollie's gaze touched over every inch of my skin, claiming me. My eyes drifted closed, and I waited for him to touch me, for his hands to make the same journey where his eyes had roamed.

I heard the mattress move before his breath hit my neck. "How about now?" he whispered, and my insides shuddered in response. "Mia?" he questioned, and the slight graze of his erection through his sweats skimmed across the inside of my thigh.

Ollie tilted my chin up, and his tongue swept along my bottom lip. "Mia has no words?" he mocked and pulled my lip between his teeth before dropping his hand from my chin. I leaned forward to kiss him, and Ollie pulled away. "No, love. It's my turn."

Though my eyes stayed closed, I heard the smile in his tone. He lifted the shirt over my head, and his warm breath fell over my nipple before his tongue circled over it. Then he blew cold air, and my head rolled back. He moved over to my other nipple, and an electric current ran through me, dropping to my core.

Ollie tucked the hair behind my ears and pressed his forehead to mine, hovering his perfect lips so close, I could taste the mint from his gum. His fingers skimmed down the length of my arms.

"The only way to cheat death is by creating a love that will last forever," Ollie whispered. My lashes parted, and we locked eyes. "That's what I wrote."

Ollie's eyes dropped to my mouth.

My pulse skipped.

He wet his lips.

I held my breath.

His fingers traced the edge of my panties.

Lower. Closer. "Breathe, Mia," he whispered.

My chest let go.

He moved my panties to the side.

The foretaste controlled my senses.

And his finger skimmed through my center.

My need for him exploded, and my hand wandered, reaching for him.

Ollie snatched my hand in his free one and squeezed. "Look at me," he demanded and pushed two fingers inside. A moan left me. Ollie let go of my hand and grabbed the back of my neck to keep me steady. He stroked his melodic fingers inside, and my sex tightened around them. "I can't," I rasped out, fighting to stand but weakening by every torturous second as he scraped his thumb against my clit, and my legs shook in response.

"I have you," Ollie rolled his forehead over mine. "I'm not going to let you go."

All it took was two more sensual thrusts of his fingers, and one more scrape of his thumb. My knees buckled, and Ollie scooped me up in one arm with his fingers never leaving their post. He kissed along my jawline, down my neck, and back up until his mouth covered mine. My sex clenched around his fingers, pulsating to the beat of my climax and Ollie refused to withdraw until I'd ultimately came undone and pieced back together.

After he pulled out of me, he slid his fingers between his lips with a smug grin.

"What about you?" I asked, cheeks still heated, and my breathing was begging to return to normal.

He fixed my panties and pulled me over the mattress. "Oh, you think that was for you?"

We made out like two crazed teens until our eyes grew heavy.

Ollie laid his head over my chest, and I dragged my fingers through his hair.

"Mia?"

"Yeah?"

He tilted his head up to look at me. "I'm the crack to your arse?"

I laughed. "Forget I ever said that."

"I wish I could, love," he laid back over my chest and wrapped his arm around me. "I really wish I could."

THIRTY

*"We're not out of the woods yet,
but let's kiss in the leaves
while we're here."*

OLIVER MASTERS

Ollie

"And then there were three," Jake exhaled as the three of us walked down the hill and toward the woods. I grabbed Mia's hand and kissed her knuckles. "To be honest," Jake continued. "I never thought it would be Crap-bag standing next to me at the end of the road."

"Crap Bag?" I echoed, and Jake interrupted me with a shriek.

"Although we've come to the end of the road," he sang.

"Still I can't let go," Mia added, causing my head to snap in her direction. *"It's unnatural."*

"You belong to me," Jake sang.

"I belong to you!" They both belted in unison.

I'd stopped walking, and the two continued singing and spinning each other around in the grass for two more rounds of whatever this song was that they shared. I couldn't wipe the stupid smile from my face. Mia's brown hair whipped through the spring breeze, and Jake leaned her back into a proper dip. She couldn't wipe the heart-stopping smile from hers, either.

They laughed uncontrollably and turned to face me.

"Don't tell me you don't know that song," Jake asked with a hand digging into his hip, catching his breath. I threw up a hand in the air. *"I'll make love to you?"* he asked, growing frustrated.

"No, thank you," I answered and walked toward the two.

"How are you with this bloke?" Jake asked Mia in disbelief.

Mia recovered and jumped on my back. I grabbed her thighs, and she laughed into my neck as she tousled my hair. "I'll introduce him to *Boyz II Men* when he's ready." She wrapped her arms around my neck.

We reached our spot in the woods, and I leaned back to guide Mia to her feet. Tyler and Jude sat over the broken tree limb, and Liam sent a nod over to Jake from the ground.

Greetings exchanged, and I took a spot over the ground and pulled my knees up, more relaxed since the first day I'd come back.

"There's this game Mia and me started on the last day last year," Jake said, taking a seat next to Liam. A pit formed in my stomach, thinking Mia had spent her last day last year without me. She had a memory I wasn't a part of. She had seven months I hadn't been a part of. "We go around and say one thing we'd been dying to say all year but was too ashamed to say. Kind of clear the air."

"What do you call this game?" I asked and grabbed Mia's waist, who began to sit beside me but I positioned her between my legs.

"Just truth. No strip. No dare. Just the bloody truth."

"I like it," I said, and kissed the side of her head. "What was yours last year?" I asked into her hair, immediately regretting it. *Did I want to know?*

Mia shifted uncomfortably, and my heart sank. It had been about me.

"Mia said *Liam* was a lousy fuck," Liam blurted with an eye roll.

345

"Why?" Mia threw her arms up and fell back into my chest.

I chuckled and grazed my thumbs over the bare skin above her waistline.

"For that, I'll go first," Liam offered. "It was sex with you that made me realize I loved dick."

The circle burst into a laugh, and Mia shook her head. "Bet you've been holding onto that for a whole year."

"As a matter of fact, yes. This whole gathering was my idea."

"Okay, okay, my turn," Jake cut in, squeezing Liam's shoulder. "Believe it or not, I'm glad Mia spilled her secrets in that journal. If she hadn't, Liam would still be in the closet."

"I suspected Jude was the prankster this whole time," Mia confessed. "Sorry, Jude."

Jude packed his cigarette pack and shrugged. "It's cool. I don't blame you. I was an arsehole."

Tyler scrunched her face. "They just didn't know you like I do."

"Nah, I should've never treated you the way I did. That's not like me."

"Fuck, this is therapeutic, yeah?" I laughed, seeing all the love pouring from the circle of outcasts. "Who knew we could've ever gotten to a place like this."

The circle went silent into deep thought.

"Bloody truth? I've fantasized about Ollie," Tyler blurted.

"And then she goes and does that." Jude shook his head.

"What?" Tyler lifted her shoulders. "This is a safe place."

"Bloody truth? I just learned your name like a month ago," I rushed in to save the moment.

"I wonder what ever happened to Brianna," Mia mumbled out loud once laughter died. Brianna had been banished from Dolor shortly after Madilyn and Zeke's death, never to be seen or heard from since that day. There hadn't been a single mention of Brianna's name either, or why she would have agreed to switch identities with Madilyn.

Everyone offered a wordless shrug.

"Bloody truth?" Tyler spoke up. "What's Officer Scott's story with you? Brianna and Madilyn both said you two were together."

The knot in my stomach increased to the size of an American football and my teeth clenched. Mia's fingers circled my knee caps.

Three.

Two.

One.

Exhale.

"There is no story," Mia said casually. "Ethan—"

"Oh, he has a name," Jake interrupted.

Mia dropped her head and narrowed her eyes in his direction. "Officer Scott is intense, but he was the only one who was there when everyone else bounced, so …" she lifted her shoulder.

Tyler nudged her head. "Earmuffs, Ollie." I flipped her the bird. Whatever she was about to say, she could say it. "Suit yourself." Her eyes darted to Mia. "You and Officer Scott had sex, didn't you? Is he really a fucking monster under his uniform?"

"Ooh, does the carpet match the drapes?" Jake asked with an anticipated smile.

Mia shook with laughter in my arms, and I didn't know if I was relieved I couldn't see her face to catch her expression, or mad about it. "You guys are horrible."

"Ah, keeping to your guns on this one, yeah?" Tyler shook her head. "That answers it."

Mia turned in my arms, and I fell back to my elbows. She blinked slowly, the complete opposite of what my heart was doing. "I love you," she whispered.

The three single words were rare coming from her lips.

She never had to remind me, but in times such as these, it was everything my body needed to relax. Mia pulled her hair over her head into a band, and stubborn strands danced in the wind. "Say it again," I demanded, wanting to hear it for a second time.

Mia's hands slid down my thighs, and the blood rushed to both heads.

"I love you, Ollie." She smiled, and I pulled her on top of me to hide my hard-on growing in my joggers from the rest of the group. Her eyes bulged. My face heated, and I shrugged my shoulders. *Yes, love. That is what you do to me.*

"I'm telling everyone," I whispered to her. She knew it had been hard for me to hold in the news that she would soon be my wife. "Can I tell them? Yeah, I'm telling them."

Mia's hand came over my mouth, and I darted my tongue out. Her jaw dropped and she quickly pulled her hand away. "Bloody fucking truth," I called out, sitting back up and wrapping her legs around my torso. "I'm marrying this girl." I pointed at Mia, who was now hiding in my chest. I pulled her head away and looked into those coffee-colored eyes, seeing the same girl I'd fallen in love with across the mess hall since day one. "And I can't fucking wait, love. I can't. I don't want to."

Gasps spread from the group around us, but my eyes stayed on her. Jake made a comment about calling maid of honor before I'd proposed. Tyler whined about not being able to go at all and how it wasn't fair.

But my gaze and lips touched all over her.

We kissed until the topic changed.

We got lost inside our own little world.

We held each other until it was just us two left out here, soaking in the sun, the breeze, and each other.

"The second we're released, I'm waiting outside those walls for you, and we're taking a car to the closest train station. We're going straight to Gibraltar. We don't have to wait." I kissed her soft lips and dropped my head to hers. "Come with me. All I'm asking is for two days before you go back to the states. This will work."

Mia ran her tongue across her bottom lip. "Ollie," she said through a sigh and averted her eyes.

"No, don't say my name like that." I rolled my forehead against hers. I felt it—the uneasiness creeping from her and crawling under my skin. "I don't like it. Don't pull back on me. Say you want this, too. Say you'll meet me outside those gates on release day, Mia."

"We shouldn't have this conversation right now."

"Love …"

"I'm scared," she admitted, unable to look at me directly.

I grabbed her face. "I have you."

"What if I go to the states and they won't let me come back?"

"Then I will come to you. Always. Wherever you are, I'll fucking follow."

"What if you can't get a passport?"

"Mia, stop. This will work out. It has to. Let me worry about all that stuff. All I'm asking is to meet me right out there on release day. That's it. I'll take care of the rest."

"I don't know if I can marry you then go back to Pennsylvania alone."

"Then you won't go alone. We'll go together. We'll go to Spain, get married, and take the first flight out to Pennsylvania."

"You live in a fairy tale." She smiled. "Real life doesn't work like that, Ollie. Something will come up. We have no money. We have no car. We'll never be out of the woods."

I had less than thirty days to get the documents in order. Too much time had been wasted already. I sent a quick nod to Jinx, pushed through the door, and picked up the receiver to dial Travis.

"Twenty-eight days," he greeted me, only reminding me my time was ticking.

"I need you to do something for me."

"Yeah, mate. Anything."

Mia

Release day—nothing like graduation days in America that you would see on TV.

I'd never had a graduation. I was homeschooled during my Senior year. My graduation day had consisted of a diploma delivered by the United States Postal Service. Not even by hand. The mailman had stuffed it into the mailbox along with the electric bill and an ad for a lawn service.

Ollie had been busy the last couple of days. Each time I'd ask him what he was up to, the only response he could give was, "Getting our shit together."

Good enough for me.

Though I had not expected to wake up on release day alone in our bed. The moon and the sun competed outside when I opened my eyes. I stretched out my arm beside me, feeling nothing but an empty cold side. Panic set in, and I sat up, allowing the blankets to bunch at my waist. The door creaked open, and Ollie came through, balancing two cups under his chin and a brown bag tucked under his arm.

"Where were you?" I asked as he kicked the door closed.

Ollie dropped the bag into my lap and shifted the cups into both hands. He leaned over and landed a kiss over my lips before sitting on the edge of the mattress. "Happy release day, love."

"Is that what I think it is?" I asked, staring at the bag between my legs.

Ollie handed me a cup. "Working on baby number three," he took a sip from his cup, closed his eyes, savored, and swallowed. It had been so long since I'd seen him do that. That small gesture told me he'd been waiting for that first sip until he got back to me. "Eat. We have no time to waste."

I scarfed down the glazed croissant before Ollie rushed me out the door. "You're freaking me out. What's gotten into you?" I asked as he pulled me down the hallway.

"I have ten minutes before the rest of the campus wakes up. Ten minutes." Ollie pushed through the door and turned to face me, grabbing two towels from the shelf with a rebellious smile. "You and I are making love in that shower one last time." He took a step forward, eating the distance between us. "I promised myself I'd never fuck you like that again, so this time will be different. I'm going to fuck you, Mia, then make sweet love to you, then go back and do it all over again. I want you fast, slow, and turn you into a pile of mess in my arms. Is that okay with you?"

My tongue wasn't working. I opened my mouth and shut it again. Ollie raised a brow. "Yeah." I cleared my throat. "Yeah, that sounds … yeah."

"Good." Ollie threw the towels over his shoulder and picked me up in his arms walking me into our stall until my back hit the wall. He flipped the water on, and ice-cold water sprayed over us, but neither one of us cared.

It happened quick—the tearing off of clothes. My legs clenched around Ollie's waist all while his tongue collided with mine. "Christ, Mia…always ready," he breathed against my mouth. "Forgive me," he rushed out before snaking his arm behind my back, and slammed inside.

The instant connection was mind-blowing.

Ollie held true to his word.

He took me hard and deep with angelic hands and the kiss of a saint.

Then we made slow, sweet love.

And then he did it all over again.

And not just in the shower—in the library, too.

"I'm going to be busy for most of the day," Ollie informed as we got dressed in our nook under the skylight. He pulled his *Poetic* hoodie over his head and pushed his overgrown hair back. His eyes hit mine, and he shook his head with disbelief in his eyes and whispered to himself, "I don't deserve you." I wrapped my arms around his neck and kissed his raw lips gently. Ollie's fingers dragged down my sides, sending shivers up my spine. "Are you going to be okay without me?"

I nodded, and his mouth inched down my neck. "What's keeping you from spending the day with me? What's so important?" I asked, struggling to hold it together while his mouth covered my nipple.

"Our future," he looked up from below, "but if you don't put your shirt back on, that will be at risk." I dropped my head back and laughed, and Ollie's hands gripped my sides as he came back up. "There are last-minute things I need to take care of." His hands drifted up to my chest, my neck, then cupped my face. "Three-o-clock, love. I'll have our bags packed and a car waiting for us. Say it, Mia. Say Three-o-clock."

"Three-o-clock."

Ollie kissed me. "I love you so fucking much."

"I love you more."

Ollie kissed me again.

My head darted over to Liam. "You can't seriously go back to that house," he whisper-shouted. "They are poison. He's going to send you away ... and what's next? Military school?"

My head snapped to Jake.

"You don't know him," Jake seethed.

Liam slammed his palm over the table in the mess hall, and my head darted back to him. "He doesn't know you! Not like I do!" Liam shouted.

My head whipped back and forth between the two as if I were caught in an episode of *Jerry Springer*, when finally, I held up a palm in both their faces. "You guys need to chill out. Take it somewhere else. You're ruining release day for me," I pouted. "Jake, what is keeping you from going with Liam?"

"Easy." He fell back into the chair and crossed his legs. "My dad would kill me."

I nodded and tilted my head. "Convincing argument."

"Bullshit excuse." Liam released his band, and his blond hair fell over his shoulders. He twisted the rubber band around his wrist nervously. "I've been gay for what? Two fucking seconds, and already both my parents are accepting and offered to open their house to you. Your dad is a coward. Hardly a man of God."

"Whoa," I cut in.

Jake's eyes bulged before he leaned forward. "My dad wasn't raised by gormless white trash, pikey. He has standards. Pardon me if those standards are over your head."

"Do you even hear yourself?" Liam matched Jake's distance, and his blond hair fell over his face. "You know ... I pity you, Jake. Really, I do. Don't be crying for me when you're standing in the desert with a SA80 strapped around your shoulder and piss running down your leg." Liam jumped up, the chair screeched against the marble, and he took off, but not before flipping the chair to the ground.

My eyes slid back to Jake, who had his lips pursed, and arms crossed firmly over his chest.

"He has a point," I stated.

"Bugger off, Crap-bag. No one asked you," Jake said, moving his head back and forth.

I stood to my feet and dropped my head, so we were eye level. "He obviously loves you, and I know you love him too. You're not choosing Liam over your father by doing this, you're choosing love. Go with him. I promise you, if you don't, you will regret it for the rest of your life. Now get your head out of your ass and go after him."

With that, I left.

Two hours left before three-o-clock, and there was one last person I had to see before making my way to Lynch's office to sign out. Tyler, Jude, and I had said our goodbyes the day before, and Dr. Conway and me had celebrated our last session last week. The rest of these two hours I'd saved for Ethan.

I searched the entire floor—every room, every hall, every bathroom. Nothing. I turned the hall, and my gaze fell on Liam and Jake in a deep make-out session at the end. From the looks of it, Jake had come to his senses, and my heart squeezed in my chest.

My feet made their way up the stairs to the third floor where the classrooms were, and again, I searched every room.

And my eyes checked every clock I'd passed to keep up with the time. *An hour and a half left.*

I pushed through the last door when I heard sounds coming from an adjoined abandoned room. When I made it to the door, I slowly pushed it open. "Ethan?" I called out.

I made it through the door and completely froze at the view before me.

Lionel, a student I'd only known in passing, hung from the ceiling, kicking his legs back and forth over an abandoned chair with a rope around his neck. I wanted to scream, but fear wrapped a tight leash around my throat. I tried to run, but my feet felt as if they were nailed to the ground.

My eyes burned. My hands shook. And finally, I spun around to see Ethan. His eyes were hazy and red—a raging fire burning inside them. He covered my mouth with his hand and pinned me against the wall. "I'm so sorry, Mia," he whispered, and I no longer recognized the man staring back at me. My eyes strained, darting back and forth to the guy struggling for his life hanging from the ceiling. "It's not what you think," Ethan chanted in my ear with his hand pressed firmly against my mouth, muffling my screams as the boy slowly suffocated before me.

Ethan pressed all his weight against me to keep me pinned.

The sight was too hard, and I squeezed my eyes closed to shut it all out.

I was confused. So, confused.

Anger rolled through me, and I snapped. My arms had a mind of their own as I fought against Ethan. I shoved him, and he pushed me ten times harder. I screamed, he squeezed my cheeks together. I pumped my knee into his groin, and Ethan took me to the ground and wrapped my wrists in one hand, putting his entire weight over my body. "I'm sorry," he repeated. "I never wanted you to see this. You were never part of the plan."

Then all I saw was black.

Ollie

I paced the road outside Travis's car, my eyes itching to check the clock every five seconds. My palms sweat, gripping the bouquet of roses in my hand. In forty-eight hours, Mia and I would be in Spain getting married. I had been waiting for this day since I'd first felt her.

I would say saw her, but that would have been a lie.

I felt her first.

Her soul called out to me first, and then I saw her.

Where are you, love?

The car was packed up with our clothes, her camera, my journal, our pictures, and the dozen or so roses Zeke and I had made her.

My Mia Rose.

The Artist green card had been mailed to my residence yesterday. Travis had brought it with—the first thing I'd asked to see. I had a way back and forth to the states. Mia had dual legal citizenship, with a little help from Lynch.

I fucking did it, and all I needed was for her to walk through those iron gates so we could get married and go home.

Where are you, love?

"Are you sure you said three?" Travis asked. His heavy glare did nothing to ease the ache rising inside my chest. I couldn't think under all the weight, and I leaned over the hood of his car and tried to breathe. The burn in my chest only intensified with each passing second.

"She's coming." I opened the door and set the bouquet of roses over the passenger side. The clock read ten minutes past three. The air was still cold, but sweat pricked my forehead. "She'll be here."

EPILOGUE

> "In the wake of death,
> a **monster** was born.
> His name was *Karma*,
> and he craved revenge."
>
> OLIVER MASTERS

Ethan

There were five stages of grief. Psychologists had figured it out in five bloody stages. I had passed denial a long time ago, but never reached bargaining—stuck in a continuous cycle of Anger.

Anger, my most trusted and loyal friend. I could count on Anger. It was there when I woke up. It was there when I closed my eyes. Anger even took me in my sleep. The rage had become a part of me—a monster—and I fed that bloody beast every godforsaken day.

Sixteen months ago

It had been a year since I'd walked up the steps of Dolor, but it seemed like just yesterday I saw her face.

"Don't you look snazzy in your new uniform," Livy says. "Are you egg-cited? I'm so proud of you." Her hand grabs mine as she always did to get my attention, and a small smile washes over her face as she looks up at me with matching blue eyes. Her use of egg-cited started one year on Easter when we were younger, but it had bled into an all year thing between the two of us.

I know Livy is proud of me, but I'm mad at her at the moment. She was taking off to a reformatory school to get help. She said I wouldn't understand, but one day I would. And all I see now as she smiles up at me in admiration is the fact she did not trust me enough to confide in me. We were supposed to be family. We were supposed to be in this shit together.

The least I could have done was thank her, smile, or given her a lick of appreciation or acknowledgement, but I had walked away, holding onto a fucking grudge against her.

A bloody fucking year.

If only I'd known what I knew now.

I waited outside the door for Lynch, when, finally, the door creaked open and he greeted me with an outstretched hand. It took me a second to swallow the beast inside and shake his hand—it took everything. Even while shaking his hand, I wanted to snap his wrist for not doing the one thing he'd promised: keep Livy safe.

"Mia is important to me," he had said over the phone when he had called me for help about a matter. I hadn't spoken to the chap since Livy's death, and he had the nerve to call me with a favor. I should've told him to go fuck himself. Livy had been important to me, too. She had been in his

care, his responsibility. He was supposed to help Livy. She was the only family I had left, and here I was, back at Dolor because he needed me.

Little did Lynch know, I had other plans in mind.

My heart warned me with every step I took up the stairs as I followed Lynch. It told me it would leave me too if I continued this path of vengeance, but the monster inside shut that bastard up.

Side by side, we walked past Livy's old wing. I turned my eyes away, anything to lessen the blow and shield myself from the memories threatening to resurrect. I'd kept those memories locked up, but now the monster inside pounded against my skull, rattling in its cage, thirsty for redemption.

Not yet, my dear friend. Your time will come.

Livy's death had reminded me there were no second chances. No rewinds. No going back in time to erase the damage. You only had one chance, and I'd missed it by a long shot.

Late, without so much as a decent excuse.

The pressure stacked heavier with each long stride down Livy's old wing. My hands fisted at my sides, and Lynch stopped in front of the nurse's station. "Her name is Mia. She has no idea I'm her father," he warned me in a hushed tone. "I prefer to keep it that way."

"I understand," I complied. Livy was my sister, and I preferred for her to be alive today, but we didn't always get what we wanted.

The door opened.

We walked through.

Mia laid there, withdrawn and dazed, clutching a phone in her hand. A large cut sliced through her eyebrow and she parted her cracked and bruised lip. Caramel-brown eyes studied me, waiting for a reaction. I fought to maintain the fact this was Lynch's daughter, and I shouldn't care, but the animal inside quieted at the sight of her. This girl scared him, too. I dropped my eyes to the floor so she couldn't see what her stare did to me. At least until I'd figured it out for myself.

Lynch spoke first and introduced me. I stayed quiet at his side.

She asked about a friend before making demands, then had the audacity to throw in a few jabs at Lynch's credibility as a dean. I laughed a little inside.

This girl was a storm.

I immediately wanted to know everything there was about her, and how she was able to control my anger when I'd spent months trying to pack its shit and move it out.

After watching the evidence Mia had captured on video, the monster inside me awakened. "Mind if I ask you a few more questions?" I asked as I bagged the phone.

Mia, despite her situation, was intimidating. When she looked at me, she looked through me. Her eyes violated me, frisked me for weapons, and rendered me defenseless—with just one fucking look. I had to know more. I had to know how she carried the same jaded look in her eyes as my sister had, and still be here when my sister wasn't. How had Mia gotten this far?

Mia's ability to tell her story with only a few shed tears was impressive, considering I was the one who had to pause her, close my eyes, and prepare for impact. Every similarity was a punch to the gut. She mentioned her uncle and what he had done to her. She mentioned her mum, and the way she had left her. And the only family she had, shipped her to Dolor.

Mia and I were one in the same, aside from the fact she was able to obliterate the anger inside just by her presence.

I'll be back, Mia.

We said our goodbyes, and as I walked away, she grabbed my hand.

By the single touch of her hand, I froze. The monster froze. I'd never been so nervous, and I found the will to turn to face her.

"I'm sorry about your sister, Ethan. She would be so proud of you," Mia said, and squeezed my hand. That was all it took for me to know I had to see my plans through.

For Livy. For Mia. For justice.

"Why don't you want her to know?" I asked Lynch back at his office. I leaned back in the chair and rested my elbows over the armrests, bringing my pointer fingers to my mouth. Lynch absentmindedly rolled a pen between his palms in deep thought, wondering which version he wanted to spit my way.

Try me, Lynch. I may have been a horrible brother, but I was a walking lie detector.

"She's smart," he finally said. *Truth.* "She will use it against me during her time here. I'll tell her, but not until her last day. It has to be her choice in whether or not she wants to accept it. It has to be because I'm not the dean of the school she's attending, but because she honestly wants to be a part in my life."

I sat back in the chair and scratched my jaw. "How long have you known?" I asked and held my arms out to the side. "That she is your daughter. How long?" *Where were you while her uncle was raping her? Where were you when her mother took her life? Where were you the last nineteen years of her life? What was your fucking excuse? Was it the same as mine?*

"Eight months," Lynch scoffed. "Bruce, her father, reached out to me about eight months ago. Told me what happened with her mum, laid a shit storm on me and confessed I had a daughter. He said Mia needed help. I didn't believe him at first, but then he sent me the original birth certificate. When she first arrived, I had her blood drawn." He tossed the pen over the desk. "She's mine, Ethan. That little girl in there?" He pointed up, where Mia lay above us. "She's my daughter. You're the only one I trust to protect her. Lord knows Livy had gone through hell and back, and I'm sorry for what happened to Livy. I know I should've checked up on you after she died. I should have been there for you. But I failed and I was scared to face my failures. I can't have the same thing happen to Mia that happened to your sister. If anyone understands, it's you. You're the only one who can do this job. I need you to keep an eye on her. Watch her every move."

Lynch was desperate, but so was I.

"I'll do it." I would watch over Mia, do what I couldn't do for Livy. I would make sure nothing ever happened to her, but in the meantime, I'd also raise hell in this fucking institution and eliminate the bastards who gang-raped and murdered my little sister.

The police had said it was suicide by hanging. Deep down, I knew the truth. Livy would've never left Tommy behind or take the life of their baby. Livy would have never left me behind.

But those were all assumptions.

The cold hard truth? I'd been the first one at the scene. The facts had screamed at me from the door of her dorm. Livy didn't have the height or strength to have carried out the suicide. It had taken Livy until the age of eight to learn to tie her shoe. I hardly believed she configured a noose in the form of a bedsheet.

The cold hard truth? I'd spent months investigating her case, reading the reports, studying her last months, visited Tommy. They didn't bother testing the skin under her nails for DNA. They didn't bother interrogating the students. And they never bothered to report the bruises or evidence of foul play that painted over her body.

They didn't fucking care.

Suicide was much easier to jot down. Investigating the truth was harder. The police wanted easy, not justice. They wanted a closed case and to go home to their families.

Crazy how one lie on a death certificate could haunt a soul daily, on top of the last memory I had of her. The memory of saying goodbye to her cold, lifeless body at the morgue. I would never forget the way her forehead felt beneath my kiss.

That chill ran through me ever since.

The cold hard truth was, if I wanted something done, I had to do it myself. It was time Livy's murderers were punished, and thanks to Tommy, one of them had been taken care of. But it was up to me to take out the last four blokes under the same fate they'd given my sister.

One by fucking one.

To be continued in ...

Now Open Your Eyes

The last book in the Stay With Me series.

And what if we all stop & listen?

I refuse to measure suicide with numbers, statistics, and percentages because at the end of the day, it only takes one to disrupt the entire world.

You can erase this stigma by how you respond to this tragic death.

For more information, please visit:
https://save.org

National Suicide Prevention Lifeline:
1-800-273-8255 (TALK)

Crises Textline:
Text **HOME** to 741-741

Acknowledgements

HOLY CRAP.
   My second publication.
      I'm still reeling.
         Give me a moment.
            … **Exhales** …
               Okay, here we go.

I can't start off my acknowledgements without thanking the **readers** first. Whether you found my books through social media, word of mouth, recommendations, or me reaching out to you, the time you've taken to read, review, share, and so much more, <u>YOU ARE THE ONES WHO BRING THIS STORY TO LIFE</u>. And with that, I can't thank you enough.

Thank you to the **ARC ARMY** and **LOVELIES**, you ladies are incredible. I am in awe of all that you do. It's amazing to a see a community of strong and passionate people from around the world sharing the same love for reading, come together by a single story. Though I'm still trying to figure out the whole social media thing, I see your messages, creations, and words, and it warms my heart of how accepting you are. And not just to me, but to each other. I literally could go on …

A never ending thanks to **Annie Bugeja**. You have made book two what it is, between beta reading, proofreading, and being an ear during my emotional meltdowns, I don't know if I could have done this one without you. Actually, I probably could have, but it would have been a huge pile of lsakjflskjfd. Thank you for loving these characters. Though we met not that long ago, I'd felt like I've known you my whole life. Is it possible to owe SWM a solid for meeting you? Would that mean I owe myself one? I'll take full credit! You are my WE.

To **K. Dosal McLendon**. My Kassy. My life support. It's crazy, really, how far we've come already. Endless thank you for everything. You knew how hard that epilogue was for me to write. You noticed a change in my writing almost immediately. Thank you for letting me cry it out, for reminding me why I started this story, for always being there and understanding my vision. I love you!

A huge thank you to **Ally Dublin** with Wasted Life Books. Damn, woman. You are the mom of PA's. Thank you for your constant reminders, keeping me on track and in line, and pushing me every single day. I think you've realized by now, I'm not like the rest of them. Thank you for accepting me with open arms.

Thank you to Michelle (Mishie) Montes, Faith Flores, Lisa Bardonski, and Lym Cruz for your time and effort put into beta reading EWIG.

Mishie, my girl, your drive and passion for the story fuels me, and I couldn't have asked anyone better to be on this team.

Lisa … (I'm laughing as I'm writing this) … thank you for your honest review of the first book. Bet you didn't think I was going to reach out and ask you to be on my team after that, did you? Thank you for catching all the missing words that ran through my head and never made it to into the story. Because of you, no word has been lost.

Faith, thank you for being there since the beginning. You are so talented and I look up to you so much. Thank you for everything you've given me, time, encouragement, advice, etc. Don't ever leave me.

An endless thank you to my husband, **Michael**, my daughter, **Grace**, and my son, **Christian**. I hear you. I see you. I feel you. I may not be there one hundred of the time, but just know you three will always be my number one. Your continuous support and patience allows me to follow my dream. I love you!

Thank you, **Amanda**, my other half for being there for my every step of the way. For celebrating every single victory, though I know at times can be annoying. Despite how hard life hit this year, you still took the time to beta read. PS: When you read this, you'll be mad I left a paragraph that you begged me to take out, but seriously … what did you expect? I'm not even sorry about it.

A huge thanks to **Kaylee**, the free-spirited one. While writing book two, you texted me one night and said how much I've inspired you to follow your dreams. The truth is, you're my inspiration. Thank you for reminding me how beautiful this world is. I thank God every day for you.

Danielle, you will probably never read this, but I love you anyway. You support me in your own way and it will always be enough.

To all the amazing Authors, bloggers, bookstagrammers, readers, and anyone else who I've missed because I'm still on a high from no sleep and deadly amounts of caffeine, Thank you!

Oh-my-God, **Mom**!
Thank you, Mom, I love you! I promise we will have breakfast …
after one more story.

ABOUT THE AUTHOR

Crafting stories and stringing words together since a young age, most times I live in imaginary worlds. Other times, I live on an *island* somewhere in Florida with my loving husband, two kids, and lazy Great Dane, Winston.

My writing style is unapologetic and emotional, striving to push buttons, hearts, and limits within romance. I would say my books fall under all sub-genres, from gothic romance, suspense, to fantasy. I want to write everything.

A lover of music, especially a good electric guitar solo, I can rap most Eminem songs, dance, dabble on the piano, but also enjoy using power tools and a paintbrush. When I'm not writing, I'm either enjoying family movie/game nights, sleeping (probably sleeping), traveling, or planning my next book adventure … with one hand on my laptop, and the other holding a can of Red Bull.

I LOVE HEARING FROM YOU!

Facebook & Instagram: @nicolefiorinabooks

JOIN THE BOOK CLUB ON FACEBOOK:

https://facebook.com/groups/littlemissobsessivebookclub

SIGN UP FOR THE NEWSLETTER

https://www.nicolefiorina.com

n i c o l e   f i o r i n a

Printed in Great Britain
by Amazon